PRAISE FOR THE

JESSICA DARLING SERIES

"Comic and wise . . . Irresistible."

—*Miami Herald*

"Judy Blume meets Dorothy Parker."

—*The Wall Street Journal*

"McCafferty looks at teen travails with humor as well as heart."

—*People*

"A springboard for McCafferty's hilarious pop culture riffs . . . The series has won her a legion of fans, from teens and college students to twentysomethings, mothers, and the occasional grandmother."

—*The Star-Ledger*

"Witty, insightful, and a good read for anyone between the ages of 15–99."

—*Ottawa Sun*

"McCafferty's debut novel became a crossover hit, equally touching teenagers and adults nostalgic about their youth. . . . [A]n exhilarating and genuine take on teendom."

—*Boston Herald*

"Smart and accomplished enough to delight all readers. Jessica's an original, but her problems are universal, and McCafferty is formidably adept at channeling her self-deprecating, wise-guy voice. If you don't see yourself in Jessica Darling, you're not looking hard enough."

—*Chicago Tribune*

"Portrays teenaged life so accurately, you can forget about putting this one down." —*Toronto Sun*

"It's Jessica, her wit and, especially, her utterly droll take on life, that draws readers (fans of the series include adult women as well as teens) into McCafferty's books. Entirely too smart for her own good, Jessica offers brilliant and cutting insights into the world of the adolescent about-to-be-a-woman." —*Chicago Sun-Times*

"The snappy writing, au courant wordplay, and easy-to-relate-to plot turns will keep eager teens—and teens-at-heart—turning the pages." —*Publishers Weekly*

"Surprisingly mature and witty . . . Should snag more than a few adult readers." —*Kirkus Reviews*

"This genre at its best; it's literature full of life, unique voices, and unforgettable characters." —*The Harvard Crimson*

"This charming series will appeal to both the young-adult crowd and women who like to look back and remember." —New York *Daily News*

"Boy, do I wish Megan McCafferty had been writing books about high school when I was young and foolish and insecure. But even now, at my advanced age, I get a huge kick out of the bright, wickedly funny, and cheerfully off-color observations of Jessica Darling." —*Miami Herald*

"Smart, tentative, and funny, Jessica is a likable and wry observer of the competitive, gossipy high-school world." —*Booklist*

ALSO BY MEGAN MCCAFFERTY

SECOND HELPINGS

A Jessica Darling Novel

MEGAN McCAFFERTY

WEDNESDAY BOOKS
NEW YORK

Published in the United States by Wednesday Books, an imprint of St. Martin's Publishing Group

www.wednesdaybooks.com

Designed by Devan Norman

Library of Congress Cataloging-in-Publication Data

Names: McCafferty, Megan, author.
Title: Second helpings : a Jessica Darling novel / Megan McCafferty.
Description: First Wednesday Books edition. | New York : Wednesday Books, 2021. | Series: Jessica Darling ; 2
Identifiers: LCCN 2021004757 | ISBN 9781250781819 (trade paperback) | ISBN 9781250781826 (ebook)
Subjects: LCSH: Darling, Jessica (Fictitious character) | High school students—New Jersey—Fiction. | Teenage girls—New Jersey—Fiction. GSAFD: Bildungsromans
Classification: LCC PS3613.C34 S43 2021 | DDC 813/.6—dc23
LC record available at https://lccn.loc.gov/2021004757

Our books may be purchased in bulk for promotional, educational, or business use. Please contact your local bookseller or the Macmillan Corporate and Premium Sales Department at 1-800-221-7945, extension 5442, or by email at MacmillanSpecialMarkets@macmillan.com.

First published in the United States in 2003 by Three Rivers Press, an imprint of the Crown Publishing Group, a division of Random House, Inc., New York.

First Wednesday Books Edition: 2021

10 9 8 7 6 5 4 3 2 1

FOR MY PARENTS

foreword

Sloppy Firsts was published in 2001, barely a month shy of 9/11. Jessica Darling—a precocious, sexually curious, fast-talking teenage girl—spun into a world in turmoil. Schools the country over watched the towers fall, understanding that for many, for the first time, tragedy in life and country were unavoidable. A place that had felt so safe—America, *home*—changed practically overnight.

It's been twenty years, and today's teens face their own crisis of country. Progress, as we've seen, bends slowly, doubles back, barrels forward. Teens take up the fight. In many ways, they are on the front lines: the future belongs to them, to *you—yes, you*—after all.

So let's talk about Jessica, shall we? I first came to Ms. Darling my sophomore year of college. Like thousands before me, I was immediately taken with Jessica's voice. This overly average girl who was anything but. Like our queen Judy Blume, Megan McCafferty draws a young woman who is unafraid of her own sexuality. Who is curious, intrigued, and annoyed by the culture of high school. Who wants to be extraordinary, but who also understands and acknowledges her own singular existence. She is no more than a high school girl. And yet—what could possibly be more powerful?

Then there's Marcus Flutie. Jessica and Marcus, Marcus and Jessica. The most perfect teenage boyfriend of all time—and the biggest fuckup (I feel like I'm allowed to swear here). The stoner kid who needs Jessica's pee (literally), and who ends up being her greatest teacher and her greatest love. Throughout the five books, we get to see not only a real, true, deep, often tragic first love, but we also get to see the anatomy of a relationship. We get to question, along with Jessica, whether first love is forever love. And whether, in fact, love itself is enough. Marcus and Jessica's relationship is never trivial, and never trivialized. Not the way they speak to each other, not the pain they feel at sometimes being apart, not the way they have sex. It's part of the reason Jessica Darling continues to appeal to adults—some of us, now, on the better side of thirty. We could all learn a thing or two from the way these two love.

Throughout the course of *Sloppy Firsts*, *Second Helpings*, *Charmed Thirds*, *Fourth Comings*, and *Perfect Fifths*, we journey with Jessica Darling from fifteen to twenty-five. We watch the world change with her. She moves to New York, a city on the brink of rehabilitation. She tries to seek employment in a tough economic time. She gets a cell phone. Her world doesn't include Twitter or Instagram. There is no Uber, or Netflix, and yet—Jessica Darling is more relatable than ever. Why?

It's simple: the specific is the universal. The more immediately you can write a character's existence, mind, heart, life, the more universal it will feel to the reader. Because in order to inhabit the world, we first need to inhabit ourselves. When we meet Jessica, she is a teenage girl uncomfortable in her own skin. When we leave her, she's a young woman on the cusp of adulthood. Just like progress, the trajectory of Jessica's growth is not linear. She is, arguably, the most lost of all when we see her in *Perfect Fifths*, the final book. But there is always the sense that the story the universe is telling—no matter how tangential the plot may get—ultimately does have meaning. That there is a humor and reason to why things unfold the way they do. That sometimes the moment when all hope is lost is the exact moment when your life begins to change.

Jessica Darling is a time capsule of her era—but she's also a timeless figure. A feminist, a leader, a daughter, a best friend. I have no doubt that in another two decades we will still be laughing and crying and swooning inside these pages. I'm jealous of everyone experiencing Jessica for the first time. Congratulations, Megan, on twenty years. And thank you, Jessica, for still being a friend. This thing is forever (whatever).

Love,
Rebecca Serle

july

June 30th

Hope,

By the time you get this, I will already be attending the Summer Pro-College Enrichment Curriculum in Artistic Learning. I think it's hilarious for a gifted and talented program to have an acronym (SPECIAL) with the exact opposite educational connotation.

While I'm psyched to escape another summer of junk-food servitude on the boardwalk, I can't help but feel like a fraud. I'm not all that interested in "experiencing the artistic, intellectual, and social activities integral for a successful career in the arts," like it says in the brochure. My motivation is simple: I know the only way to brace myself for the indignity of my senior year at Pineville High is to avoid everyone and everything associated with it for as long as I possibly can.

You know I would've stuck around this strip mall wasteland all summer if you had opted to visit me in Jersey instead of jetting around Europe. Tough choice. If you weren't my best friend, and I didn't love you so much, I would hate you. Not for your decision, but for the privilege to make it in the first place.

I know our email/IM daily, call weekly schedule will be out of whack until you get back to Tennessee. But don't forget to write. More than once a month, if the mood strikes. And if it doesn't, well, less. Even though you're going all international on me, these are still the **Totally Guilt-Free Guidelines for Keeping in Touch.** With a special emphasis on the **Guilt-Free** part.

Enviously yours,
J.

the first

I can't believe I used to do this nearly every day. Or night, rather. In the wee hours, when the sky was purple and the house sighed with sleep, I'd hover, wide awake, over my beat-up black-and-white-speckled composition notebook. I'd scribble, scratch, and scrawl until my hand, and sometimes my heart, ached.

I wrote and wrote and wrote. Then, one day, I stopped.

With the exception of letters to Hope and editorials for the school newspaper, I haven't written anything real in months. (Which is why it's such a crock that I'm attending SPECIAL.) I have no choice but to start up again because I'm required to keep a journal for SPECIAL's writing program. But this journal will be different. It *has* to be different.

My last journal was the only eyewitness to every mortifying and just plain empty-headed thought I had throughout my sophomore and junior years. And like the mob, I had the sole observer whacked. Specifically, I slipped page after page into my dad's paper shredder, leaving nothing but guilty confetti behind. I wanted to have a ritualistic burning in the fireplace, but my mom wouldn't let me because she was afraid the ink from my pen would emit a toxic cloud and kill us all. Even I can admit that would have been an unnecessarily melodramatic touch.

I destroyed that journal because it contained all the things I should've been telling my best friend. I trashed it on New Year's Day, the last time I saw Hope, which was the first time I had seen her since she moved to Tennessee. My resolution: to stop pouring my soul out to an anonymous person on paper and start telling her everything again. And everything included *everything* that had happened between me and He Who Shall Remain Nameless.

Instead of hating me for the weird whatever relationship he and I used to have, Hope proved once and for all that she is a better best friend than I am. She swore to me on that January day, and a bajillion times since, that I have the right to be friends and/or more with whomever I want to be friends and/or more with. She assured me of this, even though his debaucherous activities indirectly contributed to her own brother's overdose, and very directly led to her parents moving her a thousand miles away from Pineville's supposedly evil influence. Because when it comes down to it, as she told me that shivery afternoon, and again and again, her brother Heath's death was no one's fault but his own. No one stuck that lethal needle in his arm; Heath did it himself. And if I feel a real connection with him, she told me then, and keeps telling me, and telling me, and telling me, I shouldn't be so quick to cut it off.

I've told Hope a bajillion times right back that I'm not removing him from my life out of respect for Heath's memory. I'm doing it because it simply doesn't do me any good to keep him there. Especially when he hasn't spoken a word to me since I said "fuck you" to him last New Year's Eve.

That's not totally true. He has spoken to me. And that's how I know that when it comes to He Who Shall Remain Nameless and me, there's something far worse than silence: small talk. We used to talk about everything from stem cells to *Trading Spaces*. Now the deepest he gets is: "Would you mind moving your head, please? I can't see the blackboard." (2/9/01—first period. World History II.)

STOP!!!!!!!!!!!!!!!!!!!!!!!!!!!!!!! I don't want to have to burn this journal before I even begin.

the second

Now, here's a fun and totally not bananas topic to write about! Today I got the all-time ass-kickingest going-away present: 780 Verbal, 780 Math.

GOD BLESS THE SCHOLASTIC APTITUDE TEST!

That's a combined score of 1560, for those of you who are perhaps not as mathematically inclined as I am. YA-HOOOOOOOOOOOOOO!

I've done it. I've written my ticket out of Pineville, and I won't have to run in circles for it. I am the first person to admit that if an athletic scholarship were my only option, I'd be out running laps and pumping performance-enhancing drugs right now. But my brain, for once, has helped, not hindered. I AM SO HAPPY I DID NOT SIGN UP FOR CROSS-COUNTRY CAMP.

As annoying as all those vocabulary drills and Princeton Review process-of-elimination practice sessions were, I'm totally against the movement to get rid of the SAT. It is the only way to prove to admissions officers that I'm smart. A 4.4 GPA, glowing recommendations, and a number-one class rank mean absolutely nothing when you're up against applicants from schools that *don't* suck.

Of course, with scores like these, my problem isn't whether I'll get accepted to college, but deciding which of the 1600 schools in the Princeton Review guide to colleges I should attend in the first place. I've been banking on the idea that college will be the place where I finally find people who understand me. My niche. I have no idea if Utopia University exists. But there is one consolation. Even if I pick the wrong school, and the odds are 1600 to 1 that I will, it can't be worse than my four years at Pineville High.

Incidentally, I didn't rock the SATs because I'm a genius. One campus tour of Harvard taught me the difference between freaky brilliance and the rest of us. No, my scores didn't reflect my superior intellect as much as they did my ability to memorize all the little tricks for acing the test. For me the SATs were a necessary annoyance, but not the big trauma that they are for most high school students. Way more things were harder for me to deal with in my sophomore and junior years than the Scholastic Aptitude Test. Since I destroyed all the evidence of my hardships, let's review:

Jessica Darling's Top Traumas:
2000–2001 Edition

TRAUMA #1: MY BEST FRIEND MOVED A THOUSAND MILES AWAY.

After her brother's overdose, Hope's parents stole her away to their tiny Southern hometown, where good old-fashioned

morals prevail, apparently. I can't blame the Weavers for trying
to protect her innocence, as Hope is probably the last guileless
person on the planet. Her absence hit me right in the middle of
the school year, nineteen days before my bitter sixteen, shortly
before the turn of this century. Humankind survived Y2K, but
my world came to an end.

Here's the kind of best friend Hope was (is) to me: She was
the only person who understood why I couldn't stand the Clueless Crew (as Manda, Sara, and Bridget were collectively known
before Manda slept with Bridget's boyfriend, Burke). And when
I started changing the lyrics to pop songs as a creative way of
making fun of them, she showcased her numerous artistic talents by recording herself singing them (with her own piano ac-
companiment), compiling the cuts on a CD (*Now, That's What
I Call Amusing!*, Volume 1), and designing a professional-quality
cover complete with liner notes. ("Very special *muchas gracias*
go out to Julio and Enrique Iglesias for all the love and inspiration you've given me over the years. *Te amo y te amo . . .*")
I'm listening to her soaring rendition of "Cellulite" (a.k.a. Sara's
song) right now. (Sung to the tune of the Dave Matthews Band's
"Satellite.")

Cellulite, on my thighs
Looks like stucco, makes me cry
Butt of blubber
Cellulite, no swimsuit will do
I must find a muumuu
But I can't face those dressing room mirrors
[Chorus]

Creams don't work, and squats, forget it!
My parents won't pay for lipo just yet
My puckered ass needs replacing
Look up, look down, it's all around
My cellulite.

If that isn't proof that Hope was the only one who laughed at my jokes and sympathized with my tears, I don't know what is. We still talk on the phone and write letters, but it's never been enough. And unlike most people my age, I think the round-the-clock availability of email and interactive messaging is an inadequate substitute for face-to-face, heart-to-heart contact. This is one of the reasons I am a freak. Speaking of . . .

TRAUMA #2: I HAD SUCK-ASS
EXCUSES FOR FRIENDS.

My parents thought that I had plenty of people to fill the void left by Hope, especially Bridget. She is Gwyneth blond with a bodacious booty and Hollywood ambitions. I am none of these things. We share nothing in common other than the street we've lived on since birth.

My parents also had a difficult time buying my loneliness because it was well known that Scotty, His Royal Guyness and Grand Poobah of the Upper Crust, had a crush on me. This was—and still is—inexplicable since he never seems to understand a single thing that comes out of my mouth. I found the prospect of having to translate every utterance exhausting and exasperating. I didn't want to date Scotty just to kill time. He has since proven me right by hooking up with girl after girl, whose first names all invariably end in *y*.

My "friendship" with the Clueless Two, Manda and Sara, certainly didn't make my life any sunnier, especially after Manda couldn't resist her natural urge to bang Bridget's boyfriend, and Sara couldn't resist her instinct to blab to the world about it.

And finally, to make matters worse, Miss Hyacinth Anastasia Wallace, the one girl I thought had friend potential, turned out to be a Manhattan celebutante hoping to gain credibility by going incognito at Pineville High for a marking period or two, then writing a book about it, which was optioned by Miramax before she completed the spell-check on the last draft, and will be available in stores nationwide in time for Christmas.

TRAUMA #3: MY PARENTS DIDN'T— AND STILL DON'T—GET IT.

As I've already mentioned, my parents told me I was overreacting to the loss of my best friend. My mother thought I should channel all my angsty energy into becoming a boy magnet. My father wanted me to harness it toward becoming a long-distance-running legend. My parents had little experience dealing with my unique brand of suburban-high-school misanthropy because my older sibling, Bethany, was everything I was not: uncomplicated, popular, and teen-magazine pretty.

TRAUMA #4: I WAS UNABLE TO SLEEP.

I developed chronic insomnia after Hope moved. (I currently get about four hours of REM every night—a huge improvement.) Bored by tossing and turning, I started to sneak out of the house and go running around my neighborhood. These jaunts had a soothing, cathartic effect. It was the only time my head would clear out the clutter.

On one of those early morning runs, I tripped over an exposed root and broke my leg. I was never as swift again. My dad was devastated, but secretly I was relieved. I never liked having to win and was grateful for an excuse to suck.

TRAUMA #5: MY MENSTRUAL CYCLE WENT MIA.

My ovaries shut down in response to the stress, lack of sleep, and overtraining. I was as sexually developed as a Q-tip.

TRAUMA #6: I DEVELOPED AN OBSESSION WITH HE WHO SHALL REMAIN NAMELESS.

He wasn't my boyfriend, but he was more than just a friend. I was able to tell him things I couldn't share with Hope. When I couldn't run anymore, his voice soothed me, and I was actually able to fall asleep again. My period even returned, welcoming me back to the world of pubescence.

His motives weren't as pure as I thought they were. Whatever relationship we had was conceived under false pretenses. I was an experiment. To see what would happen when Pineville High's most infamous Dreg—who just happened to be my best friend's dead brother's drug buddy—came on to the virgin Class Brainiac. He thought that confessing his sinful intentions on that fateful New Year's Eve would lead to forgiveness, but it made things worse. I was profoundly disappointed in him—and myself—for ever thinking he could've replaced Hope.

No one can. Or should. Or will.

the third

When I was in first grade, my teacher wanted to bump me up two grades in school. I was already reading, writing, and not wetting my overalls, which apparently put me years ahead of my peers. Miss Moore told my parents that I would be more intellectually stimulated if I were with third graders. I think she just wanted me out of her sight. I was bored out of my mind in Miss Moore's class and had no problem letting her know it.

"Miss Moore the Bore! Miss Moore the Bore!" I'd sing over and over.

My parents nixed the skip idea, of course, arguing that speeding up my academic growth would have a negative effect on my social development. They were afraid that if I were two years younger than all the other kids, I would be on the receiving end of countless wedgies. With the exception of the two hours I spent with accelerated third-grade reading and math groups, I spent the rest of the school day with children my own age, learning how to play nice.

I soon found a way to combat boredom in the middle of **B** is for **B**oy and **B**aby and **B**ear lessons. I'd clutch my chunky blue pencil like a microphone and walk around the classroom conducting imaginary TV interviews, but not with the classmates

I was supposed to be bonding with. No, I'd pose in-depth questions to the chalkboard, the fern, or whatever inanimate object had a lot to say that day. *Does it tickle when we write on you? Would you like to be iced-tead instead of watered?* Thus, despite my parents' best efforts, I still ended up being a freak.

I wish my parents had skipped me, if only to provide an acceptable excuse for my inability to relate to anyone. It would have been *all my parents' fault*! As it is now, I have no one to blame but myself. More importantly, if my parents had skipped me two grades, I would already have my freshman year of college behind me, and not be prepping for a six-week-long college*like* experience at SPECIAL.

Never have cinder block walls been so inviting! Never have I been so intoxicated by the scent of industrial-strength antiseptic! Never has a glorified cot with a one-inch-thick mattress seemed so comfy! Never have I been so excited by the idea of writing for six hours a day, five days a week! Never have I been so happy to see my parents pull out of the parking lot!

My dad is still pissed off that I chose SPECIAL over cross-country camp. Angry sweat on his bald head sizzled as he tried to transform the former into the latter. He's still got the sturdy, muscular frame of the star point guard he was back in the day, but the way he moped and slumped around campus gave him the appearance of a man whose athleticism was limited to beer-guzzling weekends at the Bowl-a-Rama.

Cross-country camp is just what the doctor ordered. Literally. My orthopedist said that with the proper training regimen, I could easily get back into my record-breaking shape, completely disregarding my total lack of interest in doing so. See, as a senior, a two-year captain, and four-year varsity veteran, I have a moral obligation as a mighty, mighty Pineville High Seagull to train harder than ever to overcome the leg injury that provided my father with enough video footage last spring for *Notso Darling's Agony of Defeat*, Volumes 3 and 4 (both of which will be available on DVD any day now).

When he wasn't acting depressed for my benefit, Dad spent most of the afternoon pointing out good places for me to run. This is a supreme example of parental cluelessness, as he has no inkling that my stellar SATs have made me less inclined to break a sweat than ever.

"Those stairs are good for building your uphill strength. The perimeter around the quad is roughly a quarter mile—you can do sprints around the path. If you eat dinner at the cafeteria on South campus, you can get in six miles a day right there."

Right before he left, he gave me a six-week training schedule, forty-two hardcore workouts that I'm somehow supposed to squeeze in between my seminars. Then he kissed me on the cheek and said, "If you sit on your ass thinking about artsy-fartsy crap all summer, you'll pay for it in September."

Thanks, Dad. I love you too. I didn't even bother telling him that according to MY DAILY SCHEDULE, I will have little time to sit on my ass to *take* a crap, let alone contemplate it, which is just the way I like it. Being Busy = Avoiding My Issues. He of all people should appreciate this, as someone who hops on his bike and rides around greater Pineville (an oxymoron, by the way) for hours whenever I'm "testing his limits."

Mom may be in real estate, but I think interior design is her true calling. She was in full-on Martha mode. As with a sleepwalker, it's best not to interrupt her, or she could snap and strangle me with the behind-the-door shoe organizer. So I just watched as she buzzed around the room, blond hair bouncing, perky as the cheerleader *she* used to be. She unpacked all my clothes and arranged my closet so it would "meet its full stowing potential." She didn't think the room was "maximizing its blank space" and rearranged the beds and the desks before my roommate could arrive and protest the takeover of her half of the room.

Two hours past check-in, and she still hasn't shown up. According to the pink construction paper pointe shoe on the door, her name is Mary DePasquale. Since *Jessica Darling* is written on a yellow construction paper pencil, I would assume that the toe shoe means that the mysterious Mary DePasquale is a dancer. That is all I know about the person who will be sleeping less than a foot away from me for the next six weeks of "sharing ideas and making memories with other highly motivated, talented New Jersey teens . . . one hundred actors, singers, dancers, musicians, visual artists, and writers who will shape the cultural landscape for years to come."

Bridget is the only other student from Pineville High who was accepted to this "highly competitive, nationally recognized program," so it's pretty much impossible to buy into all the brochure's rah-rah, change-the-world rhetoric. Bridget would rather shape up her ass than shape the cultural landscape.

MEOW-ZA! Got any 'nip for my cattitude?

Bridget is still offended by my decision not to room with her. When she found out that we had both been accepted, she automatically assumed we'd stay together, exhibiting the special kind of naïveté that is sometimes refreshing—but more often annoying—in this cynical world.

"Don't you want to make a *new* lifelong friend?" I said, intentionally hitting her weak spot, which is her unwavering need to connect with people.

"And, like, *you* do?"

Valid point. But I was not going to cave. The mysterious Mary DePasquale was better than the certainty of living with Bridget. I know exactly what my summer would be like if I lived with her. Until I bonded with Hope in middle school, I spent the first dozen years of my life playing the quirky best friend to Bridget's leading lady—you know, the comic sidekick whose average appearance seems downright troll-like when sharing the frame with the incandescent, above-the-marquee beauty. Like Lili Taylor in *Say Anything.* Or Lili Taylor in *Mystic Pizza.* Or Lili Taylor in any movie, *ever.*

But turning her down did me little good. This dorm has forty rooms on four floors. Yet is it any surprise that Bridget has been assigned a room just two doors down?

"You can ignore me if you want to," she said with a pout.

I should give Bridget more credit because the acting program had more applicants than any other, but I probably won't. I'm pissed at her for crashing what was supposed to be *my* summertime banishment. Dropping out of Pineville society had a purpose, you know. This was supposed to be my test run for college, my only opportunity to practice spinning my personality into a more alluring and/or amusing alternative to the real me. I could've worked out all the kinks this summer so I don't waste a moment of real college life next September.

For example (and this is just an example, one of many possibilities), I could've written erotica and transformed myself into suburban New Jersey's underage answer to Anaïs Nin. No one would've known any better to question the authenticity. I mean, what kind of starved-for-attention sicko would make up a whole new identity for herself just for amusement's sake? Oh, yeah. That's right. One who wanted to score a book contract, a movie deal, and an acceptance letter from Harvard. None other than the trust-fund turncoat herself, Miss Hyacinth Anastasia Wallace. Ack.

Too bad Bridget's pathological honesty makes such a temporary image makeover impossible for me. I can just imagine her calling out my bullshit in front of my SPECIAL classmates. "Jess is a *virgin*. Like, what does she know about throbbing, pulsating passion?"

While I don't look forward to exhausting the energy it will require to ignore Bridget all summer, I do look forward to all the possibilities of getting out of Pineville, mainly (as much as I hate to admit it because it gives in to my girliest tendencies) the chance that I'll meet the magnetic, brilliant boy who proves once and for all that a particular Pineville High student, He Who Shall Remain Nameless, does not corner the market on magnetism or brilliance.

the fifth

The first two days of SPECIAL are devoted to orientation, during which we're supposed to meet people and get cozy with the campus. Instead of letting us meet people on our own, in a natural, uncontrived way, the powers that be organize agonizing events like last night's Get-to-Know-Ya Games.

It was during the GTKY Games that I looked into the face of pure evil. She wore blue eye shadow and hot-pink spandex leggings, and went by the name of Pammi. She had eighties soap-opera hair and a well-rehearsed bubbliness that instantly reminded me of Brandi, the school's mental health "expert," with whom I had several run-ins last year. I swear Pineville's "Professional Counselor" and Pammi were separated at birth, with only one brain between them. Pammi is one of the teachers in the acting program (lucky, lucky Bridget), but for last night she was the "Play Leader," a sort of referee for these inane games. Her main responsibilities were (1) *woo-hooing* at random intervals, (2) shouting the rules for the next GTKY game, and (3) blowing the start signal into the beak of a plastic whistle shaped inexplicably like a toucan.

For example:

"*Woo-hoo!* Find each and every person in the program who shares your birth month! Go!"

Tweet!

Then I would have to find each and every person in the program who shared my birth month until all one hundred of us were in the proper calendrical grouping.

Or:

"*Woo-hoo!* Dance butt-to-butt with someone wearing the same color shirt as you but who is not in your birth month group! Go!"

Tweet!

And then I would have to dance butt-to-butt with someone who was also wearing a white shirt but was *not* born in January.

This went on for three hours.

They can't possibly make us do this during freshman orientation next year, can they? I don't get how this is supposed to help us fit in. In theory, you're supposed to get everyone's names and become lifelong friends. I literally had contact with half the kids here last night, but how in the hell do they expect me to differentiate one of my butt-to-butt dancing partners from another? Am I supposed to randomly rub my buttocks up against people to see if we've bonded booties before? "Yes, the particular musculature of your ass does feel familiar. I remember you now!"

Now that I think about it, buttocks-bumping was an unintentionally appropriate prelude to the fun we have in store for the next month. The unspoken objective for the overwhelming majority of SPECIAL students has clearly revealed itself, and it's a lot more straightforward than the enrichment crap listed in the brochure: GET LAID.

To this end, the girls on my floor have devoted much time

to the creation of the Lucky Seven, an official designation of the most doable guys in the program. Girls outnumber guys seventy-two to twenty-eight, so the competition is fierce. SPECIAL is a haven for straight boys whose interest in the arts has inevitably led to homophobic taunts at their respective high schools. This is their chance to shine. Even after taking their hardships into consideration, only seven made the cut. Very lucky for them, indeed. Very unlucky for me. See, I made butt-to-butt contact with each and every one of the Lucky Seven, none of which was a gluteal love connection.

Take Derek, "the vocal music hottie," for example. The mere mention of my name inspired him to break out into a Broadway show tune version of the 1981 Rick Springfield tune "Jessie's Girl." This was unwise for two reasons: (1) I introduced myself as Jessica, not Jessie. I loathe being called Jessie. (Almost as much as I loathe it when my dad calls me Notso, as in Jessica Not-so-Darling. Har-dee-har-har. It's even more hilarious *now* than it was the first bajillion times he said it.) (2) The song "Jessie's Girl" is sung by a guy (Rick Springfield) who wants another guy's (Jessie's) girlfriend (name unknown). For the song "Jessie's Girl" to apply to me, it would have to be a song about Rick's lesbian envy, or something like that.

I tried explaining this to Derek, who replied, "Well, excuse me, Miss Buzzkill."

I see my reputation has preceded me.

The only other notable Lucky Seven exchange was with "the saxophone player hottie."

"I'm Mike," he said, swiveling his butt against my shoulder blades. He was nearly a foot taller than me. "What's yours?"

"Jessica."

"Jessica what?"

"Jessica Darling."

"Get the fuck out!" he yelled, bringing our butt-to-butt dance to a screeching halt.

"I will not," I said. "That's my name."

He snickered.

"Seriously, what's your problem?"

Snicker. Snicker. Snicker.

"What?"

"You look different in person."

I stood there with my hands on my hips, glaring.

More snickering.

More glaring.

"I know we just met, but now you're pissing me off."

He held out his hand. "I'm honored to meet you, Jessica Darling, the Queen of Anal as voted by the 1997 Adult Video Awards."

Jesus Christ. If telling a girl she shares a name with a porn queen who specializes in butt stuff qualifies as wooing these days, I'm signing up for the nunnery tomorrow.

The upside to all this is that at least I know for sure, on day one of orientation, that there is no hope. Not one shred of hope that I will find my true love. Not one sliver of hope that I will meet the one who will permanently erase the memory of He Who Shall Remain Nameless.

It's good to get that out of the way. Now I can just move on.

Of course, it would be much easier to forget He Who Shall Remain Nameless and move on if I stopped having XXX-rated dreams about him.

Oh, Christ. That's exactly the type of thing that warrants a journal burning.

the sixth

The very notion of being defrocked by a teacher is nothing more than comedic fodder for girls in the Pineville school district. A sorrier assemblage of men is unlikely to be found anywhere in the world. Hope and I tried compiling a list of the hottest teachers when we were sophomores, and it turned into a carnal cavalcade of freaks, starting with Mr. "Bee Gee" Gleason, the history teacher whose disco-era, irony-free wardrobe consists of polyester bell-bottoms and butterfly collars, and ending with Mr. "Rico Suave" Ricardo, my homeroom teacher, whose party-in-the-back, all-business-up-front mullet is an engineering marvel requiring no small amount of technical know-how and a complex assortment of mousses, gels, and hair sprays.

I lamented the dearth of hot male teachers, but now I realize it was a blessing. My academic record would not be as impressive had I been distracted by the likes of Professor Samuel MacDougall, who can credit three novels, two works of nonfiction, and one hot piece of ass to his name. Finally! A new Obsessive Object of Horniness. OOOH!

"Call me Mac," he said.

Mackadocious is more like it.

"For the next month, I will be your writing instructor . . ."

Lip Macking Good.

"It was Alfred, Lord Tennyson, who said, 'Words, like Nature, half reveal and half conceal the Soul within . . .'"

Big Mac Attack.

"Here, in the next six weeks, I hope you do more revealing than concealing . . ."

Oh, I'll reveal more than that if you want me to, Mac Daddy.

"You will read and write for six hours a day, five days a week. There will be a morning workshop lasting three hours. Then a break for lunch, followed by an afternoon workshop. You will be expected to share your writing and critique each other's work, which will help you become more careful readers and better blah-diddy-blah-blah-blah . . ."

That's where I kind of zoned out. Maybe it's the humidity, but Jesus Christ, Mac brings out the Van Halen in me.

Got it bad, got it bad, got it bad . . . I'm hot for teacher.

What makes it worse is that I seem to be the only student who has fallen under his hypnotic spell. True, he's not the obviously crushable type. He's skinny with thick tortoise shell glasses and curly black hair that springs off his head in all directions: *SPROIIIIINNNNNNG!* See, my idea of cute comes with an IQ requirement. It's geeky cute. It's Rivers Cuomo, not Justin Timberlake. Joseph Gordon-Levitt, yes please! Brad Pitt, no thank you.

My mental undressing got as far as Mac's boxer briefs when the class gasped in response to something he had said.

"What did he just say?" I whispered to a tall, anemic guy next to me, a dead ringer for the Grim Reaper. (Pun very much intended.)

"The seminar will culminate in a reading at Blood and Ink," he replied in a subvocal growl.

This meant nothing to me. "Where?"

"Blood and Ink."

Me, expressionless as a lifetime of Botox injections.

Grim Reaper turned to the shadowy figure sitting next to him. "She's never heard of Blood and Ink."

You wouldn't think that a girl with eight barbells in her face could be so easily horrified. I would say that all the color drained from Barbella's face, but I was pretty sure that the vampire girl sitting behind her had drained her veins already.

Thankfully, Mac stepped in before I was ritually sacrificed.

"Blood and Ink is a performance space located in the East Village in Manhattan. It is one of the last bastions of oral story-telling. Historically, it has always been a forum where writers blah-diddy-blah-blah-blah . . ."

I think the other reason I'm the only one Macking out is that my fellow students can only be bothered by the deepest, most intellectually rewarding pursuits.

"Now that you know what I expect of you in these next six weeks"—which I didn't, because I hadn't been listening—"I'd like to find out what you hope to get out of this program. Francis Bacon said, 'Write down the thoughts of the moment. Those that come unsought are commonly the most valuable.' For the next fifteen minutes, I want you to write in the moment. Answer these questions: Why are you here? Why did you willingly sign up for a program that traps you inside a classroom all summer long while your friends are at the beach? More important, why do you want to write? I expect you to share your responses with the class."

A hand shot up next to me. It was attached to another black-clad lump of a person, with skin so pale that her veins gave her a blueish hue. A vision of the Lump frolicking in the sand made me chuckle, which was not a very cool thing to do when you should be trying to make friends.

"Must I use prose? I'm a poet."

"You can write in whatever form you feel is best for self-expression," Mac replied.

So what did I write about? How did I account for my presence at SPECIAL? Well, without totally plagiarizing my application essay, I basically wrote that I wanted to escape another summer catering to attitudinal tourists at Wally D's Sweet Treat Shoppe but my parents are putting every extra penny toward my college fund and would only send me to a summer program that cost little (cross-country camp) or nothing at all (SPECIAL), so I chose mental exertion over physical and applied to the writing program because I can't sing, act, dance, paint, play the piano, or do anything else of artistic merit.

This response was deemed unacceptable by everyone in the room.

"Is that your idea of satire?" asked a guy who literally had the word LOSER tattooed in tiny letters across his forehead.

"Do you know how many *serious* writers were dying to get into this program?" grumbled the Grim Reaper.

"I know her type," murmured the Lump. "She's here so she can put one last accomplishment on her Harvard application."

And Mac clicked his tongue. "Tch."

I deserved this abuse, but not for the reasons they thought I did. My essay was the biggest pack of lies this side of Miss

Hyacinth Anastasia Wallace. It's one thing to lie to my (hot!) teacher. But I know I've sunk to a truly sad state when I'm tempted to lie in here to make myself look better to the hypothetical reader in the future who has nothing better to do but pore over this journal. (Wouldn't you rather beam yourself to another planet, or something twenty-third century like that?)

So in the spirit of full disclosure and unflinching honesty (that is totally unnecessary for anyone who has been reading this notebook from the beginning and sees my confession coming), I will reveal the truth. I am here for one reason.

Because *he* isn't.

He.

Him.

HIM.

He Who Shall Remain Nameless . . .

ARRRRRRRRRRRRRRRRRRRRRRRRRRRRRRRRGH.

This self-prescribed cognitive behavioral therapy isn't getting any easier.

According to my psych book, traumatized patients can convince themselves that a heinous event never happened. Apparently, if the delusion lasts long enough, you'll trick yourself into really *believing* that it did not occur and move on with your life. It doesn't necessarily sound like a healthy strategy, but it's not like any other approach is working for me. So I decided to remove the name of He Who Shall Remain Nameless from my vocabulary until I forget him entirely. At that point he'll still be nameless, but I won't be excruciatingly aware of it anymore.

It's been seven months and my carefully selective amnesia hasn't kicked in yet.

But I wasn't about to write about him. Nope. Just like I'm not going to think about him now. Instead I will think about Mac. And I will think about Mac *out* of his boxer briefs . . .

the tenth

W ell, after a week of endless introductions, it's official: I can't revel in my relative obscurity anymore. Until six months ago, Pineville was fairly anonymous, even to fellow New Jerseyans. If Pineville High was known at all, it was only for its proximity to other notorious high schools.

Heightstown High School, for example, the upscale enclave for Wall Street commuters' kids that saw its hoity-toity reputation plummet when it was revealed that one-third of the graduating class of 1996 had contracted syphilis at one of several Senior Class Orgies organized by the student-body president in an attempt to "boost school spirit." ("Go SCO!" was a popular motto among those in the know.)

Or perhaps you recall hearing about PHS's archrival, Eastland High School, a.k.a. the Prom Mom's alma mater. Back in 1999, she left the dance floor and dropped a six-pound, two-ounce bundle of joy in the back seat of the rented limousine. Prom Mom left him screeching and covered with amniotic slime while she headed back inside and asked the deejay to play "Boom Boom Boom." Psychologists scratched their heads over interpreting the symbolic meaning of the song choice, oblivious to the obvious explanation, which was, simply, that she was a huge fan of the Outhere Brothers.

These tabloid stories occurred at high schools less than a half hour from home, thereby providing an amusing way to pinpoint Pineville's location when introducing myself to strangers, i.e., "Oh, Pineville? It's fifteen minutes from Prom Mom." I appreciated the relative anonymity, as it spared me the embarrassment of apologizing about my origins with a reflexive, "Yeah, I know. I live in the stankiest, hairiest crook within the armpit of the nation."

Here at SPECIAL, my fears have been confirmed. Pineville is now as well known as its neighbors for not one, but two different claims to fame: (1) The inspiration behind Miss Hyacinth Anastasia Wallace's book and motion picture. (2) The birthplace of gangsta "pap" trailblazer Kayjay Johnson *and* the video bitch who broke his heart.

I refuse to waste ink on the former because it's only going to get worse in the coming months, a thought that makes me want to pull out my teeth one by one with a medieval dental instrument as my SPECIAL classmates cheer me on.

I have avoided writing about the latter because I keep hoping that he will cross over into "Where are they now?" oblivion. But it's clear that neither is going to happen anytime soon. I'm known throughout the dorm as "the girl from Pineville who knows the other girl from Pineville who went with Kayjay Johnson!" So much for me wanting to establish an identity completely separate from Bridget's.

Karl Joseph Johnson is a shoulda-been graduate of PHS Class of 1999. He was sent to juvie after the top-notch Pineville police department discovered that he was stealing his neighbors' lawn mowers and selling them for drug money. (The giveaway? The Johnsons were the only family in the Bay Gate section of town whose lawn wasn't a weedy, overgrown mess.) But unlike every one of Pineville's juvenile delinquents before him, Johnson parlayed his petty criminal status into a full-time career when he was rechristened Kayjay, one of the five demi-himbos in the "baaaaaad" boy band Hum-V.

Because it is doubtful that Hum-V will be remembered in the annals of music history, I will briefly describe their contribution to popular culture here.

Hum-V is what I predict will be the last teenybopper trifle to come off the Orlando assembly line, a group put together in a desperately calculated attempt to cash in on *TRL's* *NSYNC– Eminem polarization, squeezing every last bit of air out of the barely breathing boy-band genre. Hum-V's faux-funky jams and toothachey ballads sound as synth-cheesy as their nonthreatening, harmonizing predecessors, but their lyrics are painstakingly incendiary. Hum-V is the first boy band to earn a Parental Advisory warning label.

Kayjay was the most vocally challenged member, whose only reason for being in the group was because he had red hair and freckles. The evil geniuses behind Hum-V decided they needed a Cute Redhead Boy with the Freckles to round out the mix. The other members are: Cute Blond Boy with the Baby Face, Cute Latino Boy with the Muscles, Cute Black Boy with the Smile, and Cute Chinese-French-Canadian-Brazilian-Australian-Moroccan Boy with the DNA from Six out of Seven Continents.

Last spring, as the five Hum-V hunks pored over hundreds of eight-by-ten glossies to handpick the girls who would portray "bitches" in the video for their straight-to-the-middle single, "Bitch (Y U B Trippin?)," Kayjay instantly recognized the aspiring model Bridge Milhouse as none other than Pineville High's Bridget Milhokovich, the blond babe who was ranked number one on the Fuckable Freshmen List when he was a senior. Kayjay never got a crack at her before he was bounced out of PHS because Bridget was still with Burke, as he had yet to cheat on her with Manda. So to make his high school fantasy a reality, Kayjay picked Bridget to portray the bitch who b trippin' on him. Their portion of the video "plot" involved screaming at each other, then kiss-and-making-up in a torrential downpour, all shot in the slo-mo style that signifies heavy emotional stuff in the music video world.

Neither the wrath of his then-girlfriend, Shy'la from the Christian girl group Halo Hello, nor the fire hose rain could put out the fire of Kayjay's desire. (Hmm . . . that sounds familiar. Oh, no. I think that's a line from the Hum-V Song. Christ.) Kayjay was smitten with Bridge Milhouse and was obsessed with winning her over. Bridget is a sucker for glamour and couldn't resist his offer to be his arm candy for important PR ops like movie premieres, awards shows, and parties thrown by people he'd never met. Incredibly, it only took one such outing for Bridget to discover that fame had only expanded the dimensions of Kayjay's sphincter.

"He was, like, the biggest asshole I'd ever gone out with," she reported to a rapt audience at PHS the Monday morning after the big date.

Considering that "Bitch (Y U B Trippin?)" peaked at number 8 on *TRL* and barely cracked the *Billboard* chart, Hum-V's appearance on the covers of teenybopper bibles continues to baffle me. Apparently, Hum-V's small but intense fan base—the Hummers, as they call themselves—guarantees that Kayjay enjoys a cushy existence that has little to do with Hum-V's overall popularity. They are also responsible for the relentless haterade spewed on message boards toward "the blond ho from the video" who "broke poor Kayjay's heart" months after their one and only and very insignificant date. Bridget has vowed to never, ever date a celebrity (or quasi celebrity) again.

"Unless it's, like, James Dean back from the dead," she says.

"Well, *that's* sensible," I say.

Though the relationship tanked, this little credit on her résumé has already made Bridget the envy of all the other girls in SPECIAL's acting program. Still, I realized her notoriety had spread beyond the world of wannabe actress-models when my roommate recognized Bridget right away. My roommate just happens to be Hum-V's biggest fan, or so she shrieks.

You might have noticed my roommate's conspicuous absence from my journal thus far. Every time I picked up this journal to start writing, she'd hover over my shoulder and say, "You're writing about *me*, aren't you?"

This is just one of many quirks I've observed about the person with whom I'm supposed to share a room for the next three weeks and five days. For the time being, I will stick to irrefutable facts, untainted by my cynical analysis. We've still got a long haul ahead of us and I don't want to damn her right away with my first, second, and third impressions, as my character analyses are usually shit. I could very well find out tomorrow that she really is cool, despite surface characteristics that indicate otherwise. If I avoid jumping to conclusions now, I won't have to feel guilty about all the mean things I'll most likely write about her later.

So here are the facts and just the facts:

- **Name:** Mary "Call Me Chantalle" DePasquale.
- **Hometown:** Huntsdale, which means she is from the wealthiest town in the wealthiest county in the wealthiest state in the wealthiest nation in the world.
- **Long-Term Goal:** Principal dancer with the American Ballet Theater.
- **Short-Term Goal:** To share an unspecified "intimate moment" with each and every one of the Lucky Seven. Ack.
- **Aesthetic Icon:** It's hard to tell. Her body is so teeny that her head looks supersized in comparison, giving her the appearance of a lollipop in a tutu. She makes *me* (a boobless, assless five foot five) look like a WWF superstar.
- **Telltale Quote:** "Call me Chantalle." These were her first words to me. "Is Chantalle your middle name?" I asked. "Call. Me. Chantalle," she replied. Then she ripped Mary DePasquale's pointe shoe off the door, the only evidence that her birth name was more spinster than Parisian courtesan. This switch is fitting, considering it took her fewer than twenty-four hours to provide Derek, the vocal music hottie, with a manual release. Unspecified Intimate Moment #1. Ack. The thing that really irks me about Call Me Chantalle's name change is that it's precisely the kind of summer identity-morphing that I can't get away with. Damn that Bridget!
- **Potentially Troubling Fact:** On the bookshelves above her bed, Call Me Chantalle displays three

nutcrackers like the hero from the ballet of the same name, each one foot tall, a mere fraction of the extensive collection she keeps in a display case at home. They are all dressed in military garb but carry different weapons—a gun, a sword, a British bobby baton—as if they were guarding her virginity. They'd better be on high alert, because I walked in on her in full-frontal frottage with "the saxophone player hottie" on day five. Unspecified Intimate Moment #2. Ack.

▫ **Positively Troubling Fact:** Call Me Chantalle brought a half-dozen bottles of Summer's Eve douche, which she keeps in plain view in her closet, not to mention the Summer's Eve body wash in her shower caddy, and the travel-size Summer's Eve disposable wipes stashed in her backpack. What makes this hygienic hoarding so odd is that she doesn't try to hide it, which makes me feel like I'm wrong for thinking it's weird. But it *is* weird, isn't it? Then again, maybe there's something *I've* been doing in the privacy of my own bedroom my whole life that I think is perfectly normal but is actually illegal in thirty-two states. Call Me Chantalle could observe the way I clip my toenails and think, *My God, how can she cut the pinky toenail first, when every sane person knows you finish with the littlest piggie?*

I am doing my best to be positive by celebrating Call Me Chantalle's quirks. After all, isn't this the beauty of having a roommate? Getting a glimpse of someone else's private world and discovering that everyone is as big a freak as you are, just in different ways?

I got a postcard today from Hope, who's in London, where she has had a far more interesting assortment of cool characters to observe. I'd like to think she's got the advantage of a fascinating location, but I know it's just the way she is. At first, strangers are struck by her appearance—six feet of luminous, alabaster skin topped by wild, flame-colored curls. But then they're drawn to her warmth, sensitivity, and good humor. No matter where she ends up at college, Hope will make lasting connections with the chatty girls in her dorm, the brooding guys in her art classes, the awkward sopranos and tenors in her choir, whoever. *She* could find redeeming qualities in Call Me Chantalle, that's for sure.

I'm afraid that Hope will still be as vital to my sanity but I won't be as important to hers, simply because she will have made new friends to fill the void. I don't think she'll forget me, but she'll move beyond me, because that's the healthy thing to do when your best friend lives a thousand miles away and you can only talk to her once a week and see her once a year.

Maybe I should try to get used to this now. Maybe I should accept that this journal is the only place that's safe to express what's really going on inside my mixed-up mind. Or maybe I should give others the benefit of the doubt. Maybe, just maybe, I should stop blaming SPECIAL or Pineville for not serving up my soul mate on a silver platter with caviar on the side. Drop me anywhere on the map and I'd quickly prove that location isn't the problem—it's *me*.

the seventeenth

My trial run for college is still not going well. My classmates hate me. I should have known SPECIAL would be a haven for Noir Bards, and that they would have no tolerance for a fraud like me.

Pretentious and depressed, Noir Bards are very big on the fact that they are writers. They write a lot about writing, often rhyming words like *verse* and *hearse*. To them, black is always the new black. They spend a lot of time at poetry slams and other literary events, chain-smoking and washing down Paxil with (black) coffee. Their intricate facial hardware and goth get-ups are painfully obvious cries for help. Here's a brief archetypal member profile, very much tainted by my cynical analysis. (But that's okay because cynicism is in keeping with the true, blackened spirit of the Noir Bard.)

- **Name:** Rebecca Adams (a.k.a. Ms. Nosferatu).
- **Hometown:** Cherry Hill, by way of Transylvania.
- **Long-Term Goal:** To be the next Sylvia Plath or Anne Sexton. (Read: Suicidal, then dead.)
- **Short-Term Goal:** To creep me out.
- **Aesthetic Icon:** Winona Ryder in *Beetlejuice*.

- **Telltale Quote:** "Why is/Anyone/Anywhere?" (From her poem "Dying All the Time.")
- **Potentially Troubling Fact:** She has fangs. Genuine fangs, not those detachable ones that club kids wear to torment their elders.
- **Positively Troubling Fact:** She bares them whenever Mac calls on me in class.

I admit that there are certain aspects of my personality—my chronic, low-grade depression, for example—that would prompt Pineville High classmates to vouch for my card-carrying status in the Noir Bard camp, despite the lack of funereal tones in my wardrobe. But now that we've shared our work with one another over the past few weeks, it is clear I am not one of them.

Take today's assignment, for example. We were asked to write a dramatic monologue in which the character talked about a life-changing experience. Proving the theory that writers are a tortured bunch, I was the only student in the writing program who didn't write about being rehabbed, raped, or rejected by a parent in a viciously ambivalent child custody case. I've never felt so normal in my entire life. Of course, SPECIAL is the one place on earth where being normal is a liability.

My monologue, told from Hope's perspective about moving to Tennessee, was not very well received. After I read it out loud, Mac made it clear that I am probably the most sunshiney, super-ficial student he's ever had. This, by the way, is making it much more difficult to have a crush on him, but not impossible.

"'The harder the conflict, the more glorious the triumph,'" Mac said. "Thomas Paine."

"Uh, okay."

"Dig deeper, Jessica. Work harder. Struggle with your writing. It will be worth it."

"Uh, how?"

"Tch." Mac grabbed two handfuls of his curls, right above both ears. "Any suggestions?"

"Use her departure as a metaphor for man's journey to the grave," urged Loser.

"Make the narrator a voice from the grave," suggested the Grim Reaper.

"But she's not dead," I argued, not so eager to kill off my best friend for the sake of satisfying this bloodthirsty group.

"Do you know anyone who's moved on to the next realm?" asked Barbella.

"Her brother died of a drug overdose when he was eighteen."

"That is the best thing I've heard out of you since we've been here," said Nosferatu.

"Write it from *his* perspective," said the Lump.

There were nods of approval all around the room.

And Mac said, "Tch."

I don't think it's fair for me to steal someone else's tragedy for the sake of completing an assignment. This makes it very hard for me to "dig deeper and darker." We all know that nothing *really* bad has ever happened to me—just take a look at my Top Trauma List. Every day, I wait for that doomsday shoe to drop on my head and crush my spirit.

If my classmates have any say in the matter, that shoe will be made by one Dr. Marten.

Until the Doc drops, what can I possibly have to write about? What made the admissions people believe that I belong here? Why didn't I choose cross-country camp instead? Oh, that's right. Because I suck. I broke every school distance record in my sophomore year. The only thing I've broken since then is my leg. I'm still waiting for the day I finally shatter my father's dreams of NCAA glory.

But right now, limping through workouts seems preferable to this. I may be the best writer at Pineville High, but that really isn't saying much now, is it? I just don't have it in me. If there's one thing I've learned at the New Jersey Summer Pre-College Enrichment Curriculum in Artistic Learning, it's this: I may be SPECIAL, but I'm not all that special. Good thing I figured this out here and now instead of next year.

the twenty-first

Having lost all hope for friendship with my classmates, I've tried to expand my social sphere here at SPECIAL, not because I really want to, but because I think it would be a good run-through for college.

Spurred by Bridget's endorsements, or more likely in desperate need of an extra order to reach the Chinese delivery minimum, her acting class buddy Ashleigh knocked on my door and invited me to dine with them. I was hungry and tired of the dining hall's grilled cheese sandwiches, so I accepted. Against my better judgment, mind you, because I do not like Ashleigh.

In Ashleigh, I've discovered a unique breed of annoyingness, different from that of the Clueless Two. Manda and Sara are annoying because their whole belief system is in opposition to my own. Manda has a compulsive need to sleep with other girls' boyfriends, then uses pseudofeminist arguments to justify why her actions are a fight against the patriarchy and not just an exhibition of heinous skankitude. Sara delights in spreading the word about her best friend's misdeeds (and everyone else's, for that matter) yet doesn't think it's hypocritical to get pissed when the gossipmongering exposes her own shady debaucheries.

Anyway, Ashleigh's annoyingness manifests itself more in

form than content. Meaning, her comments aren't inherently annoying. In fact, she often says things that I've been thinking myself. The problem is, even Ashleigh's most banal observations become annoying by the irritating force of her personality. She has a compulsive need not only to be right about everything, but to stake her claim as the first genius/philosopher to have ever thought that particular thought. She will argue and argue and argue until you give in to her point of view and see things her all-knowing way.

For example, the first time I met Ashleigh, Bridget tried to speed up the bonding process by pointing out that we are both huge fans of John Hughes's earlier work.

"I've loved the Molly Ringwald movies *forever*," she said. "Not just because the eighties are trendy."

As you know, this same comment could also be applied to yours truly. But my fascination with the eighties goes way beyond John Hughes, and has long superseded all interest in my own generation. (With the exception of *The Real World*, which I still love even though it's totally predictable and corny. Like, who's the gay one this year? Who's the one who will have issues with her long-distance boyfriend? Which two are gonna be the platonic sexual-tension couple? But I still love it more than my own real world.) Ashleigh was clearly insinuating that I liked those flicks only because *Seventeen* and *YM* had approved their retro-kitsch appeal. But we had just met, and I was practicing my personable personality.

"Me too," I replied calmly. "I watched them when I was little because my sister liked them and—"

"I didn't need anyone to introduce me."

"Well, uh . . . okay."

"And it makes me mad when girls suddenly decide that *Breakfast Club* is their favorite movie, when they haven't even seen the version that isn't edited for TV . . ."

"It's pretty hilarious when they say 'Flip you!' instead of 'Fuck you!'" I said, trying to salvage the conversation. She steamrolled right over me.

"*I* didn't jump on the bandwagon. *I* discovered them on my own."

Ashleigh made this declaration as if she were Columbus, Magellan, and Ponce de León all rolled up into one ugly little package. Not so incidentally, Ashleigh uses a similarly contagious mind-over-matter to convince others she's cute. She believes in her cuteness so deeply that others see it too, despite the evidence to the contrary: flyaway bottle-blond hair, crazed, bulging eyes, and a nose that resembles a stalk of broccoli, inverted. (This is an externalized version of my He Who Shall Remain Nameless trick, which still isn't working.)

I so dislike Ashleigh's desperate need for conversation domination that I intentionally pick fights with her, even when I'm in total agreement with what she's saying. Very immature, I know. But it wasn't until tonight that my combative behavior came back to chomp me in the ass. No sooner had I looped my first lo mein noodle onto my chopsticks than Ashleigh gave the last word on the most infamously self-proclaimed virgin in the pop music community.

"Britney? No way," Ashleigh said. "She *lives* with Justin. Case closed."

It would be difficult to find someone in the Western world who disagrees with this. I mean, the only virgins left in the world are, uh, *me*, Hope, and those True Love Waits religious zealots who wear "hip" Holy Roller T-shirts with sayings like CHRIST'S MAMA WAS A VIRGIN AND SO AM I. But I just couldn't let Ashleigh go through life thinking that she's right about everything.

"How do you know Britney's motto isn't 'How about a hand job instead'?" I countered.

"Is that *your* motto?" Ashleigh asked, in the snotty way that only a not-cute-who-thinks-she's-cute devirginized girl can.

Splotches sprouted all over Bridget's face and neck, like a harvest of cherry tomatoes. Make that a harvest of cherry tomatoes with a guilt complex.

"Well, like, Ashleigh asked if you were a virgin, so, like . . ."

I didn't let her finish her sentence. I picked up my carton and left.

To add to the insult of my nonsexed status, I returned to my room to discover that Call Me Chantalle had tied one of her toe shoes on the doorknob, her way of letting me know she was "getting her wettins on." Unspecified Intimate Moment #6. Ack.

Her moans easily escaped through the walls, so the warning was totally unnecessary. Call Me Chantalle's pleasure grunts were so specific that I could tell that her partner was slurping, not screwing. Where, oh where, was the resident adviser when I needed one?

Tonight's sexile destroys all hope that my roommate and I will be anything but mortal enemies. Oh, I've seen her freak side, all right. Unfortunately, it's the Rick James, *from-her-head-down-to-her-toenails* variety. And to think my first impression of Call Me Chantalle, the one I kept to myself because I was being nice—that she was a prissy, waify nutcase with an unhealthy obsession with hygiene—was a dream compared to the reality. Call Me Chantalle is far more complex than I had thought. She's a prissy, waify nutcase with an unhealthy obsession with personal hygiene that is at odds with her freewheeling attitude about hookups.

I was contemplating my next move when I looked up and saw Bridget standing over me, chewing on her twenty-four-carat ponytail, looking sincerely apologetic.

"I'm, like, so sorry," she said. "I shouldn't have told Ashleigh that you're, like, you know, a *virgin*." She whispered the last word as if she'd said "necrophiliac" or "unicyclist." Come to think of it, it would be more socially acceptable at SPECIAL if she had.

"Ash is gone, by the way, if you want to, like, come back to my room with me."

It was better than listening to Call Me Chantalle climax with Joe, "the multimedia hottie."

"By the way, you, like, forgot this," she said, handing me a fortune cookie.

I opened it and it said: *The road less traveled will not be smooth.*

As if I didn't know that already. I should share it with Mac so he can add it to his repertoire.

the thirtieth

Since that last entry, much has happened:

1. Call Me Chantalle had an Unspecified Intimate Moment with all Lucky Seven, and two others who weren't hot enough to make the list. I hope that this hellish roommate means that next year I will blessed by the higher powers in charge of housing assignments.

2. I spend little time in my own room because it is an incubator for STDs. So I've struck up quasi friendships with girls on my floor, which gives me faith that I'll be able to suppress my naturally antisocial tendencies next year and bond with people who aren't Hope.

3. I was quite surprised by Bridget's skillful portrayal of Helena in *A Midsummer Night's Dream*. Her success in last year's spring play wasn't a fluke after all. She insists she isn't going to college but straight to Hollywood stardom. This has become our favorite ponytail-chewing debate.

4. I've heard more poems about the futility of human life than I care to mention.

5. All the evidence is in: My gaydar is broken, if it ever worked at all.

You might be wondering why I didn't write about any of these things. Well, the reason I didn't write about any of these things is that I didn't have this journal to write in. And the reason I didn't have it is so utterly moronic that it could only happen to me.

As you know, we are all required to keep a journal for class. In it, we were supposed to do a half hour of free writing a day, work on drafts of our assignments, and so on. Of course, it didn't take me very long to get back into the habit of writing only the most humiliating things in my journal, because deep down, I don't think anyone, even Hope, should be subjected to these ramblings in real life. Since I knew Mac would eventually ask for our notebooks, I started a new class journal that was highly censored, unlike this personal journal, which isn't censored enough. Both are of the traditional black-and-white-speckled composition notebook variety.

Last Friday, Mac asked us to turn in our journals so he could start reading them over the weekend. You see where this is going, so I'll just get to it:

I TURNED IN THE WRONG JOURNAL.

Psychologists would say that I did this on purpose. An intentional accident, because I wanted him to read all my ramblings, which he did, including those about him.

I think my only conscious thought in the forty-eight hours between that realization and my next class was, *HOLY SHIT*.

When I tried explaining my mortifying mistake on Monday morning, he said it was all the more reason for him to read it. Then he quoted Alexander Pope.

"'To observations which ourselves we make, we grow more partial for the observer's sake.'"

"Uh . . . but . . ."

"No buts," he replied. "Discussion over."

And it was over. For the next five days, Mac didn't say anything about the journal. In the meantime, I hoped that my pagan peers had filled their journals with malevolent blood oaths and lunar hexes. I prayed that these future cult leader manifestos were troubling enough for Mac to overlook my erotic overtures. I even considered asking the Wiccans to cast a spell involving all five points of the pentagram, one that would make these hopes and prayers come true. So what if I had to repay the debt by turning my soul over to the dark lord of the underworld? A small price, indeed.

Finally, today, Monday, as the class took a break for lunch (me) and ceremonial bloodletting (everyone else), Mac held up the wrong journal and said, "'The advantage of the emotions is that they lead us astray.' Oscar Wilde."

"Uh."

"Let's discuss this."

Sure, let's discuss that he's thirtysomething and I'm a minor and I'm lusting after him in a totally inappropriate student/ teacher "Don't Stand So Close to Me" kind of way that ruins reputations and gets people arrested and now we're alone in a classroom together and no one is around and it's very hot and sweaty and he's talking about leading me astray and I'm not wearing that much clothing and—

"Don't be embarrassed about the things you wrote about me," he started.

I wanted to say, *Oh no, I am not embarrassed at all. I believe in articulating one's deepest thoughts and feelings, even those that may be unconventional or, yes, illegal. After all, what use is a mind if we disallow freedom of expression?*

But it came out like this: "Nuhhh."

"You are familiar with my work, right?"

"Uh, sure! Of course! I love your books!" I lied. I'd never heard of him or his work before I showed up at SPECIAL.

"Then you know that my first novel, *Mama's Boy*, was a semiautobiographical account of my struggle to come out of the closet."

Out of the closet.

"And that it was dedicated to my longtime lover . . ."

Lover.

"Raul."

Raul.

"So you know I'm gay . . ."

Gay.

He's . . .

Gay.

Of course.

OF COURSE HE'S GAY.

Why would I ever lust after someone who *isn't* gay? First Paul Parlipiano, now Mac. Are all Manhattan hotties gay? How many more until I'm officially a princess among queens? This would only happen to me.

"Which means there's no reason for you to be embarrassed or uncomfortable about what you wrote."

He said it matter-of-factly, to make it so, even though he knew the exact opposite was true. I felt like a busted horse's ass, one whose only redeeming quality was that it could be shot and turned into glue.

"Now that that's out of the way, I'd like to talk to you about what I read. Why is it that nothing you've written for me in class holds up to what I read in this journal?"

I wanted to say, *What do you mean?* But instead it came out: "Wuhhh?"

"I want more of this," he said, handing my journal back to me. "This is real. This is you. If you want to be a writer, you need to stop censoring yourself. You need to write like this."

He massaged his scalp, waiting for some kind of multisyllabic response that I couldn't give him.

"The Noir Bards, as you aptly describe them, are more concerned with the stereotypical, self-loathing trappings of being a writer. But they all lack the one thing that you have: a writer's soul."

Jesus Christ. It was like Miss Haviland all over again.

"You're as bad as my English teacher," I said. "I'm here because I didn't want to go to cross-country camp or work on the boardwalk." Mac's eyebrows shot up in doubt. That's when I remembered that he had read the truth. So I switched gears. "Who says I want to be a writer?"

He removed his hands from his head. "'We are what we pretend to be.' Kurt Vonnegut."

"What's that supposed to mean?"

"You already are a writer," he said. "All you have to do is be yourself."

Huh. All this time, I thought Mac hated me and my writing. I told him this.

"The only thing you lack is life experience. Your life so far has been lived in one of those self-contained, shake-it-up-and-watch-it-snow globes. You owe it to yourself to go explore beyond your picture-perfect suburban surroundings. You owe it to the rest of us to go out into the world and describe what you see and feel from your unique point of view."

Okay. My surroundings are far from picture perfect, but I got the point.

"I pushed you because you were better than all the other kids in the class. You've only got two weeks left here; don't waste it. Don't blow this opportunity by being what everyone else wants you to be. Are you afraid of offending people? Telling them things they don't want to hear?"

"Yuh," I said, nodding vigorously.

"'If you can't annoy somebody, there's little point in writing,'" he replied. "Kingsley Amis."

"I'm afraid of embarrassing myself," I said. "I reveal excruciating things. Things like my illegal lust for my gay writing teacher. The me in my journal is a total dumbass."

This cracked Mac up.

"'The ignorant take themselves too seriously. The brilliant know better, and laugh at themselves.'"

"Who said that?"

"I did," he said, pausing long enough to shine the high beams on my stupidity. "In my second novel."

"Oh," I said, wincing. "Yeah."

"Tch."

While I'm relieved that Mac doesn't think I'm a pervy loser, his praise doesn't change the fact that I don't want to be a writer. I've already decided to major in psychology. I analyze everyone so much already, I might as well get paid for it.

I was on my way out the door when Mac called out to me.

"Oh, one last thing," he said.

"Yes?"

"Who is He Who Shall Remain Nameless?"

"Muhhh," I replied, stripped of my powers of speech. Again.

august

Hope,

Now that I've FINALLY FINALLY FINALLY got my journal back, I've been looking through it more carefully than usual for glimpses of genius. Personally, I don't see it.

What I do know is that my journal is a very shabby representation of my SPECIAL experience so far. I've been here for four weeks, yet I've neglected to write about any of the fun stuff I've done, or the cool people I've met since I've been here. No, I'd much rather dwell on Ashleigh, Call Me Chantalle, and the Noir Bards, all of whom have taught me a very valuable lesson: Annoying people are everywhere. They're at school. They're at camp. And they'll surely be in college. I might as well get used to it. But I won't. And that, my friend, is because I am a glutton for punishment.

Happy entries in my journal do not exist. Or if they do, they end abruptly with scenes and sentences left unfinished because they are too gushy in a way that is disturbing and foreign. Because of my inability to document any nondepressing developments in my life, the girls with whom I've spent the bulk of my time here at SPECIAL have gone nameless. Brooke Mars, for example. I've never mentioned her before, even though she is a very cool person. And I doubt I'll mention her again. I think the reason I didn't bother writing about Brooke is that I know, deep down in my gut, she and all the friends-4-eva that I meet this summer will drop off the edge of the universe once school starts up.

Oh, sure. I'll still be on their lists for forwarded email jokes and whatever, and there will be a few phone calls. But responding to their emails with a "LOL" is about as much effort as I'm willing to put into these friendships, which I know are just temporary time-and-place things, anyway. I know that to them, I'm just another smart-ass girl, no better or worse than the friends they see every day in the halls of their own high schools. Why make the effort to stay friends with me, someone they would have only known for forty-two days? Especially when we're all going to make a new four-year set of friends once we head to college.

I have a hard enough time keeping in touch with you—and you were my soul sister numero uno for three and a half years. You know as well as I do how exhausting it can be to have to explain everything after the fact. You should be here, watching my life happen in real time, because that's the only chance you'll have at really understanding it—and even then there's no guarantee. Even with the best intentions, growing apart might just be an inevitable part of growing up. It's no one's fault, so there's nothing to feel guilty about. It's just the way things are.

I know this letter is particularly pessimistic, but I don't see the point in putting any effort into any more long-distance friendships. Life—such as it is—always seems to get in the way.

Pragmatically yours,
J.

the fourth

I've never been a big fan of New York City. A lot of this has to do with my parents programming me to hate its dirt and crime and crowds and general seediness. When I told them I needed their permission to attend last night's big reading at Blood and Ink, they almost didn't sign the consent form. Their arguments ranged from hysterical ("Gangs target innocent kids like you for drive-bys!") to simply childish ("Giuliani, Schmuliani!"). Finally, after much whining on my part, they caved in ("Bring Mace!").

Now that I've returned from the trip, I understand why New York City has become a haven for people who don't feel like they fit anywhere else. Only in New York could I hear the sound that would change my destiny.

"I'd like a coffee, black." That voice . . .

"And a biscotti."

That *voice*. Could it be . . . ?

"Thank you."

And there, brighter than the wattage of Times Square or the Rockettes' bleached smiles, and more spectacular than anything Broadway has ever seen, was none other than the Boy Whose Name I Can Shout Out Loud . . .

PAUL PARLIPIANO!

I caused such a commotion at the milk and sugar station that I immediately attracted his attention in the most seen-it-all city on earth. But even on the off chance he recognized me, I never expected him to come over to talk to me, which is exactly what happened. So this is how, in a city of a bajillion people, and even more coffee franchises, I found myself standing face-to-face with my crush-to-end-all-crushes.

"I know you," Paul Parlipiano said.

I gulped down a chunky mouthful of air.

"Jessica Darling, right?"

I nodded.

"You're still at Pineville. You're going to be a senior."

I nodded again and forced a single word out of my throat.

"Yes."

"What are you doing here?"

"SPECIAL."

"I see."

As soon as he said that, I realized how dorky I must have sounded. He didn't know SPECIAL was an acronym. Duh.

"Summer Pre-College Enrichment Curriculum in Artistic Learning. SPECIAL. I got accepted to the writing program."

"Great," he said.

"It really isn't all that great because I don't really like the people in my class because they're all very pretentious and suicidal and we all took a trip here today to do a reading at Blood and Ink that they're all very psyched about but I'm not really and our professor who is the writer Samuel MacDougall have you heard of him? No? Well, he let us roam around for a while to take in the sights, sounds, and smells so we could write about them later so I decided to come here to take a break even though it would totally freak my parents out if they knew I was wandering around alone because they hate New York but nothing screams *dork* louder than traveling in packs . . ."

Correction: Nothing screams *dork* louder than a dork who can't stop babbling.

Thank God Paul Parlipiano pointed to a free table, because the shock of that gesture shut me up. He did it without thinking, as though it was totally natural and normal for me, Jessica Darling, to sit down and have coffee with him, Paul Parlipiano, my former obsessive object of horniness, in the middle of the afternoon, on a totally average day, in this teensy little nothing of a pastry shop in the heart of New York City, New York, USA. If this was happening, didn't it make *anything* possible? Why couldn't we fall madly in love and get married and have many babies? I don't even like babies. I have a very low tolerance for people who sit in their own feces. But something about Paul Parlipiano made me want to procreate. He gave me the urge to merge.

I sat down.

With a broad sweep of his forearm, Paul Parlipiano brushed away stray sugar crystals and muffin crumbs left behind by the previous customer. It was the sloppiness of that tidy-up gesture—one I'd watched him do hundreds of times in the Pineville High cafeteria—that reminded me of a small but crucial detail that would put the kibosh on our honeymoon: PAUL PARLIPIANO IS GAY.

This was easy for me to forget because he looked and acted the same as he always did. Trust me, I'm an expert. No one has studied Paul Parlipiano as intensely I have. But there were no signs of any coming-out clichés: No platinum highlights in his dirty blond curls. No pink triangle pins. No I'M HERE. I'M QUEER. GET USED TO IT! tattoo.

"So how do you like school?" I bravely ventured.

"I love it! Columbia was the best decision I ever made in my life," he said, running a finger around the rim of his mug. "I thought that's why you might be here."

I didn't understand what he meant.

"I thought you might be checking out colleges."

"Oh, uh. No."

"Oh," he said, his mouth forming an oval just wide enough to wrap my lips around.

"Jessica?"

"Uh, what?" I said, snapping back to G-rated reality. "Did you say something?"

"Where are you headed next year?"

Sigh.

When you're a senior in high school, it's a given that everyone you come in contact with is going to ask you a variation of that question within thirty seconds of saying "Hey." So you'd better have a fast answer. Until today, mine was: "Amherst, Boatwright, Swarthmore, or Williams."

Paul Parlipiano's face puckered as though he had just taken a swig out of a milk carton with an expiration date from the *first* Bush administration.

"What's wrong with those schools? It just so happens that all four of them are among the top twenty most difficult to get into *in the world*. In fact, it's harder to get into these schools than some of the Ivies."

Defensive much, Jess?

His face relaxed slightly, enough to reply, "They're *fine* schools."

"Then what's with the face?"

"Well, it's just that they're all kind of out in the boondocks," he replied. "How did you decide that you wanted to be on a campus in the middle of nowhere?"

"Do you really want me to get into it?"

Paul Parlipiano leaned back in his chair and made the steeple gesture with his hands. You know, from the childhood rhyme: *Here's the church, here's the steeple, open the door . . .*

I took a deep breath.

"According to the Princeton Review, there are approximately sixteen hundred accredited institutions of higher learning I can apply to. This is way too many, as having too many options always freaks me out . . ."

And thus, for the next half hour, I explained . . .

JESSICA DARLING'S PROCESS
OF COLLEGIATE ELIMINATION

STEP 1: ELIMINATE ANY SCHOOL THAT IS NOT IN THE
MOST-DIFFICULT-TO-GET-INTO CATEGORY.

Not everyone can get away with such academic snobbery. With my College Boards and jacked transcript, I can be as snooty as all get-out.

Number of Schools Left: 35

STEP 2: ELIMINATE ANY SCHOOL "IN THE RED"—IN OTHER WORDS, ANY SCHOOL LOCATED IN A STATE THAT VOTED FOR BUSH IN THE 2000 ELECTION.

While I am sure there are smart people in these red states (after all, Hope is surviving in one), I can't help but be a Northeastern elitist when 75 percent of schools in the Most Difficult to Get Into category are located in states that *did not* vote for Bush. (Note: This got a chuckle and a nod of approval from Paul Parlipiano.)

Number of Schools Left: 29

STEP 3: ELIMINATE ANY SCHOOL LOCATED IN A REMOTELY URBAN SETTING.

My parents have ruled out Columbia, NYU, UChicago, Northwestern, UPenn, Georgetown, and Johns Hopkins because they are all located in "ghettos"—which is not only offensive and inaccurate but also impossible to argue against because they are footing the bill. (Note: Pay close attention to this eliminator, as it will come into play later.)

Number of Schools Left: 22

STEP 4: ELIMINATE ANY SCHOOL IN CALIFORNIA.

The California sunshine has fried my sister and brother-in-law's brains. Bethany and G-Money were always scary, but never as much as when they moved to the dot commune. As if the state weren't overrun by blonds already, Bridget flies out there all the time to visit her dad and advance her career. Furthermore,

I find Californians' compulsive friendliness unsettling. I think these are enough reasons for staying away from that freaky state.

Number of Schools Left: 20

STEP 5: AND CANADA, FOR THAT MATTER.

Celine Dion. Enough said. (Note: Another chuckle from Paul Parlipiano. I was *on*, baby. On.)

Number of Schools Left: 19

STEP 6: ELIMINATE ANY SCHOOL THAT ANY OF MY CLASSMATES HAVE THE SLIGHTEST INTEREST IN/ CHANCE OF GETTING INTO.

My only competition for valedictorian, Len Levy, has made it very clear that he is going to Cornell. Do I even need to mention that there is only one *other* person at PHS who is smart enough to get into any of these schools? And he has kept his preferences to himself. Or maybe he hasn't. But he hasn't shared them with me.

Number of Schools Left: 18

STEP 7: ELIMINATE ANY WOMEN-ONLY SCHOOLS.

I WANT TO HAVE (HETEROSEXUAL) SEX. Is that so wrong? I'm not ready to give up and take a four-year lesbian vacation. (Note: I didn't get into the specifics with Paul Parlipiano on this one, lest he think I'm homophobic, which I'm not. It's just not for me.)

Number of Schools Left: 14

STEP 8: ELIMINATE ANY SCHOOL CONVENIENTLY LOCATED FOR UNANNOUNCED PARENTAL VISITS.

Duh.

Number of Schools Left: 11

STEP 9: ELIMINATE ANY SCHOOL WHERE I'D BE THE DUMBEST FIRST-YEAR STUDENT.

This is probably the most surprising eliminator, so I'll explain.

For my first three years of high school, I was obsessed with getting into Harvard or Yale. Then I toured both campuses last spring and discovered I was the only prospective freshman who hadn't won an Academic Decathlon or developed opto-electronic semiconductor heterostructures in my downtime, you know, for kicks. I'm not kidding. PHS hasn't prepared me for cutthroat academics. I am a big, brainy fish in a tiny, toxic waste–filled pond. I don't want to be reminded every day for four years that my SATs can only do so much in the effort to transcend my white trash roots.

Plus, there's something kind of sick about the over-the-top sense of pride my parents would get from slapping a Harvard or Yale sticker in their back windshields. My mom didn't go to college, but she wants everyone to know that her very own flesh and blood is smart enough to attend one of these super brand-name Ivies. She wants to take credit for my intelligence like a classic parensite, a.k.a. any adult who tries to leech a life out of their kid. Yikes.

Number of Schools Left: 9

STEP 10: ELIMINATE ANY SCHOOL THAT COULD NOT SERVE UP SWEET UNDERGRADUATE EYE CANDY WHILE I WAS ON THE CAMPUS TOUR.

Very shallow, I know. But let me reiterate: I WANT TO HAVE (HETEROSEXUAL) SEX. Remember, it's not like my idea of cute is brainless and beefcakey cute. So the built-in intelligence factor counteracts the shallowness of this requirement. Almost. (Of course, I kept these details to myself.)

Number of Schools Left: 4

"Amherst, Boatwright, Swarthmore, and Williams," I repeated, coming to the conclusion of my dissertation. "And that's where I stopped."

Four seemed like a manageable number to me. But I could have kept right on cutting. I'm sure if I thought hard enough, I could have come up with a deal breaker for every school in the book. I swear, I would thrive in a communist regime. See, when I have too many choices, it's my own fault if I make the wrong one. I am much better when decisions have been made for me. It not only gives me the right to complain, but a sense that I've had to overcome overwhelming odds in the struggle to become the success that I am.

Go ahead and bash my methods all you want, but it's not any more or less of a crapshoot than if I had followed the advice of my guidance counselor, my parents, or the Princeton Review. The odds are 1600 to 1 that I'll pick the perfect school. I might as well go with my own dubious logic.

When I finally finished my spiel, Paul Parlipiano looked at me and said, "You're making a big mistake."

The fact that Paul Parlipiano had formed such a definitive opinion about me and my life was too much for me to handle, and I coughed half a cup of coffee out of my nostrils. Our history made this humiliating hurl all the more so. Need I remind you that this is the same person whose shoes I puked all over at a farewell-to-summer beach party one year ago? *After* I pledged my undying love? *Before* I passed out? I shudder at the memory. The fact that he graciously neglected to mention that last regurgitative gift as he mopped up today's mess is proof that Paul Parlipiano is a perfect human being—gay or not. Oh, how I wish he were not.

After I had run out of apologies and lied about a lingering case of bronchitis that had the annoying habit of sneaking up on me when I least expected it, our conversation resumed its course.

"How am I making a mistake?"

"Well, I'm biased, of course, but you should reconsider your 'no urban setting' rule. Columbia changed my life."

"Really?"

"Yes. New York is the best place in the world for an education."

I was skeptical. This was only the second time I'd even been to the city, which is unbelievable since we live less than two hours away. And the first time barely counts because it was with my grandmother to see *The Lion King*.

"No offense or anything, but what makes you so sure I'd love living in New York? I mean, I can't watch thirty seconds of *Sex and the City* without wanting to puke."

"Well, because of the editorials you write for *The Seagull's Voice*, mostly," he said. "Like the one you wrote about the uprising in response to the social zoning in the lunchroom . . ."

"'Vegetable Medley Mayhem: A Food Fight Against Cafeteria Tyranny.'"

"And the one about the slumming socialite, Hyacinth something . . ."

"'Miss Hyacinth Anastasia Wallace: Just Another Poseur.'"

"Yeah! That's the one!"

You could've struck me dead right then and there and it would have been okey-dokey with me.

"But you had already graduated when I wrote those . . ."

"My sister sent me your columns in *The Seagull's Voice* last year," he said. "She's a big fan of yours. She loves your editorials."

"Your sister?" There wasn't another Parlipiano at school.

"Stepsister," he corrected himself. "You know her."

"I do?" How could this be possible?

"Sure you do," he said. "Taryn Baker."

Taryn Baker is Paul Parlipiano's stepsister?!

Holy shit.

Very few people remember Taryn's brief but big-time impact on Pineville society. Most have already forgotten about how she got suspended from school a year ago for peeing into a yogurt cup to provide He Who Shall Remain Nameless with a clean urine sample for his surprise drug test. I am definitely the only person (besides He Who Shall Remain Nameless, of course) who knows she was lying about having done that, and only did it in a pathetic attempt to propel herself into popularity. We—He Who Shall Remain Nameless and I—are the only two people on Earth who know who really squatted over the yogurt cup. We know who, though I doubt either one of us knows why.

I certainly don't know why I did it.

Of course, Taryn's plan backfired miserably. After a few

weeks, Pineville had erased the Dannon Incident from its collective unconscious, and Taryn in particular. Thus, she went back to being a fade-into-the-paint wallflower.

But what makes this stepsibling revelation even freakier is that I spent a bajillion hours with Taryn last spring, tutoring her so she wouldn't flunk tenth grade. I agreed to help her because I felt I needed to pay her back in some way for taking the fall for me. Of course, it helps that her parents paid *me* ten dollars an hour to ease my guilty conscience.

Taryn is not dumb. Just abysmally unmotivated to do any work in her classes—except English and band. But getting suspended by the administration, then shunned (as usual) when she came back to school, has left its mark. Taryn is the most reluctant conversationalist I've ever met. And this is coming from *me*, so you know it must be bad. Compared to her, I'm like, well, Sara. Whenever I tried acknowledging Taryn's presence when we passed each other in the halls, she focused her sad brown eyes elsewhere. She spooks me out a little bit. In fact, she's got definite Noir Bard tendencies. I still can't help but wonder how she mustered the courage to confess to a crime she didn't commit.

Even though it qualifies as bizarro behavior, it wasn't all that surprising she never mentioned Paul. She never revealed anything personal about herself. Ever. Anyway, her quasi-relation to Paul Parlipiano explained his otherwise inexplicable concern for my well-being. Thank God my mouth was empty, or I surely would've spewed more fluids all over this poor boy.

"Well, Taryn never mentioned that she liked my editorials."

"She really looks up to you."

"I had no idea," I said, strangely proud to be admired by Paul

Parlipiano's semisister. "She never mentioned that you were her sorta brother."

His face dropped slightly. "Well, she got into some trouble when she was a freshman." He was intentionally vague, but I knew all too well what incident he was alluding to. "And it made her lose her sense of self. She has no confidence."

"Yeah," I replied.

"She doesn't have a problem with my sexual orientation, but she knows that PHS isn't the most enlightened place on earth."

Now, I wasn't exactly sure how to handle this moment of disclosure. I mean, I already knew that he was gay. Should I just wink to let him know he didn't have to say more?

"That's why she loved your editorials. They made her feel like she wasn't alone," he continued. "It's tough to be different at Pineville. Whether it's her type of different, or my type of different, or yours."

"Tell me about it," I muttered.

"Coming here has been so great. It's the first place where I felt like I could finally be myself and find others who are just like me. Or people who weren't like me at all, but would accept me as I was, anyway."

Could such a place exist?

"I got involved with PACO, People Against Conformity and Oppression."

"Is that, uh, a gay and lesbian organization?"

"Well, there are gays in the group, but that's not what we're about. We're an organized resistance to a world of greedy narcissism and complacency."

"Like Key Club on steroids?"

"Not exactly."

"Are you socialists?"

"Some of us are, but we're really a true democracy. There are no elected leaders; there's no hierarchy."

I couldn't really think of anything legitimately cool to say, so I just said, "Cool."

"It *is* cool," he said, smiling. "Unlike other, more notable anarchist groups, we believe firmly in nonviolent protest. We work within the system to try to effect change, and work outside of the system to put the heat on those who can make change. Just like you did with your articles."

Wow. Wow. Wow. Holy shit. Wow.

"We don't think that your beliefs should be one thing and your actions another," Paul Parlipiano continued. "They should be one and the same."

I think so too. I really do. Yet I still manage to have an easier time *thinking* about things instead of *doing* things. Maybe an organization like this is what I need. There was something I needed to know, though.

"Do you feel like . . ." I grasped for the right word, couldn't find it, then just went with the first one. "Like a dumbass at Columbia?"

I felt like a dumbass as soon as I said it.

"Not that you're a dumbass! I mean, it's just that it was a huge deal when you got into Columbia, because it's a huge deal whenever anyone from Pineville gets into an Ivy League school, because it's only had about three students get accepted to Ivy League schools in a bajillion years, and I think two of them dropped out before the end of freshman year to go to Rutgers—not that Rutgers is a bad school or anything, but it's not Columbia, you know . . ."

He sipped his coffee while I babbled on.

"And I know I'm not a dumbass, either. But I worry that I'm only Pineville smart. And if I went to an Ivy League school with *real* students from *real* high schools . . ."

I realized that my get-into-the-Ivy-League intensity hadn't faded after all. It had just transformed itself into don't-get-into-the-Ivy-League inadequacy.

"I know what you mean," he said when I had finally faded out. "It was a little intimidating at first. I felt really ignorant about cultural things that were embedded in my classmates' DNA. But that's no reason to go to another, less intimidating school. Do you want to live in your ignorance forever? I think you could use a challenge, don't you?"

I nodded my head. Yes, I did.

"Everyone could benefit from a challenge." His voice grew stronger, with more conviction. I could imagine him rallying a crowd before a demonstration. "That's what's wrong with our society: We've all grown so content to sit on our asses and settle for what comes easy. Accept the challenge, Jessica!"

I was nodding more vigorously now.

"The admissions people know what they're doing. If they think you're smart enough to be accepted, then you're smart enough to be there." He paused. "From what I know about you, Jessica, you are definitely smart enough to be there."

My head almost came off its neck hinges.

"I'm heading back to campus. Would you like to come with me? I could show you around before my next class. Maybe introduce you to some people from PACO . . ."

He totally misinterpreted the hideous facial contortion that resulted from my stifled *happyhappyjoyjoyhappyhappyjoyjoyhappyhappiness*.

"Oh, that's right. You've got the reading at Blood and Ink."

NO! I DON'T HAVE TO BE ANYWHERE BUT WITH YOU, PAUL PARLIPIANO, GAY MAN OF MY DREAMS!

"No, it's not mandatory. So I don't have anywhere else to be," I replied as calmly as possible.

"Are you sure?"

"I've never been so sure," I said. "Can I use your two-way for a second?"

I really didn't give a damn about Blood and Ink. I never wanted to read my stuff out loud in front of the Noir Bards anyway, because I am not a writer, no matter what Mac says. So I used Paul Parlipiano's pager to tell Mac I wasn't going to make it to Blood and Ink and that I'd find my own way back to SPE-CIAL. The program was almost over anyway. What disciplinary measures could be taken against me?

Then, for the next two hours, Paul Parlipiano and I took the ultimate campus tour. Ultimate. Meaning both best and last.

I'll spare you an encyclopedic cataloging of my sensory experiences. Why? Because it wasn't the sight of PACO members of every conceivable ethnicity debating and BS-ing on the steps of Low Library, or the sound of a homeless man singing a medley of New Kids on the Block songs on the corner of 116th and Broadway, or the smell of incense, pot, and taxicab exhaust, or the acidic, stinging taste of the free wine by the carafe that came with our delicious Malaysian food, or the fuzzy rush I felt thrumming throughout my body just by being in the place where Paul Parlipiano, my crush-to-end-all-crushes, belonged, and being told that I belonged there too. It wasn't any of these experiences that provided me with the final answer to the question. It was all of them. And something more.

Okay. Let's clear the air here. I know how this looks. I know that anyone who has taken psych 101 would say I'm following in Paul Parlipiano's footsteps because I'm still in love with him. But really, I am not holding out for a gay man. Give me more credit than that.

Here's my take on this situation. Maybe my obsession with Paul Parlipiano was orchestrated by whatever higher power was in charge of these things as a way of getting me to Columbia—or rather, New York City. Paul Parlipiano wasn't the *end*; he was the means to an end. As an agnostic, I don't know who or what or why this force is pulling me toward New York. Frankly, it's beyond my comprehension. All I know is that when I set foot on that campus, I was sure it was where I was supposed to be. It wasn't a shout that reverberated inside my body until I rocked with shock. No, it was a quiet but confident voice I wasn't used to hearing, one that assured me I had just come to the place where I could be part of something great. It was the first time I'd ever felt that way in my life.

Actually, there was one other time I felt this way in my life. But it wasn't a place that made me feel at home with myself. It was a person. A person who turned out not to be worth it. But I told myself I wasn't going to write about that—about him— anymore. So I'm not. So *there*.

the ninth

Whoo-boy! Was Mac pissed about my Manhattan vanishing act. First thing Monday morning, he took me by the arm and led me into the hall to chastise me in pseudo-privacy. I'm sure this was a huge disappointment to the rest of my classmates, who have been looking forward to witnessing an act of violence against me all summer long.

It's a wonder he's not as chrome-domed as my dad, so enthusiastically did my prof pull his hair throughout his lengthy tirade, one that included quotations from Nietzsche, Emerson, and Virginia Woolf in addition to his own well-chosen words, like "wasted opportunity," "selfish short-sightedness," and "reckless endangerment of a minor."

When he was finally done telling me how irresponsible I was and how lucky I was that he was not going to tell my parents or the program directors about this (which, quite frankly, was more about saving his own—fine!—ass than mine), I replied:

"It's your fault, you know."

"*My* fault?"

"You're the one who told me I needed to bust out of the snow globe."

"What?"

"You're the one who encouraged me to go out and experience the world. Or was that a load of crap?"

"It wasn't crap, Jessica," he replied. "You do need to break out of your suburban bubble."

"But just not on your watch, right?"

He yanked on his hair.

"One unsupervised walking tour of the Upper West Side is not what I was talking about. I was talking about—"

"Well, that tour was enough to change my whole life."

He laughed. "Your life changed in two hours?"

"Yes. I've totally changed my college plans."

A not altogether friendly smile crept across his face. It was more of a mocking smile. A smile that said, *Your childish antics amuse me.*

"Changing your college plans does not mean you've changed your whole life."

"Well, for me it does."

"Then you were even more sheltered than I thought," he replied. He unsnared his hands from his hair. "Let me guess. Columbia."

It was weird to hear someone else say it. It made it true.

"Yes."

"Tch," he said.

We stood there for a moment because I didn't know what to say, but Mac hadn't made a move that would indicate that the discussion was over.

"Do you know what John Steinbeck said about New York?"

"Uh, no."

"He said, 'New York is an ugly city, a dirty city. Its climate is a scandal, its politics are used to frighten children, its traffic is madness, its competition is murderous. But there is one thing about it—once you have lived in New York and it has become your home, no place else is good enough.'"

He took a dramatic pause, as he often does after his lengthier quotations.

"Well, Jessica Darling," he replied as he opened the class-room door, "good for you."

He meant it too. More than I knew at the time, because the next day Mac handed me a sealed envelope right in front of all the Noir Bards.

"What is this?" I asked.

"Your letter of recommendation," he replied, louder than necessary, so the Grim Reaper, Nosferatu, the Lump, Barbella, Loser, and the rest of the coven would hear.

"Don't read it, though," he urged. "I don't want it going to your head."

On the envelope he had attached a Post-it that read: "'Be great in act as you have been in thought.'—William Shakespeare."

I was so stunned by this gift from my fairy godfather that I couldn't even express my gratitude.

"Thuh," I said.

"You're welcome," Mac replied.

Of course, I will probably wake up tomorrow to find that the Noir Bards have turned me into a toad.

Mac's generosity more than makes up for the lackluster reac-tion I initially got. I had wanted to share my life-changing excite-ment with someone, *anyone*, after I'd returned to campus on the train that night. The resulting exchange with Bridget (and her lamprey Ashleigh) had left a lot to be desired.

"Columbia!" Bridget screamed. "Like, Julia Stiles goes there!"

"I didn't know that."

"Oh, yeah! And Meadow Soprano got in, so you, like, shouldn't have any trouble."

"Yeah, that's exactly why I want to go to Columbia, because the fictional daughter of an HBO mob boss goes there."

"OH MY GOD! Doesn't Felicity go there?" she yelped again.

"Felicity who?"

"Duuuuhhh," said Bridget and Ashleigh in unison. "Felicity from *Felicity*."

"The TV show *Felicity*," I said, not really getting it.

"I think she goes to a made-up school . . ." Ashleigh's voice trailed off, only to come back three hundred decibels louder than before. "YES!" she screamed. "It's *just* like Felicity because *you're* following your high school crush to college just like *she* followed her high school crush, only in *your* case it's really pathetic because your crush is gay."

I shot Bridget a look.

"Well, Ash, like, asked me if you had boyfriend and I told her no, but then I told her about—"

"Never mind," I said, cutting her off. I turned to Ashleigh. "For the record, I am not trying to emulate the heroine of a WB dramedy. I don't watch those kinds of shows."

"Whatever you say," Ashleigh said in a singsongy tone that just made me want to clock her in that broccoli schnozz of hers.

"I. Don't. Watch. Those. Shows."

"Whatever."

I've learned from years of experience with the Clueless Crew that it's futile to have a constructive argument with people I hate. So I walked out of the room for the very last time, which sounds more dramatic than it really is because there were only six days left in the program anyway.

You're probably wondering what Mac's letter says, right? You assumed I steamed it open and read it. Oh, ye of little faith. I didn't—and won't—open it. And it has little to do with respecting Mac's wishes. The truth is, I'd rather not know what Mac said about me. I really can't handle reading other people's assessments of my intelligence. Like the quarterly accommodations from my teachers. They always say that they hope I learned as much from them as they did from me. Stuff like that. Excruciating. They go so overboard that I can't believe one word of it. It's hard to buy into all that crap when I know the chaos that's *really* going on inside my head.

the eleventh

I 've spent my last days in Mac's class developing a strategy for breaking it to my parents that my final answer to the question is one they don't want to hear. The four-step approach to solving my college conundrum is called the Perfection, Deception, Acception, Defection plan. I will share my PDAD plan in the hopes that it will help others who, like me, are unjustifiably stuck under the heavy thumbs of parental totalitarianism.

PHASE ONE: PERFECTION

I will act like the daughter my parents have always wanted. By smiling a lot in their presence and offering up enough information about my life that they think I'm telling them everything, when I'm really sharing nothing of any genuine importance, they will believe they have raised a happy, healthy, well-adjusted teen who has gotten over her growing pains and no longer needs parental policing of all her activities. This gives them permission to back off and leave me the hell alone so I can begin Phase Two.

PHASE TWO: DECEPTION

Meanwhile, I will complete as much of the Columbia application process as possible without my parents' knowledge. I've got Mac's recommendation and can recycle the one Haviland wrote to get me into SPECIAL. All my parents' financial stuff can be easily accessed on the computer, so I can even take care of that part too. Applying online makes this easy—no paper trail!

PHASE THREE: ACCEPTION

This is the part when I get accepted to Columbia. If I don't get accepted, I am screwed.

PHASE FOUR: DEFECTION

By the time I'm forced to inform my parents of my college plans, they will be so awed by my Perfection (see Phase One) that even they will consider it unreasonable to bar me from my first-choice university.

I'm still working out the kinks. Phase One is particularly troublesome. Perfection is much easier to strive for in theory than in practice. Within five minutes of my parents' arrival on the SPECIAL campus to pick me up and take me back to Pineville, my flawless veneer was already at risk of losing some of its luster.

Call Me Chantalle had already packed her pointe shoes and nutcrackers and douches by the time my parents walked into the room. But it was enough time to give the Darlings and the De-Pasquales an opportunity to do what all college-bound seniors' parents do when they are in a room together: brag about their offspring.

"Vassar and Boatwright are already wooing Mary for their honors programs!"

"Boatwright, Swarthmore, Amherst, and Williams will practically *pay* our Jessie to attend their honors programs!"

"Our Mary doesn't need financial incentives! She can write her own ticket!"

"Our Jessie already has! She has her pick of the Ivies!"

The one-upmanship was enough to make "their Jessie" drop out of high school and work on the boardwalk until my hands are too arthritic get a solid grip on the frozen-custard scooper.

"It's been so fun rooming with you!" Call Me Chantalle gushed, handing me a pink piece of stationery with a tea-rose border.

The sound of her voice came as a surprise to me. We hadn't spoken a word to each other for weeks, not since she neglected to put a pointe shoe on the door and I walked in on her polishing the Grim Reaper's skin scythe with her tongue.

I took a closer look at the paper, on which she had written *Mary DePasquale* in loopy, girly cursive. What? Didn't her parents know about Chantalle? Beneath it was a series of numbers, letters, and symbols which surely couldn't represent what I thought they did.

"My email and digits, silly! So we can keep in touch."

It was obvious that she was putting on a show for both sets of parents. I looked at the two very respectable, very deluded people whose genetics had produced this fraud. I wanted to say something like, *Call Me Chantalle, I wouldn't touch you without a stockpile of antibiotics.* But I knew my parents would be horrified by my candor, which, of course, conflicts with Phase One of the PDAD plan.

I waited until I got home to flush her info down the toilet, where it belonged.

I hadn't expected to get anything out of SPECIAL. To finally have something to be excited about was beyond my expectations. I now know I will get through my senior year, if only because I've finally gotten a glimpse of what awaits me once my diploma is in my hands.

the fourteenth

I thought it was bizarre that my parents hadn't driven up to visit me at SPECIAL, but I didn't want them there, so I didn't bring it up. And on the phone, they said nothing but vague, unimportant things about life back in Pineville, so I assumed nothing was going on. I should've known better. No, they wanted to wait until I was settled back into the homestead, enjoying a fine breakfast of Cap'n Crunch and coffee, before springing a month's worth of bad news on me.

"Your grandmother, Dad's mother, Gladdie . . ."

"I know who my grandmother is, Mom."

"Well," she said, clutching her teacup. "She fell down the stairs again while you were at SPECIAL."

"Jesus Christ! Is she okay?"

"Well, she didn't do any damage to her artificial hips." Mom paused to sip her chamomile. "However, it seems the fall was caused by . . ."

"By what?"

"A little bit of a stroke."

"WHAT?! How can you have a 'little bit' of a stroke? That's like saying she's a little pregnant."

"Well, she was in the hospital for only two weeks."

"*Only* two weeks!"

"The stroke impaired her motor skills. And her memory is gone."

"Mom! The woman is ninety years old! She hasn't been in her right mind in decades."

She shushed me. "Don't say that. It will upset your father."

"Where is she now?"

"Well, we moved her into an assisted living facility because she can't take care of herself anymore."

"Assisted living facility. Like a nursing home?"

She shushed me again. "Don't say that. It upsets your father."

My father. Aha! No wonder he hadn't grilled me about my workouts. He's been too distracted by his mother's little bit of a stroke.

"Why didn't you tell me about this?"

"We didn't want to worry you."

"Does Bethany know?"

My mother paused just long enough before saying yes to let me know that she was full of crap.

"Liar."

Mom frowned. "We don't want to tell your sister over the phone. And she's out in California, so she couldn't do anything to help, anyway. Why worry her? We're waiting for a more appropriate time."

Of course. Denial is how we Darlings deal with everything. Or, rather, *don't* deal with anything. Like Matthew. His birthday is two days away. He would've been twenty-one. But instead of acknowledging it, and maybe releasing some of the pain she still feels about the crib death of her two-week-old son, my mom will simply and silently pop a Valium instead. My dad will ride his bike from Pineville to the moon and back again.

We never, ever talk about it. Never will, either. It is extremely unhealthy.

Is this how it's going to be next year? My parents will save all their bad news for when I come home for breaks from whatever the hell college I'll be attending since they probably won't let me attend Columbia even after I get accepted because it is absolutely impossible for me to feign perfection in their presence.

"Would you have told us if she died? Or would you have buried her without us and waited for a more appropriate time?"

My mother placed her hands over her eyes for a few seconds, reluctant to look at me. I wasn't sure who she was more ashamed of: me for the comment, or herself for the truth in it. I found out soon enough.

"*Jessica Lynn Darling,*" she said in her best Because-I'm-Your-Mother-and-I-Say-So tone. "Just for that, I insist you go over there and visit Gladdie today."

"Will she even remember it afterward? I mean, will I get credit for going?"

Another scornful look.

"What? You said she'd lost her memory! So why bother going if she's going to forget I was there as soon as I leave?"

"Because it will make her happy while you're there. And it will make your father happy. By the way, try to be a little nicer to him, okay?"

"Okay," I said, with a heavy, stereotypically adolescent sigh.

So that's how I ended up spending my afternoon at Silver Meadows Assisted Living Facility.

To its credit, the place wasn't nearly as depressing as I thought it would be. It looked more like a well-appointed hotel than a hospital where the elderly go to die. There were lots of fresh flowers, which thankfully made the joint smell like potpourri, not pee. Bandstand music piped through the speakers. A chanteuse crooned about all the things she didn't get a kick out of: champagne, cocaine, a plane. "But I get a kick out of you . . ."

I had no problem finding Gladdie. She was sitting in an overstuffed chintz chair, holding court in the Silver Lounge, located directly across from the front lobby. She was in the middle of one of her famous stories, surrounded by no fewer than a dozen men and women who all looked as old as she did, but with far less flair. Gladdie was looking as lovely as a nonagenarian stroke victim with two artificial hips could. She was wearing a lavender pantsuit with a matching beret perched atop her salon-poofy white hair. Always color coordinated, she had her walker done up for the day with ribbons in light and dark shades of purple. She seemed virtually unchanged from my memory. She'd been ancient my whole life.

"And so I said to the fella, 'That old gray mare ain't never been what she used to be!'"

The crowd howled with phlegm-filled, ragged, lung-rattling laughter.

"Hey, Grandma," I began cautiously, well aware that I'd have to break in before she launched into her next tale. "It's me, Jessica."

She fixed her eyes on me and there was an instant flash of recognition.

"Hey, guys and dolls!" she brayed. "It's JD! The one I told you about!"

Twenty-four quad-focaled, cataracted eyes turned toward me. So Gladdie seemed to know me, but why did she refer to me as JD? No one had ever called me that in my life. Even so, I pretended that it was a nickname Gladdie had given me years ago.

"This one here has to beat 'em off with a stick, I tell ya!"

Not true at all, obviously, but it's in line with Gladdie's usual delusional view of me.

"Like grandmother, like granddaughter!" shouted a liver-spotty man in a plaid sport coat.

The crowd went into more spasms of laughter, but I clearly saw a hint of blush show through Gladdie's heavy "cheek rouge," as she calls it.

Later, when we were alone in her room, Gladdie told me that this twice-widowed charmer is Maurice, but everyone calls him Moe.

"He has a car!"

Gladdie's driver's license was taken away a few years back when she ran a dozen too many stop signs. I imagine that Moe's freedom of movement is very appealing to her. I had to laugh, though, because it's the exact same thing hot freshman girls say when they get hit on by horny senior boys who should know better.

"Moe's the pick of the litter," she confided. "*And* the cat's meow." She purred for effect.

They sure know how to have a grand old time at Silver Meadows. I stayed through bingo, Wheelchair-obics, Music and Memories, and afternoon tea and cookies. This assisted living facility seemed closer to my vision of college than SPECIAL turned out to be. You know, guys and girls hanging out, having fun, hormones flying. Only it's better because they don't have to go to class or study or write papers or anything.

Jesus Christ. I'd rather be a senior citizen than a senior in high school. A new low.

the sixteenth

My mom won't get out of bed today.

My dad disappeared at dawn, and won't pedal into the driveway until after sundown.

My sister in California will go shoe shopping, blissfully oblivious of the date.

I will sit and think about how I am a pinprick in the condom. A forgotten pill. A misplaced diaphragm. An accident. I am the second daughter they weren't supposed to have after the first son who wasn't supposed to die. I will contemplate how my very existence relied on his demise.

I will sit and say it silently, because no one will ever say it out loud:

Happy birthday, Matthew Michael Darling. Happy birthday to you.

the twentieth

I am trying to be nicer to my dad. Trying and failing.

I actually asked him if he wanted to follow me on his bike while I went on a five-mile run. If only he knew how much of a sacrifice this was for me. Not only have I always hated it when he rides along with me, but the sheer act of running has been pure torture lately.

Running used to be effortless, even when I hated it. I broke my leg last fall, but now my entire body feels like it needs to be fused back together. I feel like I've gained a hundred pounds, even though the scale hasn't budged. Every breath is labored, as if I'm running in a biohazard suit but the oxygen tank isn't working. I know I look as terrible as I feel, and I don't need my dad to point that out.

"I told you to work out at that artsy-fartsy camp! Now look at you! Do you want to get beat by freshmen again?"

No, I most certainly do not. Last season's "comeback" from my injury was a total failure. I've tried to let go of that humiliating track season, when I was beat by runners I had practically lapped the year before. I can't. Still, nothing bothered me more than my inability to come within twenty seconds of my old PRs. The way I see it, if I can't beat my former self, what's the point?

After being number one, it's tough to settle for being just one of the pack.

I want to quit. If that makes me a sore loser, then so be it.

I've never quit anything in my life. Plus, I'm the captain, a senior, and a four-year varsity vet. And captains who are seniors and four-year varsity vets do not quit.

But I really want to quit.

In fact, the only real problem I have with the concept of quitting is that no more team means no more running—period. I'd miss those middle-of-the-night solo runs around my neighborhood. They were the only things that soothed my insomnia— well, besides those late-night phone conversations with He Who Shall Remain Nameless. I felt connected to something larger than my own sorry little suburban existence. It was the closest I've ever come to having religion. It's too bad I never felt that sense of peace at practice, or at the meets—even when I won.

The other drawback to quitting would be my dad's insistence that I see a surgeon. My mom hates hospitals, which is why she has supported my decision not to go under the knife. Or maybe she sees what my fanatical father can't. She knows that an orthopedist won't be able to fix the real source of my pain: my head.

the twenty-eighth

Ack. I was malled by the Clueless Two while back-to-school shopping.

I figured the food court would be the one mall zone where I'd be safe, since the Clueless Two don't eat. Just my luck that they lined up right in back of me at Cinnabon, where I was buying a PecanBon and they were buying Diet Cokes. They could've bought Diet Cokes at any one of the thirty-eight eating and drinking establishments in the Ocean County Mall, but in a truly sadomasochistic dieting gesture, they chose to buy their Diet Cokes at Cinnabon. But I digress.

"Omigod!"

Sara's voice is unmistakably snotty. (Ha. In more ways than one. Her parents are so moneyed, you'd think they would've paid to have her adenoids yanked out of her nose, then had a bit lopped off the bridge in time for her senior portrait. Or at the very least, provide her with a travel pack of tissues before she leaves their seaside estate.)

"Omigod! Look at me, Jess! I'm skinnier than you are!"

I wasn't about to endorse her eating disorder by agreeing, but it was true that Sara had lost quite a bit of weight. More disturbing was the unnatural crispiness of her skin. Tanning was the closest that Sara came to having a hobby besides gossiping. She started every morning with a half-hour fake bake in the bed her parents bought her before the junior prom. Then, weather permitting, between 10:00 a.m. and 4:00 p.m. every day, she would soak up UVs on the beach in her backyard. The result? Even the webbing between her fingers was the color of coffee without cream.

"Do you even recognize me now that I'm *quote* a perfect size two *unquote*?"

Had an Aberzombie salesgirl called Sara "a perfect size two"? Or was Sara acknowledging she wasn't *really* a size two, but *close enough*? Or had Sara's quote/unquote catchphrase gotten to the point that she was starting to use it appropriately?

These are the types of things I think about when Sara talks at me. Her verbosity is such that my brain can take a two-week Club Med vacation right in the middle of the conversation. When my gray matter comes back, it's all refreshed and relaxed, knowing it hasn't missed a thing while it was away.

"Omigod!" shrieked Sara, taking a pink tube top emblazoned with a glittery Playboy bunny out of her shopping bag. "I will look so cute in this!"

I was not fooled by her buddy-buddy behavior. Sara was simply thrilled to have the opportunity to brag about her diet, how much weight she had lost over the summer, and all the guys she'd hooked up with as a result of her makeover blah-diddy-blah-blah-blah. Sara was very proud of her accomplishment: She had finally mustered enough discipline to become the full-fledged anorexic of her dreams. For years, she had hated herself for not having enough stick-figure stick-to-it-tiveness. Now she showed off her physique in a backless apron shirt and shorts that were so tight, I could see ample beavage. Foul.

"Omigod! I can't believe you eat that stuff. I've lost all taste for junk food."

The saliva fizzing in the corners of her mouth said otherwise. Honestly, her obvious hunger took away all the pleasure in biting into the oozy, caramel-coated, bajillion-calorie Bon.

Throughout this conversation, Manda acted like she couldn't have been more bored. She lazily skimmed her new paperback copy of *Reviving Ophelia*—she must have read the old one down to shreds. She just stood there, popping another piece of Doublemint, or reapplying her lip gloss, or slapping her ever-present pack of Virginia Slims against her palm. (Insert oral fixation jokes here, here, and *here*.) Her hair—usually dishwater brown and wavy—had been straightened and bleached the color of sweet corn since the last time I saw her. I couldn't help but wonder if this was an attempt to look more like Bridget. Unlike my beauteous SPECIAL friend, whose visage demanded overblown metaphors (sapphire eyes! rose-petal lips!), Manda's features were dull and forgettable. She didn't need a cute face, or the new hair for that matter. Just when I thought she had maxed out on hooter hugeness, it seemed that whatever poundage Sara had lost over the summer had turned up in Manda's bra.

"So . . ." Sara said in a pinched tone that tried too hard to sound nice. "What did you do all summer?"

This was good news. The fact that Sara had deigned to make an inquiry about my life meant she had zero gossip on me. If she'd had the slightest trace of secondhand info, she wouldn't have bothered asking at all. I decided to respond with the most snoring of possible answers, one that would end the interrogation right then and there.

"I spent all summer in a classroom taking a college-level creative writing seminar."

Stupefied silence. Mission accomplished.

"Omigod! Have you heard about the new hottie who's gonna be in our class?" asked Sara.

As always, Sara was good for a teensy bit of information, which makes her annoyance factor all the more annoying because you can't ignore her completely.

"No. Who is he?"

Manda shot Sara a quick, disconcerting side-glance.

"Dunno," said Sara.

Like hell she doesn't. I swear Google goes to Sara for information. Manda was just pissed that Sara had mentioned the mystery hottie in front of me. If Manda hadn't been standing right there, I'm sure Sara would've spilled the gory story I'd already heard from Bridget about how Manda and Burke's on-again, off-again sex fest had finally come to an end. Burke had dumped Manda two weeks ago, the day before he left for college, because he couldn't "be tied down by a high school girl." Yet that hadn't stopped him from trying to woo back Bridget via a series of corny, incredibly incriminating emails ever since.

The point is, Manda is currently boyfriendless and on the rebound. She is out for hot-blooded American dude companionship, but she'll settle for frozen plasma if the search takes too long. This situation is extremely fortuitous for the new honors hottie, who I will take the liberty of assuming will enjoy making the beast with two backs with a girl he barely knows. You know, like any other guy between the ages of twelve and death.

Seeing the Clueless Two for the first time since June reminded me of everything I hate about school. It's amazing. Two minutes with them is all it took to suck whatever waning optimism I had right out of me. Why do I feel that sweet taste of Columbia will only make the toxic cocktail that will be my senior year harder to swallow?

Hence my decision to apply for early decision.

I don't know why I didn't think of this before. By applying for early decision, I get all my worries out of the way. My application is out there and I'm done with it. Once accepted, I am contractually obligated to go there, and nowhere else. Surely my parents would rather send me to Columbia than suffer the humiliation of having a daughter living at home and working on the boardwalk while the rest of their friends' children are attending their freshman year of college. *Woo-hoo!* It's genius.

Now that I've made this decision, there's no point in putting it off. There's no penalty against getting it in too quickly. The sooner I get it in, the sooner I have one less source of stress.

september

Dear Hope,

This year, I'm going in prepared. If I stay focused on these objectives, my final year of Pineville imprisonment might prove to be slightly less painful.

SIX GOALS FOR MY SENIOR YEAR THAT I HOPE WILL MAKE IT SUCK A TEENSY BIT LESS, THOUGH I WOULDN'T WAGER AN *EYELASH* ON IT

1. I will not be a college-unbound senior. I will send my application to Columbia ASAP and not get caught up in the mass hysteria of the selection process.

2. I will try not to be such a buzzkill. If I succeed, I will write happy journal entries. When I get psyched about something this year, Lord knows I should document the rarity for posterity.

3. I will be nicer to Bridget and any other misguided individual who—for reasons I can't comprehend—pursues a friendship with me despite the inevitable incompatibility at its core.

4. I will ignore the Clueless Two. This requires Herculean effort, as Manda and Sara's debauched adventures are too front-page tabloid to go unnoticed.

5. I will refuse to read, watch, listen to, or take in through any other means of sensory absorption anything related to Miss Hyacinth Anastasia Wallace and her so-called Gen-Whatever masterwork, *Bubblegum Bimbos.*

6. I will accept that it is my primordial nature to focus all my hormones on one guy as opposed to taking the scatter-shot approach. I will learn from my mistakes and make a wiser choice for my OOOH (Obsessive Object Of Horn-iness) for the 2001–2002 academic year. Specifically, one who is not (a) gay or (b) He Who Shall Remain Nameless.

Dogmatically yours,
J.

the fourth

My first period class is gym. My second class of the day, which starts at 8:35 a.m., is lunch—or should I say, brunch. It takes place in the gymnasium, which is convenient because it's followed by two more back-to-back gym classes. After that, I have freshman-level basic skills English and another lunch. The last period of the day is blank. I interpreted that as a study hall.

This slacker schedule is not a manifestation of early-stage senioritis. A wonky 404 hacked into the guidance department's new scheduling program, and now not one of Pineville High's students has a schedule that makes any sense. Approximately 25 percent of the student body was in my first gym class. We all squeezed into the bleachers in a flagrant fire code violation and sat there for the remainder of the day while the guidance department tried to sort out the glitch.

"What's up, *ma chérie*?"

I turned around and was so happy to be face-to-face with someone I actually wanted to see.

"Why, if it isn't *mon bon ami*!"

Pepé and I bumped fists.

Last spring, Pepé and I bonded over the stupidity of everyone else in our French class. He's a big fan of my editorials in

The Seagull's Voice too, which I totally appreciate. We even got over our first totally awkward moment, crucial to the well-being of any friendship. I was sure his Pepé Le Pew crush would fizzle as soon as he got to know me better as a person. I mean, it's a lot easier to have a crush on me when you don't know what a total weirdo I am. So I was shocked when, after eight months of daily conversations, he asked me if I'd like to go to see a French flick that was showing at the local library's International Film Festival. I was even more floored when he decided we could still be friends after I turned him down, which I did because (say it with me now) *I will not get obsessed with anyone who is anything less than perfect for me.* This mandate pretty much guarantees that my hymen will continue to stay so intact and so airtight that it could be used as a flotation device in case of an emergency.

"Hey, Jess!"

Bridget was also in the ridiculous gym class. She was flapping her arms in the air to get my attention.

"Over here!"

Bridget was sitting alone in the gym bleachers. Sort of. She was surrounded on all sides by a ring of fawning freshmen who kept a very safe distance. The fact that they were gawking at Bridget with awestruck admiration clearly IDed them as freshmen. (All sophomore, junior, and senior girls have already moved on to bitterly envying Bridget's entry into quasi celebritydom, as evidenced by all the fingernail-pointing and *Who does she think she is?*-ing coming at her from all directions beyond the ring of fans.) Furthermore, in the attempt to put their middle school days behind them, these Clubber Babies were dressed in the most revealing items in their

wardrobes. Lucky for them, the administration was too preoccupied with the scheduling snafu to enforce the dress code.

If Bridget noticed the freshmen, she didn't let on. I started to
climb up the bleachers to sit next to her.

"You coming with?" I asked Pepé.

He shook his head. "Nah, you go ahead. She's A-list. I'm still
fighting for walk-ons. You tell her I said 'sup."

"Will do."

And with a complicated, palm-slide-slap-behind-the-back-
finger-snap-chest-thump number-one maneuver, Pepé was
gone.

"Hey, Bridget, you're being gawked at again," I said, motion-
ing to the girls, who were trying—and failing—to keep their
cool.

"Am I?" Bridget looked around, uninterested. "Whatever. How
come Percy didn't come over here to, like, say hi or something?"

"Oh, he's too intimidated by your celebrity," I said.

"That's so, like, *ugh*," she said, watching him retreat. "I don't
know why everyone acts like the video is such a big deal."

Me neither. Personally, I'd be more than a little mortified to
be the subject of false rumors involving a member of a bargain-
bin boy band. But you know, that's just me.

"So have you seen Sara and Manda yet?" I asked.

"Skank and Skankier?" Bridget replied, grimacing. "No.
Have you?"

"Not today," I said. "But I bumped into them at the mall last
week."

"Oh. I'm surprised Skankier wasn't, like, too busy snaking
someone else's man to go shopping."

I really wasn't in the mood to rehash the details of how Manda slept with Burke while Bridget was with her dad in LA. Christ, it happened two summers ago. Even though Bridget is obviously over Burke, she still relishes any opportunity to remind everyone how slutty Manda is. This vicious, girl-bashing side of Bridget was not a great look for her. I was tired of talking about it, so I seized this perfect opportunity for a segue.

"Sara seriously downsized over the summer."

"Bruiser finally lost the fat?" Bridget was so stunned that she temporarily forgot to refer to her as Skank and had regressed to using Sara's slightly less damning nickname. "Ten pounds? Twenty pounds? Fifty pounds? Like, how much?"

I've never been on a diet in my life. I have no idea how much weight would transform Sara from a stout trapezoid into a slender, rectangular shape. And I think my geometric explanation would be lost on Bridget. Math is not her strong suit.

"I don't know," I said. "A lot, I guess."

"You never help when it comes to, like, the important stuff."

According to her definition of *important*, I couldn't agree more.

Bridget stood up, using her pale white hand to shield her eyes from the sun streaming through the window. She scanned the crowd, looking for the newly skinny Skank. I remained seated and did the same. I found Sara within thirty seconds, but before I got around to pointing her out to Bridget, I discovered something far more disturbing.

"Holy shit! Is that Manda wearing Scotty's varsity jacket?"

Bridget squinted her eyes in their direction. "Skankier!"

I couldn't read the name embroidered on the jacket, but from the way Scotty and Manda started plowing their tongues down each other's throats, I thought it was a safe bet that it was indeed

Scotty's wool-and-leather varsity jacket Manda was wearing on
this 90 degree, 10 tanning-index day. Somehow between last
week and today, Manda had used her feminine wiles (a.k.a. her
penile mastery) to nab His Royal Guyness, the Grand Pooh-bah
of the Upper Crust. Revolting.

"I seriously think I'm going to blow chunks," I said.

"I thought you didn't, like, like Scotty anymore," Bridget said.

"I don't," I replied. "I never did like him as a boyfriend. But
it's just so gross that someone who once liked me, and wanted
me to be his girlfriend, is now engaging in fluid exchange with
Manda."

I still can't believe that he was my first and only ex-boyfriend.
Of course, this was back in eighth grade, years before he became
junior prom king, All-Shore point guard, and the all-around cool
guy that he is today. I never really wanted to date him. Still don't.
But when I saw him and Manda, I almost belly flopped right out
of the bleachers. *Manda.* I wonder if she'll change her name to
Mandy to match the rest of his girlfriends: Kelsey, Becky, Corey,
Lindsey, and Tory. Ack. I didn't really know any of those girls, and
that made their girlfriend statuses easier for me to take. Nevertheless, Scotty with Manda was too incestuous. I knew them both
too well.

"Ack."

I continued to freak out in this manner for the next half hour,
until Bridget found a better source of distraction.

"New hottie alert!" she exclaimed, pointing to an intriguing
guy on the opposite side of the gym. His hair was a deep, deep
brown, a color I couldn't help but hope was a reflection of his
deep, deep intellect. It was cut short on the back and sides, kept
long on top, so it flopped onto the wire rims of his brainy specs.

He possessed a subtle musculature, the kind you get from hiking alone for hours in the woods, not from pumping iron with a bunch of goons in the weight room, and a nervous smile he took back as soon as he gave it away. Pale, perfect skin, not unlike that of the naked *Nevermind* baby that swam across his T-shirt, reaching for the dollar bill, taking the bait.

OOOH. My kind of cute. Geek cute, with an emphasis on the *cute* part. Yessiree.

Was he the new honors hottie Sara told me about? PHS has about a thousand students but seems much smaller. By the time you're a senior, you either know all nonfreshmen personally or know something about them that may or may not be true. Clearly, he wasn't freshman meat. No, Nirvana was fresh *man* meat. A transfer student from another district. Or maybe he was a confused foreign-exchange student who needed a native Jerseyan like myself to give him a glorious guided tour of the Garden State.

Mere milliseconds later, I didn't give one god-diggity-damn about reaching Nirvana anymore. Because next to this honors hottie, I saw . . .

The person I had hoped to see in homeroom, but didn't, because our messed-up schedule had replaced some of the Ds-through-Fs with kids from all over the alphabet, reassigning some of the Ds-through-Fs (and one F in particular) to homerooms unknown.

I saw . . .

The Boy Who Shall . . .

Oh . . .

Screw it.

SCREW IT. I GIVE UP.

My mind games aren't working. Removing his name from my vocabulary has *not* removed him from my memory. This cognitive behavior therapy crap I read about in my psych book is officially over. Done. And to prove it, I will say and write his name.

Marcus Flutie.

That's when I saw Marcus Flutie.

There, I wrote it. I said it.

MARCUS FLUTIE! MARCUS FLUTIE! MARCUS FLUTIE!

Christ, that feels good. But not as good as it felt to lay eyes on him. I gasped when I saw him, sucking enough air into my lungs to suffocate everyone else in the stadium.

"Oh, Jess," Bridget said. "No."

Oh, Jess. Yes.

"No," she said, quietly but firmly.

Yes.

"Not Marcus Flutie again," Bridget said.

Yes. Marcus Flutie. Again. And again and again and again and again and again.

His shirt-and-tie uniform had been replaced by a plain white short-sleeved T-shirt, with something too distant, too blurry for me to read printed across his chest. The summer sun had brightened his russet hair to a new-penny shade of copper, and he'd grown out his buzz cut, so tufts rose off his scalp like a rooster. OOOH. Cock-a-doodle . . .

"Don't."

Cock-a-doodle-don't.

"What is it about him that makes you, like, totally lose your shit?"

I wish I knew. It's more than the late-night conversations we used to have about everything and nothing, the only thing besides running that helped calm me down and get a decent night's sleep. It's more than the way he seems to make things so complicated, yet helps me see things so clearly, through new eyes. It's more than the fact that he is the only guy I have ever almost had sex with.

It's probably because I know there is no way we will ever be together.

"I'm supposed to remind you that you, like, hate him."

I like/hate him. I love/hate him. I love him. I hate him.

"I hate him."

Bridget sighed. "Yes."

Bridget is the only one at school who knows that I came this-close to letting Marcus Flutie devirginize me last New Year's Eve. She's the only one here who knows that I didn't because he had the nerve to come clean about how his desire to sleep with me started out as a game, just to see if the infamous male slut of Pineville could bed the class Brainiac, then evolved into a genuine longing. She's the only one who knows how I tortured myself every day afterward, wondering how I could have even considered sleeping with Marcus when he had been drug buddies with Hope's brother, and seemingly unapologetic about Heath's overdose. She's the only one here who knows about the destroyed journal from the obsessive second half of my junior year, the one that covered these Marcus-related issues (and many, many more) in gruesome detail. She's the only one here who knows how, despite my guilt and how tired I am of being toyed with, *I can't stop thinking about him.*

I've made her promise not to tell anyone about any of these truths, and I know she'll make good on it. What Bridget lacks in depth she more than makes up for in honesty. Bridget does not lie. That quality alone makes Bridget my closest PHS ally, which really isn't saying much because my options are quite limited.

"How about this?" Bridget said all of a sudden, with renewed vigor. "Say everyone in the world had to be put in, like, one of two bins, a fat bin or a thin bin. Which bin would Sara be in?"

This is going to be a very long year, indeed.

Marcus Flutie.

Ahhhhhhhhhh. I said it again.

Cock-a-doodle-dooooooooooooooooooooooooooooooooooooo.

the fifth

Thanks to my "new and improved" messed-up schedule—
which now has one less gym, but one more study hall—the
only period that comes close to resembling a real class is English
with Havisham. (Damn. I mean Miss Haviland. Since I am well
on my way to dying a virgin, I vow to make an effort not to make
fun of her spinsterhood anymore.) A core of the normal honors
group was still intact, but we were joined by at least a dozen other
PHS students who had no business being there. Actually, *we* were
the ones who had no business intruding on *them*, because according to the schedule, it was listed as a freshman basic skills
class and not senior AP. Whatever.

Haviland relished the opportunity to reach a wider and
more varied audience than usual. I'd barely had a chance to sit
down before she climbed on her soapbox to deliver one of her
famous orations. Specifically, her speech was about how whoever
hacked into the school's computer system was obviously bright,
yet our generation tends to use its brainpower for mischief, not
good. *Don't we see that our spoiled generation takes education
for granted? That wisdom is our ticket around the world? That
knowledge is power, and these lost days will have a devastating,
long-lasting effect on our fragile teenage minds?!*

I'm generally amused by Haviland's flashbacks to her hippie protest days, but I was too distracted by the view to pay much attention. Haviland had finally abolished the alphabetical seating system, giving us the privilege of sitting wherever we wanted. And who should choose to sit right in front of me but Marcus, a development that, on principle, I refuse to waste any more words about. I just started writing his name again. I have to pace myself.

But who should choose to sit on the left diagonal in front of me but the new honors hottie, Nirvana. I thought it really couldn't get any better than that. I felt kind of bad for Nirvana, though. I mean, how many gyms and lunches were packed into his schedule? Furthermore, because this was our third year in a row with Haviland, she had dispensed with the usual back-to-school introductory garbage that's way boring to us veterans but would be essential for a newcomer. I thought that was rather insensitive of her. I made a note to go out of my way to introduce myself after class.

"I'm not a supporter of the militaristic zero-tolerance policies that are in vogue with school administrators right now," continued Haviland. "But sometimes I worry that across-the-board punishment is the only way you people will develop a sense of responsibility or accountability for your actions. What do you all think about this?"

Our class was surely thinking of how much we missed the days when all that was required of us on the first day of school was three paragraphs describing "How I Spent My Summer Vacation."

"I agree with you, Miss H," said Scotty. "That zero-tolerance stuff is bullshit."

"Why, Scott! I would be delighted if you elaborated."

"Okay," Scotty elaborated. "It sucks."

Manda—who was sitting behind him—squeezed his shoulders to celebrate her boyfriend's profundity. While that exact line might settle some of Scotty's fiercest locker room debates, it wasn't going to pass muster with Haviland.

"Why?"

"My ass got hazed when I was a freshman," he said. "Now I'm a senior. I'm the captain, and it's payback time."

Scotty paused, letting the significance sink like a cinder block in a swimming pool.

"So zero tolerance sucks because I can't touch these freshman punks when they get out of line. I can't beat any sense into them, and it's just not fair."

He leaned back into his chair and held up his palms so PJ and the rest of Scotty's disciples could high-five his brilliant contribution to the discussion. Scotty had successfully completed his transformation from jock to jerk-off. Manda quickly smooched the back of his neck. And to think I could have been his girlfriend as recently as a year and a half ago. Unreal.

For a few moments, Haviland stood motionless, undoubtedly counting her sick days in her head, wondering if they would give her enough to retire now and still earn the maximum pension package.

Thankfully, the bell rang and everyone hopped up to head to the next nonclass. I decided it was the perfect opportunity to introduce myself to Nirvana. I would be first to welcome him to Pineville High. Plus, Marcus would see that his presence had no effect on my mental stability whatsoever. *Whatsoever.*

"Hi!" I said, in my best approximation of bubbliness. "I'm Jessica. Welcome to Pineville High."

Nirvana shot a confused look first at me, then at Marcus, who was hovering behind me.

"Um . . ." he stammered. "Um. I . . ."

Wait a second. That monotone, shaky staccato . . .

"Um. Jess. Um. It's me. Um . . . And."

Those shaky, nervous "ums" that punctuate his incomplete sentences . . .

"Um. Len. Um. Levy. Um."

LEN LEVY???!!!

Jesus Christ! Nirvana *wasn't* the new honors class hottie, he was the old honors class nerd—minus the purple, pus-filled cysts, plus a new haircut. Through some dermatological miracle, he'd been transformed into a porcelain-skinned cutie with a sartorial flair evoking the golden era of grunge. Just as I made this discovery, I noticed Sara and Manda falling all over each other with laughter.

"Omigod!" Sara shrieked through her cackles. "She totally fell for it!"

Bitches. They set me up.

"Len," I said, trying to compose myself. "I'm kidding. Of course I recognized you. I didn't mistake you for someone new. I was just, uh . . ."

There really wasn't a logical lie. Not one that I could come up with under Marcus's watchful eye.

"Um," Len said.

Then he turned away, like he had to cough, then very deliberately cleared his throat, as if to hock up whatever blockage made him stutter. *A-heh-heh-heh-hehmmmmmmm.*

"Sorry about the zebra, then. That's intern lingo for an unlikely diagnosis. An old medical school saying goes, 'If you hear hoofbeats, think horses, not zebras.'"

"Uh-huh," I said, starting to regret my decision to try to make Marcus jealous—I mean, show Marcus I wasn't affected by him anymore.

Len kept right on going. "So my assumption that you thought I was a new kid, and not someone who had benefited from Accutane, was far-fetched, a zebra on my part. See, I learned a lot of medical lingo this summer. I worked as an EMT because I want to go premed at Cornell and I thought it would look good on my applications if I got to see the bright lights and cold steel of emergency surgery."

Len reminded me of a used ATV, one you had to kick-start a few times before the motor revved. Once his words were up and running smoothly, he wouldn't stop until he sputtered out of gas.

"This has been interesting, Len, but I gotta go." I started walking out the door, and Len trailed behind me, with Marcus following him silently, grinning like he didn't have a care in the world.

"Man, I saw my fair share of fascinoma. There was one LOL with SOB . . ."

Marcus broke in between us, then gently slapped Len on the forehead with the heel of his palm. I noticed then that Marcus's white T-shirt had the word WEDNESDAY printed on it in black iron-on letters. It was a more true, less blue-black than that of the unreadable tattooed Chinese characters that permanently embraced his bicep.

"Um." *AHEM!* "That's his way of telling me that not everyone is clued into ER speak."

Then Len explained that LOL with SOB meant "little old lady" with "shortness of breath," not "laugh out loud" with "son of a bitch." When he took a breath to refill his tank, I seized the opportunity to excuse myself. I mean, this could go on forever.

"Well, Len, I just wanted to tell you that you look . . ." Could I bring myself to say it? Len Levy, who started my streak of unrequited romances in third grade by not reciprocating my love in Pineville Elementary School's Valentine exchange? Len Levy, who has served as my academic arch nemesis all these years? Len Levy, whose cystic acne was so out of control that it was difficult to look him in the face until now?

Marcus was looking at me, still chuckling to himself. That sealed my decision.

"Great," I said. "You look great."

Len opened his mouth, but nothing came out. Not even an "Um."

Marcus never took his feline eyes off me. I know this because I was watching him too. The entire time.

the seventh

Len and I were chosen as PHS's Seniors of the Month for September. Our photo will grace the front lobby of our school for nine and a half months, which means it will acquire more graffiti than any of the other golden twosomes chosen for this illustrious honor. When you consider my competition, you can understand why I didn't mention it until now and won't mention it again.

I seized this opportunity at having Len's undivided attention. I was curious to hear about his makeover. And how he'd spent his summer, and with whom.

Okay. A little bit of the reason I wanted to talk to Len was because of his new cuteness. Len was looking good, that's for damn sure. But he was still stiff, stuttering, sputtering Len—a premed wannabe with delusions of rock-and-roll grandeur, for whom the defining moment of his young life was Kurt Cobain's suicide.

A whole helluva lot more of the reason I wanted to talk to him was to find out what was going on with Marcus. Len is Marcus's only real confidant—and vice versa. Had he kept a low social profile? Had he successfully made it through his first sex- and drug-free summer? Oh, and one more little thing. *HAD HE SAID ANYTHING ABOUT ME?!*

Since his makeover rivaled her own, I knew Sara would take it upon herself to find out everything about Len's transformation from spotty to hottie, including his involvement with Marcus. I could've relied on her spy skills, but I chose not to. I don't want to get back into the habit of relying on Sara for all my gossip needs, not this early into the school year. No. If I wanted the scoop on Marcus, I'd have to find it out for myself, from Len. Knowing Len's conversational tendencies, I was well aware that going straight to the source would prove to be a rather inefficient method. And I was right. While we were waiting to have our picture taken, Len told me a few things I wanted to know—and a lot of things I didn't—in one long-winded sentence prompted by the simplest of questions.

What I Asked:

"How was your summer, Len?"

What Len Said:

[*Ahem!*] "My dermatologist prescribed Accutane, the most powerful drug for cystic acne **(1)** but not without a host of daunting side effects, including changes in mood, severe stomach pain, diarrhea, rectal bleeding, headaches, nausea, vomiting, yellowing of the skin and eyes, dark urine, **(2)** and increased photosensitivity, the last of which made it impossible for me to spend much time outdoors, so when I wasn't working on hits and gomers **(3)** I was in the basement with Flu **(4)** and the band formerly known as the Len Levy Four because once Flu joined the band **(5)**, it was inaccurate and unusable **(6)** unless we were being ironic and wry, but the other band members never liked the original name **(7)** so now we're called Chaos Called Creation, inspired by a line from one of Flu's poems **(8)**, and he writes a lot because he says it's a positive way to channel the excess energy he used to waste on women and wine **(9)**, as I like to put it **(10)**, but that's all in the past **(11)**, which is good because we don't want to end up like every band on *Behind the Music* before we even get our first gig **(12)**, so all in all I'd say I had a perfectly productive summer, how about you?"

What I Thought:

1. *Too bad Accutane can't cure the bumps in his personality. Why would anyone go out of his way to remind everyone that his now-cute face used to be in a state of epidermal emergency? How could someone so hot be so socially awkward?*

2. *Christ. Is he a catch, or what? And I thought I'd have to go back to Silver Meadows to find a guy with such a fascinating list of ailments.*

3. *More EMT-speak, I presume.*

4. *Who?*

5. *Len calls Marcus Flu. Like a viral infection you can't shake until it's good and done with you. Flu. Ha!*

6. *So Marcus joined the band? No shit.*

7. *No duh.*

8. *What?! That's straight from the poem Marcus wrote me after the Dannon Incident! The one called "Fall," in which he used Adam and Eve and the Garden of Eden and other Creation imagery to tempt me into sin. Which meant sex! Marcus is still messing with my mind, even when I'm not around.*

9. *Women and wine? Did Marcus really say that? I mean, I don't doubt that he's been tempted by his favorite vices, but would he put it in those exact words?*

10. *Aha! I knew it. Marcus wouldn't use a phrase like "women and wine." Booze and broads maybe. Or nymphos and needles. But not "women and wine." That's too precious for him.*

11. *When he says "all," does he mean that Marcus has given up girls altogether? Or does he mean that he's given up recreational banging as a way to pass the time, but is still interested in the female form?*

12. *Who cares about your band? Answer my questions, damn you!*

WHAT I REPLIED:

"It was okay."

By the way, Marcus wore a T-shirt that said THURSDAY yesterday, and FRIDAY today. His new uniform, no doubt. I'm going to see the entire school year, day by day, stretched out across Marcus Flutie's chest. As if it weren't interminable already.

the thirteenth

The day it happened—the day the World Trade Center tragedy was captured on camera—I was too shocked, too numb, too afraid to write anything at all. It's been a couple of days now, and I know I should at least try to write to sort out my feelings about all this.

But everything I think is wrong.

For example, I find myself feeling nostalgic for the post-Columbine crackdown of '99, back when the biggest threat to our safety was vengeance at the hands of hypothetical, pimple-faced Harris/Klebold copycats. A time known as Pineville's infamous "No Tolerance" era, which is best remembered for its short-lived edict that simultaneously outlawed wearing a belt—because you could use it to choke a fellow student—and busting a sag—because it "glorified" gang culture—forcing us to button our pants uncomfortably at our hips. Back when we were freshmen, and PHS was ranked last in the county academically but came out on top when it came to suspensions and expulsions. When a whopping 35 percent of the student body had been booted out for one wacky infraction or another. When we were routinely herded out of the building because another anonymous misanthrope had called in a bomb threat to get out of taking an exam he didn't feel like taking, threats brilliantly called in from traceable cell phones, but that still required football field evacuations while the police dogs sniffed for keg bombs made with kerosene, paper clips, and chewing tobacco, or whatever crafty suburban anarchists supposedly used. When my biggest concern was not only having someone to sit with at lunch, but finding a bomb-scare buddy to chill with in the bleachers.

I know I sound callous and uncaring and cruel. But really, anyone with any sense knew that the average PHS dreg would *never* jeopardize losing his liquor store deposit by rigging a bomb out of a rented keg.

I can't believe I'm making jokes at a time like this. And about *Columbine*, for Christ's sake. What is wrong with me? Why do I have the compulsion to make jokes at a time when nothing should be funny? Why do I mock others for coping with this tragedy with sensationalized sentimentality, when my methods are far worse? Has my mind been so tainted by our culture of irony that I'm incapable of feeling any real emotion? Is this my way of denying the depths of the horror of what happened?

Or am I just irreversibly fucked up?

the twenty-first

Other evidence that I am a seriously disturbed individual:

1. All students were encouraged to wear red, white, and blue clothing to show our solidarity. I complied the first day but stopped on Thursday because the denim and American flag aesthetic made us all look like we were in the chorus of a Broadway musical version of *The Dukes of Hazzard*.

2. When our football pep rally was canceled in favor of a candlelight vigil, I genuinely thought the latter would be more fun. This turned out to be not far from the truth.

3. I've been glued to CNN, not because I want to see more disaster footage, but because I developed a little crush on one of the hunkier anchors. Last night I even had a dream about him in which he wore a Superman costume.

4. I'm freaking out because I have to *re*-reconsider my college choices. If this had happened two weeks from now, I
might have already sent my early admissions application
out and I would be screwed. Not like I'm not screwed
now. Because I had my heart set on Columbia, but obviously, NYC is out of the question, and I have no clue
where I want to go, or whether I want to bother going to
college at all because I feel like the future isn't going to be
there anymore, which makes no sense. This is all so small
and self-absorbed that it's beyond disgusting.

5. There is only one thing that has given me any sense
of hope, and it's not Oval Office rhetoric or stars-and-
stripes patriotism or religious zeal—the things that
seem to be working for everybody else. It's something
that probably isn't really happening at all. But in the
past two weeks, I swear I've caught Marcus looking at
me. It's not a "Can I borrow your pen?" look. It's a "Can
we talk about this?" look. The look I haven't seen since
December 31, 2000. Leave it to me to turn a national
tragedy into fuel for my sexual daydreams. I am one
horrible mofo.

Haviland has already approached me about writing an essay about
the impact of 9/11 for *The Seagull's Voice*. She thinks it will be
cathartic for me and the student body. I know I should try to sort
out my feelings by writing, but I don't know if I can. I doubt my
ability to muster a socially acceptable response out of my twisted
psyche. I told her that until I can guarantee something normal,
I'm better off not writing anything at all. This isn't an essay that

airs all my petty grievances against Pineville High. This is World War III.

And she said, "That's exactly why you need to write, Jessica. Don't get me wrong. Your essays last year were impressive, that's for sure, but they were all, perhaps, too tightly focused on Pineville High. Don't you want to broaden your scope and take on global issues? Don't you see how your classmates would benefit from having world events filtered through the observant eyes of one of their peers?"

Every time I hear myself described in relation to "my peers," I can't help but crack up.

"Don't you see how this would be a challenge, one that, if you don't mind me saying, you so greatly need to prevent complacency and boredom from making a waste of your senior year?"

Haviland, like Mac, wants me to bust out of the snow globe. I don't think it's a bad idea myself. But I'm worried about taking a nasty blow—instead of breaking through—when I hit the dome's border head-on.

the twenty-ninth

I was feeling pretty hopeless when I was living in the most mon-eyed, peaceful, and trouble-free era in American history. (At least for white, upper-middle-class suburbanites like myself.) So you can imagine how I've been since 9/11.

It's affecting me on a physical level. I'm awake for twenty-three and a half hours a day, but not really awake. I'm kind of in a walking-sleep state that makes it impossible to do . . . anything.

I got a C on my AP Physics test. I've never gotten a C in my life.

And running? My race pace is a stroll with just enough bounce to distinguish it from a walk. I haven't won a meet all season.

This has brought much grief to my father, but my mom didn't worry until she realized that I wasn't eating. I have never *not* been able to chow down.

"These tragic events have taken a toll on everyone," she said, eyeing my barely touched bowl of Cap'n Crunch this morning. "I think you should talk to a counselor. It's nothing to be ashamed of."

Ha! Our "Professional Counselor" has been unhinged lately, herself. We've all seen Brandi in the parking lot behind the school, furiously sucking on cigarettes to cope with the onslaught of traumatized students who have sought her infinite wisdom.

"Don't think so, Mom."

My mother's brow wrinkled with genuine panic. I hadn't seen her this concerned since my sophomore year, when I told her about my MIA menstrual cycle.

We both sat at the kitchen table in silence for a few minutes. During this time, my mom stared at me while I stared at a fascinating green thread hanging from my place mat. I'm telling you, I've been the walking brain-dead lately.

Finally, my mother said, "I think you should visit Gladdie."

She thought that going to Silver Meadows and talking to Gladdie and WWII vets about the 3 H's—Hitler, Hiroshima, and the Holocaust—would give me—guess what?—*perspective*. Quite frankly, I didn't have the energy to argue, so I took her suggestion. As much as I hate to admit it when my mother was right, she was.

At Silver Meadows, I was given the red carpet treatment.

"Look who it is!" exclaimed the receptionist, a chubby, forty-something lady named Linda with frosted Farrah Fawcett wings. "It's JD!"

"Uh, hi," I said. "How did you know . . . ?"

"Oh! Gladdie's told everyone about her brilliant, boy-magnet granddaughter!"

I laughed weakly. Boy magnet. Har-dee-har-har.

"Just go upstairs and follow the noise," Linda said. "You'll find her in the recreation room."

Sure enough, I could hear Gladdie's strident voice rising above everyone else's before I was halfway up the staircase.

"So I say to the fella, 'You can't make a burlap purse out of that sow's ear!'"

Riotous, pacemaker-shaking laughter. They didn't seem fazed by current events in the least.

Gladdie was sitting at a card table designed accommodate only four people, but was surrounded on all sides by an elderly coterie. Whether they were the same group as the first time, I honestly couldn't tell. I'm not ageist or anything, but old people have a tendency to look alike. However, I did notice that Moe, "the cat's meow," was sitting right next to Gladdie. A deck of cards rested on the table, untouched. The game had been indefinitely postponed.

Gladdie roared when she saw me.

"JD!"

Then, on cue, the whole group exclaimed, "It's JD!" They were so excited to see me, as if I were Bob Hope or Milton Berle or some other ancient entertainer I'm not sure is dead or alive at this point.

"Uh, hi."

After a few minutes of grandiose and grossly inaccurate bragging about her granddaughter, Gladdie asked Moe to get her walker.

"Well, guys and dolls, I gotta shuffle off to my room for some good old-fashioned girl talk with my granddaughter here."

Moans of disappointment all around.

"I'll be back in time for arts and crafts, don't you worry." Then she clasped Moe's hand and gave him a wink. "And I'll see *you* later."

Moe lifted her hand and gave it a gentlemanly kiss.

Was that . . . ? Could that . . . ? Were they . . . FLIRTING? I could barely wait to get to her room to interrogate her about what I had just witnessed.

"Grandma! Have you landed the pick of the litter?"

She looked at me with uncharacteristic coyness.

"Oh my God! You have! You have a . . . a . . ."

"A boyfriend, JD," she said. "I've got me a boyfriend."

Gladdie told me all about their courtship. The flirtatious glances over the Yahtzee cup, the long conversations in the dining room over bowls of goulash, the hand-holding during Sunday afternoon showings of Abbott and Costello. It all sounded very, very sweet, yet very, very distressing. I mean, imagine discovering that your ninety-year-old grandmother has a better shot at getting laid than you do. Not a pretty picture, now, is it?

"So! I hear you've been letting the godless terrorists get you down," Gladdie said.

"Yes."

She sighed and sat next to me on her sofa, a dusty, rusty-brown velvet job that makes me sneeze if I sit on it too long.

"Look, kiddo. We were all quaking in our boots during the Big One. Still, I had faith that our nation, the greatest nation in the world, would pull through and show those bastards what they had coming to them."

"But this is a different kind of war, Gladdie."

She didn't even listen. She kept right on going about her contribution to the war effort, how she sold war bonds and worked in the federal Office for Price Administration, whatever that was, and bartered coupons for nylons and pork chops.

"I took comfort in doing without because I knew it was all for the greater good. We all made great sacrifices, none more so than those boys who lost their lives. Tragedy was part of our daily routine. But through it all, I never understood the point of being sad when I could choose to be happy."

Of the incessant jumble of words that have tumbled out of

my grandmother's mouth over the last ninety years, I would doubt that any were more perfect, or more profound, than those.

"Don't stop doing what you love," she said, tenderly patting my knee. "Don't let your future be ruined by a bunch of loonies."

Gladdie obviously lives by the "choose to be happy" philosophy. She always seems happy, something I've long attributed to her senility. But maybe she was born that way. While it may be in her blood, it's just not easy for me. I think Bethany got all the happy genes.

I'm still scared about the future. Actually, I'm petrified beyond words, which is why I can't write about it at length. Though Gladdie did help me today. It's small and stupid, but I realized I can't keep doing what I *don't* love, starting with cross-country. I don't love competitive running. Never did. Now that my transcript is locked and loaded, why should I still participate in an activity that I hate so much? I should be doing something that's important to *me* and isn't just providing unnecessary padding for my college applications. The only glitch is that I've been living for college admissions officers for so long that I don't even know what I like to do anymore.

I need to work on that.

october

Dear Hope,

Pineville High has certainly taken our president's advice to heart. Everything here is back to normal. Our Class Character elections perfectly illustrate that point:

Most Athletic: Scotty Glazer
Best Looking: Bridget Milhokovich
Class Flirt: Manda Powers
Class Motormouth: Sara D'Abruzzi
And last but not least ...
Class Brainiac: Me (and Len Levy)

Hmm ... Sounds familiar, doesn't it? Maybe that's because we won the EXACT SAME TITLES IN THE EIGHTH-GRADE ELECTIONS. I'm surprised *you* didn't still win Class Artist. The only differences between eighth grade and now are that the yearbook staff added new categories and reversed the middle school rule that allowed only one victory per student. Scotty also walked away with Best Looking and Most Popular, the latter with Manda, of course, whose coupling with King Scott has elevated her social standing at Pineville High to nosebleed level. The Clueless Two got Bestest Buds. I got Most Likely to Succeed—again with Len. The addition of new titles made it possible for even Marcus Flutie to come out a winner. I would love to joke with him about his oxymoronic status as the universally accepted Class Nonconformist. But I can't. It's not that simple, even though I know you think it is.

Anyway, I should be comforted by Pineville High's resilient unoriginality, but I'm not. I don't want things to go "back to normal." I want things to be *better* than back to normal, because normal was never good enough for me.

Predictably yours,

J.

the second

Bridget and I sat in the auditorium, watching Scotty and Manda get rock-star treatment.

"Most Popular, up! Best Looking, on deck!" yelled Haviland, who's also the yearbook adviser.

The yearbook photographer had recruited a dozen students to gather at the bottom of a ladder that had been spray-painted gold and coated in glitter. The lowly masses gazed up at their idols, who were perched as high as their Most Popular status could take them. As I watched, I started thinking about how this degrading display was at odds with our nation's new appreciation of true courage and valor. I was figuring out how I could turn this into my first *Seagull's Voice* editorial for the year, when Bridget clogged my brain flow with one of her classically sincere questions.

"Why doesn't anyone, like, take me seriously?"

"What do you mean?"

"Best Looking." She stuck out her tongue. "Bleeech."

Jesus Christ.

"Bridge, don't make me slap you. Don't be one of those gorgeous girls who longs to be average-looking so she can be taken seriously. It's insulting to the truly average."

"It's just that—" Her voice broke.

"What?"

"It's just that, like, I did a really good job in *Spoon River* last year, right? And I was good enough to get into SPECIAL."

She *was* good in last year's play; I had to admit that. Her performance surprised me even more than Pepé's. Pepé's triumphant serious stage debut *would* have shocked me, as it proved there was much more to him than his legendary reign as Black Elvis, PHS talent show champion, and Geek from Shoot the Geek. But his predictable unpredictability has made it impossible for him to shock me anymore. Anyway, I told Bridget that she was good enough to make people temporarily forget how goddamn blond and gorgeous she is, which is the best compliment to her acting I can think of.

"Thank you, Jess," she said, the telltale redness rushing to her face and neck. She paused, and pointed toward Dori Sipowitz, who was in the corner, perfecting her pose with an oversized tragedy mask. "I just, like, totally beat her out for the lead in *Our Town*. And she's still considered Class Drama Queen."

"Are you trying to tell me that you wanted to be voted Class Drama Queen?"

"Well, like, yeah."

"Oh, come on, Bridget! Dori is a theater geek through and through," I said. "There's no way anyone at PHS would see you as one of those tools."

"Percy said the same thing at play practice," she said. Pepé—Percy—was cast as the Narrator in *Our Town*.

"He's right. You're too pretty. You're too popular. Too many guys want to get into your pants."

"That's the problem," she said softly.

I'll say it again. Jesus Christ.

"Best Looking, up! Brainiacs, on deck!" yelled Miss Haviland.

"We better get up there before Haviland starts ranting about how today's youth doesn't respect time," I said. "Don't we see that our collective disregard for punctuality contributes to the unreliable devil-may-care image that undermines our credibility as a generation?"

Bridget wasn't listening. She was too busy chowing down on what would normally be her ponytail, but was released from its elastic for the photos.

"Stop chewing on your hair, unless the saliva look is what you're going for."

She kept right on gnawing as we made our way to the stage.

Each Class Character photo is taken in front of the same red-and-white PHS logo backdrop, but with different props. For Class Motormouth, Sara yammered into a cell phone. For Class Flirt, Manda hung her hooters all over PJ, her prop/male counterpart, while Scotty glared off-camera. For Best Looking, Bridget and Scotty gazed lovingly at themselves in handheld mirrors. To her credit, Bridget rolled her eyes as she did it.

"Honey, this isn't Class Clown," the photographer said. "Now, do me a favor and look pretty, like you're supposed to."

Bridget called out to me, "See what I mean?"

It was quite nauseating.

Len was dutifully waiting for our photo, wearing a T-shirt I'd never seen him in before. Underneath a black-and-white pic of Einstein, it read GREAT SPIRITS HAVE ALWAYS ENCOUNTERED VIOLENT OPPOSITION FROM MEDIOCRE MINDS.

"Cool shirt," I said. It reminded me of something Mac would

say. I wondered if he'd be disappointed in my decision not to apply to Columbia. He'll never have to know.

Len cleared his throat, as is his custom, the signal that the babble was about to begin. "Not as perfect in its simplicity as Flu's days-of-the-week thing that he has going, but it is a fashion statement in the truest sense of the word. Did you know that Einstein wasn't a good student? In fact, I doubt he would have been voted Class Brainiac, because his teachers thought he had a learning disability, which is really ironic—"

"I get it," I said, cutting him off.

I get very impatient with his blathering. Once he gets started, he can't stop. It's best not to get him started at all. So we stood there for a moment not speaking, which is the way I like it with Len. When Len isn't speaking, I can just gaze upon his hotness and begin to forget that he's Len. I can get close to convincing myself that he's this totally new cool, smart, and geek-cute guy, but as soon as he opens his mouth: same old Len.

"This is getting to be a habit with us. You know, first the Seniors of the Month photo, now this. I have a feeling that there are going to be a lot of pictures of you and me together in the future. Um. Um. Um." He suddenly got all tongue-tied. "Um. I mean, that you and I will be winning all the big awards through-out the year and will be asked to pose with each other a lot and so we should just . . . um . . ."

Mercifully, Haviland intervened. "Brainiacs, up! Most Likely to Succeed, on deck!"

For Brainiacs, Len and I were surrounded by textbooks. This was funny, since I get all my work done in study hall and haven't lugged home a textbook since my sophomore year.

"Smile!" the photographer urged.

We smiled.

"Most Likely to Succeed, up! Nonconformists, on deck!"

"That's us," said Len and I, simultaneously.

"Most Likely to Succeed," said I.

"Not Nonconformists," said Len.

"No kidding," quipped the photographer, dripping with sarcasm.

For Most Likely to Succeed, we held a blow-up globe over our heads, which I suppose represents our inevitable world domination.

"Smile!"

We smiled.

"Um. Jessica. Do you?"

"Nonconformists, up!" Haviland shouted.

Where was Marcus, anyway?

"Um. Jessica?"

I turned to Len. "Uh, what? I'm sorry."

"How's your. Um. Cross-country season going. And?"

"Ugh. It sucks. I suck."

"Um. Do you have a meet on Saturday. Or?"

"Yeah. Every Saturday. I hate it. It sucks. I suck."

"Um. Because I. Um . . ."

"Nonconformists, you're up! Come on, Nonconformists!"

K8linnn Maxxxwelll—who had her name legally changed to this nonconformist spelling over the summer—hopped around the auditorium on her nonconformist pogo stick, looking for Marcus.

"Tra-la-la! Tra-la-la!" she sang, her nonconformist catchphrase. "Tra-la-la! I'll find Marcus!"

"Um, Jessica?"

"Nonconformists, where are you?" shouted Haviland, louder than before.

Where was he?

K8linnn boinged over to Haviland, the bells on her nonconformist jester's cap a-jangling.

"Marcus isn't here," she said, gritting her teeth, which were covered in nonconformist neon-green orthodontia. "He didn't show up. Tra-la-la."

I damn near peed my pants I was laughing so hard. Now, *that's* a nonconformist for you.

I was about to say as much to Len, but when I turned to face him, he had vanished too. But Len's disappearance didn't disturb me at all. I was thinking about Marcus. Where was he?

Where *is* Marcus?

Why can't I stop myself from asking?

the seventh

I n case you were wondering how my cross-country season is going, I still suck.

Suck, suck, suckity suck suck.

I suck worse than I did last spring. I've sucked about as badly as someone with both feet can suck at the sport of cross-country running. Last year I won the Juniors division at the Eastland Invitational. I won by eleven seconds, which doesn't sound like a lot, but it is. Today, on the same course, against all the same girls, I ran forty-two seconds slower than I did last year. I came in twenty-third place! Twenty-third! The only upside to my suckiness is that the paper only prints the names of the top twenty finishers, so my humiliation isn't a matter of public record.

After I crossed the finish line, I curled up into a fetal position on the grass with my eyes closed, contemplating how much I suck, and how much I couldn't wait for the season to be over, how much I dreaded indoor track season, and spring track season. Then I thought about how much I couldn't wait until college because only then would I be free from all this torture, which sent me into a panic, since I still have no idea where I want to go.

I didn't see my father, camcorder in hand, having just documented the race for *Notso Darling's Agony of Defeat, Vol. 5*, but I felt his presence, like a cold shadow after the sun disappears behind a storm cloud. The gray behind my eyes went black and a chill shot straight through me to the bone.

"Dad, don't say a word."

"I don't know how many more of these disasters I can take."

You would think that in light of 9/11 he wouldn't be throwing around words like *disaster*. But to him, my performance really was a disaster, which is really messed up.

"I just don't know," he grumbled again.

I knew the answer to that question: None. I couldn't take any more pain and suffering all in the name of preserving my honor as a mighty Pineville High Seagull. Screw it. I was done.

"You won't have to worry about it anymore, Dad, because I quit."

I couldn't believe I said it. Neither could he.

"You *what*?"

"I quit," I said. "I'm done with running. It hurts too much."

"But the orthopedist said that you should be fine."

He thought I meant my busted leg, so I didn't bother to correct him.

"Well, it's not. I tried and I failed and I don't see the point in trying anymore."

"Then what the hell are you going to do?"

"I don't know," I replied, without looking up or opening my eyes. "Not this."

When the darkness lifted, I knew he was gone. The wind shifted, then lifted the familiar, pungent scent of Chanel N°. 5 into the air.

"Jessie . . ."

I looked up and saw my mom, as I had expected to, but she had someone with her, who I hadn't smelled coming at all.

"Um. Hi, Jess."

Len had come to see me run. No one came to cross-country meets unless they had to. My first reaction was shock, followed by my second reaction, which was total and utter embarrassment, both over my performance and my sweaty, grimy appearance. This led to my third reaction, which again was shock. Why would I care about my performance or appearance in front of Len?

"Len was telling me that he'd been to every other type of sporting event but a cross-country meet and wanted to see for himself what it was like, so he could round out his Pineville High experience. Isn't that right, Len?"

Len nodded and my mom kept right on going.

"Especially after talking to you about it when getting your yearbook photos taken last week. Aren't you two the high achievers? Len told me that he's applying to Cornell. He's just waiting for his last round of SAT scores. Isn't that wonderful?"

My mom had taken an instant liking to Len. Not only was she talking our ears off, but she kept patting down her hair, making sure each expensive golden strand was in place. She's thrilled whenever any guy shows the vaguest interest in her younger daughter, as it brings her just the teensiest bit closer to planning her next wedding extravaganza.

"I only wish that you were so organized. I told him you had narrowed it down to Amherst, Boatwright, Swarthmore, and Williams." She turned her attention to Len. "I don't know why she's waiting until the last minute to apply, Len, dear. Honestly. I've told her to apply to them all and make her decision based on who gives her the biggest scholarship."

While my mom babbled (something she and Len have in common), Len gave a sympathetic shrug. I could tell from his reaction that his mom must do the same exact thing to him.

"It was my first cross-country meet," he said, cutting someone else off for a change.

"That's funny," I replied, "because it's my last."

"What?!" asked Len and my mom.

"I'm quitting. I mean, I quit," I said, switching to a verb tense with more finality. "I don't want to do this anymore. I don't want to spend another second on this field, so let's go."

Len and my mom wore strangely identical expressions of gaping-mouth shock.

"Len, thanks for coming to witness my last moments of agony." I got up and limped toward the car.

"See you in. Um."

"Mom, let's go," I said, my back to both of them.

My dad had opted to ride home with Coach Kiley to discuss in detail all the things that were wrong with me. Unlike my dad, who doesn't even bother trying to engage me in any non-running related conversation, my mom frequently tries to force touching mother-daughter moments—usually when we're trapped alone together in an automobile. The fundamental problem with this ritual is that she all too often relies on the stuff of which her blond bond with Bethany is made: boys, dating, shopping, and, uh . . . boys. So any bonding between us is short-term and ill-conceived—like trying to rebuild the World Trade Center with Popsicle sticks and edible elementary school paste. Thus:

"Len is so cute! And smart! Cornell! Ivy League! You should have invited him over our house!"

"I didn't want him over our house," I replied.

"And why not?" she said.

"I just don't."

"What is your problem?" she asked, strangling the steering wheel. "Why do you reject every cute catch who comes your way? First Scotty, then that nice boy Marcus who took you out on New Year's Eve and we never saw again . . ."

I started thinking about that nice boy who took me out last New Year's Eve. If my mom had any clue that I almost became his forty-somethingth sexual conquest in the back seat of his 1979 fossil-burner, she wouldn't think he was so nice, now, would she?

"But Len is so cute, Jessie. And smart! Cornell! Ivy League!" she repeated, like a TV pitchwoman. "I bet he makes his mom proud."

"I bet he does. His mom is *so lucky* to have such a great kid, isn't she?"

I was starting to get dizzy.

"That's not what I meant, Jessie, and you know it," she said, her face hard and lined like a walnut shell. All of a sudden—FLASH!—her eyes popped and her face brightened with a lightbulb memory. "Wait a minute! Is this the same Len Levy you had a crush on in elementary school?"

I groaned. I really wasn't feeling well.

"The one you gave a valentine in third grade, but didn't give you one in return?"

I was sweaty but cold.

"That's why you aren't giving him the time of day! Revenge

for being rejected! Well, Jessie. Let me tell you this, revenge won't get you a date to homecoming."

So it went for the rest of the trip. I didn't hear much, though, because her voice was drowned out by the sound of my blood pulsing through my skull. When we got home, I ran straight to the bathroom and threw up.

It was probably dehydration, or overexertion and lack of sleep. For a few seconds, I actually wished it was carbon monoxide poisoning. Anything not to be subjected to a car ride home like that again.

the twelfth

Sara thinks I quit the cross-country team because I haven't had a boyfriend since eighth grade and I'm tired of being mistaken for a lesbian.

"Omigod! Not that I think you're a *quote* muff bumper *unquote*," she said in homeroom this morning. "I know all about your *quote* undying love *unquote* for Paul Parlipiano." She paused long enough to chew on a yellow Swedish fish. "Then again, he is gay, which makes him the perfect *quote* beard *unquote*, doesn't it?" She popped another piece of candy into her huge gob, the same mouth I wanted to fill with a boxing-gloved fist.

"Sara, I'm so happy to see you eating," I replied, sweet as the cherry gummy fish she held between her fingers. "You're obviously comfortable enough with your body not to worry about putting the weight back on. Good for you." I clapped lightly.

That was mean, I admit. But it shut her up. Bonus: She gave me the unfinished school of Swedish fish left in the bag.

I shouldn't have been surprised that Sara of all people would offer an opinion, as Sara prides herself on knowing everything about everyone. It turns out that me quitting the cross-country team is already a very big deal, and people who don't ordinarily offer their amateur analyses are having no problem sharing them.

A COLLECTION OF THEORIES ABOUT WHY
JESSICA DARLING QUIT THE XC TEAM

EVEN THOUGH SHE IS A SENIOR CAPTAIN
AND FOUR-YEAR VARSITY VET

AND SENIOR CAPTAINS AND FOUR-YEAR VARSITY VETS JUST DON'T
QUIT RIGHT IN THE MIDDLE OF THE SEASON. GODDAMMIT!

Scotty's Theory:

Females aren't meant to be athletes. Unless they're hot, like
Anna Kournikova. But who the fuck cares? It's not like the star
player on the football squad quit.

Comment: I definitely agree with the who-the-fuck-cares aspect
of his otherwise sexist analysis. Though I don't think my weakness is
an inherent female thing; it's just something wrong with me.

Manda's Theory:

Whatever Scotty said, by default. She might have expressed
her own point of view, a feminist take that would have been di-
ametrically opposed to Scotty's, if only she had stopped blowing
him long enough to speak up.

Comment: Scotty represents everything Manda hates in guys—
and vice versa. Sex is the only thing they have in common.

Len's Theory:

I quit the team to devote more time to my studies so I can
beat him out for valedictorian.

Comment: I had much pleasure informing him it would require
absolutely no extra effort on my part to kick his academic ass.

Marcus's Theory:

???

Comment: None. None at all. Okay, maybe one comment...
No, Jess. No. NO COMMENT.

Bridget's Theory:

I quit the team because I want to devote more time to obsessing about why Marcus hasn't expressed his theory.

Comment: Har-dee-har-har.

Hope's Theory:

I quit the team because it was conflicting with my desire to make good on my second goal for my senior year, which was not to be such a buzzkill.

Comment: She's partly right. I wasn't consciously thinking about my goal list when I quit, but I do hope my freedom will make me less of a mopey mess.

Commiseration came from an unexpected source. Only *Percy*—calling him Pepé doesn't feel right anymore—seems to get where I'm coming from. He reminded me in French class how it shocked everyone when he quit the wrestling team last year to go out for the school play.

"*Ils s'en remettront.*"

("They'll get over it.")

"*Et s'ils ne le font pas?*"

("And what if they don't?")

He shrugged.

("Who cares?")

Percy was tired of rolling around on a mat with another sweaty, half-naked guy and wanted to try something new. So unlike everyone else who gets categorized early in our high school careers and just sticks with the status quo, he actually did something about it. He quit to try something new. And it turned out that he was an even better actor than he was a wrestler. The big difference is that he had something new to quit *for*. I don't.

I've been doing a fairly good job at avoiding Coach Kiley in the halls. I think he was avoiding me too, thinking that if he didn't put any pressure on me to come back to the team, I'd come back on my own. But as the time wound down before the team's next meet, he cornered me.

"You've only missed a few practices," he said, clamping his huge hand on my shoulder, having snuck up on me from behind. "It's not too late to come back."

There is no chance of me rejoining the team.

Need I mention that my dad is less consolable than Kiley about all this? I suspect the only reason Dad hasn't shut the garage door and turned on the car's engine is that he got a promotion at work that sucks up a lot of the hours he would've spent obsessing about me. He's hardly home anymore, but when he is, he always manages to find time to guilt the hell out of me, invariably in the form of one of the following short but bitter exchanges:

Exchange #1: You're Not Tough Enough

Dad: How can you quit? Other runners come back from injuries worse than yours.

Me: I'm not other runners, Dad.

Exchange #2: You're Passing Up
a Golden Opportunity

Dad: How can you quit? You could have gotten an athletic scholarship.

Me: I can still get an academic scholarship, Dad.

Exchange #3: You're Going to Regret This
When You're Old and Gray

Dad: How can you quit? Doesn't leadership and teamwork mean anything to you?

Me: Uh, not really, Dad.

Exchange #4: You Can't Let the Terrorists Win

Dad: How can you quit? If you leave the team, the terrorists have won.

Me: Uh, it has nothing to do with terrorism.

One of these days, in the middle of one of these exchanges, his chrome dome is going to crack open like the San Andreas Fault. But it won't be my fault when it does.

As proof that my departure was meant to be, the Monday after I quit the team, Taryn Baker (a.k.a. stepsister of peaceful anarchist and gay man of my dreams) approached me about tutoring her after school.

I felt a gentle touch on my shoulder. I turned to see Taryn, who, like always, wasn't looking at me, but at an invisible person behind me.

"Hey, Taryn. What's up?"

"Geometry."

Taryn is a true minimalist when it comes to conversation. With that barely audible whisper, I knew exactly what she needed from me.

"So you need me to tutor you after school?"

She nodded. As usual, her T-shirt and cargo pants were at least three times too large, as though she didn't want any body part to be distinguishable beneath the fabric. Dressed in all brown, Taryn never strayed from a palette of earth tones—all the better for blending in. And she was wearing a striped wool cap, even though it was unseasonably warm. For Taryn, it's 365 days of winter. I couldn't believe that she and Paul Parlipiano were quasi siblings.

"Well, it just so happens that I just quit the cross-country team and . . ."

I babbled for a few minutes about my defection. That's the thing with Taryn. She's such a nonentity that you end up talking way more than you normally would because you feel compelled to hold up her end of the conversation too.

Once it was agreed that we would meet at 2:15 p.m. in the library, Taryn noiselessly drifted away, like a phantasm. That girl is strange. Whatever. Her academic loss is my monetary gain. Ten bucks an hour, for a minimum of five hours a week. Sweet! And if she starts failing chemistry, I just might be able to buy myself a VW Beetle.

So I have no regrets about quitting the team. The sleeplessness thing isn't even a big deal anymore because I'm so accustomed to it by now. I'm used to memorizing every vein and capillary crack in my ceiling. I'm used to looking at my walls so long and so intensely that shapes—a tugboat, a ladybug, Carrot Top in profile—suddenly pop out of the imperfections in the paint. I'm used to the whirr of my fan, the hum of my laptop, and the drip in my bathroom sink converging in a nocturnal symphony that only I can hear. I'm used to getting shocked out of a dream by the alarm clock, even though I was wide awake minutes, maybe even seconds, before.

It can't be very healthy, though.

Hope suggested I replace running with yoga as my way of releasing some insomniac tension. She even sent me a book and a video to help me get started. It's from a series called "Yoga for You." I'm not sure it's for me. But if yoga mellowed Madonna into an earth mama, it should at least help me get more than my current average of three minutes of sleep every night. The negligible brain activity PHS asks from its seniors is about all I can muster right now. This is the one advantage to not attending a real high school, you know, one with academic standards.

Still, I'm pretty skeptical of the om-ing and all those other New Age-y trappings of yoga, but I should at least try them so Hope's money doesn't go to waste. I appreciate any effort she makes these days, only because I don't know how much longer it will last. It's really only a matter of time before her real life in Tennessee—or wherever she winds up—takes precedence over the one she left behind.

the fourteenth

The first, belated edition of *The Seagull's Voice* came out to-day. And my editorial, "Sycophants, Suck-Ups, and Scrubs: How High School Hero Worship Hurts Us All," was nowhere to be found. Not that anyone would have noticed besides me, of course. I stalked Haviland as soon as I discovered the omission.

"Where's my editorial?"

Haviland wrung her bony hands. "It seems the administration thought your editorial was too controversial."

"What?" I asked, truly shocked. "It wasn't any more or less controversial than anything else I've written!"

"Well, it seems that the administration couldn't condone any writing that castigates your fellow students."

"'If you can't annoy somebody, there's little point in writing,'" I replied, channeling Mac. "Kingsley Amis."

"Well, it seems that the administration thinks that in these troubled times, we need to be more sensitive and promote positive relationships among all social groups. Don't you see how your editorial might have a devastating effect on your peers' self-worth?"

"I was trying to help!" I said, literally hopping up and down in frustration. "You're the one who wanted me to broaden my point of view. I was trying to show how true heroism is overlooked in favor of treating jocks and cheerleaders and other members of the high school hoi polloi like gods."

"I see," said Haviland.

"High school hero worship screws everyone's self-worth. So-called losers hate themselves for not being like the Upper Crust. And the Upper Crust gets caught up in their own hype and are devastated when their post-graduation lives don't live up to their high school glories." I was gasping for breath, I was so worked up.

"I know, I know," she said, placing her hand on my shoulder and giving me a grandmotherly sympathetic headshake. "But we're dealing with a lot of closed-minded Puritans who don't see things the same way you and I do. I agree that we need to have agitating points of view—they are a necessary part of the conversation of humankind."

I think I started eye-rolling at this point, as Haviland was starting to get all hippie-dippy on me.

"And," she continued, "as students of the world, they should be privy to these divergent thoughts, to question them, analyze them, and critique them."

"Okay, then as my adviser, shouldn't you have fought to keep it in?"

She twitched her nose in annoyance, like I was a gnat that wouldn't go away.

"If I didn't cut your editorial, I was told I'd lose funding for *The Seagull's Voice.*"

"So it's better to have a paper that's full of nicey-nicey, sanitized crap than *not* have one that actually stands for something?"

This question didn't make much sense, so I don't blame Haviland for not answering. I'm much better making my arguments on paper. But not this paper.

"When you first persuaded me to write for the newspaper, you told me that *The Seagull's Voice* needed my voice. I guess you were wrong. I quit."

And for the second time in less than two weeks, I turned my back on the face of gaping-mouthed shock. My words and actions are finally getting in sync. Paul Parlipiano would be so proud!

I've totally reversed my attitude about quitting, by the way. For me, quitting isn't a sign of weakness. The weak thing to do would've been to keep on running, keep on writing. It takes a bigger set of balls to do the exact opposite of what everyone expects me to.

Only one problem: What to do with all this free time.

the seventeenth

I think my mom is secretly psyched that I quit the team and the paper because now I'm not at practice or meetings all the time. It provides more opportunities for her to torture me with trivialities.

"We got a letter from your sister today!" my mom sang before I had a chance to take my backpack off my shoulder.

"How's the cult?"

My mother's jaw and neck tightened. "I told you to stop saying that," she said. Then her smile widened and her eyes brightened, a facial presto chango as quick and authentic as Mr. Potato Head. "She wants us to come out to California for Thanksgiving."

"California? Are you joking?" I cried. "Even if I were willing to get on an airplane, which I'm not, there's no way I'm going back to the dot commune with those freaks."

"Don't make me reprimand you again. You know it upsets me when you call it that."

"It upsets you because it's the truth," I said.

I went out to California during spring break last year to visit Stanford and Berkeley. However, one visit to the dot commune convinced me that I could never spend another four days, let alone four years, in that state.

Bethany and G-Money lost a bundle in the tech crash but still had more liquid in their account than my parents have earned in their entire lives. Instead of seeing themselves as members of the under-thirty leisure class that they are, B&G fancy themselves as forerunners of a spiritual/financial movement in which former internet impresarios shun conspicuous materialism in favor of "the simple life." Only their idea of simplicity is . . . expensive. Bethany's letter was probably written with ink hand-squeezed out of imported Indian Ocean squid on thick linen paper cushiony enough to wipe even the most hyperallergic ass.

The stationery is just the tip of the iceberg, one made, no doubt, by purified well water pumped in via an elaborate irrigation system that cost hundreds of thousands of dollars to install. B&G's definition of a simpler life also meant selling their condo and moving into a brand new 10,000-square-foot ranch in the Marin County countryside with two other dot-bomb couples. That's 3333.33 square feet per couple. I don't need my real estate maven mother to tell me that's still a grotesque amount of footage. They have this notion that it is somehow more noble and less wasteful to buy necessities of life like salmon roe and Veuve Clicquot in bulk for six, instead of for two. Their whole oxymoronic existence makes me want to hurl. If you want to be rich, just be lousy, filthy, stinking rich!

Even worse than their ostentatious minimalism was all the BS I was forced to listen to every night at dinner. They've been brainwashed by Francis T. Upbin, PhD, cult leader and a self-described economical downturn doctor they met at a seminar called "Invest in Yourself." Dr. Frank is helping them cope with Loss of Sudden Wealth Syndrome.

"As Dr. Frank says, your portfolio isn't the only thing that takes a beating when you tank ten million dollars in an afternoon," said G-Money, taking a bite of organic guinea fowl. "I'm grieving the loss of my lifestyle, my identity, my self-worth."

Bethany and the other dot-bombers looked on, hypnotically.

"But that money was all on paper," I pointed out. "You guys are still pretty loaded."

"Dr. Frank says I need to diversify my psychological portfolio," G-Money continued, without so much as a nod in my direction. When I first met him, I thought he didn't talk to anyone because he was painfully shy. But I've since learned that self-absorption is his defining characteristic, and he simply can't be bothered by anyone else's existence.

"You also need to recontextualize your belief system," Bethany chimed in.

It was an unusually multisyllabic comment for my sister, so I couldn't help but quiz her.

"What the hell does that mean?"

G-Money answered for her.

"It means," he said, "that I'm going to invest in the life assets to which Dr. Frank and I have assigned the highest Nasdaq-proof valuations."

"Which means?"

G-Money sighed. "It means," he said, looking around at his

fellow cultists for sympathy, "I'm going on more ski trips this year."

Well, there you have it. How can you argue with spiritual transcendence through self-indulgence? Bethany and G-Money represent everything critics hate about our country. While no amount of vitriol justifies mass murder, I can't blame them for feeling it, because sometimes I feel it too.

Normally, I could use cross-country practice or the newspaper as the excuse to get me out of the trip, but now that I've quit both, I can't use them as a catchall excuses for avoiding activities that I want no part of. Tutoring sucks up Monday through Friday after school. But the weekends are still problematic. I need to work on that.

Incidentally, dabbling in ancient Eastern disciplines has taught me one important lesson already: *I suck at yoga.* Good thing it isn't a competitive sport, which I now realize is why Hope recommended it in the first place. When I lie on my stomach and attempt to arch my torso into the cobra asana—which is practically the *easiest* pose that has come out of six thousand years of practice—each and every muscle fiber holding my anatomy together screams in protest: WHAT IN GOD'S NAME DO YOU THINK YOU ARE DOING?????

I know it's not supposed to hurt like that, but I kind of like the pain, in that masochistic hurts-so-good kind of way. I can definitely forget about achieving the enraptured state of mind-body-spirit for a very long time. I've got about a bajillion poses to get through before I can reach my *toes*, let alone enlightenment. I tell myself to *breathe, Jessica, breathe,* and curse all those years of running for winding my leg muscles so tight.

The book says there is definitely a corrclation between my inflexible physicality and unbendable personality. I think the book is right.

the twentieth

I was amazed at our generation's ability to bounce back after the recent tragedies. Since we've never experienced any real hardship, I think we assume that whatever is wrong with the world will just work itself out. It's our inalienable right to live worry-free lives. (It's my opposing take on life that makes me more of a Gen X kind of girl, hence my love for all things eighties. But I digress.)

Until global chaos hit locally.

"Omigod! Did your SATs *quote* get the 'thrax *unquote*?" Sara asked.

"What SATs? What 'thrax?"

"Did the SATs you took last month get stuck in an anthrax-contaminated post office?"

"I didn't have to take them this month," I said. "I rocked them the first time around." That second part was unnecessary, but there are few opportunities to brag about my brain. Bonus: I knew it would piss Sara off.

"Omigod! I hate your guts! If I have to take them one more time, I'm going to kill myself."

I doubt she'd be so kind. The fact that she brought up the SATs at all suggests she is very unstable right now. The SATs are one topic Sara avoids the way a vegan shuns a Whopper. The D'Abruzzis have already shelled out the cost of a college tuition by hiring a one-on-one "test prep professional" to help boost Sara's scores. She's more than 200 points shy of the 1200 she needs to get into Rutgers, where she and Manda (1210) have already promised to be *roommates* and pledge the *same sorority* and date *smokin' fraternity boys* and be *maids of honor* in each other's *weddings* to said *smokin' fraternity boys* and buy *luxury homes* next door to each other in a *gated community* and be each other's *very, very bestest buds 4-eva.*

Sara isn't the only one in honors who is so devastated by the lost scores.

"Um! I'm never going to get! Um! Into Cornell!" yelped Len at my locker in between classes.

Len did well when he took the SATs last March, but 1490 just wasn't high enough for him. He took them again last May but was so convinced that he did worse than the first time that he walked right out of the classroom and called the testing service to cancel his scores. Being the academic obsessive that he is, he took them again this month.

"Now I'm going to have to take them again! I have to get at least! Um! Fifteen hundred to guarantee that I'll get! Um—"

"Len, you'll get in with fourteen-ninety," I said, cutting him off.

"Easy for you to say. Um. Miss Fifteen-Sixty." He gulped.

"Okay. It *is* easy for me to say now, but I was just as freaked out as you were last spring. *Everyone* was freaked out because our school had done zippo in helping us prepare for them."

"I wasn't, like, freaked out," said Bridget, who had come up behind us.

"That's because you didn't care what your scores were because you had this out-of-nowhere idea you weren't going to college, anyway," I replied.

"I'm, like, still not going to college," she said.

"YOU'RE NOT GOING TO COLLEGE?" Len simply didn't have enough bandwidth to process this information.

"She's going to college," I said. "She's just being dramatic."

"I'm, like, so not going to college. I want to be an actress," she said. "And if there's anything I learned at SPECIAL this summer, it's that no one can teach you, like, how to be an actress. So why pay all that money?"

Len was practically flopping on the floor and frothing at the mouth at the very notion of an honors student not going to college. He cleared his throat. *Ahem!*

"Pineville High's college matriculation rate is already the worst in the county. Only eighteen percent of the senior class, composed almost entirely of our honors group, will go on to a four-year institution of higher learning. Another ten percent will attend two-year junior colleges, in most cases Ocean County College. If honors students cut short their education, Pineville High's academic standing will sink even lower than it already is, making it even more difficult for serious students like myself, or my younger brother Donald, who currently has the highest grade point average in eighth grade, to get into top-notch schools like Cornell. What will happen to future generations of Pineville scholars?"

And then, at the point in Len's one-sided sermons when he usually keeps on going until someone mercifully interrupts him, he stopped himself. I couldn't help but stare. That was the first time I had ever heard Len complete one sentence, not to mention an impassioned oration, without stumbling over his words, or babbling on forever. It was as if he had swallowed Paul Parlipiano. Or Haviland, the traitor.

"She's going to college, Len. She already applied."

He turned back to me and said, in classic Len style, "Um. Huh? She. What?"

Bridget didn't miss a beat. "I applied to UCLA to get my dad off my case. But I'm, like, totally not going."

I know Bridget is going to college, so I don't even bother getting all riled up. I have to admit, though, that the more she says it, the more it starts to concern me. Bridget does not lie, which means she really has herself convinced that she isn't going. I figure the best way to make her change her mind is to just agree with her and get the conversation moving. I needed to calm Len down. He's the only EMT I know, which wouldn't be much help in the event of his own apoplexy.

"Okay. Besides Bridget, who doesn't count because *she isn't going to college*"—I said those last five words with just enough singsong-y sarcasm to make my point—"everyone else, myself included, was freaking out about the SATs last spring. So don't think I can't relate."

"Like, Scotty wasn't freaked out," Bridget quietly pointed out.

Thankfully, Len didn't hear her. Her comment was unnecessary but true.

Scotty was the only person I envied last spring because he was totally chillaxed about the SATs. He had already been wooed to play b-ball for the Patriot League, the only Division I conference a reasonably skilled, five-foot-eleven white guy from the 'burbs could hope for. All he had to do was fill in his name correctly to accept an offer from Lehigh. He's as hooked-up as a king should be.

After struggling through races all spring, I knew no such athletic recruitment was in the cards for me. Yet I kept the dream alive for my dad and Kiley, promising to train hard all summer to get back into my formidable form. I sort of meant it too.

That is, until I got my scores.

Nevertheless, my success has brought on a new problem. As Len pointed out, I am one of a handful of students in the history of our school whose scores might provide PHS bragging rights via a scholarship to a particularly prestigious university. Therefore, I am asked the question approximately a bajillion times a day. Teachers I've never had. Custodians. Lunch ladies. You can't not give an answer to the question when you're Jessica Darling, which is why I'm back to saying:

"Amherst, Boatwright, Swarthmore, and Williams."

I decided to listen to my mom and have started putting together applications to the original final four, the ones Paul Parlipiano disapproved of. Surely he would understand my reasons for wanting to stay safe and sound and away from New York City. I even dared to bring it up with Taryn over geometry proofs yesterday.

"So Taryn, did your stepbrother ever mention meeting me over the summer?"

She didn't lift her huge eyes off the paper.

"Well, we did. He told me that I should go to Columbia, which I had considered until, you know, everything that's happening in the world."

I could tell she wanted to pull her wool cap over her eyes.

"Has Paul ever mentioned wanting to leave the city now, you know, because he's afraid of what will happen?"

She peered through her thick curtain of hair. She didn't answer. I guess she wants to keep our relationship on a professional level.

I still can't help but feel like none of these schools are quite right. I'm trying to convince myself it's safer for me to stay within what Mac called my "perfect suburban world." Why would anyone bother bombing a snow globe?

the thirtieth

He was wearing the black shirt. It was the only exception to the days-of-the-week uniform. He'd stopped wearing that particular day-of-the-week shirt as a memorial to that unforgettable Tuesday, almost a month ago.

So it was still Tuesday when it happened.

One second, I'm lying on my bed, listening to *Upstairs at Eric's*, thinking about how much less stressed I should feel because I finally sent out applications to the final four, yet not feeling the least bit relieved at all. Life, as ordinary as it can be.

The next second, magic! Enchantment!

"Hey, Jessica."

Poof! MARCUS WAS STANDING IN MY BEDROOM.

Actually, he was leaning against my wall, six feet of long-limbed, tattooed, slouching insouciance.

My body got all tingly.

"Are you quiet because you're surprised or because you're repulsed?"

"Uh . . ." MARCUS FLUTIE WAS STANDING IN MY BEDROOM. "Not repulsed."

Yet not quite surprised, either. Just . . . otherwordly. My arms and legs didn't feel like flesh anymore. They felt like they were filled with helium, lighter than air, going up, up, up. My head wasn't too solid anymore, either.

Marcus looked around my room, taking it all in. Then he turned to me. And that's when I began to levitate.

"Look at you," he said, taking his hands out of the front pockets of his threadbare jeans to point to the mosaic Hope had made for my sixteenth birthday. "Happy."

He was right. I was a portrait of rosy-cheeked, bright-eyed bliss. I was happy then, and it wasn't a matter of choice. Happiness chose me. But I couldn't respond because I was too preoccupied with trying to anchor myself to the bed.

"I don't know if I've ever seen you that happy," he said.

This was so Marcus to just come over here, on a totally random night, after barely speaking to me for nine months, and pick up where he had left off, messing with my mind.

My heart.

I couldn't say anything because I was using all my energy to stay grounded—one hand clutching the headboard, the other clasping the quilt.

"I didn't plan to come over here tonight. Pure impulse. I was on the way home from band practice and I saw your lights on. I stopped the car, got out and knocked on your door, talked politely to your parents. Then I walked up the stairs and opened the door and here I am."

He paused and examined my bookshelf, which, sadly, is filled with more DVDs than actual books. Then he read the fine print of the cast and credit lines on my *Pretty in Pink* poster. I held on for dear life, afraid to float up, up, up and get hacked into little pieces by my ceiling fan.

He turned his attention back to me.

"Can I sit down?"

I nodded furiously, still holding on for dear life.

As he pulled out my desk chair, I did a quick once-over in the mirror. My hair was stuffed under a Williams baseball cap, a souvenir from the campus visit. My gym shorts were safety pinned at the waist. Low-riders are the thing right now, but since I've lost my appetite, mine have a tendency to slip beyond plumber's crack. Thank God I was sitting down, so Marcus couldn't see the word BOOTYLICIOUS printed across my nonexistent ass—the butt billboard was a gag gift from Hope. Worst of all, I was wearing my favorite ribbed tank top, which was practically see-through from too many machine washings. I quickly grabbed a dictionary off the floor and held it to my also-nonexistent chest, hoping it would both cover me up and weigh me down.

Marcus turned the chair around so he could straddle it instead of sitting like a normal person. He looked at my murky, gray-over-pink painted walls—the result of Hope's and my DIY project gone horribly wrong.

"Did you know that the color of your walls changed the world?"

I was too preoccupied by the fact that I was hovering an inch in the air above my quilt to respond.

"Mauve," he said.

An inch and a half up. Did he notice?

"The invention of that hue in 1856 inspired the creation of new dyes which, in turn, led to numerous scientific breakthroughs."

Two inches . . .

"Funny how something so insignificant can have such a dramatic effect on history . . ."

He let his comment hang—like me—in the air.

"That was kind of a joke," he said.

"I got it," I replied.

"I was harkening back to when we first started talking to each other."

"I know."

"And I would throw out a question."

"I remember."

"As a conversational construct."

"Right."

"To facilitate a discussion."

"Uh-huh."

He was going to make me ask the more pertinent question that needed asking.

"Why are you here?"

He clapped his hands together—*smack!*—and I came crashing back down on the bed.

"I'm here because there are two things I need to tell you. I've decided to tell you these things because not telling you has led to the current state of our nonrelationship, which consists of me not telling you anything anymore and vice versa." He paused, resting his chin so it hung over the back of the chair, which was now the front. "Is this making any sense?"

"Uh . . . no?"

He ran his fingers through his rooster tufts, making them stand up at impossible angles all over his head.

"I didn't tell you that I knew a lot about you because I had eavesdropped on your conversations with Hope when I was hanging at her house with Heath. And when I told you last New Year's

Eve, it was too late in our relationship for such a confession, so you told me to go fuck myself, which I did." He raised an eyebrow. "Metaphorically speaking, of course."

I'd actually said "fuck you." But this was not the time for parsing semantics.

"Of course," I replied instead.

"Literally speaking, that would be quite a feat." And he paused, no doubt imagining himself in whatever contortionist pose would accomplish such an anatomical impossibility.

"So the two things I need to tell you are as follows."

He stopped speaking again, and in the silence in between one Yaz song and the next, I could hear the scratch of his chin stubble against the leather. I thought about his razor-sharp cheekbones, and how they could slice that chair straight through to the stuffing. I held my breath. I had no idea what he was about to say. None.

"Number one: I know your grandmother, Gladdie."

"What?"

"The old fogies' home, where I work—"

"Is Silver Meadows?"

"Yes."

Holy shit.

"I didn't know that she was your grandmother until the other day, when you visited her. I happened to see you walking down the hallway together. Suddenly, everything I'd been hearing about her granddaughter, 'the smart cookie with great gams,' made perfect sense. You were JD."

Smart cookie with great gams. Marcus had effectively complimented me on both an intellectual and superficial level. Sort of. Right?

"So you've been talking to my grandmother? And my grandmother has been talking to you? About me?"

"Yes, yes, and yes," he replied, his dark eyes daring me to
look away. "I wanted you to know that so you couldn't accuse
me of doing it all on purpose and tell me to go fuck myself
again."

"But why would it matter? We aren't . . . or . . . uh . . . weren't . . ."

Which is it, Jess? Aren't or weren't? Present or past tense?
Now or then?

"We *haven't been talking* to each other."

Past imperfect tense. How appropriate. Ha. In more ways
than one.

"No," Marcus replied.

"So you could've kept this to yourself. Or waited for me to
find out on my own. Why tell me this at all?"

He rose from the chair. "There's too much tension in the
world," he replied solemnly. "What hope is there in the Middle
East if you and I can't make peace?"

This whole scene was just so bizarro that I had no clue
whether he was kidding or not. I had no idea what to say. Alison
Moyet's voice filled the silence.

"*Sometimes when I think of the move and it's only a game /
And I need you . . .*"

Christ. I was falling now. Falling, falling, falling.

"*And number two . . .*"

Oh, dear Lord. I'd forgotten there was a second thing he had
to tell me.

"Len likes you," he said.

Marcus was almost out the door when he turned to say one
more thing.

"Be easier on him than you were on me."

And with that, he was gone. *Poof!*

A millisecond later, my mom was knocking at my door, bubbling over the possibility that another "catch" was courting her younger daughter.

"Jessie, that was the nice b— Why are you on the floor?"

At some point during my conversation with Marcus, I'd sunk so low, so deep, that my molecular makeup was indistinguishable from that of the carpet.

"I like it here."

My mother didn't know where to even begin interpreting this, so she blithely pressed on. "Was that the nice boy from New Year's Eve? Marcus?"

"I believe so," I replied. "Yes."

"What did he need to talk to you about?" Mom kept doing and undoing the top button on her cream-colored cardigan, a clear sign that she was getting impatient. "What did he say?"

"I don't know."

She rubbed her temples. "Honestly, Jessie. Why can't you ever give me a straight answer? Why do you have to make things so difficult?"

I wanted to ask Marcus those same questions. Even at his most candid, he's confusing.

Then Mom babbled about having just gotten off the phone with Bethany and how she and G-Money have decided to fly out to New Jersey for Thanksgiving and how *marvelous* it is that the whole family is getting together and how she *can't wait* to see the golden couple because she simply *could not imagine* celebrating another holiday without them. . . .

When I didn't respond, she walked out the door in a huff.

The song came to its end, with the last plinks and plunks of the synthesizer, with the final line.

"And all I ever knew," she sang. *"Only you."*

I stayed on the floor for a long, long time.

november

Hope,

"We are what we pretend to be."—Kurt Vonnegut (via Mac)

Halloween is a fascinating holiday. Costumes almost always reveal the wearers' secret or not-so-secret desires. Who or what they choose to be on October 31 reflects who or what they want to be during the other 364 days of the year.

Scotty was an FDNY firefighter, which I thought was appropriate considering my unpublished hero worship editorial and all. It turns out that Manda (done up as *Like a Virgin*-era Madonna) made him dress like that because it "turns her on." Ack. Ack. And more ack. Sara was a generic Miss America in a low-cut evening gown, stilettos, and a crown. Bridget was Gwyneth Paltrow at the 1998 Oscars. Len was John Lennon, but he had to tell people which of the Fab Four he was trying to be. Until the administration made him take it off, Percy was a reservoir-tipped condom ribbed "for her pleasure," one of the god-diggity-damndest sights ever seen.

But there is no example better than Marcus, whose costume consisted of jeans and a new black T-shirt decorated with white iron-on letters. It barely deviated from his days-of-the-week uniform. Instead of WEDNESDAY, the shirt read, GAME MASTER.

That's right. You read that correctly. GAME MASTER.

Not even self-proclaimed lifelong lovers of all things eighties (like Ashleigh) know about *Midnight Madness*. In fact, I daresay there are only three people on earth who don't need an explanation for the shirt, and that's you and me and Michael J. Fox. We are the only three people on earth who would recognize the GAME MASTER T-shirt as the costume worn by the Leon character in Michael J. Fox's film debut, the obscure 1980 college comedy *Midnight Madness*, which you and I enjoyed during a particularly memorable Friday Night Flick and Food Fest. And since you and Michael J. Fox were unlikely to grace the hallways of Pineville High, I can guarantee with 100 percent certainty that Marcus wore the costume for my benefit alone.

At least this time I can explain his actions; it's not a case of inexplicable intuition. I know he must have seen the DVD on my bookcase when he came to my bedroom the other night. He didn't even have to know anything about the character or the movie itself. All that mattered was that *I* knew what it meant. This brings me to the more significant point, which is how this costume perfectly sums up Marcus's life ambition: messing with my mind. So I responded to the Game Master's maneuver by not responding at all.

So there!

What did I wear for Halloween? Well, it just so happens that I didn't wear a costume. I went to school as myself. If you buy into my whole theory, it was indeed the perfect costume, wasn't it?

Inauthentically yours,
J.

the third

decided not to make a move, even though it was my turn. I swore that I wouldn't give in to the Game Master.

This lasted three days, thirty-six hours longer than I thought it would, which is pretty damn good.

This morning, however, I just couldn't take it anymore. I just had to tell Bridget all about the Game Master costume and getting ambushed in my bedroom and the news that Len liked me. I was already agitated, and since Bridget is the only other person who ever saw the "Fall" poem, I figured I might as well vent about how much it bothered me that their band's name is Chaos Called Creation. What's with that, anyway? There's no way that of *all* the lines, in *all* the poems he's ever written, Marcus just happened to choose a line from the poem he wrote with the sole intention of seducing me. You know, the one Marcus wrote to "thank" me for peeing into the yogurt cup. The one that began, "We / are Adam and Eve / born out of chaos called / creation." And ended, "I know we will be / together again someday / Naked / without shame / in paradise / My thanks to you / for being in on my / sin." *That* one. It's been ten months since the New Year's Eve cockblock, but he's still thinking about it.

This is more or less a synopsis of the rant I greeted Bridget with when I arrived at her house this morning. Her response? She thwacked me on the head with a copy of the fall fashion issue of *Vogue*—which is nine hundred pages thick with advertisements, mind you.

"Get over it. He's a Dreg."

"But he doesn't use anymore," I argued.

"Once a Dreg, always a Dreg," she said.

Bridget was just expressing the opinion shared by the Pineville High majority. Once you're put into one of PHS's neat little categories—be it Upper Cruster, Jock, Groupie, IQ, 404, Clubber, Piney, or Dreg—it's difficult, if not impossible, to get reassigned.

"And Len?" I asked.

"He's cute. He's smart. And he's a virgin," she said. "You're, like, a match made in heaven."

"How do you know he's a virgin?"

"*Everyone* knows Len is a virgin," she said, as matter-of-fact as A-B-C and 1-2-3. "Just like *everyone* knows you're a virgin."

I was outraged. "And how does *everyone* know I'm a virgin? Maybe I shared very specific intimate moments with the Lucky Seven this summer! Is that so unfathomable?"

"Yes."

"Why?"

She laughed. "If you were getting laid, you wouldn't be so, like, tense," she said. "And neither would Len."

This is coming from my closest friend at Pineville High. In all of New Jersey, actually. Make that the Northeastern Seaboard. Very sad.

Then again, maybe she has a point.

"So you still haven't, like, talked to your grandmother yet?"

"No."

"Well, you should. You never know what that freak might talk to her about."

"Or vice versa!"

Gladdie has never been discreet. Throw two strokes into the mix and there was no telling what she would say. Or what she had already said. Once I realized this, I couldn't drive over to Silver Meadows fast enough. Literally. By the time I got there, I was already too late.

"This is the dollface I've been telling you about, Tutti Flutie," Gladdie bellowed. "My granddaughter JD!"

Marcus, Gladdie, Moe, and a very sour-looking woman wearing a Richard Simmons *Sweatin' to the Oldies* sweatshirt were in the middle of a card game. Cards are a spectator sport at Silver Meadows, as is anything that involves my grandmother.

"You're here on purpose," I said.

"Well, yes," he replied.

"Aha!" I blurted, thrusting an accusatory finger in his face. "So you admit it!"

"Of course I'm here on purpose," he replied. "I work here." Duh.

"You two know each other?" Moe asked.

"Yeah," I replied, glaring at Marcus. "We know each other."

"Well, that's just swell because now you can replace Irene here, and we can get down to playing a real game of hearts."

"Would you, Jessica Darling, care to join me in a game of hearts?" Marcus asked, wearing an expression that was as aggressively innocent as those posters of babies dressed up like bumblebees and sunflowers.

Game of hearts. Har-dee-har-har.

"Well," I replied, "you are the Game Master, aren't you?"

"What? You don't like hearts?" Moe asked, oblivious to the staredown. "Then let's play poker."

"You with your poker," chastised Gladdie. "You just don't like it when I shoot the moon."

Marcus sat there, coyly batting his eyelashes at me.

"You liked my costume, huh?"

"Yeah, I liked it as much as I like your days-of-the-week T-shirts," I said. "What's with that, anyway?"

"Well, I've always admired days-of-the-week underwear," he replied.

I'll bet he has. I'll bet he's admired many pairs of days-of-the-week underwear. Three dozen girls' worth.

"But, you see, I don't wear underwear."

Gladdie and Moe rocked with ribald merriment.

"Whoo-wee!"

"Yowza!"

"I'm just joshin'," Marcus said when the din died down. "See?" He then lowered the waistband of his jeans so we could all get a totally gratuitous look at his boxers. More whoops, cackles, and wolf whistles, but only from Gladdie this time.

"So are ya in or are ya out?" Moe asked, holding up the cards. He was clearly put out by Gladdie's fondness for the youthful patch of flesh above the boxers and below the navel. And so was I, quite frankly. So was I.

"Thank you, Moe, but I'm not in the mood for cards. Gladdie, do you mind if we escape to your room for some good old-fashioned girl talk?"

"But it's so pleasant out here with the boys!" Gladdie said, flirtatiously placing one hand on Marcus's hand, and the other on Moe's. "Don'tcha want to stay awhile with Moe and Tutti Flutie?"

Oh, Christ. I really was too late. *Tutti Flutie* had already charmed the hell out of my grandmother. And my grandmother, being who she is, wouldn't want to give up a single second of attention from a guy more than seven decades her junior.

I declined with as much grace and dignity as I could muster.

"Looks like you're back in, Irene," Moe said.

Irene lifted her finger and twirled it in the air in the universal signal that means "Whoop-dee-do." I think I would like Irene if I got to know her.

"Gladdie, Moe, Irene, it's been a pleasure. I'll see you again soon." Then I turned to Marcus. "May I have a word with you please?"

"Sure," he replied, without making a move.

You know, I'd forgotten that Marcus can be a huge pain in the ass when he wants to be, which is all of the time.

"Oh, you mean in private?"

"Yes, I mean in private."

"Ohhhhh . . . ," he said, as if all the world's mysteries had just been answered. He gave everyone at the table a knowing glance. "It must be about Len, then."

Gladdie, Moe, and everyone else oohed and ahhed. Obviously, *someone* had already informed them about Len.

"It's not about Len," I said. "It's about you."

An even louder chorus of oohs and ahhs.

"You know what? Forget it."

As I walked out of the rec room, I recalled how I once thought Silver Meadows was like college. I was wrong. It's more like preschool. I'm now thoroughly convinced that maturity starts to reverse itself as you close in on a century of life.

the sixth

I had no choice. Really.

I wanted to talk to Gladdie alone. I had to talk to her in person because she refuses to pick up the phone—the only proof of a genetic connection between us.

I needed to know whether Marcus would be working today. If the answer was yes, I'd postpone my visit. Normally, I would ask Len. "Hey, Len. Do you know if Marcus is working at the fogies' home today?" Simple as that. Only it wasn't so simple anymore. Inquiring about Marcus's whereabouts would be rather insensitive, you know, if what Marcus said about Len liking me is true.

This is what happened when I called Silver Meadows to find out if Marcus Flutie was working today:

"WHAT?!" a Geritolic gentleman's voice yelled into the phone. "YOU WANT TO KNOW IF THE *MARKET PHOOEY* IS WORKING TODAY?"

"No. I want to know if *Marcus Flutie* is working today."

"*MARKET PHOOEY*? WHAT IN THE HECK IS THAT? SOME KIND OF NEW-FANGLED SLANG?"

"No. It's the name of a guy who works—"

The voice consulted someone in the background. "HEY, DO-

RIS! DO YOU KNOW WHAT IN THE HECK THE *'MARKET PHOOEY'* IS? I GOT A GAL ON THE PHONE ASKING IF THE *MARKET PHOOEY* IS WORKING TODAY."

I hung up the phone. They really shouldn't let the residents answer the front desk phone when Linda is taking a cigarette break.

So, as I said, I had no choice.

"Hey, Jessica," Marcus said after the second ring.

This totally threw me off. I hadn't anticipated the possibility that the phone would betray my identity, which is sloppy on my part, since it's not like caller ID is some super high-tech innovation in telecommunications. I had hoped he would pick up and say "Hello" like a normal person. And I would've said, "Yes. Hello. Is the Game Master there?" which would've shown him that I wasn't intimidated one bit.

"Jessica?"

"Uh. Hey. Hi. Uh . . ."

Damn that caller ID!

"I assume you're calling to have our overdue conversation about Len," he said.

"What?"

"Isn't that how it works?"

"How *what* works?"

"How *it* works. Dating."

"I'm not following you."

"The girl goes through the best friend to get the guy?"

Stumped. I knew I was the girl in the scenario.

Stymied. But who was the best friend?

Stupid. And who was I trying to get to?

"I let you in on the open secret about Len's affection for you. I did that because he isn't too confident with the ladies and would never get around to telling you himself. That's why I stepped in. He needs my wisdom. He needs my help."

Flashback: A conversation with Marcus last fall, back when our midnight phone calls used to soothe my insomnia. *Subject:* What Marcus did to pass the time now that he didn't drink or drug anymore. *Answer:* "I use my wisdom to help Len get laid."

He's using his wisdom to help Len get laid.

"Are you using your wisdom to help Len get laid?!"

He chuckled. "Hey, whatever happens between you two is your business, not mine. If there's one thing I've learned about dealing with you, Jessica Darling, it's that I shouldn't get too involved in your personal, private business."

This was unbelievable.

"Don't you think it's sort of a conflict of interest?" I asked.

"What?"

"Less than a year ago, you wanted to get into my pants!"

"That's not fair, Jessica," he said. "First of all, it was ten months ago, which is Paleolithic by high school relationship standards. Second, your pants weren't the only thing I was trying to get into. And third, when you said 'Fuck you,' I took it as a subtle hint that you didn't want anything to do with me anymore. So even if I wanted to get into your pants at one point in time, I had to stop."

"Stop what?"

"Wanting."

"Oh."

"So there's no conflict of interest."

Then he proceeded to tell me that he and Len have gotten tight over the past year, especially when he joined the band this summer. After many rehearsals, Len finally confessed to Marcus that he admired my intelligence and my bravery for standing up for myself in my editorials (R.I.P.). He also happened to think that I was "quite attractive." So Marcus revealed that we had been sort of friends last year, and knew quite a bit about me. Then Len begged Marcus to help him woo me or whatever and Marcus agreed. Now here we were.

"But I didn't give him details about all the things we talked about," he said. "I gave him generalities. Let him find out the juicy stuff for himself."

"Marcus, why are you doing this?"

"Because that's the way dating works. Len's my friend. You're my . . . well, we *were* friends, and now we're friends on the mend. If I can help you and Len get together, why shouldn't I?"

Why shouldn't he, indeed? There was no reason why this shouldn't be true, other than the fact that it came from his lips. I couldn't quite buy it. This whole conversation was just too logical to be right. His answers came too quickly, too correctly. It made the whole thing suspect. I just knew that Marcus wasn't telling me everything, but I wasn't about to beg him for details.

"I guess so."

Then, right as the conversation was drawing to a close— BAM!—instantaneous mental clickage. I don't know why I didn't think of it sooner. This insight didn't give me all the answers, but helped me muster just enough moxie to have the final word.

"Again, I must compliment you on your costume."

"You liked it."

"You saw the DVD at my house, so you knew that I would," I replied. "But there's just one thing that doesn't make sense."

"And what's that?"

"Well, if you're really looking out for Len's best sexual interests, I can't help but wonder why you didn't tell *him* to dress like Leon to impress me. Think about that for a while."

And I hung up.

Marcus doesn't really want me with Len! He only wants me to think he wants me with Len!

Why???!!! I have no idea! But it doesn't matter right now! Victory is mine! I'm too excited! I must stop this abuse of exclamation points!

Calm down.

I won the phone call outright. By the way, it felt better than every first place in a race combined and multiplied a bajillion times over. It was only after I put the phone down that I remembered that I never found out whether he would be at Silver Meadows today. I decided not to risk my champion status with a rematch, so I stayed home. Gladdie wouldn't miss me. She's got Moe to keep her company.

the tenth

Marcus has backed off ever since I blew a hole in his "I'm helping Len" alibi. Silently and simultaneously, we decided to take a nonantagonistic yet not-quite-tight approach to dealing with each other. We talk, but not *really*.

"Hey, Jessica," he says.

"Hey, Marcus," I say.

"How's Len?" he asks.

"Len's fine," I reply.

"That's good," he says.

"I guess," I say.

And so it goes.

At the same time, Len has stepped up. This is not a coincidence. He's been going out of his way to talk to me more. In class. In between classes. At lunch. He's called me twice. I did my part by not being phonephobic and picking it up when I saw his name. The second time, he asked me out on a sort of date. Not a real date. A sort of date.

"Um. I know you can't run anymore. But would you like to go hiking? Um. With me?"

It was all very sweet, so I said sure. My defenses must definitely be down.

So today—much to my mother's delight—Len and I went for a long walk around the windy, sandy trails of Double Trouble Park. It's really the perfect time of year to do something like this, because the leaves are as vibrant and varied as the sixty-four box of Crayolas. There's that crisp hint of chill in the air that reminds you winter is coming and you'd better get outside while you still can without freezing your ass off. Perfect cross-country weather. While I don't miss the team one bit, I have missed being outside and moving my body and feeling alive.

Len and I walked for two hours. And we talked. A lot.

The actual content of our conversations isn't necessary to rehash here, as they can always be traced back to the headlines in the *New York Times*. (If you're interested, just check the NYT archives for November 7 through November 10, 2001.) Len's end of the conversation always takes one of two forms: (1) long-winded and rambly or (2) start-and-stop stuttery. He's very dependable in that way.

My reaction varies.

Sometimes I can get past the shoddy presentation and focus on what he's saying. When I listen, I appreciate that Len's observations are intelligent and almost scientific in their factual accuracy. Spontaneous or emotional, they are not. Still, they are a far cry from the gaseous emissions that pass as conversation among his guy peers. I come away from the conversation better informed about current events.

Other times, I purposely tune out so I can just appreciate his cuteness. I try to forget that this cute guy with the cute bangs falling oh-so-cutely into his cute eyes is Len Levy.

This is harder to do on the phone.

Most times, I think about how much easier my life would be if I could just fall madly, passionately in love with Len already. The end result—our mad, passionate love—would more than make up for its less-than-romantic roots. Falling madly, passionately in love with Len would compensate perfectly for the fact that I only let him into my life to annoy Marcus, who, I'll repeat, for the sake of clarity, *doesn't really want us to be together, but only wants to make it seem like he wants us to be together,* for reasons I can only attribute to the brain-fry incurred from his falling into one K-hole too many in middle school.

About halfway through our hike, we hit the graffiti bridge. I have crossed it a bajillion times on training runs, but I'd never stopped there before.

"Let's take a break for a second," I said.

We braced ourselves on the beam overlooking the water. The wood was weathered gray and carved with almost illegible initials and names. Len and I looked at the water in the kind of comfortable silence that only exists between good friends. It was nice, actually. The mud floor and cedar foam made the creek look like a dark, bitter brew swirling in a cauldron.

I turned to him and said, "Do you remember breaking my heart in third grade?"

"Um. I did? What? Um."

"You did."

Then I reminded him how I gave him a valentine and he didn't give me one in return, the first devastating event of my loser love life.

He looked at me very seriously. "I'm sorry I did that. Um. I would never do that to you now."

It was a very sweet thing for him to say. And if he felt like kissing me, it would have been the perfect moment for him to do it. But he didn't.

the fifteenth

Now that my college applications are out to the original final four, I don't have much else to do to pass the time in school. There's only so much energy I can funnel toward making sure that Paul Parlipiano's silent, spine-chilling stepsister doesn't flunk her junior year.

I was looking forward to a little Marcus-Len intrigue. Marcus may not want us to *really* be together, but I don't think it has anything to do with him wanting to be with me. I mean, if Marcus wanted to be with me, I think he would just say something, or do something. Why get Len involved? So I kept waiting for Marcus to do something, anything, when he saw me and Len together. But he did absolutely nothing.

Life around PHS had flatlined. Boring, boring, boring. I was dying for something to happen to *anyone*, if not me.

Today I was rewarded with more cranial commotions than one person can deal with. Now I can't think straight. It's not like I need my brain for anything else right now, so it's better than being bored.

It all started, as most scandalous things do, with a bitchy bulletin from Sara in homeroom.

"Omigod! So you've found a new way to vent now that you're through with *The Seagull's Voice*, huh?"

"What the hell are you talking about?"

"You know what I'm talking about."

"I have no idea what you're talking about."

"A *quote* temporarily ectomorphic scandalmonger whose college acceptance will be purchased at no small price by her Mafioso father *unquote*?"

I laughed. "That's pretty funny," I said. "Who said it?"

"You did."

"I wish," I replied. "But I didn't."

"Omigod! Who else would write something like that? Who else would call Manda a *quote* pseudofeminist who has fellated her way into the upper echelons of high school society *unquote*?"

I laughed again. "Where did you read this?"

"*The email*," she said, in about as close an approximation of a whisper as she can get, which is still an eardrum banger.

I check my email once every day, at night, to see what Hope has to tell me. The fact that I have no interest in 24/7 two-way communication is another prime example of how I was born about a decade too late. Regardless, there had been nothing out of the ordinary in my inbox lately.

"What email? If it's hot nude pix of Haviland and Rico Suave getting it on, I don't want to see it."

Sara shushed me. "The newsletter," she said. "*Quote Pinevile Low unquote*."

"Bruiser, I really have no idea what you're talking about."

She scrutinized my face for eight loud exhalations. A total mouth breather, Sara can't even aspirate without being annoying.

"Then why weren't *you* slammed?" she asked, finally.

"Why wasn't I slammed *where*?"

"In *Pinevile Low*," she hissed.

"What is *Pinevile Low*?" I practically screamed, gathering the attention of the rest of homeroom, even Marcus, who rarely looks up from his notebook, which is brimming with lyrics for Chaos Called Creation, something I know via a secondary source. Len.

"SHUT UP!!!"

Sara looked like she was about to have thirty-six back-to-back heart attacks. After she regained her composure, she said, "I'm going to drop this until I gather enough evidence to prove it isn't you. I can't take any chances."

At this point, I was still convinced it was something trivial, or that Sara was messing with me. Yet that didn't stop me from lingering in my seat long enough after the bell rang to time my exit out the door with Marcus and ask him about it.

"Did you know what I was talking about?" I asked.

"Usually, yes," Marcus replied. "But in this case, no."

Then I realized that even in the spirit of making peace with the past, I can't tell when Marcus is being straight with me. It was a pointless question, really. I decided to ask a more reliable source.

"Bridget," I said loudly, getting her attention in the crowded hallway. "What's with *Pinevile Low*?"

She shushed me even more violently than Sara. "You didn't get it?"

"I don't think so."

"Uh-oh."

"What?"

"Listen to me, Jess. Don't say another word about this until you get home and check your email."

"So you got the email too? Why didn't you say something this morning?"

"Because, like, I can't," she said. "I was pretty much spared and I don't want it to get worse. But, like, that's all I can say until later."

"What the hell is going on? Is it a conspiracy?"

"I'm serious! Not another word," she replied, teeth gritted into a nervous smile. "Go home, check your email, and then we'll, like, talk. Maybe."

This was getting annoying. My only choice was to turn to the one person who wouldn't be able to withhold information from me, what with my irresistible feminine wiles and all. It might take him six hours to spit it out, but I'd get it from him.

"Hey, Len," I said. "Do the words *Pinevile Low* mean anything to you?"

I had the answer before he even cleared his throat. His blank face told me that he hadn't gotten it, either.

"Forget it," I said, before he got his first word out. I was about to turn on my heels and hurry to class when he called after me.

"Um. Jess?"

"What is it, Len?"

The warning bell rang.

"Later."

"Okay."

The rest of the day was very strange. It was like Sara, Manda, Scotty, and everyone else in our class was making an extra effort to act normal. There was a falseness to all the talk about homecoming and the big Thanksgiving football game. It was like the new reality entertainment trend that Bridget has told me about, in which *real* people play the *fictional* roles they inspired. It was like everyone was cast as themselves but weren't giving very convincing performances.

Rampant paranoia. No one knew just who knew what I didn't know yet.

Reread that last sentence. *This is what senior year is doing to me.*

The only class that was somewhat normal was French III, and that's because it's filled with juniors. Apparently, the only non-senior student at PHS who knew about *Pinevile Low* was Percy. The cool thing about French class is that Percy and I can talk freely and no one in the class has the skills to translate what we're saying. This is one of the greatest advantages of our friendship. I'm glad that I waited until sophomore year to take French I as an elective, otherwise I would have never gotten to know him.

"Tu l'as écrit!"

("You wrote it!")

"Quoi?"

("What?")

"Pinevile Bas."

("Pinevile Low.")

"Il n'est pas moi! Je ne l'ai pas écrit!"

("It is not me! I did not write it!")

"Eh."

("Eh. I don't think so. I know you really wrote it, you filthy liar you!")

"Où est-ce que tu l'as vu?"

("Where did you see it?")

"Bridget me l'a montré."

("Bridget showed me.")

"Oh!"

("Oh! Why would she show you and not me? You're *my* friend! Not hers! Why are you hanging out with her?!")

I must admit, I felt, well, not jealous exactly, but territorial.

I'd known Percy for three years now. He was my friend, not hers. Yet she shared the email with him, but she wouldn't with me. I bet they even have their own inside jokes. I wondered if that's just how things got when someone who has a crush on you asks you out and you turn him down for no good reason other than the fact that he's not absolutely perfect for you.

But who is, really? Who is perfect?

No one.

I guess I was thinking about that when Len came up to me at my locker after tenth period.

"Um. Jess, can I talk to you? Um. Now?"

"Sure."

And for the next forty-five minutes, Len proceeded to ask me to next week's homecoming dance.

I don't need to go into detail, because it was a very underwhelming proposal that dwelled a lot on his apologies for asking me on such short notice, which really hadn't occurred to me at all because homecoming isn't something I waste any time thinking about. I guess the important thing for you to know is that I said yes.

You're shocked, aren't you?

I figured, why the hell not? I've already done the stay-home-on-homecoming-night thing for the last three years. Why not just go? And I bet Len will look cute in his suit. If the music is loud enough, maybe we won't even have to talk.

When I got home, I checked my email. Sure enough, I had been left out. No email from anyone about anything.

"Why didn't I get the email?" I mumbled to myself.

My dad happened to be in the office, looking for some wonky techie thingie.

"What email?" he asked, which were probably the first two non-running-related words he's said to me since I ruined my life by renouncing my status as a Pineville High Seagull.

"Oh, some email that everyone got at school that I didn't get," I replied, as unsnotty as possible.

"Did you check your bulk-mail folder?"

"Huh?"

"I've put a pretty high junk mail filter on there, so it might have been funneled into that folder." Then he intelligently exited the room, probably well aware he'd be pushing his luck if he pursued a lengthier conversation with his daughter.

I clicked on my junk mail folder, and there, among the porn site spam (BARELY LEGAL LESBIANS, REAL LIVE NYM-PHOS, XXX!!! J. LO!!!XXX) was the message I was looking for. The subject: Pinevile Low. The sender: blank. The message:

I'VE UNCOVERED THE DIRT, THE SHAKY FOUNDATION
THAT KEEPS THIS SCHOOL TOGETHER.

Then, ten blind gossip items that were so exquisitely detailed you knew exactly who they were about but would probably hold up against defamation-of-character charges in court. Among the most notable (besides the items Sara had mentioned that slammed her and Manda) were the following:

WHAT VIDEO VIXEN'S HEARTBREAK LEFT HER BELIEV-
ING THAT PINEVILLE BOYS ARE BENEATH HER, AND IS
NOW RESPONSIBLE FOR A RAMPANT, RAGING BLUE BALLS
EPIDEMIC?

Bridget!

WHAT POPULAR, BEST LOOKING, MOST ATHLETIC GUY
HAS IMPRESSED COLLEGE RECRUITERS WITH HIS LAYUPS
ON THE COURT, BUT CAN'T GET IT UP FOR HIS SEXU-
ALLY DEMANDING GIRLFRIEND-OF-THE-MOMENT?

SCOTTY!!

WHAT TYPE-A BRAINIAC HAS VOWED TO FINALLY HAVE
SEX FOR THE FIRST TIME ON HOMECOMING NIGHT?

LEN!!!
(And indirectly, ME!!!)
Then, the comically ominous sign-off.

YOU WERE CHOSEN TO RECEIVE THIS EMAIL FOR A REA-
SON. SHARE THIS WITH ANYONE AND YOU'LL FIND YOUR-
SELF OUTED, OR YOU'LL GET IT WORSE THAN YOU DID
THIS TIME AROUND. AND THERE WILL BE A NEXT TIME.
MY EYES AND EARS ARE EVERYWHERE.

I know this sounds nuts, but I was kind of relieved that I
wasn't totally overlooked, as it proves that I register as a blip on
the Pineville radar. As much as I don't care about those things,
I think it's human nature to not want to feel totally insignificant. Besides, I've got nothing to worry about. There's nothing to
out about me. Besides pissing into an empty yogurt container to
provide Marcus with a drug-free urine sample sophomore year,

I've done nothing of any scandalous importance. No one knows about the Dannon Incident but Marcus and me, and I doubt anyone would believe him if he decided to narc on me after all this time. The point is, I'll go unscathed for as long as I continue to lead this sad, sexless existence.

And it will be sexless too. I'm not taking what *PL* said about Len seriously. I mean, he can barely muster the courage to talk to me, and he blew a perfectly good opportunity to kiss me, so I seriously doubt he has any designs on my bod. It was just someone's idea of a joke. I forwarded it to him, though, because I think he deserves to know that someone is talking smack about him. I guess that's the sort of thing that you're supposed to do once you accept someone's invitation to a formal. Maybe I should consult Bridget on the etiquette.

the seventeenth

This morning I called Len to talk to him about *Pinevile Low*. He needed to know that I didn't think any less of him or anything. Plus, I was interested in knowing what he thought about it.

"Um. Okay. Weird. I'm surprised you sent it to me. Um."

"Well, I thought you had a right to know."

"Um. Right."

"So don't worry about it, okay?"

"I'm not. Um. Worried."

"So we're cool, then."

"Yeah."

After I got off the phone with Len, I went over Bridget's to discuss who it could be.

"You can drop the act, Jess," she replied. "You wrote it, didn't you?"

"That's exactly what Percy said!" I cried.

"I know," she said. "We've already talked about it. We both know you pretty well and, like, we think it's you."

"Bridget! It's not me! Why does everyone think it's me?"

"Look at the evidence," she replied.

The Evidence

1. The perp is probably not someone outed in the email. ("You weren't outed in the email," Bridget said.)

2. Yet to disguise their identity, they might have outed someone she was friends with in a benign way. ("Like me," Bridget said. "What was said about me wasn't all that embarrassing. And Len's sexual quest makes you look kinda good.")

3. The perp is highly intelligent and/or has access to the kind of techie know-how that would disguise the sender. ("Hello, Class Brainiac! And your dad is a computer nerd," Bridget said, with increasing Sara-variety know-it-allness.)

4. The perp has a way with words. ("You're only the most infamous editorial writer in the history of Pineville High!")

5. And a hatred for the Upper Crust. ("Hello?!")

6. And needs a forum to vent. ("Who just lost her column in the school paper?")

By the end of her analysis, I was half-convinced that I had indeed written it. But I didn't. Unless I've developed a whole new dozing disorder to replace my insomnia. Maybe I sleep-write, like those sleep eaters who scarf an entire fridge worth of food without revving out of REM mode.

"Bridget," I said. "I swear to you, it's not me. I'd actually like to find out who it is."

This is the truth. Whoever wrote it seems like someone I'd like to get to know.

the twentieth

Pineville High makes the news again! The *Pinevile Low* email made the front page of the *Asbury Park Press*. Oh, I'll be so proud to tell my fellow college freshmen next year where I'm from.

According to the article, an anonymous "concerned mother" was doing her daily snoop through her kid's email in-box, found it, then forwarded it to all the Pineville powers that be. Of course, this is the same group of technological geniuses who required almost a month to undo the hacked class schedules, so it's no surprise that the sender of the email has not been found.

"Omigod! I'm totally gonna prove it's you," Sara hissed.

"I'd like to see that," I replied.

In related news, the Big Walk-Out was scheduled to begin after homeroom, and it would last as long as it took for justice to be served. Hundreds of PHS students stormed the doors and flooded the parking lot, carrying painted signs saying, TWO WRONGS DON'T MAKE A RIGHT! and THE PUNISHMENT DOESN'T FIT THE CRIME!

What were these rabble-rousers protesting? The war in Afghanistan? Hell, no.

Listen to their cries of freedom:

"*WHAT DO WE WANT?*" shouted Scotty.

"*HOMECOMING!*" screamed the crowd.

"*WHEN DO WE WANT IT?*"

"*FRIDAY!*"

It brought tears to Haviland's eyes. Tears of despair. Marcus, Len, Bridget, and I watched the Big Walk-Out from Haviland's classroom on the second floor. We were the only ones in honors who hadn't joined the cause.

Despite this never-before-seen show of solidarity, the administration stuck to their decision to cancel the homecoming dance for the first time in our school's history. It was schoolwide retribution in response to the refusal of the person behind *Pinevile Low* to come forward and claim responsibility for the painfully public humiliation it caused our school district.

Hence, the protest. When it was in full swing, Masters made an announcement over the loudspeaker.

"Any student who does not get back to class by the next period bell will be suspended."

No one moved. No one cared.

"And will be permanently restricted from all after-school activities."

No one moved.

"Which includes participation in all sports, and the big football game against Eastland on Friday afternoon."

I haven't seen students run that fast since PJ tested his lactose intolerance by chugging a milkshake.

"We should do something else on Friday," Marcus said, grinning down at the melee.

"What do you mean?" I asked. What I really meant was, *What do you mean by "do" and "we"?*

Bridget piped in. "Like, we should organize an alternative event to homecoming!"

"Exactly," Marcus said, nodding his approval.

"Like what?" Len asked.

"Len, I think this is the perfect time for Chaos Called Creation to get out of the basement."

Len turned green. "Um. Flu. Um. We're not ready for a show."

Bridget jumped up and down with excitement.

"What's the point of being in a band if you don't play?" Marcus asked.

"We play."

"For the four walls of wood paneling in your basement. But I'm talking about people."

"I don't know. Um," said Len, glancing in my direction.

"I think it's a great idea, Len. I can't wait to hear *Chaos Called Creation.*" I said the last few words with an unintentionally sarcastic emphasis that resulted in a spontaneous exchange of looks between Bridget and Marcus. Len didn't notice.

"Um. Okay. Where?"

Silence all around.

"I got it," Bridget exclaimed. "Bruiser's house."

Groans all around.

"Her house is the only one that's big enough," Bridget said. "And she's, like, the only person I can think of who will be able to promote the party on such short notice."

Bridget was right. Sara's huge oceanfront homestead was the only domicile in the Pineville school district that actually looked like those colossal party houses in the movies. Everyone else threw parties in dark, damp, cramped basements or similarly crowded quarters with inadequate pissing facilities. Bruiser had become quite the party-throwing expert. She knew to set up several booze stations throughout the house so no one would have to wait in line to get liquored up. She knew to put party slipcovers on all the furniture, and to put temporary rugs on the hardwood floors and other high-traffic areas. She knew to lock all her parents' valuables in an off-limits room, usually her dad's home office because it didn't have a bed, and all beds were always put to use at one of Bruiser's parties. So I hear. I had stopped going to her bashes a long time ago.

"You're right. Um. But she'll never do it."

"She wished death by overdose on Marcus, remember?" I chimed in.

Marcus turned to Bridget and said, "These two make a perfectly pessimistic pair."

"They, like, totally do," Bridget replied.

Len and I just stood there awkwardly, praying they would get back to the original subject. Bridget finally did.

"Look, Bruiser will do it because she'll, like, be worshiped for rescuing homecoming. She'll find a way to take credit for the whole idea. Be persuasive—you know, like the way you used to be in your editorials. Only not such a downer."

"*Me*? Why me?" Why was the fate of Pineville High's homecoming weighing heavy on the shoulders of the most antisocial person in the history of the school? Besides Taryn Baker, that is.

"Because you're the only one of us she deigns to talk to," Marcus said.

The moment he said it, I knew he was right. Of course I'd

have to do it, since I was the only one of us on speaking terms with Sara—and that's using the phrase loosely.

"You'll just have to, like, kiss her ass a lot."

"Lucky me."

Protestors straggled into the classroom, defeated.

"I'm sorry," Len said.

"Yeah, I'm sorry I have to kiss Bruiser's ass too."

"Um. No. I mean that our plans are ruined. And. Um."

Oh, my tragic fate: I'll never attend a Pineville High homecoming dance. He had no idea how much I didn't give a damn.

"I'm not crushed, really," I said. "We can still have fun, I guess."

"We can?"

Fun is a foreign concept to both of us. We really do make quite a pair.

"Look, I didn't go last year either and I didn't care one bit. I even went out with my mom to buy an anti-homecoming dress—"

Oops. As soon as I said it, I regretted it. I didn't want anyone else in the room to remember the blue shirtdress I wore last New Year's Eve, a relic from the Paleolithic era of high school memory.

"That's it. Um. We'll call it the Anti-Homecoming. If you don't mind me swiping your idea."

"No, there's no copyright on it."

"Um. Copyright. That's so funny."

Nothing indicates unfunniness more than the phrase "That's so funny" unaccompanied by even the quietest peep of legit laughter. Len does this a lot with me.

"You can even wear. Um. Your Anti-Homecoming dress."

Marcus and Bridget nearly fell out of the window when he said that. I almost jumped.

Oh, poor Len. He was the only one in the room who had no idea why I could never wear that dress again, because it reminded me too much of a night that changed my life, but not in the way I had planned, that it reminded me too much of, well . . . you know. Him.

There's no need for me to belabor the point, now, is there?

the twenty-first

need a skin graft. My lips are permanently damaged from the amount of ass-kissing I did today.

Bridget was right. Once I played into Sara's ego as the savior of homecoming, she was all for hosting the party. It was not so easy to persuade her to let Chaos Called Creation make their debut.

"Omigod! Why should I let Krispy Kreme set a freaky foot in my house?"

It always sounds strange whenever someone refers to Marcus by his old nickname. He hasn't dunked any new doughnuts as far as Len knows. Then again, why would Marcus be any more honest with Len than he was with me? Marcus could have banged any number of girls in his spare time and admired their days-of-the-week underwear.

"I'm waiting for an answer," Sara said, tapping her foot. "Why should I let in that freak?"

Freak. Freak show. Aha!

"Because a band will draw a major crowd to the party, just like the talent show that's always SRO every year. Kids will come because of the freak factor. Many will come to see if Chaos Called Creation is any good. Even more will come to see if they suck."

Sara thought about this for a second. While I think my talent show argument was a strong one, I think the real reason she agreed is that she still thinks I'm the Mystery Muckraker behind *Pinevile Low*. She's afraid that if she pisses me off, I'll write something even worse about her, especially since I have been privy to many things about her that are indeed so much worse than what was already said.

"If they suck, I'm pulling the plug and putting on some real music."

"Then you'll let them play."

"Yes," she said. "They can play in my game room."

Sara's house has many superfluous rooms. The game room, as she puts it, is a miniaturized version of one of her dad's many arcades. It even has a little stage for karaoke. But for the Anti-Homecoming, it would be the platform for Chaos Called Creation's debut. The game room for the Game Master. How perfect.

"Cool," I replied. "I'll let them know."

Then she ran over to Scotty and Manda, who took a break from probing each other's uvulas to listen to her say, "Omigod! I'm totally saving homecoming. I'm throwing the *quote* Anti-Homecoming *unquote*."

"What the hell is the Anti-Homecoming?" Scotty asked.

Then Sara explained how *she* thought an alternative event for homecoming needed to be planned and blah-diddy-blah blah-blah. Manda was psyched.

"The best thing about it is that I can still wear my fuck-me dress!"

Scotty suddenly became very interested in fashion. "Fuck-me dress?" he said, with a raise of his eyebrows and a knowing smirk. "I thought *every* dress was your fuck-me dress."

Manda's face twisted with hurt. Only *she* is allowed to acknowledge her skankiness. That's what makes her a powerful woman, or so her theory goes. She smacked Scotty straight through to the skull with her notebook. "Shut up, you prick."

I guess after three months together they aren't so blinded by sex anymore. Scotty and Manda are starting to see each other for what they really are. The enemy. I can't wait until they break up.

"And guys can still wear their suits!" Sara said.

"I'm not wearing a fucking suit," Scotty muttered, almost to himself. "And PJ won't want to, either." PJ was supposed to be Sara's date.

"Ooh, honey," Manda cooed, smoothing the hair she had mussed only seconds before. "But you look so hot in a suit." She lowered her voice, but it was still loud enough to hear. "And you know what happens when you look hot . . ."

We *all* know what happens. To think that I helped orchestrate the event that will provide their precoital entertainment tomorrow night. That is, unless they shed all their inhibitions and have sex at the party, which is really not all that different from the display they put on in the halls every day. Ever since *Pinevile Low*, Scotty and Manda have been going out of their way to prove to the public that—yes!—he *can* get it up. It's really nasty. They get more action during any one of their four-minute trysts between classes than I will get in my entire life. I'm not exaggerating. Seriously. There are a lot of eyewitnesses—teachers and students alike—who will back me up on this.

When I think about sex in the Scotty-and-Manda sense, I'm so relieved that I'm still a virgin. The fact that I haven't done the nasty things (and with them it is nasty, because it's them) that they have done and continue to do with shocking regularity gives me a sense of peace.

I'm not like them.

But then I get really horny and I know I'm just kidding myself.

At least Hope understands what I'm going through. She's the only other virgin I know. I mean, I think she is. Sometimes I worry—irrationally—that she's done it too, and just hasn't told me. She's dated a few guys in Tennessee. but none have been serious enough to warrant a devirginization, she says. And the fling she had with a Parisian last summer didn't go any further than the kind of kissing France is famous for. But if Hope has had sex, she'd keep it a secret, not out of shame, but because she knows the news would be a devastating blow to our friendship. It would be one less thing that distinguishes Hope and me as the *us* against *them*. Sometimes loyalty requires lies. Think of all the things I've neglected to tell her over the past two years.

The point is, I've waited this long, so I might as well just keep on waiting. Waiting for the right person, the right time. When it makes sense to have sex, that is, when the timing is right, and timing is almost everything, I want to know beyond a shadow of a doubt that no one else should be inside me.

This is why I am going to die a virgin.

The right person is not Len, that's for sure, his homecoming deadline be damned. I thought Marcus was right. And I was wrong. Wrong. Wrong. Wrong. I couldn't have been more wrong. I must have been out of my mind. I read that teenagers' poor decision-making can be attributed to an overproduction of cells in the cerebral cortex, the "thinking" part of the brain. Our gray matter gets all clogged with new cells and we can't possibly make rational choices.

My cerebral cortex must have been gridlocked last New Year's Eve.

Combine brains gone all gunky with cells with bods jacked up on hormones and it's no wonder we drink and drug and screw and get body parts pierced that should be nowhere near a man wielding a gigantic needle.

Oh. By "we" I mean teenagers. But it's really more accurate for me to say "they," isn't it?

A joke to get my mind off my nonsexed status.

Q: *How do you make a hormone?*

A: *Tell her you'll wear a suit to the Anti-Homecoming dance.*

Har-dee-har-har.

I know I'm being a bitch about this but . . . Ack. I'm losing it. Everything but my virginity, that is.

Har-dee-har-har.

the twenty-second

Run! Flee! Before little G-Money, Jr. starts his eighteen-year reign of terror! Oh, Christ! What if it's a girl? A baby Bethany—just like Dr. Evil and Mini Me!

AHHHHHHHHHHHHHHHHHHHHHHHHHHHHHHHHH.

Yes, it's true. Bethany and G-Money have made a little monster! Boy or girl, it's bad.

Mr. and Mrs. Doczylkowski barely got their coats off before making the announcement.

"We're expecting!"

I can't describe the deafening screech of joy that came out of my mother.

Dad clasped G-Money on the arm in a manly-man, bro-bonding gesture.

Gladdie turned to Moe (whom she had insisted on bringing because "he's like family now") and said, "I told you Sonny's boys could swim!"

I just stood there, dumbfounded. This news was really the last thing I was expecting to hear out of my sister's mouth. Mommy Bethany was a ludicrous concept. She's too self-absorbed. And lazy. I mean, this is a person who recently got her eyelashes permed so she wouldn't have to endure the tragic inconvenience of curling them manually with a Maybelline doohickey.

Bethany's lack of baby lust was one of the very few things we had in common, besides our very compatible eighties CD/DVD collections. I don't have one teensy-weensy bit of a maternal instinct. Maybe this is my body's way of coping with the fact that I am destined to die a virgin.

"I wanted to tell you right away," Bethany said, patting her still-flat stomach. "So you wouldn't think I had gotten fat."

I don't know how many times I'd heard her declare that her uterus was a baby-free zone for that very reason. "As soon as wives pack on the pregnancy fat, their husbands leave them," she'd say. "That's not going to happen to me." Her fear of flab would overcome thousands of years of biological programming. Or so I'd thought. I couldn't resist bringing this up.

"Bethany, I didn't think you wanted to have a baby."

Big mistake. You should have seen the looks of revulsion and loathing. It was as if I had screamed: I HATE BABIES. KILL ALL THE BABIES. ALL BABIES MUST DIE, DIE, DIE!!!!!!!!!

I now know what it's like to be OJ Simpson or Taryn Baker—shunned. No one talked to me until we sat down to enjoy our Thanksgiving meal, at which point Gladdie got on my case about not visiting her lately. It turns out that my absence at Silver Meadows for the past month was more conspicuous than I had thought.

"So why ain't ya gracing us with your face lately?"

"I've been busy with, uh, tutoring," I said unconvincingly.

"That's not what Tutti Flutie says," she cawed.

"Really? And what does Tutti Flutie say?"

"He says ya got yourself a boyfriend!"

Up to this point, my mother hadn't added much to the

Thanksgiving Day conversation other than shouting "My baby's having a baby!" at random intervals that grew more frequent as Chardonnay replaced the blood in her veins. But upon hearing the word *boyfriend*, she suddenly gave me her full attention.

"Jessie! You've got a boyfriend! Who is it?"

"I don't have a boyfriend, Mom."

"That ain't what I heard," said Gladdie.

"Me neither," chimed in Moe.

"Well, you can't believe everything you hear," I responded. "Especially if it comes out of Marcus Flutie's mouth."

"I'm sorry, kiddo! But he said that you and this Len fella were going to the big dance," Gladdie said.

"YOU HAVE A DATE TO HOMECOMING?" shouted Mom and Bethany simultaneously.

"No!"

"That ain't what I heard . . ."

Then I had to go on to explain that Len had asked me to homecoming, but it was canceled, so we organized some Anti-Homecoming festivities for tomorrow night instead.

Just imagine the eviscerating shrieks of horror as my mother and Bethany contemplated a world without homecoming.

"I don't know about this Len fella," Gladdie said after the wailing had quieted down. "But that Tutti Flutie is a firecracker, ain't he?"

"Yes," I agreed. "He is."

"Too bad Tutti Flutie ain't interested in you."

"He said that?"

"Oh, yeah," she said. "He likes your brain, JD, but he ain't attracted to you, which is just a cryin' shame, if you don't mind me sayin' so."

No. How could I mind the truth? It was a cryin' shame, and my tears almost dripped right into my stuffing. No matter how much it hurt to hear it, this is good news, right? Now I know for sure that Marcus doesn't want me anymore. His intentions with Len are pure.

"That Len fella, he's got hot pants for you," Gladdie said with a snicker and a wink of a wrinkly eye.

Then she, Mom, and Bethany launched into a fit of giggles.

Throughout this conversation, G-Money, Moe, and my dad were totally engrossed in their own discussion about Michael Jordan's return to the game. It's at times like this that I wish *everyone* in my family were addicted to ESPN. Myself included.

the twenty-third

The Anti-Homecoming will go down in Pineville High history as one of the all-time biggest, best, and most debaucherous blowouts.

The Anti-Homecoming will go down in my personal history as one of the all-time bizarro nights of my life, from the moment Len picked me up to the second he drove me home, and including all the moments without him in between. Especially those.

Let's fast-forward past my mother and sister's futile attempt at a fashion makeover, when I vetoed all of their superfemme sartorial suggestions in favor of my favorite dark rinse low-riders and a pristine, child-sized T-shirt from the Jacksons' 1984 Victory Tour that I scooped up on eBay. Let's bypass the mortifying prelude, during which Mom, Dad, Bethany, G-Money, Gladdie, and Moe lined themselves up *Brady Bunch*-style on the staircase to watch me greet my "new boyfriend." Let's skip right over the part where Len and I exchanged awkward pleasantries for the benefit of our viewing audience and headed out the door to the car. Len drives his dad's navy-blue Saturn, a very dependable vehicle that lacks the personality of, say, a titanic brown seventies-era Cadillac.

Len started talking.

(*Author's note:* Pay very close attention. When this entry is finished, you'll probably want to refer back to this conversation, as well as my conversation with Len documented on November 17, to make sense of our misunderstanding.)

"Jess? I can't do. Um. It," he said as soon as he turned the key in the ignition.

"What? You can't perform?" I was talking about his show.

"Um . . ."

"You can do it, Len!"

"It's just a lot of. Um. Pressure."

"I know this whole night is kind of riding on how good you are . . ."

Len whimpered. I swear to God.

"Relax, Len! You'll be great. You've been practicing a lot, right?"

Len's hands shook on the wheel. "WHAT?!"

"Believe me," I said, gently putting my hand on his shoulder, "you'll be fine."

He whimpered again, like a Doberman that just got its ass kicked by a French poodle.

Len had set up and soundchecked earlier in the afternoon, so all he had to do was chill until go time, a metaphysical impossibility in his torqued-up state. It only got worse when we arrived. Bruiser's circular driveway was jammed with cars and kids. This party was well on its way to becoming a legend. Not only was the senior class in near-perfect attendance, but underclassmen and even some graduates had shown up for the sex, drugs, and rock and roll. Everyone was in a particularly festive mood because Pineville had beat Eastland in the annual Thanksgiving gridiron grudge match, 21 to 7.

"Omigod!" Sara screamed when she saw me and Len. "I'm

so psyched to see you!" She planted a yeast-and-hoppy kiss on my cheek. She obviously had beer-blasted her brain cells.

"Omigod! Len! Tonight's the big night, huh?" She elbowed him in the ribs, almost knocking him over.

"Um. I have to get away. Um. Until the show. Sorry. Okay."

And he scurried off with his guitar slung over his shoulder. I don't know where he hoped to get some time alone, as the house was packed. Within five seconds, I spotted Scotty—looking very unhappy in his suit—and Manda—looking very on display in a black jersey backless, almost-frontless, slit-up-to-the-crotch dress. It was so barely there that it seems more accurate to call it a dress *concept*, rather than an actual dress. Neither of them said anything to me, as they had their mouths full of each other's saliva.

However, I knew that this party had reached mythological proportions when I saw that even Taryn Baker was in attendance. Guess who she brought with her?

"Hey, Jessica!"

"Hey, Paul!" I was quite proud of how cool I was. So cool that I would acknowledge Taryn, who was hovering silently and sullenly behind his shoulder.

"Hey, Taryn. How goes the quadrilaterals?" This, in reference to our latest tutoring session.

She shrugged and scanned the room as if she were searching for something specific, like she was on a scavenger hunt and would get ten points for finding Billy Bass the singing fish.

"So did you send your application to Columbia yet?" he yelled, in between sips of beer.

BEER! Oh, God. I hoped that the concept of me and beer didn't bring back the visual of me puking on his shoes.

"Jessica?!" he shouted louder, thinking I hadn't heard him. "Did you apply to Columbia yet?"

"Actually . . ."

He slapped his palms against his cheeks in shock. "Jessica! I'm surprised at you!"

"Uh, what?"

"You're letting 9/11 stop you!"

"I got freaked out!"

"That's what they want!" His arms were flailing all over the place. He was all riled up, as I imagine he is at his PACO meetings. "Don't you see? Fear is the greatest form of oppression. The best way to rise up in protest is to live your life to its fullest!"

Taryn whispered something into his ear.

"Look, I gotta go now. Remember, it's not too late to change your mind." Then he looked me dead in the eyes and said one last time, "Columbia."

Columbia. Columbia. Columbia.

New York City. New York City. New York City.

Death! Terror! Fear!

"Was that, like, *the* Paul Parlipiano you were talking to?" said Bridget, snapping me out of my hysteria. She and Percy had been watching the whole thing. I was actually very relieved to see them.

"So was it?" Percy asked, handing me a cup of beer.

"The same," I replied. I took a long swig and was pleasantly surprised to find that it didn't have the familiar cat piss bouquet that Milwaukee's Best is famous for.

"What is it?" I asked.

"MGD," Percy said.

"No Beast? Pretty classy for a Pineville party."

"Truth," he replied, and we bumped fists.

"Is he, like, still gay?" Bridget asked.

"I'd assume so," I said.

"Too bad," she replied.

"What's too bad?" another voice asked.

I looked to my left and Marcus was standing next to me.

"It's too bad that Jessica's, like, future husband is gay," Bridget replied.

"Yes, that is unfortunate, isn't it?" he said, holding my gaze a little longer than necessary.

"Good luck, Marcus," Bridget said.

"If you get nervous, just imagine everyone in their under-wear," Percy said. "That's what I do when I'm onstage."

"It's easier to do with some people than with others," Marcus said, looking right at me.

How did I become a part of yet another conversation about Marcus and underwear?

"Truth," said Percy, glancing at me, then zoning in on Bridget.

The truth hit me like a dodgeball to the face: I'd been re-placed as his older-woman object of lust. Fortunately, Bridget hadn't heard any of this banter because she was distracted by Dori Sipowitz and the rest of the theater crowd convening in the corner. Obviously, there's no hope for Percy and Bridget. Like me, Bridget enjoys Percy's sense of humor and his company, but she will never see him as dating material. I'm going to have to talk him out of it. One friend to another.

"Let's, like, bond with the rest of the cast," Bridget said as she whisked Percy away.

Marcus and I were alone. Alone surrounded by a hundred screaming, scamming, shot-slamming buffoons. Our peers. The walls were vibrating. The air was thick with smoke and the airborne form that beer takes on at parties, so it hangs heavy over everyone's heads.

"Aren't you going to ask me how Len is doing?"

Marcus complied. *"How's Len?"* he asked with dramatic emphasis.

I matched his tone.

"Len is fine."

"That's good," Marcus replied.

"I guess."

Our conversation had already become a parody of itself.

"Nice shirt," he said.

"Thanks," I replied, sincerely flattered that *someone* appreciated its awesomeness. "I was about to say the same to you."

For the Anti-Homecoming, Marcus was wearing another one of his custom white T-shirts. This one said: COMINGHOME. If I'd had an adequate number of beers, I probably would've pressed my fingertip to one of the letters, to feel the soft fake-velvety texture.

"Thanks. I ironed it myself," he replied.

The image of Marcus toiling over an ironing board was too domestic for me to handle.

"I happen to be very crafty," he said, laughing along with me, knowing exactly what I had thought was so funny.

I glanced at the plastic cup in his hand. The liquid was dark and bubbly.

"That better not have any alcohol in it," I said disapprovingly.

What was I doing? Why was I saying this to him?

"Do you want a taste?"

Why is it that everything that comes out of that boy's mouth

sounds like a come-on? Because it *is*?! No! I still can't believe it.
The Game Master was just messing with me.

"Sure." I took his cup, put it to my lips, and let the liquid wash
over my tongue. Mmmm. Plain Coca-Cola. No Jack. No Bacardi.

"Aren't you tempted?"

"I'm tempted all the time by lots of things," he replied. "But
alcohol and drugs aren't among them."

I was about to ask what tempts him when Len broke in.

"Hey, Jess. Um. Flu, Sara wants us on soon. It's almost. Um.
Time."

"Cool," Marcus said, handing me his cup as Len headed toward the Game Room. "You can finish this for me."

He is maddening.

Sara stumbled on the stage, her tube top slipping so dangerously low that it was almost a belt. Her lipstick was smeared
from nose to chin, a sure sign that PJ—or someone else—had
discovered the only surefire way to shut her up.

Sara shouted into the mike so loudly that when her words
were amplified by the sound system, they (with the exception of
the occasional "Omigod!") came out totally garbled and unintel-
ligible, or so I thought. When she paused, the crowd cheered, as
if they understood.

Percy had miraculously found me again in the crowd.
Knowing how good he is with languages, I consulted him for
a translation.

"She said that if the band totally sucks, it's—omigod!—totally
not her fault and that the audience should totally throw things at
them if they totally want to."

Leave it to Sara to promote civil disobedience at her own
party.

Then Sara screamed something else, the band took the stage, and the audience roared.

Len stepped up to the mic. I remember thinking that standing in front of the mic, guitar strapped over his shoulder, in a Nirvana *Bleach* T-shirt, Len looked really hot. I also remember thinking that I would forget about how hot he looked the moment he opened his mouth.

"This is the Anti-Homecoming!" Len said. "We're Chaos Called Creation!"

No stuttering. No babbling. Remarkable. I was wrong. He still looked hot.

Then the band launched into their first song.

Marcus stayed stage left, almost completely hidden behind the speaker. I was surprised by this. I thought for sure he'd want to be up front and more conspicuous.

I don't know if it was Marcus's addition to the band, the extra rehearsal time, the clear skin, or what, but Len was a smoother, more confident front man for Chaos Called Creation than he ever was for the Len Levy Four. He looked and sounded less tortured. And the band sounded great in that loose, loud, guitar-heavy way. It was too punk for dancing, too pop for moshing. Perfect for hopping and head-bopping. I'd say they were kind of like the Clash, though everyone else would probably compare them to the Strokes. I prefer eighties synth pop, but I was obviously in the minority. When they finished their first number, the audience went apeshit. Sara grabbed me from behind by my shoulders and shook me violently, both with her hands and her voice.

"Omigod! They totally don't suck! Omigod! I can't believe it!"

Even Manda was impressed. "They rock!"

"I scored the winning touchdown in today's game," slurred Scotty, dejectedly. He had gotten very drunk and disheveled since I last saw him. He had ditched the jacket and was wearing the tie around his head like a kung fu master.

"And their songs are all about how women are the superior sex," continued Manda, ignoring her boyfriend.

"Really?" I hadn't been able to understand any of the words.

"Yes! I am so impressed!"

She wasn't the only one. There was a lot of commotion after the band finished. Chaos Called Creation was swarmed by fourteen-year-old Clubber Babies who were wearing more body glitter per inch than actual clothing. It was gross. Just gross. You know what? Seeing those little girlies push up on Len made me want him for myself. He was *my* geek cute guy, not *their* guitar god. And if he wasn't brave enough to make a move, then goddamn it, I was going to do it for him.

I stole Percy's beer and pounded it. Then I snatched Bridget's cup and did the same. All in less than sixty seconds.

I know, I know. Liquid courage backfires because when you wake up with a hangover, you're back to your same old self, and your problems are still there, only now you've got to deal with them with a debilitating jackhammer headache blah-diddy-blah-blah-blah. Sometimes knowing something is bad for you isn't enough to stop you from doing it. This was one of those cases. Besides, I wasn't drinking to obliterate, just to loosen up. I didn't want another puke-on-the-shoes scenario.

It worked fairly well. When Len and Marcus finally approached us, I grabbed Len by the arm and said, "Let's get out of here."

When we got in the car, I remember thinking that we were alone for the first time since we arrived. I was about to tell him how much I liked him when Len cleared his throat.

"Look, Jessica. I like you."

"I was about to tell you the same thing."

"Um. Yes." He barked out a cough, to get himself back on track. "I'm so happy that you like me back and I'm flattered and quite frankly flabbergasted that you wanted to lose your virginity to me tonight and were nice enough to let me know your intentions by forwarding me the *Pinevile Low* email, but I wished you had felt comfortable enough to discuss it with me directly . . ."

I wasn't getting it. And it wasn't the alcohol that slowed my synapses, no. It was the shock value of what he was saying.

WHAT TYPE-A BRAINIAC HAS VOWED TO FINALLY HAVE SEX FOR THE FIRST TIME ON HOMECOMING NIGHT?

I assumed it was Len. And Len had assumed it was me. HA-HAHAHAHAHAHAHAHA. I defy you to tell me that's not the funniest *Three's Company*-style high jinks and shenanigans you've ever heard in your life. But he was too busy babbling for me to clear things up.

". . . which is why I simply can't go through with it. I have quite strong feelings for you, but I feel I should tell you that I have decided not to have sex before I am married, not because of religious beliefs, but because I cannot afford to jeopardize my future with an unplanned pregnancy or a sexually transmitted disease. Not that I think you have a sexually transmitted disease, I'm just speaking in the broadest terms. And I know abstinence contradicts everything that I'm supposed to do as a teenage guy, but even if I did believe in sexual relations outside of marriage, I can't help but think that having sex with you tonight would be wrong when we haven't so much as kissed yet."

There only seemed to be one logical, rational response to this, Len's first spontaneous, emotional, and factually inaccurate speech.

I leaned over and kissed him. And he didn't stop me.

december

Dear Hope,

Today was the start of the second marking period. For seniors, this means the class we've been waiting for since fifth grade: Health and Human Sexuality. A whole marking period devoted to penises and vaginas, brought to us by none other than the always-bubbly Brandi, "Professional Counselor" and Certified Sexpert Extraordinaire. Why they wait until our senior year to "teach" us about sex is beyond me. I mean, the only people in our class who still rely on secondhand sex education are me and, appropriately, Len.

I should be relieved, right? His no-sex stance makes things a lot less complicated. I know for sure that he's not just being nice to me so he can dick me over. Besides, even if Len were a typical bootyhound, I doubt I'd be in a hurry to hump him. Hearing Brandi gush about the magnificent mons pubis and the delightful vas deferens is all the negative conditioning I need to delay my devirginization by another decade or two. At least.

It's weird having a boyfriend. Or maybe it's just weird for *me* to be a girlfriend. I'm not very good at it. Like, I have to remind myself not to bolt out of class when the bell rings—I'm supposed to grab Len's hand, *then* bolt. Or I have to remember to call him before I go to bed, and to pick up the phone when he calls me. I have to remember that I'm supposed to be thinking about Len.

You might be wondering why I bother. Sometimes I wonder too. Then I remind myself that Len is smart, focused, and driven to go somewhere and do something in life. He has goals beyond Pineville High, and it's nice to have that in common with someone. His babbling and/or stuttering doesn't distract me so much from his hotness anymore. He's not a bad kisser, either.

Most important, I know Len likes me in an uncomplicated, straightforward way. I'm tired of playing with (and being played by) Marcus. Game over.

Forfeitingly yours,

J.

the fifth

I finally understand why the whole Marcus thing happened last year. I needed Marcus to lead me to my true love, Len Levy. My elementary-school crush wasn't just a crush, it was the first chapter of our complicated courtship. Now I just have to love him. Right now I'm stuck somewhere between liking him enough and liking him a lot. I didn't go into this thinking I'd come out as Len's girlfriend, which is why it is just so meant to be. Really.

Then, the day after the Anti-Homecoming, Len launched into a list of reasons why he's happy I'm his girlfriend.

1. I'm smart.

2. I'm focused.

3. I'm driven to go somewhere and do something with my life.

4. I see life beyond Pineville High, unlike most girls.

5. I have a very attractive figure.

(Yes, this bears a vague resemblance to the list I gave Hope. So I cribbed it. Sue me.)

Never in my life has a member of the opposite sex so thoughtfully and so thoroughly expressed his appreciation for my virtues. I was touched. So much so that I told him to come right over. He said he'd be there in ten minutes. Len does what he says he'll do—he was on-the-dot punctual. Precisely ten minutes and thirty seconds after I had hung up, we were hooking up.

I've realized that all that stuff about seeing Fourth of July fireworks is bullshit, propaganda promoted by the people responsible for Meg Ryan movies and the *Men Are from Mars, Women Are from Venus* books. I haven't seen so much as a lit match.

That doesn't mean that I don't like kissing Len, because I do. I'd say on the scale of guys I've kissed, he comes way ahead of Scotty, and pulls a squeaker against Cal (though Cal got points taken off by assuming our one and only kiss meant that he could jump my bones right there on the golf course during my sister's wedding reception). Len's lips are soft and pleasant. He pays attention to what my mouth, lips, and tongue are doing to him, and responds in kind with an almost technical precision. I'll bet Len takes the same approach to fooling around as he does to academics. He studies hard, applies himself, and eventually masters the material. It's a good thing he's a quick learner. And when it comes down to it, kissing him is more enjoyable than not kissing anyone.

It's also a good way to get my mind off my Columbia dilemma.

Ever since I saw Paul Parlipiano at the Anti-Homecoming, I can't get Columbia off my mind. I see a future for me there. Whenever I've tried to superimpose Amherst, Boatwright, Swarthmore, or Williams in the visual, it never works. Then again, when I try to picture myself as Len's girlfriend—which I *am*—I have trouble doing that too. My mind's imaginings obviously have little do to with reality.

the eleventh

This is how Bridget greeted me this morning:
"AAAIIIEEEEEEE!!!"

I didn't even have to look at the magazine to know what had inspired this kamikaze outburst, but I did anyway. Miss Hyacinth Anastasia Wallace was in *Harper's Bazaar*, clicked at some fashion designer's thirtieth birthday party, wearing what appeared to be a red leather Band-Aid.

> Wild child turned writer/actress Cinthia Wallace flaunts her less cerebral assets in Gucci. Filming is about to begin on the celluloid adaptation of her soon-to-be-released novel, *Bubblegum Bimbos*. Both the book and the movie are inspired by the six months the Princess of the Park Avenue Posse went undercover at a New Jersey high school.

"AAAIIIEEE!" Bridget shrieked again. "I am, like, so sick of seeing that fat, ugly moonface!"

With the release of *Bubblegum Bimbos* just days away, Hy had been popping up all over newspapers and magazines in full-on promo mode. Bridget's sanity was tested with each additional photo and caption. She's pre-ordered a copy of the book, so she'll be nice and nutty on the fifteenth. Oh, joy. I myself refuse to read it and I've warned Bridget not to say one word about it when she does.

I took the magazine out of her hand, rolled it up, and thwacked her over the head.

"Ow! Why did you do that?"

"I'm trying to knock some sense into you!"

"*Her* people called *my* people!" she said, repeating the line I've heard a bajillion times. "*She*, like, totally wanted *me*! Not vice versa!"

"I told you not to audition," I said. "I warned you."

But Bridget hadn't heeded my advice. Nope, she let it all go straight to that bubblegum, bimbocious, blond head of hers.

It all started last June, when Bridget's agent informed her that she had gotten a call from the agency that represented Cinthia Wallace. After seeing her work in the Hum-V video, Hy had specifically requested that Bridget Milhokovich audition for a very specific role: Gidget Popovich.

"Isn't that, like, so cool of her?"

"Bridget Milhokovich. Gidget Popovich." I had paused, hoping it would be easier to get through to her. It wasn't. "Doesn't this sound the least bit weird to you?"

"What?"

"She's asking you to audition for the role of *you*!"

"She's not me."

The scary thing about Bridget's inability to lie is that it means that she actually believes every idiotic word that comes out of her mouth.

"Describe her, then."

Bridget instinctively picked her ponytail off her shoulder and started chewing on it, a sure sign of guilt.

"Okay. Like, Gidget is really beautiful on the outside but super-insecure on the inside."

"And?"

"And, like, her parents are divorced."

"And?"

"And . . ." She continued gnawing. "Like, she's got this boyfriend who cheats on her."

"Oh no, Bridget. *Gidget* doesn't sound like you at all."

She spit out the ponytail. "Okay," she admitted. "She is kinda, like, inspired by me."

"Inspired? She *is* you! Don't you think that's messed up?"

"Why should I? Like, Hy is playing the role of debutante-turned-reporter Rose Karenna Williams."

That's when I started to lose it. "Hyacinth Anastasia Wallace is portraying Rose Karenna Williams?"

Bridget continued, unfazed. "My agent said it's, like, the next step of this whole reality-entertainment trend. It's all about getting the real-life people who, like, inspired the characters to play the characters in the movie."

I let this comment dangle in the air for a moment before cutting it loose.

"If that's true, why hasn't anyone called Sara to play the role of Tara, the, uh, gossipmongering rich girl with severe body image issues? Why haven't they called Manda for the role of, uh, Panda, a big-boobed feminist who thinks promiscuity is the best way to battle the patriarchy?"

"Actually, the characters are named Kara and Randa," corrected Bridget, totally missing the point as usual.

"Why haven't they called *me* to play the role of *my* alter ego?"

Bridget looked away.

"What's her name, by the way?"

"Whose name?"

"My alter ego's name. There is a character inspired by me, right?"

By then, Bridget must have trimmed an inch off her ponytail, so thorough was her chewing.

"Bridget! I'm going to find out eventually," I said. "You might as well tell me now."

Bridget sighed. "There is a character named . . ." She paused. "Jenn Sweet."

Jess Darling equals Jenn Sweet. My God. That was all I needed to hear. There was no escaping it: Hy had turned my life into a bad low-budget indie flick. Though I'm sure her crafty lawyers advised her to disguise me enough that a defamation of character suit would never hold up in court. (Kind of like the person behind *Pinevile Low*.) Still, anyone who knows me will know. *I'll* know, and that's one person too many. This is why I refuse to read it. No way will I contribute to her royalties.

Maybe Hy had originally intended to get metafictional, then changed her mind after seeing Bridget's lackluster audition. Or perhaps Hy planned all along to humiliate Bridget by telling her she wasn't talented enough to play herself. All I do know is that as bad is it will be in four days when the book hits stores, the movie is going to be even worse. I don't look forward to the day that Bridget innocently heads to the multiplex to see the new Julia Roberts romantic comedy and is driven to madness when the trailer for *BGB* seizes the screen.

There was no need to encourage Bridget's Hy-steria today. I tried to steer the conversation elsewhere, the only place my mind has been since the Anti-Homecoming. Just as Bridget's insanity

intensifies with every day it gets closer to *BGB* arriving in book-
stores, my own mental stability gets shakier as the deadline for
Columbia draws near. January first is not that far away. I've got
to make up my mind.

"So Taryn actually talked to me yesterday," I said.

"Really? I thought she was, like, a mute or something."

"She usually is, but she went out of her way to tell me that Paul
was very disappointed that I decided not to apply to Columbia."

"Why are you, like, bringing this up?"

"I don't know . . ."

She looked at me seriously. "It's like you're looking for, like,
permission or approval or something."

My argument got stuck on the tip of my tongue. She was
right. I have been looking to other people to tell me that I should
apply and accept admission. I've been looking for as many people
as possible to assure me that if I decide to attend a school in New
York City, I won't die, because at this point in history, anyone's
opinion is as valid as anyone else's. Since 9/11, no one knows
anything about *anything*. All bets are off. Pundits can talk and
talk and talk, using this piece of data and that bit of evidence to
assure the American public that this is all going to play out in our
favor. But when it comes down to it, they've got about as much
credibility as Miss Cleo, pay-by-the-minute TV psychic.

I was—and still am—completely unprepared for true tragedy.
I don't think any of us can be ready for it, and those who say
otherwise are lying. I didn't know what to say on that infamous
day because I couldn't wrap my head around the enormity of it
all. I knew life would never be the same again, but I didn't know
how. So I did what I always do when I can't handle something:
I made it manageable by being petty and small. I'm not proud

of how superficial I sounded in the days after 9/11, but I won't destroy the evidence. I'll hold on to it because it was real. Flawed and fucked up, but real.

Kind of like this journal as a whole.

Anyway, now that things are eerily "back to normal," I have even less of an idea of what the future will be like, which is why I have no idea what to do about Columbia.

"Well, like, Percy and I both think you should go for it," Bridget continued. "What's the harm in applying? If you get in, you, like, don't have to go."

See, that's where she's wrong. If I get in, I'll have to go. If only to fulfill my fate. But if I don't apply, I don't have to worry about getting in, going, and dying. She and Percy just couldn't convince me to apply, but I thanked her for her opinion, anyway.

Later, when I brought it up to Len before health and human sexuality, he told me I should definitely apply to Columbia because it's ahead of Amherst, Boatwright, Swarthmore, and Williams in the latest *U.S. News and World Report* rankings, plus its Ivy League cred will go very far with recruiters in whichever field I wish to pursue after I graduate.

That wasn't enough, either, which is why I am not a good girlfriend.

When Len was talking, Marcus shifted in his seat, as if he was about to say something to me. I really wanted to hear what he had to say. Another reason I'm not a good girlfriend.

"Marcus," I boldly ventured. "Do you have something to contribute to this conversation?"

This was a big deal. It was the first time either one of us had gone out of our way to get the other's attention since Len and I started going out. We'd even stopped our daily parody of a conversation.

Marcus turned halfway around.

"I don't," he said.

"Oh," I said, more defeated than I had wanted to sound.

"But," he surprised me by continuing, "Gladdie might. You should talk to her about this. She gives good advice."

"I'll take that under advisement," I replied flatly.

"You know, you really should visit her more," he said, fully rotating so I could look him in the face.

"How do you know? I could be there every day you're not," I replied. Linda, at my request, had provided me with his work schedule so I would know when it would be safe to visit.

"Because I know you're not."

He'd called my bluff. I'd only visited Gladdie once since Thanksgiving.

"Gladdie tells me," he said. "She tells me lots of things."

Before he could elaborate, Brandi held up this thing that looked like a sandwich baggie.

"What is this?" she called out. No one answered, but that didn't stop her. "Right! A bit of Reality! Reality female condom, that is!"

While Brandi sang the praises of alternative forms of contraception, I tried to imagine what Gladdie and Marcus talk about. Clearly, Marcus's persuasive appeal spans the generations and Gladdie can't stop herself from telling Marcus things the way that I can't stop myself from telling Marcus things. Or used to, that is. Before I knew better. But Gladdie? She's defenseless. I can only hope that Marcus doesn't take the senile ramblings of a ninety-year-old stroke victim too seriously. And vice versa.

the fifteenth

To steal Hy's gossipy thunder . . .

WHAT BUXOM CHEERLEADER'S AFFECTIONS HAVE TURNED AWAY FROM HER BALLER BOYFRIEND, AND TOWARD A RECENTLY REFORMED GUITAR GOD?

MANDA!!! And Marcus!!!

ℭ

"Are you gonna drop me for that fucking Dreg?" yelled Scotty before health and human sexuality.

"Scotty! Stop being such an alpha male! I will not tolerate this mental or physical abuse!"

"*Are you?*"

"Puh-leeze."

"*ARE YOU?*" he said, grabbing her arm.

"Well, if I did drop you, it would be for someone with more feminine sensitivity!" Then she bit his hand until he let go, and ran to the classroom.

I guess listening to Brandi talk about fallopian tubes and

foreskin for forty minutes made Scotty and Manda sufficiently hot and bothered for a reconciliation. As soon as class ended, they dry-humped and made up. They spent the rest of the day walking hand in bandaged hand.

Still, I'm certainly not convinced that Manda is uninterested in Marcus. I couldn't help but ask Marcus what he thought of the item.

"I didn't get the email," Marcus said. "I guess I'm not part of the inner circle."

"Um. What email?" Len had overheard me.

Len hadn't gotten *Pinevile Low* this time either, and it hadn't even crossed my mind to tell him about it. I'm such a sucky girl-friend.

"*Pinevile Low.*"

"What did it say?"

"Well, among other things, that Manda wants Marcus."

"Manda wants you?!"

Len's voice crackled with fear. Of what? Manda ripping the band apart, just as things were getting good? Was Manda another Yoko?

Marcus shrugged.

"Why would she. Um. Want you?"

"It happens," he replied lazily.

"But she hated you."

"It happens," he said again, only this time through a yawn.

Sure, it happens all the time, doesn't it? Girls hate you, then want you. No big deal. Yawn. You've grown *so* weary of girls hat-ing you, then wanting you, then maybe hating you again. You're so *tired* of girls and their hating, wanting, hating that all you want to do is fall right into bed. And if Manda, or any one of the other girls who want you, happen to be waiting, spread-eagled, under the sheets, well, it's easier to fuck than it is to fight, right? Get her in and out of your bed. Yawn. To make room for the next girl who wants you.

Christ. This journal is dangerously close to becoming barbecue fuel.

Quick change of subject: I was kind of surprised that my hookup with Len didn't make it into the newsletter. But then I realized that the coupling of the Class Brainiacs isn't exactly whoop-de-doo news.

Whoever is doing this knows a lot about technology. I know this because I asked my dad about it, since he's about as wonky as they come. My curiosity was only half responsible for the attempt at communication. My mother had gotten on my case about us not talking, worried that this "silly cross-country thing" was going to cause "irreparable damage" to a "father/daughter relationship" that was already on "shaky ground." Thus coerced:

"Hey, Dad?"

Grunt.

"I have a technical question for you."

Grumble.

"About computers."

"What is it?" he said, his voice bitter and his blue eyes dimmer—ever since that *tragic* day his daughter destroyed his track-and-field dreams.

I explained how *Pinevile Low* was sent anonymously from a public computer and the administration couldn't trace it back to the author blah-diddy-blah-blah-blah.

My dad perked up a little bit, and used terms like "compromised routes" and "free proxy" and "erased logs" until my eyes glazed over.

Then I said thank you and walked out of the room not really understanding the situation any better than before I had asked. If from nothing other than the length of my dad's explanation, I did glean that it's fairly sophisticated stuff. Whoever is doing this has done his or her homework. It's probably the same person we have to thank for our messed-up schedules back in September, which resulted in an additional two weeks being tacked onto our school year in June.

Who could it be? I've already ruled out the two people at PHS who are smart enough to pull this off. Len has the brains but would never jeopardize his acceptance to Cornell. And Marcus loves mischief, but he's about as anti-techie as I am. Quite frankly, *Pinevile Low* just isn't his style.

All I know is this: If Manda and Marcus get together, it proves that there is no rhyme, reason, or meaning in life.

I'm exhausted too. Between the possibility of Manda banging Marcus, the application crisis, *Bubblegum Bimbos*, and all the effort I have to put into being a good girlfriend, I'm . . . done.

the eighteenth

I wasn't going to read it. I wasn't going to give in. This lasted three days.

On day one, Bridget *tried* to respect my wishes by not saying anything much about it.

"Jess, it's not, like, that bad."

"Stop! I don't want to hear anything about it!"

"Okay," she replied. "But you have nothing to get upset about. It's actually kind of flattering."

"Not another word!"

"Okay."

I knew this was a moot gesture, since no such command would shut Sara's yap. Even she shocked me by saying how the characters in *Bubblegum Bimbos* weren't like real-life people at all.

"Omigod! *Quote* Kara *unquote* is supposed to be fat. I am not fat! And my family has been loaded for more than three decades, so we are not *quote* white trash with new cheddar *unquote*."

"Okay," I said, her arguments not entirely convincing me that "Kara" and Sara were unalike.

"*Quote* Randa *unquote* can't get any guys to fall in love with her, which is the exact opposite of Manda."

"Okay." This was closer to being inaccurate, but was, in essence, still pretty true. Manda doesn't get guys to fall in love. She gets them to fall in lust.

"And *quote* Gidget *unquote* is really pretty, like Bridget, but she's a pathetic loser. Omigod! Everyone knows Bridget is the most sought-after piece of ass in school!"

Knowing Bridget like I do, that sounded *exactly* like her. Bridget is the most sought-after piece of ass in school, but that hasn't done much to help her feel any less lonely.

"But *quote* Jenn Sweet *unquote* is totally not you. She rocked her SATs, like you, but that's about it."

"Oh. Okay," I replied.

"So . . ." Sara said, dangling the hot-pink-covered book in front of my face. "Don't you want to read it?"

"No," I replied, averting my eyes.

"Okay," she said. "Your loss."

On day two, I couldn't get those hot pink swirls out of my eyes. I asked for more info.

"What's Jenn Sweet like?"

"Omigod! She's smart, but that doesn't stop her from partying and being the coolest girl in school. *Quote* Rose-slash-Hy *unquote* even kind of worships Jenn."

"Really?"

"Yes! So she's NOT LIKE YOU AT ALL," Sara said, with pleasure. "No offense."

"Oh, none taken."

How could I take offense? She was right. Jenn Sweet didn't sound anything like me.

By day three, the neon blurs bouncing on my retinas had gotten too distracting. So I asked to borrow Sara's copy.

"Omigod! I knew you would give in and read it!" She handed it over. I glanced at the jacket copy:

> Rose Karenna Williams was the undisputed don of the Madison Avenue Mob, the trendy trustfunders who tore through Manhattan nightlife the way that only pretty, unsupervised girls of privilege can. Rose is a Page Six favorite at thirteen. Illegal consort to underwear models at fourteen. Rehabbed at fifteen. Burned out by the whole scene at sixteen. The daughter of a billionaire banker father and a celebrated artist mother, she longs for the normal life she never had. She bravely goes undercover in the strip-mall wastelands of New Jersey to find out whether these simpleminded Bubblegum Bimbos have it better than she does . . .

That kind of says it all plotwise.

Surreal is the only word I can use to describe the sensation of reading her "fictionalized" take on my world. I must have put the book down a bajillion times, not in anger, but in squirmy discomfort. How does one draw a line between fact and "fictionalized"? Even when Hy, the author, did make things up completely, her imagination seemed more true to life than the reality.

Despite the throw-down interruptions, I read *BGB* in three hours. At least I didn't pay for it. It's now beyond obvious that the only reason she's getting so much attention is because of her privilege. It's gross and I should have called her out on it in person, when I had the chance. That's on me.

I learned a lot about denial by reading this book. Hy's descriptions of Bridget/Gidget, Manda/Randa, and Sara/Kara

could not have been more accurate. But they didn't recognize the truth when they read it. Why? Because she exposed
aspects of their personalities that they try to keep even from
themselves.

- Sara/Kara: "Fatty chick who catches the vapors and
  can't stop cluck cluck cluckin'." (*Bubblegum Bimbos*,
  p. 22)
  - Translation: Overweight, ignorant gossipmonger
    who gets caught up in everyone else's business and
    can't stop babbling about unimportant nonissues.
- Manda/Randa: "Sketchy skeeza who will push up on
  your man before you can say 'punany.'" (*BGB*, p. 43)
  - Translation: Two-faced promiscuous girl who will
    try to have sex with your boyfriend before you can
    say "vagina."
- Bridget/Gidget: "Wack for thinking her golden grill is
  why she gets jerked." (*BGB*, p. 18)
  - Translation: Crazy for thinking her beauty is the
    source of all her problems.

So you think Hy would've gone off on me, right? My neuroses
could provide enough material for a trilogy, at least. Maybe even
a Harry Potter–style septet.

But Hy didn't exploit my angsty annoyingness. No. She did
something far worse than presenting the real me, flaws and all.

Take this passage, for example:

> Jenn's got mad wisdom and steelo. Her bean's bouncin',
> so she never lets triflin' shorty bullshit get her off the hizzy.

She's pimped the system and her name to become the sweetest
female in school. But she's the only girl who's too flex to care.
(BGB p. 89)

Translation:

Jenn's really smart and stylish. She's so brainy that she
never gets unnerved by trivial high school nonsense. She's
used the system to her advantage by exploiting her name and
has become the most envied girl in school. But she's too cool
to care.

No wonder no one would mistake Jenn Sweet for me. Jenn
Sweet is the Jessica Darling I *want* to be. The me I could be if
I only had the *cojones*. Maybe from now on, when faced with a
dilemma, I should ask myself WWJD? What Would Jenn Do?

the twenty-third

Hy's book has made me even more introspective than usual, if that's even possible.

Other significant descriptions of Jenn Sweet, the girl I'd like to be:

". . . goes balls-out in everything she does." (*BGB*, p. 57)

". . . her eye is on success, the platinum ring, the only bling she needs." (*BGB*, p. 93)

". . . won't let anyone jerk her." (*BGB*, p. 198)

The realization that I am not any of these things—superconfident, clearly focused on my goals, or unaffected by the actions of others—coupled with the fact that the Columbia application clock is quickly winding down has made me more freaked out than ever about my future.

In search of an answer, I dug through all my stuff from SPE-CIAL to find that unopened envelope from Mac, my Columbia-only letter of recommendation. And this is what it said:

To Whom It May Concern:

As Jessica Darling's writing instructor at the Summer Pre-College Enrichment Curriculum in Artistic Learning, I read her work with pleasure, exhilaration, and even envy. Her journals vibrated with the verve, energy, and life that can only be found in the young. Having her in class made me long to go back to that time myself, when I was emboldened by the unawareness of my own naïveté.

Jessica is one of the most gifted young women I have ever met. As I'm sure you are aware, there are many gifted high school students vying for admission to Columbia University. I imagine there are few who would so greatly benefit from the education your university can provide, both in and out of the classroom. Jessica's shining intelligence is in danger of being dimmed by lackluster life experience. Having read her most intimate writings, I can vouch that even her deepest observations— though funny, vivid, telling, and true—are appallingly shallow.

Jessica is obsessed with the petty banalities that are the hallmark of high school life, simply because she hasn't been exposed to anything else. She needs an eye-popping, high-voltage shock to her system, which she would no doubt get if she could plug into the eclectic electricity of Columbia and New York City. This intellectual and emotional jolt is the life force she needs to make her mark on the world. Without it, I'm afraid she'll never get beyond suburbia.

As Confucius says, "Real knowledge is to know the extent of one's ignorance."

The best thing that could happen to Jessica is for her to learn just how much she doesn't know. And the best place I can think of for such an education is at one of the greatest institutions located in the most indefinable city in the world.

Sincerely,
Samuel MacDougall

So I was right all along. Mac did think I was superficial. Ah, but with potential.

You might think I'd be offended by this. I'm not. Backhanded compliments are definitely the way to my heart. The fact that he was so honest about my intellectual shortcomings makes his praise all the more believable. He's right. I *am* superficial with potential. Is it me, or did Mac make it sound like going to Columbia could turn me into the person I'm supposed to be? A.k.a. Jenn Sweet? Does it make sense to find my "life force" in a place where I'm likely to be murdered live on television? Or am I just being melodramatic? I mean, do the next four years of my life really merit so much deliberation? Will choosing the wrong school really have that much of an impact on the rest of my life? Especially when the odds are 1600 to 1 that I *will* choose the wrong school?

But what if Columbia is the right one? The "1" of 1600 to 1.

WWJD? What Would Jenn Do? I know damn well what *she* would do. But—as has been gleefully pointed out by anyone who has cracked the spine of *Bubblegum Bimbos*—she is not *me*. I don't know who the hell I am. I'm definitely not the Jessica Darling I used to be. I mean, who is Jessica Darling if she doesn't run on the track team and doesn't write for the school paper anymore? Weren't those my defining traits? Who am I now without them?

Hope thinks I'm putting too much pressure on myself, because I'll thrive academically wherever I go. She's completely overlooking the social variables, but it's not her fault. It doesn't matter whether she gets into Parsons or the Rhode Island School of Design (her top two choices) because she can find ways to be happy *anywhere*. She's very much like Gladdie in that way.

With all this weighing on my brain, I consulted Len. You know, my boyfriend, the person I've been sucking face with on a semiregular basis, the person I'm supposed to turn to in times of personal crisis.

I told him all about how I visited the Columbia campus last summer and just felt like I belonged there, for reasons I can't quite explain. How after 9/11 I got freaked out by the idea of going away to a primary terrorist target, and how my parents hate all cities, even before the WTC gave them a legitimate reason, and probably wouldn't let me go to Columbia even if I got in.

"Yet despite all this," I said, wrapping up, "I'm thinking that going to any of the other schools I've applied to would be a mistake."

"Um. Well. Of course it is." No, our boyfriend/girlfriend relationship has done little to relax his verbal skills. He coughed, then cleared his throat. "Of course going to those other schools is a mistake, because Columbia outranks all of them on all of the most important lists—Peterson's, *U.S. News and World Report*, Princeton Review, to name a few. And going to an Ivy League school, like Columbia, or in my case, Cornell, will be an invaluable asset when it's time to enter the job market, as recruiters are always impressed with—"

This is exactly what he said the first time I consulted him.

"I don't know, Len," I said, interrupting him. "I'm kind of afraid of New York."

Marcus tapped me on the shoulder. I was expecting him to admonish me about Gladdie again, but he didn't.

"Not going to New York won't protect you from harm," he said. "You can die at any time."

"That's. Um. Morbid."

"Not really," Marcus replied. "The way I see it, if you're going to die, and you will eventually, you might as well die happy."

"Is that would Gladdie would say?" I asked. A valid question, considering her "choose to be happy" philosophy.

"Probably," he said. Then he turned back around in his seat.

So there it is. The argument that convinced me to apply to Columbia. Yet another example of how I'm not good at being a girlfriend.

the thirtieth

I DID IT! I APPLIED TO COLUMBIA!

This application required a lot more effort than all the others combined, since I actually cared about it. I'm so paranoid that I sent an online *and* snail mail, postmarked, and insured hard copy version, just in case.

There's no going back. I did it. Now it's up to the admissions office to do their duty. Won't it be funny—not ha-ha funny but funny like a swift kick in the groin—if after all this *Columbia is my destiny* talk, I DON'T GET IN? Like, they've already filled their quota of white, Anglo-Saxon, Catholic, National Merit Scholar, wannabe psychology majors from New Jersey who are superficial—ah, but with potential.

I emailed my gay Manhattan mentors to thank them for helping me see the light. Neither has responded, which kind of surprises me. Unless . . . Maybe Paul Parlipiano and Mac already know something I don't! Maybe they have gaydar of an entirely different sort. The kind that intuits whether someone is Ivy material or not.

Oh, God. I am going to be in full-on freak-out mode until I get accepted. This sucks. Suckity, suck, sucks. Let's face it. I could have gotten a *perfect* score on my SATs and I'd still be in a panic about getting accepted to Ocean County College if it were my number-one choice. When I really want something, I mean, really, *really* want something, I just can't believe that I'll ever actually get it. I think that's why I so rarely really, *really* want something. I try not to address my desires. If I deny, deny, deny, then I have no reason to be disappointed when I don't get it. Right?

I don't know how I got this way. I highly doubt Jenn Sweet would react like this.

In other un-Jenn-like behavior, I ended up not telling my parents about the application. It was probably Len's positive influence that had me even considering it. The other day, when I was taking a TV break from my application, I was given an indisputable sign from MTV to keep my mouth shut: Mom walked into the room while I was watching *The Real World*.

As you know, the show returned to none other than New York City for its tenth season. As Mom and I were watching, the *Real World* group was getting smacked at a bar called the West End, which just happens to be located at 114th and Broadway—*practically on Columbia's campus*. I couldn't believe it. My breath caught in my throat as I waited for her response.

"I can't believe their parents let them do that," she said.

Too vague. She could've been referring to (a) living in New York, (b) appearing on the show, (c) underage drinking, or (d) all of the above.

"Do what?" I asked innocently.

"Leave home to live in the most dangerous city on earth!"

Whammo! We've got a winner!

"Mom, the show was taped way before 9/11."

"Even still," she said. "I wouldn't want any child of mine living there. Ever!"

Could you get any clearer than that? I think not.

Knowing that I've just done something that will take decades off my parents' lives with worry, you'll excuse me for not getting into the *fa-la-la-la-la* Yuletide spirit this year. There really isn't much to tell. The only difference between Christmas 2001 and Christmas 2000 is that I don't have a visit from Hope to look forward to. And Bethany's baby belly is expanding. Oh, and now Gladdie doesn't need to ask a bajillion questions about my boyfriend, because she's already gotten the dirt from You Know Who.

"Tutti Flutie says you and this Len character are getting serious!"

"He does, does he?"

"Tutti Flutie says that you two make him want to be with someone he loves."

"Really? He said that?"

"He sure did!" Then she turned to Moe, who was by her side, as always. "From what I hear, Tutti Flutie used to be quite the lady-killer, like you back in the day!" They both slapped their arthritic knees in laughter.

"Then what happened?"

"I got tamed by a tigress," Moe shouted. Gladdie purred. Oh, Christ.

"No, I mean to Tutti Flutie," I said.

"He won't say," Gladdie said. "If you ask me, I think some dumb girl broke his heart!"

I refuse to take whatever a senile ninety-year-old double-stroke victim says as fact.

"Len is such a smart, cute, and polite boy," my mom piped up, dulled by Chardonnay and a few steps behind in the conversation.

My mom is right, you know. Len is all those things. He gave

me the *Best of Morrissey* CD, *Fast Times at Ridgemont High* on DVD, and a yoga mat as nondenominational tokens of his affection. SO PERFECT. I bought him—SO MORTIFYING!—a tie. A very nice, not-too-shiny blue silk tie from Banana Republic, one that he said he'd need for his Cornell interview next week. But Christ, it's still a tie. I am so girlfriendly inept.

Len's family celebrates some vague combination of Christmas and Hanukkah, hence the nondenominational gift-giving. Len's dad was Jewish. He was a cardiac surgeon who died of a heart attack when he was forty-three years old. If that's not ironic, I don't know what is. He died a few months before Kurt Cobain, and I can't help but think that Len's obsession with the latter has something to do with the former. Len doesn't talk about his dad's death, just like my family never talks about my dead baby brother, Matthew, and Hope's family never talks about Heath. I think this is how our parents' generation would like to deal with everything: deny, deny, deny! I only know what I know because I asked, and Len very reluctantly told me.

Anyway, Len's mom, Sandra, is Catholic. I haven't met Mrs. Levy yet—too busy perfecting my application—but I will tomorrow night, before we head to Sara's New Year's Eve party. Chaos Called Creation was such a hit at the Anti-Homecoming that she asked them back. I'm so lucky to be the girlfriend of a guitar god. Or so the freshman Clubber Babies tell me. Anyway, Len says his mom is very eager to get to know the girl who is dating her son. Yikes. This freaks me out because it kind of makes this real.

Looking over my entries for the past month, I realize I have not written much about Len. I would love to say it's because I have no words to describe my birds-are-singing, bells-are-ringing

so-in-love delirium. But this would be untrue. In my nondocu-
mentation of my relationship with Len, I have realized that I am
unable to write about not only happy moments, as I've already
pointed out, but *any* moments that do not fall into the angsty category. Things are going well, I guess. We hang out, make out . . .

The physical aspect of our relationship is progressing at a
reasonable rate. Long kisses, vertical. Longer kisses, horizontal.
Hands over the bra. Hands and mouth under the bra. Hands over
my skivvies. Under . . . Ack.

I'm kind of relieved that's as far as it will go, if only because I
would have no idea how to document my devirginization. I can't
go into detail about stuff like this when it's about me. I make it
sound a lot nastier than it really is. Plus, when I describe it like
this, in the most basic terms, it shows just how selfish I am about
sex stuff. I'm making Len do most of the work. He doesn't seem
to mind that I'm taking advantage of him. Wouldn't Manda be
proud?

Speaking of, my skankiest classmate seems to think that we're
not moving fast enough. On the last day of school before break,
after Len and I gently kissed each other good-bye before French
(me) and accounting (him), Manda marched up to me and asked,
"Have you guys fucked yet?"

"That's none of your goddamn business," I snapped.

"They haven't fucked yet," she said matter-of-factly to Sara,
who was hovering behind her. Then Manda turned back to me.
"You better do it soon. The longer you wait, the bigger a deal it's
going to be. You're going to regret building it up so much." Then
she sauntered off, her ass shaking with every step.

As much as I hated to admit it, I couldn't stop thinking about
what Manda said. I told Bridget about it later that day.

"Maybe she's right," I replied. "Maybe I have built it up too much."

Bridget gently placed her hand on my shoulder. "When it's with the right person, it's, like, totally worth waiting."

"How would you know? You didn't hold out on Burke very long and he definitely wasn't the right person."

Bridget chewed on her ponytail instead of responding. I guess it was kind of cold to throw her dubious sexual decisions in her face like that.

"Do you think Len is the right person? I mean, if he were willing?" I asked. "Like you said, we're both cute, smart, uptight virgins."

"Come on, Jess. Only you can answer that."

She's right. But as history shows, my whole concept of love is usually for shit. I don't know. I like him. I really do, even if I have to stifle the urge to complete all his sentences. My relationship with him is secure. Easy. Reliable. Len doesn't cause me any angst, which is why I don't feel the need to write about him. With him, I don't have to exorcise my demons by scribbling maniacally page after page after page. I won't be shredding any notebooks devoted to my obsession with him anytime in the near future, that's for sure.

january

Dear Hope,

I'm waiting for Len to pick me up for Sara's New Year's party. While I do, I'll make another futile attempt to better myself.

Six Goals for My Senior Year That I Hope Will Make It Suck a Teensy Bit Less (2002 Edition)

1. I will not be a college-unbound senior. Now that I've completed my application to Columbia, I will not get caught up in the mass hysteria of the college selection process. I mean it. No more Peterson's paranoia. None.

2. I will try to write, if not happy, then less miserable journal entries. If I'm lucky enough not to be completely pissed about something, Lord knows I should document the rare occasion for posterity.

3. I will be nicer to Bridget and any other misguided individual who—for reasons I can't comprehend—pursues a friendship with me despite the inevitable and immutable incompatibility at its core.

4. I will ignore the Clueless Two. This still requires Herculean effort, as their adventures are too front-page tabloid to go unnoticed by the anonymous author of *Pineville Low*.

5. Now that I've read Miss Hyacinth Anastasia Wallace's so-called Gen-Whatever masterwork, *Bubblegum Bimbos*, I will try to be more like the me I could be if only I were braver... bolder... ballsier. Applying to Columbia was a good start, but I need to do more.

6. I will try to appreciate my boyfriend, especially since he is not (a) gay or (b) He Who Couldn't Remain Nameless.

Dubiously yours,
J.

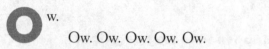
the first

Ow.

　　Ow. Ow. Ow. Ow. Ow.

My *face* hurts.

OWWWWWW.

It's 4:32 a.m. The light from my clock is like a laser, boring right through my brain.

OWWWWWWWWWWWWWWW.

I'm in my own bed. How I got here, I do not know. I'm still wearing my clothes from last night.

Last night . . . ?

Oh, Christ, my bra is missing. Uh-oh.

It's too early to call Len. Maybe I can IM him. OWWW-WWWWWWWWWWWWWWWWWWW WWWWWW.

Oh, sick. A flavor most foul. The Pineville High marching band performed a halftime show on my tongue. In stanky tube socks.

I just tried to get up. And I learned something else about my current situation.

I'm still wasted.

OWWWWWWWWWWWWWWWWWWWWWW.

I just washed down ibuprofen and a multivitamin with a liter of Coke. I'm sort of waking up.

My bathroom smells like puke. And did I mention that my bra is MIA?

Oh, God. What the hell did I do last night? OWWWWW-WWWWWWWWWWWWWWWWWWWWWWWWWWWW-WWWWWWWWWWWWWWWWWWWWWWWWWWWW.

Whatever it was, I can wait until later to find out. Ow.

What Happened to Me Last Night

The following timeline was cobbled together through author flashbacks, eyewitness testimony, and other conclusive forms of evidence, i.e., missing undergarments.

7:30 p.m. Len arrives at my house and chats with my parents. The word *Cornell* comes out of my mom's mouth at least a dozen times. My dad smiles and gently punches Len in the arm. The subtext behind this allegedly good-natured gesture: *Don't have sexual intercourse with my daughter tonight.*

7:45 p.m. Len drives me back to his house. We talked about the AP Physics test we took before vacation. We both know we aced it in a way that only two Brainiacs can.

8 p.m. I meet Len's mom. I note that Mrs. Levy has an unfortunate figure: a size six on top, but she's packing at least twice as much down below. I almost make the mistake of mentioning Columbia, which I can't, because one can never underestimate the power of the parental gossip pipeline. Even without Ivy League cred, I win her over with my wholesome, overachieving charm. (Ironic foreshadowing.)

8:15 p.m. We drive to Sara's house. On the way, I brag about how I've obviously won over his mother with my wholesome, overachieving charm. (More ironic foreshadowing.)

8:45 p.m. We arrive at Sara's. The scene is very much like the one described in the Anti-Homecoming entry, only Percy and Bridget aren't there. (Bridget is in L.A. with her dad. Percy is enigmatically MIA.) Not surprisingly, as this is a more exclusive party, Taryn and Paul are also absent.

9:30 p.m. Len kisses me, then leaves me to set up his guitar god gear. I look around for someone to talk to and don't see anyone worth the effort. I feel very loserish and lonely, wondering how I could be a senior in high school and have so few people I can talk to.

9:35-ish p.m. An inebriated Scotty comes up to me and goes off on how my boyfriend's band "ain't shit no matter what Manda says," and how he wants to "kick the livin' shit out of that fuckin' Dreg Marcus" for even thinking he has a shot with his "hot piece of ass girlfriend." I fear there will be a brawl before the night is over.

10 p.m. Chaos Called Creation goes on. Len looks damn good. *Damn good.* I must say that I'm sort of psyched to be his girlfriend at that moment. Marcus's T-shirt says OXYGEN. It takes me a few brain-banging minutes, but I eventually get the joke. $2002 = '02 = O_2 =$ the chemical symbol for oxygen. Very clever. Nothing about this or him reminds me of what I was doing on last New Year's Eve. And yet I find myself thinking about my private tour of the Five Wonders of Pineville: the Champagne of Propane, the Augie's Auto Parts Car-on-the-Roof, Der Wunder Wiener, the Purple Dinosaur, and finally, the Park That Time Forgot . . . but I cannot. (Ironic foresh—Oh, Christ. Forget it.)

10:30 p.m. Midway through the set, I spot Scotty, who is doing the heterosexual jock version of dancing, i.e., swaying his arms, shuffling his feet, and clapping at irregular intervals. He smiles serenely and sweats profusely. Tonight he has obviously added E to his andro stack.

11 p.m. Show over. I go to kiss and congratulate Len in a very girlfriendly fashion, but he and the rest of the band have to pack up their stuff. They are distracted by Clubber Babies and older G-string Groupies. Manda is among them, and I want to hurl. I can't handle watching her shove her tits in Marcus's face. I'm feeling very, very tense.

11:03 p.m. I look at my watch and all of sudden I remember something very significant: Hope moved to Tennessee exactly two years ago. Seven hundred and thirty days have gone by and I'm no better now than I was one minute after her car pulled out of the driveway. Wherever she is ringing in the New Year, she is surely having more fun than I am.

11:04 p.m. I am totally, completely, irreversibly alone.

11:05 p.m. I wander around the party—sticky with beer, sweat, and sexual tension—and somehow end up next to Scotty, who is ignoring his girlfriend's horny display.

11:15-ish p.m. I ask Scotty how he's doing and he responds by wrapping his arms around me and telling me that he loves me, and he loves everyone, even Marcus and the rest of the band, which he has decided doesn't suck after all even though he really loves this Gorillaz song that is now vibing through the speakers, spreading its happiness and gladness and sunshine-in-a-bagness. But what he would really, really love more than anything is if I danced with him. I ask him what he's on, even though I already know. Only Ecstasy could reverse Scotty's testosterrific rage in just under a half hour. I look over toward the stage and see Manda pushing up on Marcus while Len looks on. Scotty's eyes are closed and his mouth is open as if to say, "Ahhhhhhh . . ." I want to feel as mellow and untroubled as he looks. I've never tried any illicit drugs before. What Would Jenn Do? *I'm useless but not for long.* This could be the night for my sole experimentation, the harmless one I get out of the way so I can say, "*Yes,* I've tried it, but I didn't like it," when asked next year at college. What Would Jenn Do? Trying something once does not make me Heath or Marcus or a common PHS Dreg. It does not make me a bad person. It does not make me a weak-minded individual who gives in to peer pressure to fit in, because I am not giving in to peer pressure. I am giving into me-pressure, the only kind that can squeeze my brain like an orange juicer and leave nothing but a pulpy mess behind. What Would Jenn Do? E kills memory, and I sort of hope that it will help me forget about last New Year's Eve, even though I know the memory loss is really more of a long-term effect and not a one-time-user effect. What Would Jenn Do? I ask Scotty if he has any more and he beams. I ask him if he is willing to share the love and his mouth explodes with pearly-white pleasure. He doesn't balk, even though it's me, Jessica Darling, textbook goody-goody and Class Brainiac asking him to help me do something very unlike the me everyone thinks I am, myself included. He hands me a pill with a Nike swoosh. *Just Do It.* And I do what Jenn would do. I wash it down with beer. I wait. *The future is coming on . . .*

11-whoknowswhat p.m. I am enamored with my sweater. I can't stop stroking my arms, it feels so soft and warm and good. *So good.* I feel the music more than I hear it, each note singing and zinging through my body. My eyes feel fizzy like two flutes of champagne, yet colors are clearer and everything seems sharper, like the edges have been outlined in Magic Marker, then filled in with colored pencil. I look at Scotty and thank him for sharing this gift with me. He hugs me and his body is warm and so is mine and even his sweat smells clean, like nature and grass and fresh mud, and it mixes with my sweat and we're now bonded on a molecular level and I think about how deep that is and he's telling me that he loves me, he's always loved me, and I place my hands on either side of his superhero jaw, then start stoking his sideburns and tell him I miss the friend he used to be to me and I say, "Oh Scotty," even though no one calls him Scotty anymore, everyone calls him Scott because it's more manly, but he says he likes hearing me say his name like that because it's been such a long time since I've said anything to him and I almost want to cry I'm so happy to be there with him and I think about how the tears would mix with our sweat and how humans are 90 percent water and the earth is 90 percent water and how this may prove that God really does exist and . . .

Midnightish. Len's face appears and Scotty fades away and Len's hand is on mine and I feel like I'm immersed in a Jacuzzi all warm and bubbly and then we're upstairs overlooking the crowd and even though I know it's pure chaos, the party looks like a frame from a film, still and bright and overexposed, but then starting with "Ten!" the film moves in slow mo, then gets faster and faster and faster with each backward number, so when it reaches "One!" there's an explosion of sound and motion that climaxes with Len kissing me, and his lips hit every erogenous zone, even ones I never knew I had, like my left nostril, and I look at Len and I love him, I love, love, love him and I don't even think about Marcus or who he's kissing as the ball drops . . .

??? Len and I are in his car parked on a dark indigo road in the woods where I hear each leaf shimmy against the bark as clearly as I hear Len's breath and my own hums of pleasure coming up up up from deep inside me and my skin is searing and his mouth is wet and cold and everywhere and nowhere at once and it gives me chills it's so good good good it's all good and we're together not quite here in the woods but somewhere else beyond Pineville beyond the globe even and it's how I imagined it being like last year on the eve and I know it's all connected last year this year it's all connected not being with him last year was meant to be it's all connected we're all connected this is what the yoga book calls

samadhi when you experience the entire universe as an interconnected whole and this is how it's supposed to happen it's
my time to shed everything my clothes my inhibitions my regrets and just be with Len the way I'm supposed to be the way
this is supposed to happen *samadhi samadhi samadhi* and as
I'm thinking this in my head Len says something about how
this is supposed to happen a question maybe waiting for an
answer and I am euphoric because this is all the proof I need
that Len and I really are connected we have shared a moment of cosmic telepathy and I think yes this is how it's supposed to happen with Len yes Len and not with Marcus as
I have deeply believed to be an inevitability every single day
for 365 days half the time that Hope has been away and even
though I didn't want to believe it even though I shredded all
the pages that proved it I still believed in Marcus and me
until now right now and as I finish that thought I'm suddenly
hurtling through the air crashing out of the sky smashing
into stars as I tumble toward earth until the ground reaches
up not in an embrace but to smack me hit me slap me for
thinking all of this because when I finally recover from my
fall I look up and see the sad sad sad expression on Len's face
and I realize that I've been saying all of this out loud and he's
heard every word especially the ones I never wanted anyone
else to hear.

the second

I am never doing drugs again.

Don't get me wrong. I'm not about to start making public service announcements against the evils of drugs. I think my troubles have more to do with being *me* than doing E. Heath's death certainly wasn't the only reason I'd never experimented. Even before I knew he was using, I had a feeling that my body chemistry would not take well to any illicit substances. I mean, I'm not a very good drunk, so why would I do any better at getting high? I think some people are more successful experimenters than others. (Take Marcus, for example. He was able to kick all his habits no problem.)

I was never afraid of turning into a character from one of the hilarious videos that Brandi shows in HHS class—you know, the tweak freak who thinks she can fly and flings herself off the roof with wildly flapping wings, or the innocent girlfriend who goes from pothead to smackhead to crackhead in one long, druggy weekend with her bad-news boyfriend. No, my concerns were far less dramatic than that. I was worried that any drugs, any drug, would reveal things that I'd rather keep undercover.

And I was right.

The by-product of unburdening myself of BS has been one huge, hemorrhoidal pain in the ass that started with Scotty and shows no signs of clearing itself up.

Proving that her Len loyalty only goes so far, my mom waltzed Scotty right up to my bedroom yesterday even when I told her I was too exhausted from bonding with my peers to socialize with anyone until I went back to school.

"Look who it is, Jessie!" Mom stood in back of him so he couldn't see her mimicking a bodybuilder and mouthing the words: *HE'S STILL A CATCH.*

"Jess, we've gotta talk about what happened last night," he said when my mom shut the door behind him.

A lot had happened, yes. But nothing that could explain why Scotty was in my bedroom.

"We were getting pretty close last night. You know, dancing and hugging and stuff."

"Is this about Manda?"

"Sorta."

If my skull wasn't being held together with Scotch tape and a prayer, I would've laughed. Manda had some nerve to be jealous. What about the way she was shoving her hooters in Marcus's face?

"She of all people should never accuse anyone of flirting too much," I replied.

Scotty laughed. "Oh, I don't give a fuck about what she thinks. I know I've been pussywhipped, but not anymore."

I had no idea where he was going with this. "So what's this all about, then?"

He swooped down next to me on the bed. He smelled like Right Guard and the leather sleeves of his varsity jacket.

"I'm still into you."

"Uh . . ." I picked up the shattered pieces of brain matter off the floor and put them back together again. *"What?"*

"I'm as serious as a motherfucker," he said oh-so-poetically as he slipped his jacket off his shoulders. Scotty has muscles on top of muscles on top of muscles. He has subcategories of muscles scientists and personal trainers haven't classified yet.

"Scott," I began.

"Scotty," he said, stretching his meaty arms over his head so his T-shirt scooched up and revealed his happy trail and the bottom third of his six-pack. "Call me Scotty like you did last night."

"Uh, okay. *Scotty* . . ."

He flashed what my mom would call a winning smile, but to me it was too rehearsed, too cheesy—a game-show-host grin. He put one bulky limb around me and I lost track of what I was going to say.

"We connected last night, Jess. You felt it too."

True, Scotty and I had a moment. It was the first time since sophomore year that I had been able to look at his face and see the old Scotty, the sincere, sweet stud-in-the-bud with a crustache, bedhead, and boogers in his nose. That gawky little boy was far more appealing than His Royal Guyness.

"It was just some really potent stuff," I said while sliding out from under his weight. "It wasn't me, it was E."

"I've done E a dozen times and it never made me feel like that."

I saw what was going on. His "relationships" have been so devoid of any substance that he was mistaking our drug-induced bonding as something more than it really was. It was kind of pathetic, actually.

This is what I was mulling over when he grabbed my face with his hammy hands and tried to kiss me. I leapt across the room like a character crafted by Industrial Light & Magic.

"Scotty! What the hell?"

"Oh, that's right," he said dismissively. "You don't want to cheat on Len."

To be honest, Len was the furthest thing from my mind. I was just reflexively repelled by the idea of recreating the nasty kiss that sounded the death knell for our eleven-day eighth-grade relationship. But I used his excuse, as it was less likely to piss him off.

"Right! I can't cheat on Len. *My boyfriend.*"

"That's why I'm here," he said, too busy watching himself flex his pecs in the mirror to look at me. "Now that you know how I feel, you can do something about Len."

"What do you mean 'do something about Len'?"

"Break up with that chode," he said.

Break up. All day I had been debating that very course of action, yet hearing it from Scotty made it sound like the least desirable thing on earth.

"You think I'm going to break up with him just because you've offered yourself to me?"

Scotty's look of self-admiration in the mirror didn't change.

King Scotty thought I would drop Len in half a heartbeat to go out with him. Christ, it really pisses me off that someone like Scotty feels so superior to someone like Len, and that his delusions of grandeur are perpetuated by all the morons at school. If only Haviland had published my "Sycophants, Suck-Ups, and Scrubs" editorial, maybe this would've never happened. But no, since all Pineville High has gotten down on their knees to pay

homage (or *hummage*, as the case may be) to the Grand Poobah
of the Upper Crust, he has no reason to believe that there are
dissenters in the kingdom. When he walks down the hall, into
the classroom, or onto the court, all eyes are on him, his own
included. Scotty has a steroidal case of self-love, and God help
me if I was going to pump him up even more.

"I'm not breaking up with Len," I replied, suddenly appreciat-
ing his awkwardness in the presence of such balls-out machismo.
I hadn't talked to Len since he dropped me off at my house, and
now it was the only thing I really wanted to do. I wanted to set
things straight, but I had to get this meatballer out of my room
first. I got up and opened the door to show Scotty out.

He chuckled as he got up from the bed. "Okay, Jess, play hard
to get," he said. "But you can't deny what we have."

Oh, Christ. What we have is a jock jacked on his own delusions of grandeur, and a girl who has been a fool to take her
lovely, sensitive boyfriend for granted. As I dialed Len's digits, I
wanted to kick myself for not having tried to talk to him sooner.
His mom answered.

"Hi, Mrs. Levy," I said, trying my best to muster wholesome
overachieverness.

"Oh, it's *you*," she said dryly.

"May I speak to Len please?"

She smacked her lips together. "Well, if it were up to me, I'd
say no," she said. "But Len is an adult and can make his own
decisions, so I'll let him decide whether or not he wants to talk
to you. Heh-heh-heh."

Her laughter was cheerless and eerie. She must have been
joking because I couldn't imagine any parent saying that to me
and really meaning it. So I laughed weakly too.

After about two minutes of waiting, Len finally got on the phone. I have never been so happy to hear his voice.

"Len!"

"Jess," he replied, his voice as fixed and chilly as an uncracked tray of ice cubes.

"Uh . . . I . . ."

"We need to talk about last night," he said without stammering.

"Uh . . . that's why I called . . ."

"Let's meet at Helga's Diner at six."

"Oh. Okay. I thought we could—"

"Helga's at six," he said, cutting me off. "See you."

I knew Len would arrive exactly on time, so I got there ten minutes early to compose myself. I had my excuse in my head: I didn't remember what I said. I remembered what I did—what we did, or rather, what we *almost* did—but not what I said. A white lie, for the sake of saving the relationship, which I really wanted to save. Really. Len wasn't an asshole or a player. He was an honest, upright guy, which is hard to find at Pineville High, or anywhere for that matter. I was lucky enough to have him and I wanted to keep him. As for what I said about Marcus, I would explain how I didn't remember saying it, and that drugs are unpredictable and unreliable and have nothing to do with reality, which is why people take them, but I apologize for taking them, and he can rest easy knowing I'll never do it again, and what I said about Marcus was nothing, nothing at all . . .

Little did I know that there would be a third party in this summit and that he would already be seated at a booth when I arrived.

"What did you do last night?" Marcus asked, genuinely baffled.

"Oh, shit." I slumped into the banquette across the table from him. "What did Len say?"

"Nothing. He's really upset but won't say why. He just told me that we all had to be here. What happened?"

Where to start? What to say?

"I think he's mad because I did E last night," I said.

Marcus's eyes popped. "That would do it. Len is so straight edge that he won't even take Tylenol when he has a headache."

"Uh-huh. I know." I couldn't even look at him. I picked up the wrapper from Marcus's straw and folded it like an accordion.

"So did you like it?"

"Well, you've done E, so you know what happens when you're on it," I responded, intentionally avoiding the question.

"It's different for different people," he said. "Did you like it?"

I shrugged. "I don't like the fact that Len's mad at me." That was true.

"Good enough," he said, taking his straw out of his soda. "But why am I here?"

"Uh . . . I . . . Uh . . ." I couldn't talk to Marcus about this. I couldn't tell him how close Len and I had come to having sex in the back seat of his Saturn last night. I couldn't tell him that the only reason we didn't have sex is that I let it slip that for the past year, I couldn't picture losing my virginity to anyone but Marcus, who just happens to be his best friend.

As all these thoughts swirled inside my head, Marcus released a few drops from his straw on the paper I had just folded. The coil sprang to life, like a snake. I remember more lines from the infamous "Fall" poem:

I taunted and tempted
you
with my forbidden fruit

does that make
me
the serpent too?

Before I could answer that question for myself, Len arrived at the table.

"Hey," said Marcus.

"Hey," said Len.

"Uhohheyimsohappytoseeyou!" said I.

I jumped up to hug him. He kept his arms at his sides at first but then returned my embrace. He sat down next to me, which was a good sign, I thought.

Len cleared his throat. *A-heh-heh-heh-hehmmmmmmm.*

"Last night, under the influence of Ecstasty, a drug that is often referred to as a truth serum for its ability to weaken one's defenses and reveal one's innermost desires, Jessica said something that disturbed me a great deal . . ."

Len continued talking for a very, very long time. During which I couldn't take my eyes off the snake.

"In conclusion, I need to know what happened between you two that made her say what she said. You are my best friend," he said, glancing at Marcus. "You are my girlfriend," he said, turning to me. "I should hope that you will extend me the courtesy of honesty."

Marcus and I didn't say anything because we weren't sure if Len was finished or not. He wasn't quite.

"So the question remains," he said calmly. "What happened between you two?"

Now he was done. Marcus and I were still silent because neither of us had an answer for such a simple question. We looked at each other haplessly, helplessly.

Finally, Marcus stepped up.

"Nothing happened between us."

Len coughed any remaining reservations right out of his larynx. *Ahem!* "Then what was she talking about?"

Marcus looked at me. "I'm going to tell him," he said, very seriously.

"Uh . . ." I replied, not knowing what he was going to say.

"Last year, I tried to sleep with Jessica."

The snake was just a soppy blob at this point.

"But she turned me down," he said. "It was pretty humiliating, actually."

Len put his hand on my arm. "Is that true?"

"Uh . . ." I replied.

"So nothing happened, Len," Marcus said, sensing my hesitation. "Don't worry about anything Jessica might have said under the influence. Take it from someone who knows. Drugs have a way of really fucking with your subconscious in a way that bears little resemblance to what's real. It's why people do drugs to begin with."

This argument sounded so much like the one I had rehearsed in my head that I almost thought that I had presented it out loud. But I know I didn't.

Len was now scrutinizing my face so intensely that I almost couldn't handle it.

Ahem! "What about now, Flu?"

"What about now?"

"Do you still want to have sex with my girlfriend?"

Marcus took his lighter out of his pocket and flicked it open and shut. Marcus had stopped smoking, but he couldn't stop his hands from reaching for the lighter when he was . . . what? Nervous?

"Don't take this the wrong way," he said. "But I never *really* wanted to have sex with your girlfriend. I just wanted to see if I could."

Click. Click. Click. Like bullets spinning in the barrel of a gun. Click. Click.

"That was back when I was still using," he said, casting his gaze at me. "I didn't know you then like I know you now."

And I was thinking, *Oh, now that you know me, you would never sleep with me?*

"I didn't know that you and I would become friends, Len, or that you two would be so right for each other. So please know that whatever Jessica said about me has nothing to do with what's real, and how she feels about you. I happen to know for a fact that she's into you. Isn't that right, Jessica?"

His question caught me by surprise. Marcus was right, wasn't he? It was right, me and Len. *We* were right.

Right?

I looked at Len's pale, china-smooth skin, eyes as green as Heineken bottle sea glass, and delicate, guitar string-callused fingers. Geek cute to the bajillionth degree. If Len were going out with *anyone* but me, I would be madly, passionately in love with him. Or, at the very least, madly, passionately obsessed with him to the point where I'd fill, then flambé, a journal devoted to him and only him. I just know it.

"Right," I replied, hoping to make it so.

Len leaned over and kissed me for a little bit, which was rare for us because we are against PDAs.

Len is against them because he feels it is an inappropriate

breech of etiquette to let your hormones and emotions get the better of you in a public setting. I am against them because I usually
can't handle seeing anyone I know get physical with anyone else
I know. I get all skeeved out. So why should I be any exception?

I'd like to think Len kissed me in front of Marcus because he
was moved by the power of our reconciliation. Most likely, he did
it to mark his territory—me. And it worked, I guess, because when
my eyes flickered open, I caught a glimpse of Marcus watching us
with what I swear, I swear, I swear, I *swear* was a moist glint in his
right eye. A tear.

A tear?

One that was gone a few seconds later when Len and I broke
away. One that I've since decided must have been a figment of
my imagination, a drug-induced flashback hallucination maybe,
and was never, ever there at all. Just another one of my delusions.

I live a lie. I really do. The pathetic thing is that I thought
I'd been doing a pretty good job at being real ever since I wrote
that editorial "Hyacinth Anastasia Wallace: Just Another Poseur"
last year. After all, I stopped being friends with the Clueless Two,
quit the cross-country team and the bogus newspaper, applied
to my number one school even though I know my parents won't
approve, etc. But my E-scapade revealed that when it comes to
love, I've been as big a bullshitter as ever.

Since the summit, I've been devoting as much energy as I
can toward this relationship, to really give Len a chance. If I open
myself up and let Len in emotionally—the way I haven't allowed
myself, the way I let Marcus in when I didn't know better—there
won't be a need to white-lie about the depth of my feelings anymore. I'll really be feeling them.

Right?

the fifteenth

Suicide Tuesday" is the term used to describe the malaise that kicks in a few days after a weekend E spree. For me, it's turning into "Suicide January."

I've been vaguely concerned about what would happen when the next edition of *Pinevile Low* hit inboxes. After all, it was the first time that the Mystery Muckraker had Darling dirt to dig up.

Scotty assured me that he was keeping quiet about it so as not to get Manda's tits in a snit.

"Oh, I'll keep doing her until you come around," he said in a rare moment when Manda wasn't on his lap or in his mouth or otherwise attached to him. "You can't deny what we have." Scotty said that last sentence in what I know he thinks is his "sexy voice." Ack.

I was pretty positive that Marcus wouldn't say anything, if only out of respect for his best friend. Though when it comes to Marcus, I never seem to know anything.

When I casually mentioned to Len that I didn't think anyone else was privy to my idiocy, he, well . . . let's just let the conversation speak for itself.

"Um. My mom knows."

"WHAT?!"

"Um. I told her about it."

"WHAT?! WHY?!"

"I tell my mom everything. Um. Almost."

Then he cleared his throat and delivered a sermon about the importance of respecting one's elders, especially those who brought us into the world and have fed us and clothed us and provided shelter for us, so it behooves us to be fine, upstanding members of the household, and in order to do that, we need to be truthful.

"SO YOU TOLD HER THAT I GOT HIGH AND ALMOST HAD SEX WITH YOU IN HER CAR?" I said this a lot louder than one should say something that one wants to keep a secret.

"Um. Yes."

No wonder Mrs. Levy has been treating me like a drug-addled skank who wants to deflower her fine, upstanding son. BECAUSE THAT'S WHAT I AM. AND SHE KNOWS IT. I am going to have to launch into wholesome, overachieving overdrive if I want to win her over, which I do, mostly because every parent who has ever met me has loved me, and I can't stand the idea of Len's mom not loving me, especially since I'm the person dating her son.

As disturbing as this is, it doesn't explain how the Mystery Muckraker found out about New Year's Eve. This morning, in Times New Roman glory, my misdeeds were made public.

WHAT NEVER-DO-WRONG BRAINIACS DELAYED THEIR DOU-
BLE DEFLOWERING AFTER HE FOUND OUT THAT SHE HAD
GOTTEN HIGH WITH THE MOST POPULAR, BEST-LOOKING
ATHLETE?

My decided course of action: deny, deny, deny! I never considered for one second that I'd be issuing denials of an entirely different sort.

"Omigod!" Sara wailed, clutching the email in one hand and pointing a plump finger with the other. "It's totally you!"

I had anticipated this, but that didn't stop me from gnawing on my lip. "What is totally me?"

"This proves that you are totally behind *Pineville Low*!"

"What?"

"Omigod! You are so totally the one writing all this stuff! I swear I am going to hire a detective! I swear it!"

"How does this prove that it's me?" I asked, perplexed by her logic.

"Because you know we're on to you! So you posted items about yourself!"

"Why would I want to damage my reputation like that?"

"Puh-leeze!"

Manda had emancipated herself from her homeroom for this confrontation.

"Puh-leeze, what?"

"No one would ever believe that Pineville's very own virgin queen would ever do anything illegal or immoral! Miss Perfect! Miss I Don't Do Anything Wrong!"

Manda's strident hysterics revived Rico Suave from his pre-coffee coma. "Miss Powers, where are you supposed to be right now?"

Manda was not about to be silenced. "But if you think I'm just going to let you boost your ego with false claims about my boyfriend, you are sadly mistaken." And she marched off, leaving Rico Suave and the rest of the class to wonder what the hell had just happened.

When the bell rang, Marcus came up to me and said, "Told you so."

He had, you know. Told me so. Only I didn't write about it

when it happened because I felt like it conflicted with my efforts to focus all my energy on Len. But now it seems sort of necessary.

I felt like I had to thank Marcus for how he handled himself at Helga's. His version of our history wasn't the full truth, but it wasn't exactly a lie, either. Quite frankly, I don't know how I would describe what happened between us if I was hooked up to a polygraph.

Not to get all philosophical, but what is reality anyway, when no two people can ever see the same thing in the same exact way? Reality is a lot more subjective than people like to think it is. People like Len want to believe that there are definitive answers to everything because it gives the illusion of order in what is really just a chaotic, messed-up world. When it comes down to it, isn't reality just a matter of one person's opinion versus another's?

That said, Marcus's version of our history, in *my* opinion, is as good as any, only better because it managed to salvage my relationship with Len.

I was paranoid about *Pinevile Low* and had given up any hope of conducting any conversation of substance at school. So this past weekend, I showed up at Silver Meadows when I knew he'd be there.

"Well, well, well," Gladdie yowled. "Lookie who we've got here!"

"Hey, Gladdie," I replied, looking around the crowded rec room. It was almost time for bingo.

"Who ya lookin' for, JD?" she asked in a too-innocent tone that betrayed her knowledge of the answer.

"No one," I lied. "I'm here to see you!"

Gladdie laughed heartily at that one. "What are ya gonna do next? Try to sell me the Brooklyn Bridge?"

"Huh?"

"You shyster, you," Moe said.

"Why don'tcha just fess up that you're here to see Tutti Flutie?"

"Uh . . ."

"He was just here, ya know. But he cleared out when he saw you pulling into the parking lot."

"He did?"

"He said he was respecting your privacy."

"He *did*?"

"Yes he did, didn't he, Moe?"

Moe nodded vigorously. "He sure did."

"Where is he?"

"Well . . ." Gladdie said, scratching her head, or rather, the beret on her head. Only then did I notice that it was orange and her pantsuit was green. I glanced at her walker. Purple ribbons. Not even close to her trademark color coordination. I briefly wondered how long this had been going on.

"He's downstairs," she said, breaking out into a full-dentured smile. "In the library."

"Thank you."

"Oh, no, JD," she said. "Thank *you*. Now get on with you!"

I went downstairs, and sure enough, Marcus was in the library, reading to a small group of old biddies. He looked up at me when I entered the dark, woody room. He never stopped the narration, but a fireplace crackled and illuminated the surprise on his face. I sat down in a leather armchair and listened.

"'As the brawny stableboy approached the countess, she felt a quickening in her loins. Stephano's urgent, turgid love could not wait a moment longer . . .'"

Ack! Paperback soft porn!

"'They tumbled onto the hay, clawing at each other's gar-ments and grunting like animals.'"

Marcus was certainly giving them their geriatric jollies. As for me, well, I've got a boyfriend who won't give up the goods. At this point, I get damp from reading the back of a box of Cap'n Crunch. Almost.

Anyway, when the chapter was finished, he shut the book. "To be continued," he said with a sly grin. The old biddies groaned in protest.

"Sorry, ladies," he said, pointing in my direction. "I have to talk to a friend."

The gray and white and, in one case, blue, heads turned to look at me, the competition. They were not impressed. As they shuffled out, I heard them tut-tutting about my jeans and my Chucks and my utter lack of regard for personal grooming.

"Would it do her any harm to set her hair before she leaves the house?"

"Or apply a touch of cheek rouge?"

"Honestly. These girls today don't know how to present them-selves."

They were almost as bad as my own mother. Almost.

"Hey," I said. "Nice reading."

"I do my best with the material that's given," he replied, and sat down on the hearth opposite my chair. "I'm surprised to see you here."

"Yeah, uh. Well, I just wanted to tha—"

"Look, you don't have to thank me," he cut me off. "Len's my friend and I want to see you guys happy together. I said what I had to say."

"Well, I appreciate it."

"Don't worry about anyone finding out about what really happened, the drug stuff and everything else," he said, being mercifully vague. "No one would ever believe it. Just like no one would ever believe Taryn if she told everyone you were the one who pissed in the cup, not her."

An instantaneous full-body clench undid all the good that I've achieved through three months of yoga. "What do you mean? Does she know the truth? Has she asked you to tell her?"

"Not exactly," he said. "It's just . . ."

"What?"

"She approached me one day in study hall, and it was the first time we had ever talked. I'm looking at her and she seems so innocuous and harmless, and I just can't help but sort of feel sorry for her."

"Right," I said.

"I think she wanted to look sad and pathetic so I'd let my guard down. Maybe I would apologize for what happened to her. Maybe I would explain what happened. The truth."

"But you didn't?"

"Of course not. I promised I wouldn't narc on you and I never renege on a promise. Besides, as I said, no one would ever believe that you would do anything so *baaaad*." He mocked the last word, of course.

I just hope he's right. But when has Marcus been wrong about anything?

Except me.

the nineteenth

A SPECIAL BIRTHDAY SONG

(SUNG TO THE MELODY OF THE TRADITIONAL BIRTHDAY SONG)

Happy birthday to me,
I just turned eighteen,
I'm a virgin no more,
Thanks to Len Levy.

Gotcha! I'm kidding. I am totally still a virgin. I asked Len for a double deviriginization and he gave me a triple set of DVDs instead.

Not that I don't appreciate his present. He put together a little John Cusack box set. The combination of obvious (*Say Anything*) and not-so-obvious (*The Sure Thing*) and not-obvious-at-all (*Hot Pursuit*) selections made the overall gift perfect. Just perfect. I am so relieved that his birthday was in August, before I was his girlfriend, because the pressure to live up to his excellent gift-giving is just too much for me to bear.

Still, I did think that maybe I had a shot at having sex with him tonight. How did I become the sort of girl who dreams about losing her virginity on landmark days like New Year's Eve and her birthday? I don't know how I became the sort of girl who obsesses about losing her virginity at all. I guess this is what I get for deciding to date the only eighteen-year-old boy on the planet who is saving himself for marriage.

The thing is, it's not just about losing my virginity. If it was just about losing my virginity, I would stop "denying what we have" and jump on Scotty. That's about as sexy as earwax.

So it's not just about sex. It's about sex that means something.

This is probably where I'm going wrong. I mean, it doesn't seem to mean anything to Manda, Sara, or Call Me Chantalle. What makes me think it will be any different for me?

Anyway, sex was a nonissue tonight since we watched the movies at his house and his mom treated me like a drug-addled skank despite my carefully chosen Gap khakis and Ralph Lauren turtleneck. Could you get more All-American than that?

"Hi, Mrs. Levy!" I gushed as wholesomely and overachievingly as I could. To help my cause, I had actually applied makeup to fake the face of apple-cheeked, bright-eyed innocence. It didn't work.

"Oh, it's *you*."

"It's. Um. Jess's birthday today."

"I'm eighteen," I chirped. I cocked my head to the side, hoping that my bob would bounce with freshly shampooed purity.

"You better watch yourself, then," she said coolly. "Now you can be tried as an adult for your crimes. Heh-heh-heh."

Len said she was just joking, but I knew better. She wasn't joking then, or on the phone, or ever. She ends all her sentences with eerie, cheerless laughter, especially when she is completely unamused.

She made me feel humiliated, horrified, and totally unhorny. It's no wonder Len and I barely touched each other tonight. I didn't even get turned on during *Say Anything* in the scene where Lloyd Dobler and Diane Court are devirginizing each other in the car and they're shivering and in love.

Len had never seen *Say Anything* before, which I simply couldn't believe. Not even the edited TNT version. When it was over, I asked him what he thought.

"Um. It was okay."

"Okay? Just okay?"

"Kind of. Um. Unrealistic, don't you think?"

"How so?"

"They barely knew each other. And they call that love?"

I chalked his comment up to his logician's mind-set and left it at that.

Later that night, when I was on the floor in my room, twisting myself into my nighttime asanas, I started to think deeply about Len.

He got the second-best SAT scores in our class. He wants to go to Cornell because that's where his dad went. He wants to be a cardiac surgeon because that's what his dad was. That's all I know about his dead dad because that's all Len will say about him. He gets along well with his brother, who is a miniature version of Len, which means he's a mini-mini version of their dead dad. He has an unnaturally close relationship with his psycho mother, who hates my skanky drug-addled guts. He had a debilitating stutter as a kid, and speech therapy taught him to blather or splutter but not how to do anything in between. He doesn't know he's hot because he still sees purple cysts on his face when there aren't any there. He likes to play guitar and can write music but not lyrics.

He likes Nirvana and Pearl Jam and respects both bands for not selling out, but does not respect Kurt Cobain for killing himself. He hates *Episode One* but loves the original Star Wars trilogy. His favorite author is J. R. R. Tolkien. He believes in obeying laws and following etiquette. He hates anything that can't be explained, and didn't see the irony of fronting a band named Chaos Called Creation until I pointed it out to him. He does not appreciate irony or sarcasm. He likes me because I am smart and driven and want to do something with my life. He tells me I'm funny, but I've never once heard him laugh at anything I've said. His best friend is Marcus Flutie.

This isn't much. I've been dating Len for three months and I barely know him. But unlike Lloyd and Diane, it's not love. Not even close.

the twenty-fifth

You know what I'm thinking about a lot lately?

S-E-X.

Part of the problem is that I have to think about it in order to pass that damn health and human sexuality class.

Today's topic: The Bush Administration's Abstinence-Only Initiative.

"There is a movement in Washington to provide funding only for programs that promote abstinence until marriage," Brandi said.

"So that means no condoms in schools," Manda said.

"Right!" gushed Brandi. "No condoms or any other information about alternative methods of birth control. The message? Sex outside of a monogamous marriage is hazardous to your health."

Sarcastic "Yeah, rights" came forth from the Upper Crust zone inhabited by Scotty and his meatballer buddies.

"So how do you all feel about this?"

To my utter mortification, my boyfriend raised his hand.

"Yes, Len?"

He cleared his throat.

Oh, Christ.

"Young people need to learn how to make the right choice between self-restraint and self-destruction. Abstinence-only programming is the only form of sex education that makes sense. Abstaining until marriage is the surest way, and the only effective way, to prevent unwanted pregnancies and sexually transmitted diseases . . ."

"Sucks for you, Jess," Scotty said with a snicker.

Everyone laughed. Har-dee-har-hard-on.

Then Manda raised her hand and said, "I agree with Len."

Scotty rolled his eyes and made a harrumphing noise of annoyance.

"It's not just a moral issue, it's a matter of public health."

This coming from a girl whose moral compass is in the form of two erect nipples pointing toward the nearest penis. I burst out with a spitty, bullshitty snort that caught Brandi's attention.

"Jessica, would you like to contribute to this discussion?"

"Uh . . ." ALL EYES ON THE VIRGIN AS SHE GIVES HER VIEWS ON A SUBJECT SHE KNOWS NOTHING ABOUT! "It seems that the abstinence-only people are kidding themselves."

"How so?" Brandi asked.

"Well, for one, people are waiting longer to get married. It's very unrealistic for the government to think that we're going to wait until we're thirty to have sex."

Though not very unrealistic for me because I am going to die a virgin, but that's beside the point.

"Secondly, hormones are very powerful things. Teenagers are going to have sex. Without some kind of formal sex education, we're going to turn to less reliable sources for information, like the internet. Or friends. To me, it makes the most sense to give us the most comprehensive information available, so we have the power to make informed, intelligent decisions."

There was a moment of silence. Then the entire class—with the exception of Len and Manda—burst into applause. It would have made a killer editorial. Oh, well. I was so awed by the appreciation of my classmates that I didn't notice that Marcus raised his hand.

"Yes, Marcus?"

Oh, Christ.

"Jessica is right about the hormones," he said. "But she's wrong about everything else. I can't speak for the girls, but the typical teenage guy's sex drive is so powerful, it has the ability to override the best sex ed class. If a guy is in an intense situation with a girl, and he's aroused but—oops!—doesn't have a condom handy, he'll still try to find a way to get off, even though he knows he's not supposed to."

Scotty and PJ nodded their heads in agreement.

"Ignorance isn't the problem," he said. "Some very smart, informed people make some really stupid decisions about sex."

"You should know, Krispy," said Sara, who was immediately high-fived by Scotty.

"You're absolutely right," he replied, looking her right in the eye. "I do know."

Even though the bell rang, the discussion wasn't over for Len.

"So. Um. Do you really think I'm kidding myself?"

"I didn't mean it that way," I said. "I just—"

Then Len walked away without bothering to hear my explanation.

"He's really narrow-minded about his beliefs," said Marcus, who had overheard the exchange. "You're either with him or against him."

"I know."

"That's how I knew he really liked you," he said. "When he forgave you for New Year's."

"Yeah, I know. Marcus?"

"Yes?"

I wanted to ask him if he regrets his stupidity.

"Nothing," I said instead. "Forget it."

"Don't worry," Marcus said with a small, sympathetic smile. "Len will let it go."

"Yeah."

But Len had a difficult time letting it go today. He was huffy for the rest of the afternoon, and didn't stop by my locker after tenth period.

You know what? I wasn't nearly as worried about our first fight as I should've been.

the twenty-seventh

So guess what I'm thinking about right now? Yes, sex. Good guess. But more specific.

I'm thinking that there is only one other person I know whose name could have also made the last line of my birthday song rhyme. I know he's not saving himself for marriage. Last night, I had a bodice-ripping daydream that he was a stableboy and I was a countess. Inside my mind, I'm a way bigger sex fiend than Manda. The Mystery Muckraker is destined to find out about this somehow, and expose my secret, skanky dreamscape to the whole school.

february

February 1st

Dear Hope,

I appreciate your advice. Truly, I do. Though yoga has helped me show a marked improvement in the sleep department, it hasn't helped my sex problem. Think about it: Any method that showcases heavy breathing and increased flexibility will be of little help in getting one's mind off getting laid. My chakras are quaking and I'm hornier than ever.

Sorry. Too much information. I know. I crossed the line.

Where is the line, anyway? Wearing a tank top to school is a dress code violation because it's a "sexual distraction." Yet it's perfectly acceptable to use class time to fill out a sexually explicit survey? You should have seen this questionnaire Brandi passed out on the last day of health and human sexuality class. "An anonymous survey designed to provide information to more effectively identify resources to assist our community's youth to grow in a healthy, caring, responsible way." Yeah, right. Check out some of these questions:

Do you think someone who gives or receives oral sex is a virgin?

Have you ever engaged in sexual activity with a legal adult (over the age of eighteen)? If so, were you a minor (under the age of eighteen)?

Have you ever engaged in sexual activity under the influence of drugs or alcohol?

Off-the-charts ack factor. Not only did I resent a reminder of my non-sexed status, which had the administration's approval, I was totally offended by the potentially incriminating nature of the questions. For all its anonymity, it screamed entrapment to me. What's worse, we all had to fill it out because it was mandatory to pass the class. (I can't help but think about the editorial that could've been: "Pervy Survey: Stopping School-Sanctioned Smut.") Even though I know it's totally irrational, I filled it out because I don't need a third marking period senior-year failing grade to keep me out of the Ivy League. Imagine me failing health and human sexuality. Ha! How appropriate.

I lied about everything—including the personal info—just to screw up the results. Masturbation? Ten times a day. Threesomes? Hell, yeah! It was pretty funny. Len, of course, answered honestly, which only he could because he's never done anything wrong in his life. I couldn't help but wonder how the questions were answered by my fellow classmates who actually have incriminating backgrounds. But I stopped myself before I wondered too much because that's precisely the kind of daydreams that I'm trying to stop having.

I know this is going to sound like a crazy question—especially since you aren't currently dating anyone—but I'm going to ask it anyway: You would tell me if you did it, right? I used to think that I *wouldn't* want you to tell me—because my nonsexed status would make me feel left out and alone—but I've changed my mind. I know that the kind of sex that you would have is the kind that I need to hear about—romantic, right, and real. Hearing about a devirginization like that would validate my decision to wait. So I hope you tell me when it happens. And I promise to do the same, if I'm not too senile with old age and can remember how to use a telephone.

Virginally yours,

J.

the fourth

I got accepted to Boatwright University today. They even offered me an honors scholarship that covers half my tuition and gives me priority housing and class scheduling. In any other situation I'd be psyched. I have no intention of settling for Boatwright or any of the others until I hear from Columbia, but I can't tell my parents that.

This sucks. It really sucks. Especially since I made the mistake of mentioning to my parents that Boatwright was my number-one choice. Dumb. Dumb. Dumb.

"Jessie!" my dad said. "I am very proud of you."

This was a very magnanimous gesture on his part, since we do not speak.

"We are so proud of you!" my mom said, enveloping me in a hug. "You must call Len! We must go out to dinner and celebrate!"

"Yes," my dad said, "it would be nice to have something to celebrate."

(Subtext: Since you've done nothing of importance since ruining your life by quitting the cross-country team.)

Of course, I can't have any part of such a celebration.

"Actually, I was kind of leaning toward . . ." I tried to guess which acceptance letter would come last, the one that would buy me the most time until I found out from Columbia. I went the alphabetical route. A, P, S, W. "Williams."

"Williams?!"

"Williams?!" echoed my father. "Since when is your first choice Williams?"

"Uh . . ."

Okay, Jessica. Come up with something good. Come up with something really, really good. Something your parents won't be able to resist.

"Since I applied for an honors scholarship that pays full tuition?" My voice went up at the end of the lie unintentionally. And I was gnashing my lips down to the gums. Guilty! Guilty! Guilty!

"You did?!"

"Why didn't you tell us?!"

"I didn't want to get your hopes up?" Again, a question more than an answer.

"As the ones footing the bill for your education, young lady, we need to know these things," my dad said.

"Right," I said, feeling as guilty as ever about Columbia. "I'm sorry."

But not sorry enough to tell them the truth.

After a quasi-celebratory dinner (pizza ordered in, not eaten out) I called Len to tell him about my Boatwright/Columbia problem. He wasn't home—he must have been at rehearsal. Of course, I did the really mature thing of hanging up when his mom answered.

Caller ID. Duh.

Like Mrs. Levy needs another reason to despise me. I know Len told her all about our health and human sexuality abstinence argument because he tells her *everything*. That woman is as unbalanced mentally as she is physically. When it comes to parents, I think total honesty is overrated. (And look how healthy my relationship with my parents is!) But this is just another topic on which Len and I have agreed to disagree.

I don't think this is a bad thing. That must have been why I wasn't worried about it the day it happened because the occasional fight is healthy for relationships. Because if you don't fight, you don't care at all.

This is the problem with Bethany and G-Money, I think. They never fight. Ever. But it's not because they share a romantic soulmate mind-meld or anything. It's because they don't really talk to each other enough to have anything to fight about. I think that's worse than not fighting at all.

My parents fight, of course. But it's hard to take comfort in this, since they are usually fighting about me.

the fourteenth

Imagine the coldest, cruelest, most cringe-worthy episode of MTV's *Dismissed*.

One in which the guy pretends to like one girl, even though her competition for the guy's affections is hotter than she could ever be. So the guy really plays it up, and the ugly girl thinks she has a shot, even though it's obvious to everyone else—the hotter girl, the camera crew, the viewing audience—that she will be humiliated—harshly—at the end of the half hour. But the ugly girl doesn't see this; she's blinded by the guy's charms. And she gets excited thinking about how personality has won out over hotness, and fantasizing about her future with this great guy. Then when it comes time for the Dismissal, the guy who has restored her faith in the opposite sex turns to the girl and says, "I wouldn't do you if you were the last piece of pussy on the planet." And then he looks right into the camera and laughs and laughs and laughs.

That's about one-bajillionth as bad as what happened to me today, when Len did the thing he assured me he would never do. He broke my heart on Valentine's Day. Again.

Len's Dumping Speech:

"It's not you. It's me. And it's also my mom. She really

doesn't like you very much, and it's made it difficult to spend time with you, and I thought it was counterintuitive to continue a relationship with someone I can never see. Also, my future is very important to me and I can't help but feel that since I've been with you, my priorities have shifted but not in a positive, productive way. Lately I have realized that we have opposing views on important subjects, including, but not limited to, sexual relations before marriage. I feel that I've gotten all I can from this life experience, and that the best thing for both of us is if we put an end to this now, so we can move on to a more fulfilling future."

When I didn't respond, he shook my hand in a very business-like way, then departed.

LEN broke up with ME. ON VALENTINE'S DAY.

I guess it's better than his breaking up with me the day after Valentine's Day, knowing all along that he wanted to break up with me on Valentine's Day.

NO, IT'S NOT. IT STILL SUCKS.

Len breaking up with me today was like a daisy cutter bomb. Both go by a seemingly harmless name. Both contain fifteen thousand pounds of explosive power. Both drop in plain sight. Both result in total obliteration.

I was so traumatized that I was even willing to talk to my mother about it. I figured I would vent about Len, and she would go off on how any guy who doesn't appreciate her perfect daughter is obviously undeserving of her company—you know, predictable parental bullshit that I really, really needed to hear.

"He broke up with you? How dare he? Who does he think he is?"

"I know," I said, all sniffly and pathetic. "I know!"

My mom, being so utterly conventional, followed her half of the dialogue to the letter—until the phone rang.

"Bethie! How are you? How's my future grandchild? Still kicking? You're coming to visit? Oh! I couldn't be happier!"

Babies win out over everything, every time. Even breakups. They're cute for that very purpose, you know. Otherwise no one would bother with them.

She pulled her mouth away from the receiver to address me. "Bethany is flying out here and might stay for the remainder of her pregnancy! Isn't that the best news? Doesn't that cheer you right up?"

"You betcha," I said, flashing a double thumbs-up before retreating to my room.

Hope keeps reminding me that I never really liked Len all that much. If that's true, then why does this hurt so bad?

the fifteenth

I t got worse. Worse than I could have ever imagined.

WHAT VIRGINAL GUITAR GOD BROKE UP WITH HIS
BRAINIAC GIRLFRIEND ON VALENTINE'S DAY SO HE COULD
CARRY ON WITH THE VERY EXPERIENCED SUPER-FEMME
HALF OF THE CLASS COUPLE?

You read it right. Manda wasn't after Marcus. She was after
Len. And she got him. Just like she gets every guy she's ever gone
after. Ever. ARRRRRRRRRRRRRRRRRRRRRRRRRGH. And I was
too obsessed with the idea of her seducing Marcus to even notice.

Serves me right. How did my life become tabloid fodder?
Because I'm a dumbass. Take my brain for scientific research; I
apparently don't need it.

You know what the worst thing is? Worse than realizing that tits
always win? Worse than losing my faith in men? Worse than being
betrayed by someone who seemed incapable of such a thing? Worse
than knowing that Len beat me to what I wanted to do all along?

The worst thing is this: that whoever is behind *Pinevile Low*
knew the truth before I did.

That's what makes me want to crawl under the covers and
never, ever come out again.

the eighteenth

Being pissed off expends a lot of energy. So after staying under the covers for who knows how long, I went downstairs this morning for some nourishment. In the kitchen, I discovered that someone had busted into the Chubby Hubby ice cream before I did.

"Bethany, what are you doing here?"

"I was here all weekend," she said. "If you had left your room, you would know that."

It was true. I hadn't left my room since Friday night. My bedroom and its adjoining bathroom was its own self-sufficient little ecosystem. I'd lost all track of time in the outside world.

"Fine," I said, in a tone that reflected how much I resented that she was here, homing in on my mope time. "But why are you here at all?"

"Grant's away on business and I don't want to be alone," she replied in between licks of the spoon.

I want to be alone.

I thought I could stay in my room forever—until my stash of miniature Baby Ruths and Cap'n Crunch ran out. And it was practically encouraged by my mom, who would have let me stay home from school today even if it wasn't Presidents' Day. Funny how my mom wouldn't tolerate my post-Hope-move moping yet was totally tolerant of this highly melodramatic self-banishment simply because it was about a boy. Funny how I couldn't muster one-bajillionth of the emotion I'm feeling now while me and said boy were together.

"But you're not due for another three months," I said finally. Truth is, Bethany's bulging belly looked ready to pop at any second. Make no mistake, my sister was still beautiful in that rosy-cheeked, radiant way that pregnant women are supposed to be. And she'd scored the only other benefit I can see to getting knocked up: mammoth mammaries.

"I feel better when I'm around people," she said, putting her hands on her basketball belly.

I feel better when I am not around people. When I am alone, alone, alone.

Bethany turned the question of the moment on me. "What are *you* doing here?"

"I live here."

"Don't be cute," she said.

"Oh, don't worry, I'm not cute," I said. "That has been made abundantly clear lately."

"You do look *terrible*," she said, emphasizing the word in a way that someone who has never suffered a bad-hair day can.

I looked at my reflection in the spick-and-span kitchen window. Greasy pigtails, shadows under the eyes, an archipelago of acne dotting my forehead. I hadn't showered or changed out of my tank top and PHS XC sweatpants in four days. I looked like I smelled. Terrible.

I shrugged, grabbed a spoon, and dug into the pint.

"I didn't mean it that way," she said. "It's just that you shouldn't let yourself go like this."

I crammed as much ice cream on the spoon as I possibly could, then shoveled the whole thing into my mouth.

"I know this is about the boy who dumped you. *On Valentine's Day.*" She involuntarily shuddered at the thought.

My tongue was cold, but I didn't taste the salty-and-sweet, chocolate-vanilla-peanut-buttery goodness.

"I'm sorry, Jessie," she said, setting down her spoon. "Len seemed so nice too. So not the type to do something like that."

"He also didn't seem like the type to start banging the class slut, and he's doing that too."

"Really?!" she gasped, clutching her midsection.

"Um-hm." The ice cream simply didn't taste as good as I needed it to. Maybe I should have brushed my teeth first to get rid of three days' buildup of mouth muck.

Bethany watched me for a few seconds before shaking her head slowly with pity.

"I know how you feel," Bethany said in a soothing, big-sisterly voice.

"YOU KNOW HOW I FEEL?"

"I do."

"How? Nothing like this ever happened to you!"

"How do you know?"

"Because you loved high school! You were the type of person who makes high school hell for people like me."

"That's not fair, Jess. I had problems. Life was not always a bowl of cherries for me."

"Whatever."

I knew better. Bethany was the Manda of the Class of 1991: Most Popular, Best Looking, and one-half of a Class Couple who broke up immediately after graduation.

"Do you still have Trapper Keepers?" she asked.

"What?"

"Trapper Keepers. Do they still make them?"

"Yeah, I guess so."

"Well, when I was in school everyone had Trapper Keepers. And the thing to do was to cut open the plastic and replace the boring Trapper Keeper background with a collage of all the labels from the brand-name clothing you wore. If you didn't have enough ESPRIT, Benetton, or Guess? labels, forget it. You were over socially."

She mistook my silence for understanding.

"I was desperate to keep up. No matter how many labels I had, it wasn't enough. Especially since we didn't have as much money back then and Mom always insisted we buy things on sale. Or at Marshalls, which was just not cool. Not cool at all. So I'd go through the mall, secretly ripping the labels off clothes and slipping them into my purse. I was shoplifting labels for my Trapper Keeper!"

I let this sink in.

"Bethany," I said.

"Yes?"

"That is the most unhelpful help I have ever received."

I thanked her for her company, grabbed a new box of Cap'n Crunch and a bottle of Diet Coke for sustenance, and shuffled back upstairs. There I stayed for the rest of the day.

I know that Bethany was trying to bond with me over the tyranny of the Trapper Keepers and all, but it so paled in comparison to what I was going through.

the twentieth

Six Fun Activities for When You're Playing Hooky and Feeling Very, Very Sorry for Yourself

1. Count the *bleeps* on Jerry Springer.

2. Arrange your tresses into a Mohawk. Then—using a stopwatch from your running days—time how long it stands up, unaided by any hair products other than your all-natural scalp grease.

3. Email your gay mentors to find out if they are aware of any hypnosis that cures people of *hetero*sexuality.

4. Play toe-lint football.

5. Lie on your back on the floor for hours. This is known as Savasana, the corpse pose. It's the only yoga asana you have truly mastered so far, which is okay because it so aptly describes how you feel.

6. Write in your journal about your virgin ex-boyfriend

who dumped you on the most lovey-dovey of holidays so he could bang the class slut. Write about how you never saw this coming, and how you never thought it would hurt this much even if you did. Then tear out all the pages you've just written and torch them with a Zippo. If you don't have a Zippo because it's down-stairs, and you can't go downstairs because that's where people are, tear the pages into tinier and tinier and infinitesimal pieces until not even a single letter of a single word is discernible, not a trace of this *thing* that has made you into the mess you are for no good reason at all.

the twenty-second

In my entire academic career, I have never, ever stayed home from school for more than one day in a row. I rarely get sick. My white blood cells kick ass, which is one thing I've got going for me, I guess. Playing hooky was out of the question in elementary school because I loved school so much and couldn't stand the thought of my classmates learning without me. As I got older, I realized I'd be *smarter* if I stayed home, because doing so would spare the obliteration of countless brain cells. But then my participation in cross-country and track and other after-school activities dictated that I attend, whether I wanted to or not.

Unlike those mystery students who are on absentee lists with stunning frequency and anonymity, it was very conspicuous for Darling, Jessica to miss an entire week of school. Yet even after a week's worth of ignored phone calls, IMs, and emails, I was still surprised when Bridget and Percy showed up in my bedroom tonight.

"P.U.!" Bridget said, pinching her nose.

"It smells like ass in here," Percy added.

Bridget stepped over the depressing detritus—the Diet Coke cans, candy bar wrappers, Cap'n Crunch crumbs, and shredded pages from this here notebook—to open the window. The cold, fresh air hit me before I could complain. It felt better than expected. Clean.

"What are you guys doing here?"

"We're your friends," said Bridget.

"And we're worried about you," said Percy.

"I'm fine." Then I meant to laugh a silly, carefree kind of a laugh, but it came out more maniacal than intended. "*HAH-hee-hee-hee-hee-hah-hah-hah-HAH!*"

Bridget and Percy exchanged terrified looks.

"Look, Jess," Bridget said. "What Len did was—"

"Len? You think this is about Len?"

"Well . . ."

"This isn't about Len," I said, while expertly doing the corpse pose on my unmade bed. "I never really liked Len, so how could this be about Len? Oh, no. This isn't about Len. It's about me. I'm just taking some *me* time. A vacation for the soul. A Jessication! Yes! Time out from the stress of school to get back to *me*. It's all about me, me, ME!"

Another lunatic laugh followed.

"Well, it's not working," Bridget said, pulling me up from the mattress and pushing me in front of my mirror. "Look at you!"

Gasp!

I hadn't looked at myself since when I was in the kitchen the other night, and I actually gasped when I saw the greasy, zitty, stinky carcass I had become.

And that's when I started to cry. I was crying not because of what I looked like—because a shower and some clean clothes could change that—but because of the fact that I had let myself sink so abysmally low. I was a zeta-female. And over Len. LEN!

Len, whom I dated for all the reasons I said I *wouldn't* go with Scotty last year:

So I'd have something to do on Saturday nights now that Hope is gone.

So I'd have a boyfriend like all normal straight high school girls are supposed to.

So I'd have a living, breathing outlet for the sexual tension that has built up all these years.

How did I let myself get into a relationship I never really wanted in the first place?

"How did I let this happen?" I asked out loud, in between sniffles.

"Getting dissed is a bitch," Percy said, handing me a tissue, misinterpreting the question.

As I honked out the snot, I realized that this was the first time Percy had ever been over my house. He was more than my French buddy. He was a friend. A friend who had asked me out and—

"Oh, God!" I said. "I am so sorry I rejected you!"

Percy shot Bridget a glance. "It's cool, *ma belle*. I bounced back."

"And that's what you have to do," Bridget said.

Then they went on to explain that Monday was the perfect day to make the transition from hermit to high schooler because Len, Manda, and Scotty wouldn't be there. Apparently, Scotty opened up a can of whoop-ass on Len when he found out about him and Manda. Hence, Scotty's two-week suspension. After round one had been broken up and Scotty was being led to the principal's office, Len hauled off and gave him a buck fifty to the face. Hence, Len's two-week suspension. When Scotty went nuclear after Len, Manda tripped him, then kicked him in the teabags. Hence, her two-week suspension.

"It would serve Len right if he got negged from Cornell because of this," Bridget said.

"Ha!" barked Percy.

"Hmm." I was thinking about something else entirely. "I was kind of hoping Len didn't want to have sex with me because he was gay."

Percy and Bridget glanced at each other nervously, unsure of how to react.

"You know I have a thing for gay men."

Now they were actually smiling. I was showing signs of life.

"Come back," urged Percy. "We miss your face."

"You couldn't possibly miss this face," I said.

"Well, not *this* face, but, like, the nontoxic version of it," said Bridget.

"You can't hide forever," Percy said.

I was touched by this. I really was. Percy and Bridget cared in a way that I thought only Hope could, or would.

"Okay," I promised pathetically.

But there's something I have to do first. Well, second. After I take a shower.

the twenty-fourth

The millisecond I stepped foot inside Silver Meadows, I knew that word of the infamous Valentine's Day dumping had already spread among the over-sixty-five set. I was met with hushed tones too soft for hearing aids, pruny, pointed fingers, and embarrassed, toothless smiles.

I found Gladdie in the rec room, as usual. The only difference was that everyone except Gladdie and Moe hurriedly hobbled off when I arrived, as if they would catch breakup cooties from me.

"Buck up, bee-yoo-ti-ful," Gladdie said.

"Do you want me to teach him a lesson?" Moe asked, raising his hand, which, due to arthritis, he couldn't close into an official fist.

"No," I said. "There has already been too much violence over this." And I went on to explain all the brawls, balls-kicking, and suspensions.

"Look on the bright side, JD," Gladdie said. "There are plenty of fish in the sea. And your first fish ain't your last."

Gladdie gently patted Moe's hand, and he smiled at her like she was the most bee-yoo-ti-ful woman in the world, even though she had ninety years of wrinkles and her eyebrows were drawn on crookedly and her lipstick had melted past her mouth line and her beret was red and her pantsuit was blue and her walker was still resplendent in purple. Maybe she mismatched on purpose. Red and blue make purple. I was about to ask her when his voice snuck up on me from behind.

"Hey."

"Tutti Flutie! Fancy seein' you here."

"Hey," he repeated. "Hey, Jessica."

"Hey," I said, without facing him.

"Can we talk?"

I nodded. When I turned around, I looked down at his feet. Same old Vans with the hole in the toe. I couldn't bring myself to look him in the face in this state. I followed him down to the empty library. The fire was out and the room was cold and dark and smelled like musty, wet pages. I slumped into the leather armchair and he sat on the hearth facing me wearing his COMINGHOME T-shirt. The fake-velvet letters had faded and flattened out. I'd missed my chance to feel their softness with my fingertips.

"I'm sorry."

"For what? You didn't dump me on Valentine's Day to fuck Manda." My voice was not nearly as lighthearted as I had wanted it to sound. And as soon as I said *fuck*, I felt bad for saying it. I didn't feel like I should curse in a home for the elderly you know, with so many of them ready to pass on and all. It's about as close to church as I get.

"He's not f—" Marcus stopped himself from making my mistake. "He's not having sex with her."

I snorted in disbelief.

"No, really," he said, shifting his weight off the hearth so he was leaning toward me, balancing his weight on the balls of his feet. "He's not. He has no intention to, either. Apparently Manda feels that she misused her feminine powers and now wants to abstain from sex."

"She wants to be a born-again virgin?"

"Apparently."

"This is some tenth-wave faux feminist bullshit!"

"Classic," he said, nodding his head in agreement.

"Well, I hope they are very happy not having sex together. But what I don't understand is why he had to break up with me to *not* have sex with her."

The more I talked about this, the less it made sense. Marcus knew there was no use arguing with me until I finished, so he just bounced up and down in his sneakers.

"Why didn't he just *not* have sex with both of us?"

He shrugged.

"Why did you try to get us together in the first place?"

He leaned in close and put his hand on my knee. And just like the first time he put his hand on my knee—on the cot in the nurse's office, right before I peed in the cup—a current of electricity shot from my knee, buzzed my bod, and overloaded my circuitry.

But unlike that first time, it was a gesture meant to communicate sincerity, not sin.

Right?

"I tried to get you together because I thought you could make each other happy," he said. "I really thought you two could be happy together."

"Really?"

"Really."

"I don't think I was ever convinced of that."

"Then why did you bother dating him at all?"

It got very quiet in the library as I tried to come up with an answer. In the silence, I could hear a familiar melody coming from the rec room. It really was time for Musical Memories because that sweeping piano and those swooning vocals could belong to only one adult contemporary artist.

"Barry Manilow," I said.

Marcus cocked his head to the ceiling, then smiled.

"Yes. It's none other than the showman of our time."

Christ, this conversation was getting nostalgic.

"Do you still have that *Greatest Hits* eight-track in the Cadillac?"

His eyes darted around the room. "Can you keep a secret?"

"You know I can."

"I listened to it so much," he said, lowering his voice to a conspiratorial whisper, "it blew up. Literally. Smoke and everything."

"You're lying to make me laugh!" I said in between no-holds-barred cackles.

"I wish."

When I remembered what question I was avoiding by talking about Mr. Copacabana, it got quiet again. Barry sang: *"I'm ready to take a chance again / Ready to put my love on the line with you . . ."*

"There you have it," I said, clapping my hands together.

"Have what?"

"The answer."

"Elaborate."

"I was taking a chance. I decided to be very unlike me and take a chance on Len. And look what happened. I, unlike Barry, don't think I'll be ready to take a chance ever again."

Marcus slid his butt back on the hearth. He pulled out a lighter. *Flickclick-flickclick-flickclick.*

"Did you know that during the teen years, the brain goes through an intense developmental phase comparable to that of a newborn baby?"

"Is that another conversational construct?" I asked.

"No," he said. "I have a point."

"Make it."

"During that phase, the cells and connections that are frequently used survive and flourish. And those that aren't used just die away."

"Point, please."

"It was good you gave Len a chance, even though it didn't work out. You had to exercise that part of your brain, the part that lets you fall for someone, otherwise you'd never be able to fall in love with anyone. Ever."

I gazed up at Marcus, who was now standing long and lean in front of me, all mischievous half-smile, sly eyes, and glass-cut cheekbones. I wanted to ask, *Hey, Marcus, what happens to people with the opposite problem? The ones who fall three dozen times, plus three?*

Instead I said thanks for the psych lesson and left.

Later, when I got home, I consulted my textbook and found that Marcus wasn't bullshitting about the brain stuff. The frontal cortex overproduces cells during puberty, and the brain has to get rid of some of them. *Doing* strengthens neural pathways and the cells survive. *Not doing* weakens them, and the cells die. So Marcus was right about the use-it-or-lose-it theory.

But the application—love!—was dubious at best.

march

March 1st

Dear Hope,

I NEVER thought I'd see the day when two of your emails sandwiched a message from none other than PAUL PARLIPI-ANO. My crush to end all crushes! Gay man of my dreams! OOOH!

I still can't believe it. And how sweet was it that he apologized for not writing back sooner? Between the World Economic Summit and the Salt Lake City Olympics, he's had a lot of nonviolent protests to organize this semester. Since I last talked to you, he actually INVITED me (via email) to join him in PACO's biggest nondiscriminatory demonstration against all forms of tyranny, the Annual Snake March (for the month of March, get it?).

I was like, "Yes! I'll be there! That is so COOL!" even though a trip to NYC could interrupt the Toe Lint Super Bowl and I had no idea what the hell a Snake March even was. Thanks to Google, I now know that it's when a huge crowd walks haphazardly around the streets to cause traffic jams and other forms of low-level mayhem. It's an antiauthoritarian march that reflects democracy because there's no line leader and everyone decides which direction the group goes.

SOUNDS LIKE FUN FUN FUN! More fun than moping in my bedroom at least. And it's right in the middle of spring break, so I won't even have to skip more school to make it. How fortuitous is that?

By the way, he still thinks I'm a shoo-in for Columbia, which is another thing I needed to hear. He assures me that I shouldn't worry, that the school is notoriously unorganized and famous for sending out its acceptances long after every other Ivy League school. I hope he's right.

Leave it to a gay man to get me out of my guys-suck malaise. Is it me, or are gay guys the only good guys? Or am I just a masochist?

Nonviolently yours,

J.

the fourth

Today was Len, Manda, and Scotty's first day back to school after their suspensions. I had a week without them to practice conducting myself with quiet, dignified grace.

"That's the classiest way of dealing with bein' jilted," Gladdie had assured me during my last visit.

"Gladdie," I said skeptically, "I've never seen you conduct yourself with quiet, dignified grace."

"That's 'cause I ain't never been jilted, JD!"

"Who would dump a gal with a mug like this?" Moe said, holding Gladdie's face in his hands and placing a loud, smacking kiss on her wobbly, painted lips.

"I guess I have a dumpable mug," I said.

That would have been the perfect moment for Marcus to come up to me from behind and offer me some kind of assurance that everything was going to be okay. Something like, "Jessica, I would never dump your mug."

But he didn't. He wasn't anywhere to be seen in Silver Meadows that day, not that I was looking. (Okay. I was looking a little bit.) Marcus hadn't said much of anything to me since our library chat. He avoided eye contact and barely said "Hey" to me. I figured his loyalties were with Len after all.

Anyway, I vowed not to give Len, or Manda, or the PHS gossipmongers the satisfaction of seeing me upset. However, I didn't even get to homeroom before I realized how difficult this was going to be to pull off.

"Omigod!" Sara shrieked when she saw me in the hall before homeroom. "Don't you just want to die when you see Len and Manda together?"

"I haven't seen them."

"Look!"

Then she grabbed me by the shoulders and spun me in the opposite direction, just in time to see Len gently kiss Manda on the hand in parting, like he was a knight and she was a goddamned damsel or something.

Quiet, dignified grace, I thought to myself.

"Omigod! Don't you want to *die*?"

"No," I said calmly. "Not really."

"If *my* boyfriend humiliated *me* the way Len leveled *you*, I would want to *die*!"

"Well, it's a good thing that you don't have a boyfriend, isn't it?" I replied in a tone as sickly sweet and artificial as Equal. "Come to think of it, you've *never* had a boyfriend, have you?"

That shut her up and sent her stomping into homeroom.

I had my eyes closed and my head pressed against my locker door when I felt a tap on my shoulder. I had a very definite idea of who I wanted it to be.

"Um. Jess."

Instead I got the last person I wanted to see.

Quiet, dignified grace, I reminded myself as I opened my eyes.

"What is it, Len?"

"I just want to. Um. Apologize for hurting you."

I held up my hands to cut him off.

"First of all, spare me your apology because it's more about making yourself feel less guilty than it is about looking for forgiveness. Second of all, don't flatter yourself by thinking you hurt me. You're either an egomaniac or out of your mind like your mother if you think you hurt me."

Yeah, that's right. I sunk to a yo mama level. Whatever. He deserved it.

"You blindsided me, that's for sure. And I was pissed off. Not so much about you hooking up with Manda, because everyone knows you're just her latest fling. No, I was pissed for only one reason: You broke up with me before I had the chance to break up with you. And that makes me an even bigger asshole than you are. But at least *I* know it!"

When I finished, there was applause. I was so taken with my tirade that I hadn't noticed the crowd of onlookers. Bridget, Percy, Scotty, Taryn, and a whole bunch of faces I didn't even recognize were all clapping as Len slunk away, feeling every inch the huge sphincter he is.

The last bell rang, and the bodies scattered toward their respective homerooms. That's when I finally heard his voice from behind.

"So much for quiet, dignified grace," Marcus said, his lips pressed together, and his arms folded against the faded black MONDAY on his chest.

"Not my style," I said. "I'm more of a loud, offensive mess."

"Yes," he said, slowly breaking into the grin I know so well. "Yes, you are."

As we walked into homeroom together, I decided that his assurance of okayness was better late than never.

the ninth

I just came back from the innermost circle of hell, and it's decorated in Laura Ashley florals.

My parents forced me go to the Boatwright University tea being held for New Jersey applicants they are trying to woo into their honors program.

"But I already told you, my first choice is Williams."

"Jessie," my mom said. "Boatwright is throwing money at you!"

"And as the ones footing the bill for your college education," my father said, for the bajillionth time, "we are telling you to go."

I should have told them about Columbia. I should have just ended this whole charade right then and there. But I didn't. Because I suck.

"Fine," I said with an exhausted sigh.

I dragged myself upstairs and got dressed.

I will take this opportunity to mention that all the months of no running and yoga have finally paid off. I've gained some weight, but in a good way. I don't know how much because I never weigh myself, but it's enough flesh to fill out the butt of my cords and stretch the straight and vertical lines of my ribbed turtleneck into two almost-A-cup arcs. Percy actually commented on the former last week.

"Damn! *Tu es belle!*"

("Damn! You are fine!")

"*Vraiment?*"

("Really?")

"*J'aime une fille avec un peu de jonque dans le tronc.*"

("I like a girl with a little junk in the trunk.")

"*Comment?!*"

("What?!")

"*J'ai dit, 'J'aime une fille avec un peu de jonque dans le tronc.'*"

("I said, 'I like a girl with a little junk in the trunk.' ")

"*Il y a un problème avec la traduction.*"

("There's a problem with your translation.")

"*J'aime une fille avec un booty.*"

("I like a girl with a booty.")

"*Oh. Je le reçois maintenant.*"

("Oh. I get it.")

"*Oh, tu l'as reçu!*"

("Oh, you got it!)

Junk in the trunk must be why Percy has this hopeless crush on Bridget, who has looked bootylicious and legal since seventh grade. It took me eighteen years, but I finally look like a girl, albeit one five years younger than I am, but even this is an improvement. The point is, when I looked in the mirror, I thought I looked pretty good. For me.

Unfortunately, I did not pass my mother's white-glove inspection.

"You can't go dressed like that."

"Why not?"

"Because it's a *tea party,* Jessie," my mom said, "not a keg party."

"But look," I said, lifting my leg. "I'm not wearing sneakers."

"You go upstairs and change into something more appropriate this minute!"

"*Mooooooommmmmm*," I whined unattractively. "I thought this was appropriate."

Then my mom hustled upstairs and made a beeline for my closet. "No, no, no, no . . ." she said as she pushed hangers from one side to the other until she reached the inner recesses of my closet, the darkened corners reserved for clothes I never, ever wore.

"Mom," I said. "There's nothing back th—"

"This is perfect!" she said, whisking out one of Bethany's cast-offs, a charcoal-gray suit covered in dry-cleaning plastic.

"No way!" I shrieked. I was completely horrified at the prospect of looking like someone who works on Wall Street. Make that the *non-working* wife of someone who *used* to work on Wall Street.

"Jessie," she said. "This is from *Barneys*. It's a very expensive, very well-made suit. You're lucky your sister got her colors charted and discovered gray doesn't suit her hair or complexion." She chuckled, pleased as punch about her discovery. "*Suit* her. That's funny."

There was nothing funny about this.

"It was very nice of her to give it to you, and since you've put on some weight, it just might fit."

"I've already got the scholarship, Mom," I argued. "I don't see why I need to dress to impress."

Then my mom went on and on about how the tea was being held at the home of Ms. Susan Petrone, a very highfalutin Boatwright University alum, Class of 1986. She's a big-time district attorney, and even if I chose not to attend Boatwright, she could be a perfect addition to my Rolodex (?!) and someone I could turn to for a reference four years from now when I need a job blah-diddy-blah-blah-blah.

"You never get a second chance to make a first impression," she said.

I love it when my mom drops deodorant commercial wisdom.

"Mom?"

"Yes?"

Another perfect opportunity for my Columbia confession.

"Nothing."

That's right. I pussed out and put on the itchy, ill-fitting suit. I suck.

"You look very professional," my mom said when she looked me over.

Yes, it's very important to look professional when the only job on your résumé is serving frozen custard and other heart-attack snacks at Wally D's Sweet Treat Shoppe on the Seaside Heights boardwalk. Christ. How did I let myself get into this?

So we drove to Oceanhead, which is a very hoity-toity waterfront town. It's probably the classiest town in Ocean County, which is really not saying much. Ms. Susan Petrone lives in one of those slate-and-blond-wood houses with floor-to-ceiling windows exposing grandiose views of creamy sand and crashing surf. It's a private beach that has never seen a cigarette butt, beer cooler, or a bennie's plastic flip-flop.

Needless to say, my mom was very impressed. "Do you have any idea how much I could sell this for?" she asked, drooling over the potential commission. "Three mil at least."

Also needless to say, I was the only fool wearing a damn suit. The room was awash in pastels and floral church dresses.

"Why aren't any guys here?" I asked myself out loud.

"This is a tea for the girls of Westlake College, Boatwright University," said Ms. Susan Petrone, a tall, lean woman with newscaster hair, tasteful jewelry, and a no-nonsense demeanor.

"But Boatwright is a coed school—"

"Indeed," interrupted Ms. Susan Petrone in the very authoritative tone she must use in the courtroom. "One of Boatwright's greatest strengths is the coordinate system of education, which enables you to grow and share with each other in a women-only environment."

"Oh," I replied, vaguely remembering reading something about this in the brochure last year. At the time, when I was fed up with Marcus and men in general, and not in my right mind, the coordinate system had sounded like a good idea.

"Gather round, ladies," she said, "as I explain to you the benefits of the coordinate system, one of the most misunderstood components of the Boatwright University educational experience."

For the next half hour, she went on to explain that Piedmont was the only coed school in the nation that separates the sexes on campus. Much like at summer camp, guys and girls reside on opposite sides of a lake, the guys on the Boatwright University half and the girls on the Westlake College half. They have separate dormitories and student governments, but all classes are coed. According to Ms. Susan Petrone, the greatest advantage of the separate-but-equal living arrangement is that it allows women to live and work together without "the pressures of the patriarchy."

That is exactly the kind of backward, pseudofeminist bullshit Manda slings. I've never understood the grrrls who believe that the only way to get ahead as women is to exclude men. Don't get me wrong, the Y-chromosome set is teeming with total ditzes.

But how can we expect to make our mark on the world if we alienate half its population? It's like Paul Parlipiano said about PACO: The best way to change the system is to work within it. (He'd be so proud of me! Less than three weeks until the Snake March! Whee!)

The oddest thing about Ms. Susan Patrone's pro-separation-of-the-sexes spiel was that it drew so much attention to what made the coordinate system a fundamentally doomed concept. I don't think it's a coincidence that the glossy, colorful Boatwright University brochure mentions the coordinate system almost as an afterthought. I think the publicity people know the truth: If a single-sex environment is your thing, fine. But why would any guy—or girl for that matter—go to a school where two thousand menstrual cycles get in sync? What a nightmare!

It made me hate the Boatwright publicity people for being so underhanded and sneaky about something that could have such a huge impact on happiness—especially since I almost bought into it. It just goes to show you how little we really know about the schools we pin our hopes on. I can't believe I actually considered going here before Paul Parlipiano intervened. I don't know if I know Columbia any better, but I do know this: It's the diametric opposite of Boatwright, which is a step in the right direction. Thank you, Gay Man of My Dreams, for helping me narrowly avert certain collegiate catastrophe. (Just nineteen days! I'm so excited! I'm *sooooo* excited that I won't even dwell on how absolutely pathetic it is that the highlight of my spring break social calendar is attending a social protest! When other girls are island hopping, I'll be protest hopping!)

And isn't part of the point of going to college getting to know all different kinds of people, including—horrors!—guys?

At Columbia (if I get in, please let me get in), I'll be peeing next to the opposite sex on a daily basis because even the *bathrooms* are coed. I can't see how Boatwright could possibly pro-mote anything but unhealthy relationships between the sexes. Guys are lazy dogs. They are not going to leave the comfort of their own dorms, walk a mile—across a bridge, over a lake, and through the woods—just to hang out and watch television. No, the only reason they would walk a mile, across a bridge, over a lake, and through the woods, would be if they knew they were going to get their hobs nobbed *while* they watched television. In summation, the coordinate system rewards emotionless hook-ups, which really would make it the perfect school for Manda, wouldn't it?

Speaking of heinous skankitude . . .

"Look who I found!" my mom said brightly. "Isn't this a co-incidence?"

Call Me Chantalle. And her mom.

Holy shit.

This was not a coincidence. This was a sign. Any second now, I expected Ashleigh, she of the broccoli schnozz and aggressively annoying personality, to show up, saucer in hand, nibbling on a dry, tasteless shortbread cookie.

"Maybe we could be roommates again!" Call Me Chantalle gushed.

I looked around the room. It was full of chattering, excited girls. This was unreal. Why was I here, wearing an outfit I hated, putting on a happy face for my mom and the likes of Call Me Chantalle?

"So it's true," I said.

"What's true?" asked Call Me Chantalle.

"That psychosis is a symptom of advanced-stage syphilis," I whispered so only she would hear.

"What do you mean?"

"Because you've got to have a sexually transmitted brain-eating virus to think I'd ever live with you again."

Call Me Chantalle's huge head turned red with anger and she looked exactly like a stop sign. I was pretty sure I could take all seventy-five pounds of her in a catfight, but I didn't want to stick around to find out. My mother and Mrs. DePasquale were too busy bragging about the scholarships Boatwright was offering their daughters to notice the tension. I grabbed my mother by the arm and told her it was time to go.

"But Jessie, honey," she cooed. "We just got here."

"Which has already been long enough for me to realize that I will never, ever go to this school with these people," I replied, without breaking my stride.

When we got to the car, my mother attacked.

"What has gotten into you? I've never seen you behave so poorly in my life!"

"Mom, I have no intention of going to Boatwright," I said. "I should never have agreed to go to this inane event."

"Then why did you even apply?"

This was the third perfect opportunity to tell the truth. *I applied to Boatwright because at the time, I was too scared to apply to the school I really wanted to attend, the one you won't let me attend even if I get in.* That's what I should have said.

But for the third time, I pussed out. And I pussed out because I suck. Suckity suck suck.

the fifteenth

Finally, a Jessica-free edition of *Pinevile Low* I could enjoy.

WHAT RICHIE-RICH THROW-DOWN THROWER RECENTLY
EXPLODED OUT OF HER PREMIUM DENIM JEANS BECAUSE
SHE STILL THINKS SHE'S A SIZE 2?

Sara, of course. Ha!

With one less thing to worry about today, I decided to finally have a talk with Percy about Bridget. He's been hanging around her a lot lately, and I just can't stand to see him crushed. I'm very sensitive to these types of heartbreaks for obvious reasons. When I accused him of having a crush on Bridget, Percy issued denials faster than a celebrity publicist after a client's bout of "dehydration."

"*Connerie! Bridget a eu un boyfriend célèbre!*"

("Bullshit! Bridget had a famous boyfriend!")

"*Elle a eu un rendez-vous avec Geai de Kay. Et il n'est pas si célèbre.*"

("She had one date with Kayjay. And he's not that famous.")

"Pourquoi un POA chaude comme Bridget me choisirait? Je souhaite!"

("Why would a hot POA like Bridget choose me? I wish!")

"Bien, uh . . . Elle ne va pas. C'est pourquoi je t'ai dit de l'oublier."

("Well, uh . . . She wouldn't. Which is why I told you to forget her.")

"Ne t'inquiètes pas de moi. Je suis copacetic."

("Don't worry about me. I'm copacetic.")

Later, I tried to urge Bridget to spend less time with him so she wouldn't lead him on.

"I would never carry on a secret relationship with anyone, especially someone I've *worked* with," she said.

"Are you sure? I think he might be hot for you."

"Jess, that's so, like, unprofessional."

"But . . ."

Bridget wasn't about to explore this topic any further because she had revenge on her mind.

"But nothing. We've got more important stuff to, like, think about!" she said, holding up a page torn out of the *New York Times.* "We are going to finally face off with Hy!"

I looked at the clipping. Miss Hyacinth Anastasia Wallace was doing a reading and signing at a bookstore on March 28 — the same day I'm supposed to meet Paul Parlipiano in NYC.

"I'll take the bus with you, since I'm going in that day already," I replied.

"Oh," she said. "Is that the day of the big Lizard Walk?"

"Snake March," I said, so aglow with the prospect of spending the day with my crush-to-end-all-crushes that I could easily

ignore her nonchalant ignorance. "It's PACO's biggest nondiscriminatory demonstration against all forms of tyranny."

Bridget sighed. "He's gay, Jess."

"I know. What does that have to do with anything?"

"It's just that since Len dumped you, you've kind of, like,
gotten re-obsessed with Paul Parlipiano."

"Uh . . . I have not!"

She stuck her ponytail in her mouth and mumbled a "Whatever."

Okay, maybe I have gotten a little too excited about the Snake
March, but I was just publicly humiliated by my ex-boyfriend and
Skankier, whose hand-holding and pecks on the cheek are too nauseatingly chaste to be for real. Is it so wrong for me to want to focus
my energy on someone who seems to have only the best intentions
for me? It's merely coincidence that he just happens to be my former obsessive object of horniness, my crush-to-end-all-crushes.

"I *know* he's gay and that there's no chance of anything happening," I said. "It's just that I think it's cool that I've received
an invitation from someone I thought would never, ever know I
even existed."

"A *gay* someone," she clarified unnecessarily.

I just glared.

"Well, if your nondiscriminatory protest with your gay date
doesn't, like, rock your world, you can always meet up with me
at the bookstore to give Hy a piece of your mind."

"Maybe," I said.

"Aren't you, like, still pissed?" she asked, her aquamarine eyes
blinking madly, beautifully. "Don't you want to vent?"

I shrugged.

"Percy is helping me to write a script," she said. "So my telling her off will be like a role I'm playing. That way I won't, like, screw up or lose my nerve."

Bridget is the only other person who remembers that Hy's book came out at all. It's funny how little impact *Bubblegum Bimbos* ended up having on our school. The sad fact is, Pineville's population doesn't read. We've got six Wawas and eight liquor stores, but you have to drive twenty miles outside town limits to find a bookstore. PHS students just couldn't take a time-out from their kegging to read it, opting to wait for the movie, which is due in theaters sometime in 2003. But who knows if they'll even go see it? With the exception of Sara, who never forgets anything, Pineville High has a notoriously short attention span. If Hy really wanted to make maximum impact, she would've sold her rights to MTV and had *Bubblegum Bimbos* turned into a twenty-two-minute mini-movie wedged between *Cribs* and *Becoming*.

I'm still sort of working through my whole Jenn Sweet identity crisis. It's been pretty depressing to admit that I will never be one-bajillionth as cool as my alter ego. Jenn Sweet is not the kind of girl who gets publicly humiliated by her ex-boyfriend and the resident boyfriend-stealer. That's because Jenn Sweet is not the kind of girl who would have gone out with Len in the first place if she knew deep down that he was not the right person for her. Or maybe she would have given him a chance, but she certainly wouldn't have stuck it out with him as long as I did. I don't know. I still find myself asking, "What Would Jenn Do?" even when I know that trying to be like her (like I did on New Year's Eve) will only lead to certain disaster.

But it's not like being myself does me any better. Maybe I should ask Percy to script my whole life, so I never screw up or lose my nerve.

the seventeenth

After the Boatwright fiasco, I thought my parents would refuse to go out in public with me ever again. Unfortunately, I was wrong. They joined me at Silver Meadows today for its annual St. Patrick's Day celebration.

I was happy to see that Gladdie's outfit and walker were completely color-coordinated in shades of green. I had started to worry—that her mismatching was a sign that at ninety-one, she was finally slipping. But there were no signs of any new slippage today as she did a modified, walker-aided jig with Marcus to a tin-whistle ditty about sassy Irish lassies.

Marcus was wearing a KISS ME I'M IRISH T-shirt.

"Nice shirt," I said.

"It was a gift from your grandmother," he said.

"Pucker up, JD!" Gladdie bellowed.

What my grandmother lacks in subtlety she makes up for in volume.

"I'm not convinced that Marcus here is really Irish," I said.

"I'm one-quarter Celtic," he said, tipping his green plastic hat. "And just take a look at this red hair."

"PUCKER UP!"

"I'll give you one-quarter's worth of a kiss," I said, kissing my palm and blowing it in his direction.

"Oh, you disappoint me, JD," Gladdie said, shaking her head.

And Marcus, very uncharacteristically, didn't say anything at all. That is, until my mother swooped in and asked the inevitable question.

"Soooooooooooooo, Marcus," she cooed, fluffing out her highlights. "Where are you going to college next year?"

I had been wondering the same thing. The last I had heard from Len, back when we shared these things, was that Marcus hadn't even taken his SATs.

"I'm not going to college," he said.

"What?!" my mom, dad, and I asked simultaneously.

"I'm not going to college."

I played along. "Why aren't you going to college?"

"I don't need a degree to get by in life."

"Well, that's convenient," I replied. "Now I can visit you *and* Bridget at McDonald's next year."

"Just because you're conflicted about your college plans doesn't mean you should project those fears on me."

My parents jumped on that one.

"She is conflicted, isn't she?" my mom pried.

"One minute it's Boatwright, the next it's Williams!" Dad said, turning purple with frustration.

"Oh, it's Williams now, is it?" Marcus asked.

I shifted in my seat.

His eyes darted toward my parents, then returned to me.

"If I *were* going to college, however, I would definitely consider going to school in New York City."

WHAT WAS HE DOING??????? AND HOW DID HE EVEN KNOW TO DO WHAT HE WAS DOING????????

"May I talk to you for a moment?" I asked, through clenched teeth.

"It was nice seeing you again, Mr. and Mrs. Darling," he said politely while shaking my dad's hand.

He pulled me over to a quiet corner.

"Len," he said, before I even asked. "I know about Columbia through Len."

Len had become such a nonentity in my life that I had forgotten there was ever a time I tried to confide in him simply because he was my boyfriend.

"Why do you always have to step in where you're not wanted?" I asked. "This whole Columbia thing is very complicated already and I don't need you making it a bigger clusterfuck than it already is."

He opened his mouth to say something, then snapped it shut. "*What?*"

"Nothing," he said, turning away from me. "Nothing at all."

Ha! If there's one thing I've figured out, it's that when it comes to Marcus and me, *nothing* is "nothing at all."

the twenty-first

Scotty burst into the library after school today, all muscle and bluster.

"Yo! Jess! How come you haven't returned my phone calls?"

"Scotty, I'm trying to help Taryn pass her geometry test," I said.

Scotty could hardly waste his precious time by so much as glancing in Taryn's direction. She slunk lower into her seat and never took her Frisbee eyes off the parallelogram on the paper.

"So are we going to the prom or what?" he asked, his chin dimple twitching.

Ever since Sara informed me that Scotty was going to ask me to the prom, I had been artfully dodging him. I steered clear of the weight room and the cafeteria and hid in all the places I thought he didn't know even existed, namely the computer lab and the library.

"Oh, when you ask me like that, how can I resist?"

"Fuck yeah!" he said, not getting that I was being sarcastic.

"Fuck *no*," I replied.

"*What?*"

"I'm not going to the prom with you."

As soon as I said it, I could feel mini versions of my mother and my sister sitting on my shoulders, like in cartoons.

"YOU SAID NO TO THE MOST POPULAR, BEST-LOOKING CLASS ATHLETE?" screamed my mom.

"WHAT BETTER WAY TO GET OVER LEN?" screamed my sister, who weighed heavy on my left shoulder.

Then, in unison: "YOU DESERVE TO BE UNHAPPY!"

Maybe I do. I just know that I would've been far unhappier if I had said yes.

"What happened to you, Scotty?"

"What do you mean?"

"I mean, to you, what happened to the nice guy you used to be?"

"Gimme a fucking break, Jess," he said as he walked out.

He didn't even give me a chance to tell him that I would've gone to the prom with the old Scotty, the one who was sweet, a little goofy, and occasionally gross in a boogers-and-farts kind of way. The one who would have been just another jock at our school, but who had kept his integrity intact. But Scotty had made a choice two years ago. When he was crowned His Royal Guyness for the Class of 2002, all the testosterone necessary for that title left little room for sweetness or sincerity.

I think this is very sad.

But is it any worse than the roles any of us play to get through the day? I mean, I've been trying to be as vibrant and daring as Jenn Sweet for the past three months, which is just as loserish and pathetic as a pathetic loser can get.

"All you have to do is be yourself," Mac told me last summer. But anyone who has been to high school knows that being yourself is probably the most impossible thing in the world.

the twenty-eighth

This day ended up nothing like I thought it would, which is pretty much par for the course for me.

"Well, aren't you up with the sunshine this morning," my mom sang as I walked into the kitchen.

"I didn't think we'd see you until noon," my sister chimed in. Bethany is a huge and permanent fixture in our household as her due date draws near. This has made it much easier for me to go about my shady business, since my mom is too busy being a future grandmother to pay attention to me.

"Today's the day I'm going to see Hy in New York with Bridget," I said.

This, as you know, is factually accurate but not *really* true.

"New York?" my mother gasped, placing her hand to her chest. "Jessie! You didn't mention that the bookstore was in New York!" She started fanning herself, as if it were noon in August on the sun. "I don't like the idea of this!"

"Mom," I said. "You encouraged me to mend fences with Hy. Well, this is my opportunity."

"Why can't you do it closer to home?"

"Ever since her little undercover investigation, Hy breaks out into hives whenever someone so much as mentions New Jersey,"

I replied. "So until the entire state becomes hypoallergenic, I doubt she'll come back."

"Oh, I don't like this. Bethany, what do you think?"

"Is she taking mass transit?" Bethany asked my mom.

My mom turned to me. "Are you taking mass transit?"

"You can tell Bethany that yes, I am taking mass transit."

"Oh," Bethany said. "I've never taken mass transit. Grant always hired a car service."

Fortunately, Bridget breezed in through the back door, radiating a golden aura that has a spellbinding effect on my mother and my sister. I really think that deep down, my mother and sister are convinced that Bridget and I got swapped in our infancy, when all babies look identically red and squishy.

"Good morning, Mrs. Darling. Hey, Bethany," Bridget said. "Jess, are you ready?"

"Bridget," my mother said, "you know your way around the city, right?"

"Oh, sure," Bridget said, waving a porcelain limb. "Like the back of my hand."

My mom and my sister sighed in relief.

"Bring the cell and call if you have any problems," my mom said, kissing me on the cheek.

"I will."

"And don't talk to strangers."

"I won't."

"And keep your eye out for any suspicious individuals."

"I will."

"And don't leave Bridget's side."

"I won't."

"And—"

"Moooooooooooooooooom . . ."

"Okay. Go. Have fun." My mom got up and kissed me on the cheek again. "While your mother sits here and has a heart attack all day."

When we were in the car and out of earshot, I was ready to goof on my mom.

"Your mom—" Bridget began.

"I know, she's a total freak," I replied. "I'm sorry."

"No," she replied. "It's nice. She cares. My mom, like, never knows where I am ninety percent of the time because she's always working at the restaurant."

"You think it's nice because you don't have to live with her," I said. "And she only seems to care when it's convenient for her, like when she's not buying bassinets, binkies, and other baby crap for Bethany."

"Well, it is, like, a big deal, the first grandchild and all. Aren't you excited about being an aunt?"

"Not really," I replied. "We're talking about Bethany and G-Money's spawn here. Perpetuation of the beautiful species. Ack."

"I'm, like, sure her mommy instincts run deeper than that," Bridget said.

She's right, you know. The other day I actually asked Bethany why she wanted to be a mother, when she had seemed so uninterested in a vocation that would put an end to her string-bikini days.

"What greater joy can there be than bringing a baby into the world, a little person who loves you unconditionally?"

"Okay. But kids can be pains in the ass," I said. "I mean, I'm not even *bad* and I'm a pain in the ass."

"Yes, I know," she replied, rubbing her belly. "But the benefits far outweigh the troubles."

Maybe my parents would have an easier time seeing things that way if I had been planned.

Anyway, Bridget and I arrived at the bus station with just a few minutes to spare. Bridget warned me that the post-rush-hour weekday bus trips into New York are generally full of Highly Irritating Passengers. Again, she was balls-on.

AN INCOMPLETE CATALOG OF HIGHLY IRRITATING PASSENGERS ON NJ TRANSIT BUS #76

- **Species:** Snotnoses Rugrattus
  - **Distinguishing Characteristics:** Under three feet tall. Will cry and shriek if not given candy, or toys, or attention, or whatever they want. Too immature to control their own bowel movements, yet sophisticated enough to master a Game Boy.
  - **Natural Habitat:** Chuck E. Cheese.
- **Species:** Showtunicus Lionkingus
  - **Distinguishing Characteristics:** Dressed in "fancy clothes," i.e., shiny, artificial fabrics. Will chatter on and on about all the musicals he/she has seen. Often sings songs from said shows, particularly "I Dreamed a Dream" from *Les Miserables*, which the Showtunicus Lionkingus invariably calls "Les Miz." (Note: On return trips, is never seen without a yellow-and-black *Playbill*.)
  - **Natural Habitat:** The soundtrack section of Borders.

◘ **Species:** Nasticus Pervertus

    ◘ **Distinguishing Characteristics:** Trench coat, greasy hair, and dark sunglasses. Will sit across from the most attractive teenage girls (who happen to be the only attractive travelers) and leer silently. Has the uncanny ability to give one the willies.

    ◘ **Natural Habitat(s):** Porn shops and playgrounds.

Bridget and I didn't talk much during the trip because we were all too acutely aware that simply hearing the voices of teenage girls gives Nasticus Pervertus a boner. We couldn't get to the Port Authority and off that bus fast enough.

"So you know where you're going, right?" Bridget asked.

"I know."

"Just take the one or the nine straight up to 116th Street, the Columbia University stop."

"I know."

"Don't get off any sooner."

I sighed. "Did you swallow my mom?"

Bridget giggled. "Remember, I've got my cell and you can meet me at Union Square if the Snake March, like, sucks."

"It won't suck," I assured her.

Famous last words.

I was about to head for the subway when Bridget turned and asked me a question that, quite frankly, startled me.

"Like, whatever happened with you and Columbia?"

"What? How did you—?"

"Last summer, remember? You had your big moment with Paul Parlipiano at the coffee shop."

"Oh, right," I said. I had totally forgotten that I had ever told Bridget about Columbia.

"So, what happened? Did you end up applying there?"

Bridget has never lied to me. Never, ever, ever. So the least I could do was return the favor. Wasn't I going to have to face the truth within the next five to thirty days, anyway?

"Yeah, I did," I said. "I'm still waiting to hear."

Bridget raised an expertly tweezed eyebrow. "Your parents are going to, like, *kill* you."

The truth hurts, doesn't it?

"Go get her," I said.

"Oh," she said, rubbing her palms together. "I will."

Throughout the twenty-minute trip uptown, I hoped and wished and prayed that it was the first of countless times I'd be taking this ride in the future. I didn't feel the least bit nervous about traveling by myself. I felt like I knew where I was going, even though I had never been to the address Paul Parlipiano had emailed me, the one I had printed out and clutched inside my coat pocket like a talisman. I wasn't freaked out by the ride, simply because I was too busy imagining what it would be like if I got into Columbia and Paul Parlipiano became my fabulous gay best friend in New York City, the Will to my Grace. We would go shopping at swanky shops on Fifth Avenue that neither of us could afford! We would squeal with delight and hit the dance floor whenever we heard the intro to Erasure's "Chains of Love"! We would dish about boys we liked and bitch about ones we didn't! We would be more devoted, dependable, and dedicated to each other than any mere boyfriend could ever be!

This fantasy would prove to be even more farfetched than the one that involved us getting married and having many babies.

PACO HQ was a graduate student's apartment. I buzzed the intercom three times before anyone responded.

"What?" said a very shrill woman's voice.

"Uh . . . I'm here for the Snake March."

"You sure?"

"Uh . . . yeah."

She buzzed me up without saying another word.

The door to apartment 3B was open, but I could barely make it inside because there were protest signs on the floor and leaning against the walls blocking the doorway. WE WALK FOR THOSE WHO CAN'T, said one. WALKING NEVER HURT ANYONE, said another. These slogans were hardly any better than the ones on the lame signs Scotty and Manda held during the unsuccessful Homecoming Walk-Out. However, since I was the novice here, I kept my opinion to myself. One thing was for sure: There seemed to be more signs than people to hold them.

"Are those jeans from the Gap?" I heard Paul Parlipiano's mellifluous voice ask. Not exactly the greeting I was hoping for, but whatever.

I swiveled around, actually convinced that the aesthetics of my new ass transcended sexual preference. "Yes, they are!"

He heaved an exasperated sigh. "Gap is Crap!" he said.

On instinct, anyone within earshot instinctively repeated his chant. "Gap is Crap!"

Then he went on to explain how the Gap relies on sweat-shops that break about a bajillion child labor laws.

"I didn't know."

"Ignorance is no excuse, Jessica," he said.

"Uh, okay. Sorry."

Then things were okay for thirty seconds as Paul introduced me to some of the other PACO members: a Black, buzz-cut, hippie-skirted lesbian named Kendra; an elfishly short, goatee-sporting Latino hipster named Hugo; and a dreadlocked, Birken-stocked granola white boy named Zach. For people so concerned about human rights, they seemed pretty much uninterested in my very existence.

I fortified myself with a swig of Coke from the bottle in my backpack and was about to volunteer to do something when Paul said, "Are you drinking Coca-Cola?"

I looked at the label dumbly.

"Choke on Coke!" he shouted.

"Choke on Coke!" shouted Kendra, Hugo, Zach, and every-one else. He went on to explain how Coca-Cola is the most insid-ious promoter of corporate imperialism. I wasn't used to seeing Paul Parlipiano outside of Pineville's oppressive environment. The freedom made him very . . . *opinionated*, to say the least.

"Sorry," I replied. "I didn't know."

He gently rested his hand on my shoulder with great pity. "Ignorance is no excuse, Jessica."

"Why not?" I asked. "How could I know something if I, uh, didn't know it?"

Duh. Genius debate, Jess.

Then Paul Parlipiano launched into this whole pedagogical argument about how it is our generational imperative to celebrate the ties that bind our society instead of the differences that divide us, that all the peoples of the world should aspire to live as one in global unity and blah-diddy-blah-blah-blah. It was exactly the line Haviland gave me when she told me my divergent opinions would no longer be needed for *The Seagull's Voice*.

"What do you have to say to that?" he said when he was finally finished.

What did I have to say to that? WHAT did I have to say to THAT?

"Well . . ."

There he stood, Paul Parlipiano, my crush-to-end-all-crushes, the gay man of my dreams, looking down his nose at me like I'd Snake Marched through a pile of dog shit. He was getting off on his cosmopolitan superiority, but hell, I knew where he came from.

"I think that kind of thinking promotes conformity."

Paul Parlipiano's deep, deep brown eyes bulged out of his perfectly symmetrical skull.

"What?!"

"PACO is all about accepting people of different races, religions, and lifestyles, which is good. But when it comes down to it, you're a bunch of like-minded people who want to talk to other like-minded people."

He just stood there, eyes still half out of his handsome head.

"You don't want anything to do with anyone who doesn't share your politically correct point of view. You filter out any opposing thoughts that might undermine your cause, whatever it is."

I felt the whole room glaring at me, but I pressed on.

"I mean, you don't even know what you're protesting today, so you're protesting everything!"

An icicle dripped from the tip of my nose in the subzero silence.

"To single out any injustice for the purposes of our protest would be insulting to all those who suffer in the world," responded a flabbergasted Paul. "How can we measure one's oppression versus another's?"

"But you're not really taking a stand against *anything*!"

"You are wrong," Paul said, finally regaining his calm.

"See? That's exactly what I'm talking about. I'm entitled to my opinion."

"Not if your opinion is wrong," he said.

"It's my *opinion*," I huffed. "By definition it can't be wrong."

"Well, it is," he said.

How could this be happening? This was Paul Parlipiano, my former obsessive object of horniness, gay man of my dreams, my crush-to-end-all-crushes.

At that moment, I discovered a fundamental truth about this and all crushes-to-end-all-crushes: It's so much easier to convince yourself you're madly in love with someone when you know nothing about him. Now that I've seen Paul Parlipiano in his element, and have really gotten to know him, I've realized that we are truly not meant to be. You think the whole gay thing would've tipped me off to that inevitability, huh? No, that wasn't a big enough deal breaker for me. I could've dealt with his physical revulsion at the sight of my vagina. But what couldn't I deal with? His preachiness. I just don't like people telling me what to do.

"Paul, I never thought I'd say this, but I don't think you and PACO are for me. I'm out of here."

His response threw me off guard. "Are you venting your anger about my sister?"

"Taryn? Why would I have any reason to be mad at her?"

He pursed his lips. "Well, that's something you need to find out from her," he said, showing me the door.

"Okay, fine."

"No hard feelings," he said, regaining his impeccable manners. "Maybe I'll even see you around here next year."

"Yeah, maybe," I said, wondering whether Columbia was such a good idea after all, if this is how people here reacted to me and vice versa.

"I must say, though, that I am disappointed in you, Jessica."

"Likewise, Paul. Likewise."

I tried calling Bridget's cell phone, but she didn't pick up. For all I knew, she was still on the subway, so swift was the PACO in-and-outroduction. I figured I'd meet her at the bookstore, even though I had no desire to see Hy. Of course, when I got there Hy was in my face and all over the place. Huge pictures of her and blow-ups of that hot-pink book jacket covered all the store's windows. I took a deep, bracing breath before I walked in.

I followed the sound of Hy's voice, amplified by a microphone, until I found her. There were about fifty people—mostly college-age girls—lined up, waiting for Hy to sign their copies of *Bubblegum Bimbos*.

Bridget was not among them.

Hy looked just as non-Jersey as she did back when she was undercover at PHS. Her glossy black hair was spliced with shades of pink (surely to match the cover of her book) and cut in a piecey bob (which looks like bedhead but requires the touch of a celebrity stylist). She wore a peasant top and leather skirt that had a thrift-shop vibe (but were no doubt kustomized-with-a-k, which, I know from reading Bridget's *Vogue* over her shoulder on the bus, is vintage stuff that's been given a new zipper or a new hemline so the "designer" can jack up the price a bajillion percent). Her skin was tan and her cheeks were rosy, as though she had just come back from vacation. (Or "holiday," as her kind call it. Bali, no doubt. Or some island that isn't even on the map.) Her very white, very perfect teeth provided a stunning backdrop for her shiny hot-pink lips. Lips that were talking about Jenn Sweet, the cooler-than-I'll-ever-be version of me.

I stood patiently in Science Fiction until Hy had finished signing everyone's copies of *Bubblegum Bimbos*. When the last girl walked away with an autograph, Hy looked up and waved me over. She had a smile on her face, like she was genuinely happy to see me.

"Hey," I said.

"Hey," she replied, standing up and leaning across the table to hug me. Much to my chagrin, I let her. "I always hoped you'd show up at one of these things."

"Well, uh, yeah."

I. Am. So. Slick.

"You read it, right?" she asked.

"Uh-huh."

"And?" And.

"And . . ."

And what, Jessica? What?

"And . . . I read it expecting to hate you more than ever," I said. "But . . ."

"But?" she asked curiously, somewhat surprised that I wasn't going to continue on the hate trip.

"But I guess I have to thank you, in a way," I said.

"For?"

"For, well, as uncomfortable as it was for me to read, you kind of showed me who I could be—that is, if I weren't such a dumbass."

"What are you talking about?"

"Well, how you took a lot of artistic license with the Jenn

Sweet character, you know, making her a lot of things I am, only better."

"How better?"

"Better. Cooler. Someone who stands up for what she believes in, yet everyone still likes her, anyway."

She squinted at me, then shook her head in disbelief. "Girl, that's how I always saw you."

"What?"

"I always saw you as the girl who had it going on," she said. "But you just didn't know it because you were stuck in an area code where your brain doesn't get the respect it deserves."

"Are you high?" I asked, in utter disbelief.

"Not anymore," she laughed.

"How could you say that Jenn Sweet is me?"

"I can," she said, pulling out a pack of cigarettes and tapping it against her hand. "Because I'm the one who wrote it."

It's unreal, isn't it? How other people see you versus how you see yourself? Ever since I read Hy's book, I've felt inadequate when compared to my cooler alter ego. And here Hy was telling me that I *was* my alter ego.

I was about to protest, when I thought about what had happened an hour before this conversation. I had told off my crush-to-end-all-crushes, my former obsessive object of horniness, the gay man of my dreams. Yet he still seemed to like me, anyway. What more evidence did I need that she was right? Hy was right. I *am* my alter ego. I'm just not used to seeing myself that way. Powerful. Confident. And not a social outcast.

I may feel like a social outcast, but I'm not *really* one. Taryn, now, *she's* a social outcast. I think I'm an outcast inasmuch as I want to be left alone by people I can't stand, which isn't really the same thing as true social ostracization, now is it?

I dare say not.

Why did it take me until my last marking period of high school to figure this out? Because I'm me. That's why. (You probably had this all sorted out a bajillion pages back.)

"'We are what we pretend to be,'" I said, with finality.

"Kurt Vonnegut," Hy replied.

"Of course you knew it. That's a pricey private school education for you."

"Speaking of education, where you headed next year?"

The question. How odd that my first face-to-face with Hy in over a year had so quickly become so comfortable as to follow the required conversational patterns for seniors in high school.

"I'm still waiting to hear," I said. "I'd rather not jinx it by telling you."

"No big," she said. "But you're stressing for no reason."

If only she knew. "What about you? Harvard?"

"Maybe," she replied. "I don't know if I'm down with Cambridge. When you're born and raised in the best city in the world, living anywhere else just isn't an option."

Funny, how living in the *least* best city in the world could make me come to the same conclusion.

Hy's "people" soon came over to tell her that she was late for her next appointment.

"I'm out," she said.

"Yeah, me too," I replied.

"Later," she said.

And you know what? I knew that she was right.

"Later, Hy," I said. "I'll see you around."

When I met up with Bridget back on the bus to Pineville, she was hanging her head in shame.

"I bailed," she said. "I, like, totally bailed when I saw her."

"It's okay, Bridge," I replied.

"I couldn't do it," she said. "I couldn't go off like I wanted."

"It's okay. I couldn't go off on her either for some bizarre reason."

"I guess we don't have it in us to be bitches," she sighed with resignation.

"You say that like it's a bad thing," I replied.

"Well, in high school," she concluded, while pensively chewing on her ponytail, "being too nice can get you in more trouble than being a bitch."

Again, Bridget spoke the truth.

april

April 1st

Dear Hope,

Let me say it again: I AM SO HAPPY FOR YOU! Congratulations on getting into the Rhode Island School of Design. I still
wish that you had picked Parsons, but if I get into Columbia,
we'll be eight hundred miles closer than we've been in the
past two years! Woo-hoo!

See what's happened? I wrote "if." *If* I get into Columbia.
With every day that goes by, I am less and less certain that I'll
get in. Karmic punishment for all my college cockiness.

I am dreading the Williams letter. My final non-Columbia
acceptance could come any day now, and I've run out of stall-
ing tactics. I'm no Scheherazade, that's for sure. My parents
are still so pissed about Boatwright that they will not tolerate
any more ifs, ands, or buts. As their reaction to my recent visit
proves, they will never be in a New York state of mind. They
are the only people in the tristate area who did not run out
and buy I ♥ NY paraphernalia after 9/11.

Why do I do this to myself? Why do I always want what I
can't have? And why do I never want what I can get?

Because I, my friend, as we have well established, am a
masochist. I don't need an Ivy League degree to know that
much. Now I must go and celebrate the holiday that is specif
ically targeted at fools like me.

Masochistically yours,
J.

the twelfth

In homeroom this morning, Sara was showing off the thick envelope she received in the mail from someone who, according to the return address, is named S. Jones. S. Jones had stapled it more than a dozen times, requiring Sara to wrench it open with brute force. This was the desired effect. With one quick pull, Sara told me, the envelope exploded, showering the D'Abruzzis' plush carpet with glittery, multicolored shrapnel. Sara had been letter-bombed with beach-themed confetti: green palm trees, yellow suns, blue ocean waves. Her living room couch had taken the harshest hit, and I knew her stepmother would be unamused. No matter how thoroughly the housekeeper vacuums, years from now, long after Sara's college days are over, she will still be finding tiny, shiny coconuts or beach umbrellas in the cushions.

But nothing could dampen Sara's excitement. Apparently she had gotten over the fact that she hadn't scored high enough on her SATs to attend Rutgers with Manda.

"OMIGOD! THIS! IS! SO! COOL!"

S. Jones is Sandi Jones, a senior at Harrington College and Sara's "Freshman Initiation Counselor." Sandi had cleverly turned a favorite picture of herself into a sticker and attached it to the bottom of her greeting letter. She had beauty queen beauty, the kind of perfection found in Miss America pageants back when the swimsuit competition was worth more points than the interview. She had shoulder-length blond hair, no bangs, blown smooth and curled under. She was wearing a silver lamé strapless gown and a toothpaste-commercial smile. A disembodied man's hand rested on her shoulder.

"OMIGOD! SHE! IS! SO! BEAUTIFUL!"

In her letter, Sandi revealed that the manly hand was attached to a Sigma Chi brother—as she was designated the fraternity's official "sweetheart." This entitled her to a plastic cup of beer fetched at a moment's notice. No keg lines for the sweetheart of Sigma Chi. No siree.

The letter itself was a marvel. Each word of the two-page document was written in a different-colored Magic Marker. The pattern: pink, blue, purple, teal, yellow, red, orange. Repeat. This wasn't color-copied at Kinkos. It was done by hand. Multiply this by, say, ten others in Sandi's Freshman Initiation group, and that meant approximately one bajillion Magic Marker switches. I couldn't imagine Sandi getting ink on her soft, paraffin-treated hands. She must have had someone else do it—an assembly line of Delta Gammas each designated her own Magic Marker color to trace Sandi's faint pencil letters into a rainbow of welcoming. A sorority sweatshop.

"OMIGOD! I! WANT! TO! BE! HER!"

What Sara didn't realize, but I did, was that Sara and Sandi Jones were already the same person. In fact, I would bet that Harrington College was composed entirely of Saras. A college full of superficial, moneyed daddy's girls who weren't smart enough to get into better schools, all of whom would bring out each other's worst eating-disordered, stucco-butt fears.

The letter also clued Sara into all the bizarre Southern rituals she'd have to know by heart before she attended the Freshman Induction Ceremony. According to Sandi, a white dress topped the list of must-brings. This was the required dress for the Proclamation Night ceremony. The details of said ceremony were kept very hush-hush, but Sandi Jones did say that it is a time-honored tradition, when all freshmen are initiated into the college. Apparently, they all wear white dresses (girls) and white shirts with red ties (guys) and walk in single file down a brick path that's lined on either side with identically dressed seniors, carrying candles.

"That would creep me out," I said.

"Why?"

"I mean, there's something very satanic about that."

Sara flipped me the bird.

Sara was expected to memorize a song before she arrived, to be sung along with the seniors.

Harrington, Harrington
This is the song
That will be sung
By you, it's true
Four years and forever
Harrington

"Are you sure you got accepted to a college and not a sorority?" I asked.

Sara flipped me the bird. Again.

Still, as much as Sandi Jones's letter scared me, I couldn't help but get a little jealous over Sara's unadulterated excitement about the next four years of her life.

I'm insanely jealous over everyone's acceptance letters. Hope and RISD. Len and Cornell. Manda and Rutgers. Scotty and Lehigh. Bridget even heard from UCLA, which is really unfair because until she got the acceptance, she had insisted that she wasn't even going. But now that it's here, guess what? She wants to go. That's the great thing about being Bridget. Her mind is so uncomplicated that it doesn't take much to change it. It works out for her, but sucks for me because I was relying on her to be the one person who was not caught up in college excitement.

WHY HAVEN'T I HEARD FROM COLUMBIA YET????

the fifteenth

WHAT RECENTLY DUMPED BRAINIAC IS FUELING
SAPPHIC RUMORS BY REJECTING THE MOST POP-
ULAR, BEST LOOKING CLASS ATHLETE'S PROM
INVITATION?

I hate the Mystery Muckraker. I really do. Why should *my* business be anyone else's business? This violation of my privacy pisses me off. Jesus, I wish I could write an editorial. Something along the lines of "Gutless Gossip: *Pinevile Low* Author Finds Safety in Anonymity."

While I'm hating people, I hate everyone who has been accepted to college.

I hate Mac and Paul Parlipiano for making me care so much about Columbia. I hate them for making me want this so much. I'm much better off when I don't really want anything. Only then can I maintain the ironic detachment toward my whole life that keeps me from going certifiably insane.

Though this college thing has been a nice way to get my mind off other things, like how Len and Manda are severely disappointing me by not breaking up. And how it kind of bothers me when Bridget isn't home to field my Columbia freak-out phone calls. And how Marcus has been more distant and silent than he's ever been.

the seventeenth

**MY EDUCATIONAL OPTIONS FOR NEXT YEAR
SINCE IT IS CLEAR THAT COLUMBIA DOESN'T
WANT ME (AND I DON'T WANT TO GO TO ANY OF
THE OTHER SCHOOLS I'VE BEEN ACCEPTED TO)**

1. **Boatwright University.** Room with Call Me Chantalle and major in Intimate Moments. I'll just have to suck it up. (Ha. In more ways than one.)

2. **Ringling Brothers Clown College.** My moniker could be Dinky Dumbass.

3. **McDonald's University.** I am very familiar with their Dollar Value Menu.

the nineteenth

Ringling Brothers Clown College closed last year! DAMMIT!!

the twenty-third

The mailman is Satan.

the twenty-seventh

hy is it that I'm never allowed to get excited about anything?

I've been wired, wired, wired—so wound up I couldn't even
do sun salutations without feeling like I was going to snap into a
bajillion pieces. My body has been buzzing with excess energy
and I knew there was only way to get rid of it. I tried to ignore the
urge through deep-breathing techniques and mini-meditations,
but nothing, nothing could stop me today from doing the un-
thinkable.

I laced up my sneakers and went for a run. That's right. I've
damned the downward dog to hell and have finally accepted the
truth: I am not a yoga person. No one was home, so I figured
no one would ever have to know. Even if I did get caught, who
cared? It was too far into the track season for my father to insist
I rejoin.

I hadn't run in about six months. And for the first few hundred steps, my body rebelled.

*OM SHANTI!!!! OM SHANTI!!!! WHAT THE HELL ARE
YOU DOING?????*

But I forced myself to keep going. By the time I was out of
sight of the house, I fell into an old but familiar rhythm. I realized

how much I missed doing this. Not the competitions, just this. For myself. This is who I am: a runner.

For the duration of my forty-five-minute run, I barely thought about the answer to the question or anything else. Little did I know that it would be waiting for me with clenched teeth, sweaty brows, and a lot of yelling.

"WHAT'S GOING ON HERE?" my father yelled as I walked through the door.

"I felt like going running," I replied, assuming that's what he was freaking out about. After all, if I could run the streets of Pineville, I could certainly run circles around the track. But that's not what had incited this riot.

"WHAT IS THIS?" my father screamed while wildly waving an envelope in the air.

I grabbed it from him. A thick envelope from Columbia College, Columbia University.

"Jessica Lynn Darling! What is this?" my mother shouted.

It was already torn open.

"Well, you've already violated my privacy by opening it, so why don't you tell me?"

"You are not going to school in New York City!" they yelled in unison.

I pulled out the letter on top. It began, *Congratulations! You have been offered a spot in the Columbia College Class of 2006.*

Oh my God.

We apologize for the delay. The late mailings and website postings were the result of a technical error . . .

OH. MY. GOD.

. . . and we regret any inconvenience this might have caused.

Inconvenience, schminconvenience! The torture of waiting was nothing compared with the torture of getting accepted, as my parents' reaction was about as awful and closed-minded as I had imagined in my worst nightmares.

"You are going to Boatwright on scholarship."

"No I'm not. That place sucks."

"We are not paying for you to go to a school located near Ground Zero!"

"Columbia is nowhere near Ground Zero! It's more than a hundred blocks away!"

"That's not far away enough!"

The fighting stopped only when we'd all screamed ourselves into laryngitis.

I am not backing down. No way. I don't care if I have to take out a bajillion dollars in loans, work a thousand minimum-wage jobs. The struggle will be worth it. I know it.

the twenty-eighth

I thought bridal showers were the most excruciating custom in modern society, what with all the toilet-paper-wedding-dress traditions and break-a-ribbon, make-a-baby superstitions.

But today I discovered that there is one thing worse.

Baby showers.

No one likes them, especially the mama-to-be, whose sweaty tumescence was extremely disconcerting to me but didn't seem to bother anyone else. Bethany couldn't unwrap more than three presents in a row without having to waddle to the ladies' room to pee. This made the already slow and excruciating ordeal even slower and more excruciating.

As if the shower didn't suck enough, my mother was putting on her super-dee-duper nicey-nice tone to cover up the fact that she was still supremely pissed off about Columbia. Whenever a great-aunt or a second cousin or anyone else with whom I am blood related (but barely know) asked me the question, my mother singsonged the same annoying response.

"Jessie got accepted to every school she applied to!" she'd say, putting her arm around my shoulder, squeezing a bit tighter than necessary. "She's still undecided. We'll let you know as soon as she considers her offers."

And I would just stand there smiling a wax dummy's frozen, artificial smile.

Finally, Gladdie came to my rescue.

"JD! Park yourself over here!"

She was wearing a baby-blue pantsuit with a baby-pink beret. Her walker was still St. Patrick's Day green, which really bothered me. Couldn't *someone* at Silver Meadows help her stay color-coordinated if she couldn't do it herself anymore?

"Whatsa matter, JD?" Gladdie asked. "Your face is all screwy."

"Oh, I hate stuff like this," I said, plopping down in the seat next to her.

"Why? Whatcha got against showers?"

Bethany opened a box wrapped in alphabet wrapping paper. "BOTTLE WARMER!" she announced to the crowd.

Gladdie squinted at her baby shower bingo card. "Does this have 'bottle warmer' on it?"

"Yes," I replied, pointing to the upper-left-hand-corner box. "Right here."

"Bottle warmer!" she roared, crossing off that box on her grid. "Hot damn!"

"Anyway," I continued, "I just hate all these stupid rituals. These big events are supposed to be fun and memorable but are really boring."

"People need rituals," Gladdie said.

"DIAPER GENIE!" Bethany announced.

Gladdie scanned her card. "Do you see 'diaper genie' on here, JD? I can't see so good."

"No," I said.

"Crooks!" Gladdie yelled to no one in particular, then turned her attention back to me. "This is the stuff that gives people something to look forward to."

"BABY MONITOR!"

Gladdie pushed the card toward me, and I crossed off "baby monitor."

"We're gonna win this thing, JD!"

I sighed, my head not in the game. "I never look forward to anything."

"And why is that?"

"Because whenever I look forward to anything, it ends up sucking. The buildup inevitably leads to a letdown. It's safer to lowball my way through life."

"BUMPER SET!"

Gladdie put her hand on mine, and the contrast was striking. Mine—large, smooth, unblemished. Hers—shrunken, wrinkled, spotty and mottled, bumpy and blue-veined. Ancient hands. "And how happy has this made you?"

"Not very," I admitted.

"ONESIES!" my mom yelled, since my sister was taking another potty break.

I crossed off "onesies."

"Ain't ya looking forward to takin' a bite out of the Big Apple?"

"Well, my parents probably won't let me go," I replied.

"You gotta do what you want to do. If New York is what you want, you gotta go for it. If I've learned anything in my ninety-one years, it's that you definitely won't get happy going through life kowtowing to every Tom, Dick, and Harry."

"It's not so easy, Gladdie," I replied. "You know how your son is."

"He's a hothead," she replied. "He got it from his father, God bless his soul."

Then I realized that this conversation shouldn't have been happening at all, that Gladdie wasn't supposed to know anything about Columbia. It must have suddenly dawned on her too.

"CAR SEAT!"

"'Car seat,' sweetie?" Gladdie asked, innocently.

"Don't change the subject," I snapped. "How did you know about Columbia?" The question, of course, was moot, as I already knew the answer.

"Jeez Louise," Gladdie said, wringing her hands. "Tutti Flutie only told me 'cause I asked."

"He had no business telling you. He wasn't even supposed to know. He's always doing this. Butting in where he doesn't belong."

"Don't use this as another excuse to push Tutti Flutie away. How many hoops you gonna make him jump through? When's the dog and pony show gonna end?"

"Huh?"

"Don't lowball this one, JD. He's a sure shot."

"NIPPLES!"

I checked off another box as Bethany waddled back to her seat.

"But he's not interested," I said, completely flustered. "You said he wasn't interested."

"He's more than interested, JD. Even a half-blind old broad like me can see that. But I knew that you're just like me in that you don't like anything that comes too easy. You should see what I made your grandfather, God rest his soul, go through when we were courting. And Moe? That poor man still doesn't know what hit him!"

"BREAST PUMP!"

Another box.

"So I only told ya he wasn't interested to get you all fired up."

"Well, it worked," I said, sweaty, red, and burning up with the news, not sure how I could cool myself down.

"No it didn't," she replied. "You ain't together, are ya?"

"Uh . . . no."

"And why not? Because you're scared of what will happen? Don't be a fool, JD. You gotta take chances in this life or you're already dead."

Before I could respond, Bethany yelled, "STROLLER!"

I crossed off a box that completed the middle horizontal row on the grid and held it up for my grandmother to see.

"BINGO!" Gladdie howled, her voice reverberating throughout the restaurant. We were victorious.

may

April 30th

Dear Hope,

I'm going to have to put in about fifty years of indentured servitude to my parents to pay off our last phone call, but I'm not
quite done venting yet.

Marcus's latest intrusion is about as surprising as a card-
board box of devil heads at the Osbournes'. He just cannot
stop mucking up my life. He intentionally told Gladdie about
Columbia (*something he wasn't even supposed to know about*)
in the hopes that she, in her uncensored, doublestroked senility, would spill the news and cause much parental pain and
suffering. It didn't quite work out that way—my parental pain
and suffering came via an alternate route—but that doesn't
make his inability to stay out of my life any less infuriating.

I don't know how you expect me to believe that it's "his
way of showing he cares." No offense, but that's easy for you
to say because you're not here to see what he's REALLY like.
He's the GAME MASTER, Hope. He's an EVIL GENIUS who
messes with my mind and my life because he has NOTHING
BETTER TO DO now that he's (allegedly) living a life of chas-
tity and temperance. Thank God there's only two months of
school left, because I really don't know how much more of
this I can take.

I have to ask you this on paper because I'm a wuss and
couldn't bring myself to ask you on the phone: Why don't you
hate Marcus? Don't you hate him for doing everything Heath
did, but living to tell about it? Don't you hate him because he's
still here and your brother is gone?

Here's the thing that's keeping me awake: If you don't hate

Marcus, then it's difficult, if not impossible, for me to make a case against him. And where does that leave me?

Bafflingly yours,
J.

the second

I saw her just four days ago. Alive.

And now she's dead.

Gladdie died the dream death, in her sleep, at ninety-one. Yet that doesn't make it any easier for me to accept that she's gone.

Grandmothers die. Matthew and Heath and other brothers who are too young to die, die.

Read today's obituaries: A college girl playing beach volleyball on a cloudless spring day gets struck by lightning in front of all her teammates and dies. A thirty-six-year-old nonsmoking father of four gets lung cancer and dies. A seventy-five-year-old retired police officer gets hit by a drunk driver and dies.

Everybody dies, eventually. We're all doomed, and I don't like it. I don't want to die.

You might think that's an obvious thing to say, but the truth is, I didn't always have this aversion to death. Not that I was suicidal or anything, but if I died, I thought, I wouldn't be that upset about it. Not that I'd have any conscious thoughts about the matter, because I'd be dead.

But I really don't want to die. Not now, when I finally feel like I'm so close to escaping Pineville and living my real life in New York, the life I've been waiting for so long to live.

Then I remember: Thousands of innocent people whose only mistake was showing up for work early on a September morning died.

No one in my family has ever been religious. I always saw religion as a kind of a crutch, something people used to make themselves feel better about their own mortality. I don't blame anyone for doing this—in fact, I wish I were able to buy into it all. But I can't. I wish I believed in the afterlife. I wish I believed that Gladdie was up there on a white puffy cloud, her husband at her side, entertaining all the angels with her stories.

But I don't believe that. I don't believe in anything. I believe that when you're dead, you're dead. And sometimes, as Gladdie prophetically pointed out to me the last time I saw her, sometimes you're dead even when you're alive.

Why is it that the place I fear the most is the only place that can set me free?

It doesn't make any sense.

Four days ago, Gladdie was laughing, joking, playing games. Today she's in a coffin. This also makes no sense to me. Maybe I should find comfort in the utter absurdity of life and death. I can't outwit something that only plays by one rule: It will win in the end. No matter which way I choose to move, death will always come out the victor, so I should just try to enjoy the game of life as I'm playing it. Isn't that the point Gladdie was trying to make while she was alive?

I think it would make Gladdie happy to know that I've learned something from her passing. She was a firm believer in better late than never. I just wish I believed that I'll get a chance to thank her someday.

the third

What is wrong with me? I am the most fucked-up grand-daughter in the history of procreation.

My grandmother's wake was today. I know I should write about how much she meant to me, but I can't. Something even bigger than death happened to me today.

Before I go any further, let me try to explain my state of mind. Wakes are horrible, horrible customs.

In theory, I guess I can understand why some people would want to get a look at the deceased one last time, but not when she didn't look anything like the Gladdie we knew and loved. Her face was waxy, and yet too pale and powdery at the same time. Her makeup was applied perfectly, which is to say, her eyebrows weren't drawn on crooked and her lipstick didn't smudge beyond her lip line, so she didn't look like her usual nutty self. And they had her hands folded politely across her lap, which is something she would never do when she was alive. Whoever dressed her didn't put on one of her signature crocheted berets. The more I looked at this coffin version of Gladdie, the more upset I got.

The only people who mourned properly were my dad and Moe. Both of them sat in the front row, not really talking to anyone, deep within their own thoughts, their own memories of this woman they both loved in their own ways.

Everyone else was so chatty about everything but the reason why we were there. My mother was flitting around the funeral home like it was a goddamn cocktail party, telling second cousins and great-aunts "how lovely" it was to see them again so soon after the baby shower, albeit for such a "sad occasion."

But it was Bethany who really stole the show. Mourners lined up to pat her baby bump. "It's tragic she will never get to meet my firstborn," Bethany said over and over again, making Gladdie's death more about herself than about Gladdie. It really was sickening.

When I finally couldn't stand it anymore, I headed to the only place I could be alone for a few minutes, the bathroom. I had my hand on the doorknob when someone grabbed my other hand and followed me inside. I didn't even have to turn around to know who it was.

"I'm . . . so . . . sorry."

Again, stronger and clearer.

"I'm . . . so . . . sorry, Jessica. I . . ."

It was Marcus. At a loss for words.

"I know," I murmured.

"Gladdie was classic," he said. "A real original."

"I know."

"I liked her immensely."

"I know."

"I'm really going to miss her."

"I—" was all I could get out before I turned into a blubbery blob.

Marcus put his arms around me, and I buried my face in his chest and sobbed. I breathed in deep to take him in, his scent, which evokes burning leaves in late fall.

When I exhaled, I shot a snot rocket all over his blue-and-white polka-dot tie.

"Oh, Christ!" I groaned when I realized what I'd done. "I'm a disgusting mess."

"It's cool." Marcus laughed, and stroked my hair. "It's an old tie, remember?"

I did remember. It was the same one he was wearing the first time we spoke in the Caddie, when this whole thing between us, whatever it was, or is, began. I knew he had worn it on purpose.

He pulled me tighter, closer than we'd ever been.

"Marcus," I said.

"Jessica," he replied.

And . . .

And.

Jesus Christ.

Without knowing who started what, our mouths met—his and mine, ours—moist and messy and . . . perfect.

As we kissed, it was as if I were returning to somewhere safe. We kissed, and it was like coming home after a long, grueling odyssey. Marcus and I kissed, and kissed, and kissed, and I never wanted to leave this familiar place again.

KNOCK KNOCK KNOCK.

I de-suctioned myself from Marcus, to whom I was so forcefully vacuum-attached that I swear we made a lovely, lid-off-the-Tupperware air-sucking belch.

"Is there someone in there?"

Bethany!

"Holy shit!" I whispered.

"Jessie, is that you in there?" my sister asked.

Marcus had my lip gloss all over his chin, as though he'd spent the morning sucking on a greasy pork chop.

"It's not nice to keep a woman who's nine months pregnant and has a full bladder waiting!"

I looked in the mirror.

"Holy shit!" I whispered again.

My face was all red and raw with razor burn. And was that . . . ?

"Oh, shit! Shit! Shit! You gave me a hickey!" I mouthed, pointing to the grape-colored map of Florida he'd left behind on my neck.

He shrugged, smiling, still holding my hand.

Pound pound pound.

"Jessie! I am going to explode if you don't get out of there this instant!"

"Just a second!" I called out nervously to my sister.

"I don't have a second!" whined Bethany.

"What are we going to do?" I mouthed to Marcus.

"We are going to walk out that door," he said out loud, so anyone on the other side of the door could hear him.

"Jessie . . . is there someone in there with you?"

"No!"

And before I could stop him, before I could devise a plan that involved him busting a hole in the ceiling and crawling through the air conditioning shaft to safety, before I could even turn up the collar on my shirt eighties-style to hide my goddamn hickey, Marcus opened the door and said, "She's a terrible liar, isn't she?"

My sister was so stunned that she temporarily forgot that her bladder was about to burst.

"She thinks she's such a great liar," Marcus continued, "but she's really terrible at it."

I swear, I don't know why Bethany's water didn't break right then and there with the shock of it all.

"We've occupied the lavatory long enough," Marcus said. "Please, let us get out of your way."

And Marcus, leading me by the hand, cleared a path to the toilet.

And Bethany—still unable to confront the fact that her little sister was getting it on with this lanky stranger in the bathroom of the funeral home that was hosting her dead grandmother's wake—lumbered past us and shut the door.

"That went well," Marcus said, smiling so bright that his eyes twinkled and crinkled in the corners.

I don't know what made me angrier, the fact that he had tricked me into hooking up with him, or that he was being so blasé about it after the fact. I mean, I usually don't believe in God and the devil, but at that moment, my agnosticism was replaced by the certainty that when my time came, I should be buried in flame-retardant underwear, because I was surely spending all eternity in hell.

"Go."

"Jessica . . ."

"*Just go*," I growled.

He blinked once. Twice. Three times.

"I mean it!" I snapped. "GO!"

His smile fell, his eyes got murky, and very un-Marcus-like, he slunk away without another word.

Did I mention that his mouth was as soft, succulent, and sweet as a slice of mango? And that I can't stop licking my lips, hoping for one last taste?

AHHHHHHHHHHHHHHHHHHHHHHHIIIIIIIIIIIIHHH.

the fourth

I am a skank."

I had shown up unannounced at Bridget's house at 9:00 a.m. to spill the whole sordid story. And this is the conclusion I had come to.

"How are you a skank?"

"I made out with someone I'm supposed to hate at my grandmother's wake. That makes me a heartless skank."

I was laying facedown on her flowery bedspread, my arms shielding the morning sunlight, in agony.

"You were, like, under emotional duress," she said. "You weren't thinking straight."

My eyes were shut so tight that I could see psychedelic floral patterns swirling across the retinal blackness.

"I don't even know his middle name."

Bridget didn't respond.

"Did you hear me? *I don't even know his middle name.*"

This seemed very significant to me.

"So? Like, what does that matter?"

"I made out with him at my grandmother's wake," I replied. "I should at least know his middle name."

"Ask him the next time you see him."

"Bridget, you're missing the point!"

"What's your point?"

What was my point? Was I feeling sinful because I made out with *anyone* at my grandmother's wake? Or was I feeling dirty because I made out with Marcus, of all people, at my grandmother's wake? Or was I feeling hypocritical because I had just spent a bajillion hours on the phone trying to explain to Hope why he was an evil genius, and it would be extremely messed up for me to have this intense kissing episode with someone I considered to be an evil genius? Or was I feeling idiotic for putting off such an amazing total-body blissful kissing episode for so long? Or was I feeling guilty BECAUSE I GOT CAUGHT?

When I told Bethany that Marcus and I had been *talking*, that I wanted some *privacy*, so he could help me *cope with my grief*, she simply said, despite all the evidence to the contrary (the razor burn, the pork-chop lip gloss, the hickey), "Whatever you say," and left it at that. I can only attribute her coolness to a nine-months-pregnant hormonal cocktail. However, it didn't make the situation any less mortifying. The only thing that makes me even remotely okay about this whole thing is knowing that my making out with Marcus would've made Gladdie extremely proud. It's exactly what she always wanted to happen.

My thoughts were interrupted by the *whoosh* of the front door downstairs.

"Your mom?" I asked.

Bridget barely shook her head. Two sneakers pounded up the stairs and showed up as crimson footprints all over Bridget's neck.

"Good morning, *mon amie!*"

In this context—specifically, Bridget's house at 9:00 a.m. on a Saturday morning, I couldn't quite place the voice. Even when

I saw Percy in the doorway, I still had trouble piecing things together.

Bridget's face was redder than a thermometer in a heat wave. They shot each other nervous looks before Percy finally said, "Look who it is. My two favorite senior girls!"

The ease with which Percy had entered the bedroom made it clear that he had been here many, many times before. Then it hit me. This wasn't a hapless crush. This was real.

"Holy shit! You two are going out!"

Percy and Bridget exchanged sheepish smiles.

"BRIDGET! YOU LIED!"

She bashfully held up her palms in resignation.

I still couldn't get over this. Not so much that they were a couple, but that Bridget had lied about it. About anything. Bridget NEVER lies.

"*YOU LIED!*"

Percy sat down next to her on the bed and held her hand.

"She did," he said.

"You lied," I said again, quieter.

"We both did."

"How long has this been going on?"

"Since the play," she said. "October."

"Holy shit! You've kept this quiet since October?"

"Trying to," Percy said. "But *Pinevile Low* isn't making it easy."

"But why? Is it, uh, because Bridget is white and you're . . . not? I mean, I don't care. But you know, Pineville at large . . ."

They both laughed at how awkward I was being about this.

"We didn't do it because of the black-and-white thing," Bridget said.

"We did it to keep it real," Percy said.

"So no one would, like, get in our business."

"So no one would spread rumors."

"So Skankier wouldn't jump his bones."

"That girl is busted. I'd never leave you for her," Percy said while tenderly stroking the inside of her wrist.

"A girl has got to be on guard, though, because it's, like, only a matter of time before she gets tired of Len," Bridget said.

I sat there for a moment, still taking all of this in.

"Why don't I ever see anything coming?" I asked, almost to myself.

"What?" they asked.

"I mean, I consider myself to be a pretty observant person. I see *too* much going on, which is why I can't sleep at night. But why am I always shocked by people, even when their behavior seems so obvious after the fact?"

It was a rhetorical question, really. I hadn't expected Bridget or Percy to have an answer, which just proves my point.

"Maybe it's because you're, like, too busy thinking about yourself," Bridget offered.

I must say that I was taken aback by this attack on my character.

"Excuuuuuuse me?"

Bridget tugged on her ponytail. "You kind of, like, see people as you want to see them, as they fit in with your view of things," she said. "And you're so busy seeing people from that angle that you can't see what's really going on."

"Do you agree?" I asked Percy.

He nodded.

"Like with Len dumping you," Bridget continued. "You were

so busy worrying about Manda sleeping with Marcus that you didn't even notice how much attention she was laying on your boyfriend."

"Uh-huh."

"And with us. I think you were, like, so set on seeing Percy as your French friend who had a crush on you, and me as someone who only dates pop stars and football players, that you couldn't accept us as a couple, even though we didn't do much to hide it in front of you."

I wanted to change the subject because I did not like the fact that Bridget of all people had just psychoanalyzed me with such accuracy. Maybe *she* should study to be a shrink in college.

"But you lied," I repeated dumbly.

"I, like, had to," she said, turning to Percy. "He was worth lying about."

Then she went on to explain how she hated how personal things got so public. Like how last year, everyone in school found out that Manda slept with Burke when he was supposedly so true to Bridget, or how her one stupid, insignificant date with Kayjay Johnson was still inspiring Hummers to drag her reputation through the dirt. She was tired of it. So when she and Percy started falling for each other, they figured the best way to keep their love from getting tainted by outside influences was to keep it to themselves.

"You won't tell anyone, right?" Bridget asked when she finished.

"Of course not," I replied.

Then Percy leaned over and kissed Bridget on the cheek, which skeeved me out.

It's not just them. I can't handle seeing any people I know sharing any form of intimacy. No surprise when it comes to nasty couples like Manda and Scotty, Manda and Len, or Manda and *anyone*, for that matter. But even with sweet couples that I'm rooting for, like Percy and Bridget, I get grossed out when I see them holding hands or exchanging the driest kisses.

I used to think that my inability to deal with others' PDAs meant that I was jealous, or maybe just incredibly immature— that is, until I caught a glimpse of myself in action, and got even more freaked out than I did when I saw someone else. I'd catch glimpses of Len and me fooling around in his rearview mirror and it was like, EWWWWWWWWWW. *Who are those people?*

I knew not to open my eyes yesterday, because if I caught a glimpse in the mirror and saw what I was doing and what Marcus was doing—what we were doing—I knew I wouldn't do it anymore, even though every last cell in my body was telling me to please, please, please keep going, going, going . . .

Gone.

the fifth

You are not going to believe this. I still don't believe it myself.

Gladdie left behind nearly half a million dollars in cash and investments.

No one in my family knew she was so loaded. Not even G-Money, whom she had consulted for financial advice years ago. He had no idea that she'd actually listened to his investment strategies. What's more, unlike G-Money, *she* had the sense to cash out before the crash.

An even bigger kick in the head? Her financial savvy was well known at Silver Meadows.

"She loved the stocks," Moe said.

"She did?" asked my dad, mom, sister, and I.

"It was a hobby for her," he said.

"It was?" we asked.

"She'd spend hours poring over the bulls and the bears in the *Wall Street Journal*," Moe said. "That's what she called the stock indexes. The bulls and the bears."

"Really?"

"And she never missed the Money Honey on CNN," he said. "Gladdie loved that gal."

The Darling/Doczylkowski family just stood there, mouths agape. Some money was left to charities, but most of it was for the four of us, the next of kin, with a huge chunk of it—seventy-five K!!!!—going to yours truly.

And in classic Gladdie fashion, she was very specific about how I should use it:

"This money is to be spent doing what it is that you want to do, JD. If you don't know what that is, don't spend it until you figure that out. And don't let your parents try to talk you into using it how they want you to use it."

To me, this meant one thing: college.

Seventy-five grand would pay for tuition, room, and board for about three and a half semesters at Columbia. I could take out loans and do work study for the rest. I don't need my parents' permission, approval, or pocketbook. I can—and will—do this on my own if I have to.

Finally, I can be free.

So why do I still feel trapped?

the sixth

To me, the revelation about Gladdie's secret pastime is ultimately more shocking than the money itself. It started me thinking about how little you can actually get to know about a person. You can talk to someone, spend time with that person, share experiences and emotions and bond in all the ways that we like to think we're bonding or whatever, but it still doesn't get you any closer to someone's secret self. All couples through the ages have been kidding themselves. No one ever really gets to know anyone in this world. It's a collective delusion that makes love (or lust, for that matter) possible.

All of these thoughts have everything to do with the fact that I had to face Marcus in school today.

I kissed Marcus, but do I know him any better now than I did before? Not at all. I only know the Game Master, but that's not really him. He doesn't know me any better now, either. I wasn't really me when we were fogging up the bathroom mirror. I was, as Bridget pointed out, under emotional duress, which means Marcus was taking advantage of me at my weakest. That was a really shady thing to do, wasn't it?

We kissed. So what? Kissing is nothing these days. Kindergarteners kiss. Did it really mean anything? No. Did it bring us any closer? No. Do I understand him any better? No. Does it make a difference in our lives? No.

Since this was a totally insignificant nonevent, I decided that I wouldn't say anything about it at all. I would just ignore that it happened. I would say "Hey" to Marcus as usual, maybe even thank him for coming to Gladdie's wake, but that's as far as it would go.

Why I thought the Game Master would make it that easy is beyond me.

"Hey, Jessica," Marcus said in a voice that was softer, more careful than usual.

"Hey, Marcus," I replied casually. "Thanks for coming to Gladdie's wake. It was very nice of you."

I gathered my books to head to homeroom, but he stopped me in my tracks, simply by standing there with his hands rattling inside his pockets.

"You okay about . . . everything?"

"Uh . . . I'm still sad, of course."

"Naturally," he said. "But I meant, you know . . ."

I tried to avert my eyes, not wanting to go where he wanted to go with this conversation. So I took an alternate route.

"Did you know Gladdie was a financial genius?"

His posture relaxed, but his hands stayed in his pockets.

"Everyone knew."

"Then why didn't you tell me?"

His clasped his hands in front of his chin, as if in prayer.

"Because you told me to stay out of your business," he said.

I snorted. "That never stopped you before."

He squeezed his hands tighter. "Jessica, I want to talk about what happened."

"No," I said, getting hot and jumpy. I don't know what it was about his not telling me about Gladdie that had anything to do with anything. All I knew was that I was upset by the notion of his knowing something about my own grandmother that I didn't. "I want to talk about this. You claim that you want to stay out of my business, but then you go ahead and get involved, anyway."

"I can't believe you're getting upset at me. I only wanted what was best for you."

"That's not your responsibility," I said.

"And why not?" he asked, his body rigid with tension.

"Well, you're not my boyfriend."

"Being your boyfriend will not make this any more real, Jessica. I've been the boyfriend of dozens of other girls, and none of those relationships were real."

"Well, neither is this one."

He took a step toward me, and I backed away. He leaned in so only I could hear him.

"When are you going to stop doing this?"

"Doing what?"

"Pushing me away."

"I am not pushing you away," I said shakily. Gladdie had accused me of doing the exact same thing.

"Oh, yes you are," he said, louder this time, placing his large, calloused hands on my shoulders to keep me in my place. "You are doing your best to push me away. And you know what? I'm finally going to do you a favor and not push back. You want me out of your life? Consider me out."

Then he walked away.

"Omigod!" Sara screamed. "Holy shit! I knew something was

up with you two! The *quote* Class Brainiac and Krispy Kreme *unquote*."

I ran down the hall, out of the building, across the campus, past my house. I ran as far, as fast, and as long as I could. But it wasn't far, fast, or long enough to escape his words repeating themselves over and over again inside my head.

the fifteenth

Ever since Marcus's very public declaration of whatever he was claiming to "feel" for me, I've become the subject of countless finger-pointing rumors.

I heard he's taught her everything he knows, so she can do every position in the Kama Sutra *at college.*

They meet every morning at her house for a pre-homeroom hump.

He's turned her into a nympho.

Bridget and Percy assure me that there is no such talk going around school, that it's all my imagination, but I know better. As long as Sara is alive and in possession of vocal cords, such bullshit is an inevitable part of the Pineville High experience.

At any rate, I thought for sure that *Pinevile Low* would have something to say about Marcus and me, which is why this Marcus-related item was so bizarre.

WHAT FORMER DREG AND ALLEGED GENIUS FINALLY THANKED THE JUNIOR WHO CONFESSED TO FAKING HIS DRUG TEST BY MAKING HER HIS LATEST DOUGHNUT?

HUH?! Marcus and Taryn?!

I didn't buy it for one second. (And not for any reasons that had anything to do with me and whatever "feelings" Marcus was allegedly having about me.) No, I didn't believe it for this reason: Why would anyone bother to write about Taryn, someone so insignificant? Even if it was—against all odds—true, why would anyone care, really? Why would the Mystery Muckraker, who, up to this point, only chose high-profile students to out in her column, suddenly shift gears and write about someone who would make little to no impact on Pineville High's psyche? Any salacious interest generated by Marcus would be negated by Taryn's minus-zero status. Not to be cruel, but really. The Dannon Incident proved no one cared about Taryn Baker. So who would care now, nearly two years later?

Then it hit me with the force of a sumo wrestler belly-bumping me out of the ring. I suddenly understood what Paul Parlipiano had meant when he made that strange comment about getting back at his stepsister. It all made sense: The only person who would write about a nobody was the nobody herself.

I cornered Taryn in the library.

"Pinevile Low."

When she shriveled like a Shrinky Dink, I knew I was right. TARYN BAKER IS THE MYSTERY MUCKRAKER BEHIND *PINEVILE LOW.*

"Why?" I asked.

"Paul," she said, in her typical one-word fashion.

"What?"

"Paul," she repeated, cowering down in shame. "And you."

"What?! Me?!"

"You."

"You're going to have to give me a lot more than that," I said.

Taryn sat hunched over in her chair and stared at a stain in the carpet as she spoke.

"Paul was always getting on my case about not taking a stand against anything," she said. "He can be very—"

"Pushy," I added.

"Right," she said, brightening a little. "I also admired how your articles took a stand and made a difference. You told it like it was. And I wanted to do that too. When you stopped writing, I wanted to take your place, in a way. I knew I needed another forum, so I sent emails instead. Only I wasn't as brave as you because I couldn't bring myself to take credit."

I'd never really thought of myself as brave before. I always saw myself as more obnoxious than brave.

"If you admire me so much, why did you write about me?" I asked. "Why didn't you just stay out of my business?"

"I do admire you," she whispered. "That's why I only wrote stuff I knew was true."

"The thing you wrote about me and Len and homecoming wasn't true," I said.

"It was true when I wrote it," she said. "About him."

"Really," I said. "And how did you know that?"

"I overheard him telling Marcus about it in study hall," she replied, smiling wanly.

"Well, just because something is true doesn't mean you should broadcast it to the world. I used to think like you, Taryn. I'd go off on people just for the joy of pointing out their faults to the world."

Then I babbled on and on about a yogic practice called satya I learned from the book Hope gave me. It's about telling the truth all the time, but in way that doesn't hurt people's feelings. Basically, choosing words carefully so they do the least harm and the most good. I know I'm not perfect, because my words still tend to piss off their targets. But you know what? Sometimes—like with Paul and Hy—it *has* worked, which is a very encouraging start.

"Otherwise, what's the point? So you piss people off by pointing out their faults. But there's got to be more to it than that."

"Maybe you're right," she said solemnly.

I was feeling very superior in my maturity. "So how did you find out all this stuff, anyway?"

"You'd be amazed the things people say right in front of someone who isn't really there."

"What?"

"People speak openly right in front of me because they either didn't notice I was there or didn't give a damn."

I remembered how Scotty had blurted out his prom proposition without even acknowledging Taryn's presence in the room. Taryn was a nobody at Pineville, so she didn't even *have* to eavesdrop. Her very insignificance made her one of the most powerful people in school.

"There was only one bit of information I was never able to get, which is why I wrote this last item."

"And what's that?"

"Who *really* peed inside the cup," she said. "Because it wasn't me."

"Really?" I said, pretending to be shocked, but without overdoing it. I was very aware of how even subtle hand gestures or facial tics could give me away.

"I lied because I thought it would make me popular," she said with a grimace. "Obviously, I was wrong."

I patted her shoulder sympathetically.

"I thought that if I wrote this item, perhaps Marcus would maybe, I don't know, reveal the truth to squelch this rumor . . ."

"And if he didn't?"

"Then I'd have a hot rumor going around about me, which is more than I could ask for on a regular day."

How sad. Really. Outwardly, Taryn does everything within her power to go unnoticed. Yet she secretly harbors this irrational desire to be popular. If there's one thing I can say about myself, it's that I've been blessed by a complete disregard for popularity. I've never really wanted to be popular. All I've ever wanted was one person who totally understood where I was coming from— who wasn't a thousand miles away.

"But I guess I'll never know who did it," she said. Her huge eyes fixed on me, unblinking.

"I guess not," I replied.

the thirtieth

Wow.

Yesterday, little Marin Sonoma didn't exist. Today she does.

I love her despite her completely ridiculous name, which is a testimonial to her cuteness. She's the tiniest, pinkest, baldest thing I've ever seen, and when I held her, this sleepy six-pound, four-ounce bundle, I cried.

Yes, me, the girl least likely to get ga-ga over goo-goo. I can't explain this transformation. All I know is now that she isn't just a concept, now that she's an actual living, breathing little person, my whole outlook has changed. I want to be the Cool Aunt, the one who takes her for weekends in the city and whisks her off to Broadway shows, museums, and Central Park. I want to be the one who spoils her and makes her mom seem like a clueless dork. I look forward to this.

Strange, isn't it?

Even stranger is the profound effect this event has had on me and my dad. That's right. My dad.

My mom was still at the hospital, and we were alone in the car on the way home. I can't remember the last time we were alone anywhere together.

"I remember the night you were born like it was yesterday," he said.

I didn't say anything, so unaccustomed was I to my father's voice sans his typically antagonistic tone.

"We were so happy to have you."

"Really?"

He looked at me with surprise. "What do you mean, 'really'? Of course we were happy."

"It's just—" I cut myself off, not knowing whether this conversation was possible or appropriate.

"What, Notso? What?"

"It's just . . . after Matthew died, I kind of always thought you were too sad to have another baby."

He inadvertently hit the brakes, sending us both lurching toward the dashboard. After apologizing he proclaimed, "You couldn't be more wrong! We were thrilled to have you! What ever gave you an idea like that?"

I stared straight ahead.

He took a deep breath but never took his eyes off the road.

"Notso, I know it hasn't been easy between the two of us, but I want you to know that I have always loved you. I worry about your well-being. I want what's best for you. I still don't understand why you stopped running or why you would give up something you were so good at, but I've had to let it go. I still don't agree with your college choice, but I have to respect your opinion. I won't lie to you, I wish I could still hold you for financial blackmail, but my dear mother thought you needed this. And out of respect for her and you, I have no right to stop you from doing what you want to do."

This was the most my father had said to me . . . possibly ever. And he wasn't done yet.

"On the way to the hospital that night, a song came on the radio. Whenever I hear that song, to this very day, it always reminds me of you."

"What song is it?" I asked, expecting from his tone that it must be something deep and significant.

"'Flashdance,'" he replied.

"'Flashdance'?"

He tried—in vain—to sing the line *"What a feeling!"*

Our lack of musical ability is something we have in common, so I burst out laughing. As soon as I did, I was afraid it would start another battle about my insensitivity and immaturity. But my dad started laughing too.

"That movie really tugs on those old heartstrings," I said.

"I know, it's really sentimental, huh?" he said, still chuckling. "But whenever I hear that song on the radio, I remember the joy of that night."

When we pulled into the driveway, I realized I will probably not have another conversation like this with my father for another eighteen years. I didn't really want it to end, but I didn't really know what else to say. I guess I could have taken advantage of the moment and tried to explain why I quit the team, and why I'm able to run now, on my own, for myself, without the pressure of having to win, but I just couldn't. Maybe someday, but not today.

My dad broke the silence.

"It could have been worse," he said. "It could have been 'Maniac.'" And we both cracked up some more, enjoying our new— our *only*—inside joke.

I'd like to think that this is the first of many, but I'm not holding my breath. We're more alike than we are different, but that doesn't guarantee we'll get along. After all, he's still my dad. And I'm still me.

june

Hope,

Remember when we were freshmen? We thought the seniors were so damn mature, and we couldn't wait to be them. All of Pineville culture revolved around them—senior athletic awards banquet, senior powder puff football, senior prom. The seniors ruled the school. So why do I still feel like a clueless freshman? Could it be because I've exiled myself to bystander status with all of the above and more? But would participation have given me a sense of belonging? I doubt it.

While I'm happy to be running again, I don't regret quitting the track team. Even after Kiley went out of his way to tell me that a freshman broke my school record in the 1600. All my records will be broken by someone, someday, whether I ran this year or not. Someone, someday, will break that freshman's record too.

And I don't regret not joining the powder puff football team either, even though it would've been the perfect school-sanctioned opportunity to slide-tackle Manda and Sara.

As I said on the phone, I don't regret turning down Scotty, guaranteeing that I will make it through all four years of high school without ever having attended a formal. It's only slightly disconcerting, though, knowing that I'll go through the rest of my life hearing the horrified cries of *WHAT? YOU NEVER WENT TO YOUR PROM?* whenever the subject comes up in adult, post-high school conversation. If you spend any amount of time with my mother or sister, you know that it does indeed come up with startling frequency.

Only twenty days left of school. When I think about everything that happened in the past month—my first family death, my first birth, my first real conversation with my father—I realize that twenty days is more than enough time for *anything* to happen... almost. You know what I'm *not* talking about, the only rite of passage that I—that *we*—have yet to make. But I've sexiled myself to bystander status on that front too, and twenty days is definitely not enough time.

Wistfully yours,

J.

the second

KNOCK. KNOCK. KNOCK. It was my mother's knock, one that went from the knuckles straight to my skull.

"Jessie, Bridget is here to see you," Mom said. "She said it's urgent."

I popped out from under the covers.

"Send her in."

The last time Bridget arrived at this early an hour on a Sunday, it was to break the news about Miss Hyacinth Anastasia Wallace. So I knew whatever it was that was bringing her to my door was indeed urgent.

Bridget walked in, her face as deep and red as a gash without a Band-Aid.

"What's going on?" I asked.

She coughed up her ponytail.

"What? Did you see a trailer for *Bubblegum Bimbos* on the internet or something?"

"No. It's . . . like. Okay."

"Bridget, what is it?"

"I can't go to the prom with Percy!"

Of course. What could be more important than the prom?

"Why not?" I asked.

"I've got, like, this really big audition in L.A. for a TV movie about OxyContin abuse the next day," she said. "It's, like, a really juicy part, and as much as it kills me not to go to the prom, Percy is insisting that I don't pass up the opportunity."

"Okay, so what does this have to do with me?"

"Will you go with him instead?"

I shrank back under the covers.

"Jess! He's already put down his deposit for the tux, and I've already paid for the ticket, and we don't want them to go to waste."

"Why would Percy want to go to the prom with me when you're his girlfriend?"

"Because you're, like, his best girl friend," Bridget said. "And you're, you know . . ."

"What?"

She sat down next to me on the bed. Her eyes got a little moist. "Well, you're, like, my best friend too, and I'd like to see you go to the prom with someone fun."

I didn't quite know what to say. I had never really thought about my relationship with Bridget. With Hope's best friend status still secure, who was Bridget to me? My childhood playmate? The one friend who has known me since diapers?

But thinking back over the past year or so, Bridget has been more than my former best friend. She was the fallback person I went to whenever I needed to have a face-to-face heart-to-heart. But I had obviously penalized her for one reason: She wasn't Hope. So what if she wasn't my intellectual equal? So what if she's sometimes more ditzy than I can handle? Bridget was still the only person at Pineville I completely trusted, even if she wasn't my actual best friend. She was indeed, as she had said, "like" my best friend. Sometimes that's good enough.

"Okay," I said. "I'll go to the prom with your boyfriend."

She clapped her hands enthusiastically, proving that you can take the girl out of cheerleading, but not the cheerleader out of the girl.

"And I'll try not to sleep with him too."

With that, Bridget squealed and smacked me in the face with a pillow. I yelped and whacked her back. Thus began a very girly pillow fight, the kind that's the fuel of countless adolescent boys' fantasies.

the fifth

I very intentionally did not tell my mom right away that I was going to the prom. As it is my mother's custom to obsessively ask about any school-spirited PHS function, I figured I would wait until she brought it up, then have a lot of fun by stunning the hell out of her by blithely mentioning that yes, after four years of abstention, I was finally making her dreams come true: I was going to attend a high school formal, and I needed to shop for a dress. Not an anti-prom dress. An actual prom dress.

Although I am loath to admit it, I was kind of looking forward to getting an eat-your-heart-out kind of dress. Whose four-chambered organ I wanted to dine on, I'm not so sure. Truth is, once I agreed to go with Percy, the prom actually seemed like sort of a fun idea.

Watch for lightning.

However, my mom, in a unique spin on her usual annoyingness, and being preoccupied with her darling first grandchild, did not ask. So today, two days before the prom, I was still dressless. As much as I didn't want to run to my mom for help, that's exactly what I ended up doing.

"Uh . . . Mom?"

"Mmmm," she said. She was distracted by the latest pictures

of itty-bitty Marin. I leaned over to take a look. Bethany and G-Money had put one of those awful lacy headbands on her. Babies are cute enough as they are, so why do parents feel the need to decorate them like a Christmas tree? I could tell from the sour expression on her face in the pic that Marin did not enjoy the accessorization. Either that or she was crapping her diaper.

"Uh . . . Mom?"

"Mmmm."

"Mom, I thought you would like to know that I'm going to the prom on Friday night."

My mother slapped down the pictures. "You're going to the prom???!!!"

"Yeah."

She just stared at me all bug-eyed and in disbelief.

"I was asked, so I decided why not?"

"By who? Scotty?"

"Mom, how many times do I have to tell you that Scotty is a total jackass and that I would never go out with him?"

"*Jackass* isn't a nice word, honey," she said.

"Well, he's not a nice person," I replied.

"Then who? Len?"

"He's still with Skankier," I replied.

"*Skank* isn't a nice word, Jessie," she said. "It's disrespectful to all women."

"Well, so is her compulsive need to sleep with everyone else's boyfriends."

She tapped her forefinger to her temple, deep in thought. "That boy from Silver Meadows? Marcus?"

I snorted. "Definitely not."

"Then who, Jessie?"

"Percy," I replied.

"Who is Percy?"

"He's a junior in my French class."

"You've never mentioned him."

This was true enough. Isn't it funny how I could sit next to someone every day for three school years, form a friendship with that person, yet never, ever mention him once in front of my parents? It just goes to show you just how little they really know about my life, even the stuff that wouldn't be such a big deal to mention.

"We're French-class friends."

"You must have made quite an impression on him if he asked you to the prom."

"Not really."

"Oh, Jessie," my mom said, girlishly swatting my wrist. "Don't be so modest."

"No, really, Mom. He's Bridget's boyfriend."

Now my mom was stumped. "Why would Bridget's boyfriend want to go the prom with you?"

Then I told my mom the whole complicated story.

"This is all very strange, Jessie," my mom said.

"Yes, it is," I replied. "But it doesn't change the fact that it's two days before the prom and I'm still dressless."

My mom took off her reading glasses and shook her head with pity. "Well, it's too late now."

"What do you mean it's too late?"

"You cannot buy a dress this far into prom season."

"And why not?"

"Why not?" she said, exasperated by my ignorance. "Why not? I'll tell you why not. When Bethany was a freshman and started dating that senior boy—what was his name? Well, whatever his name was, he broke up with his girlfriend and started dating Bethany right before the prom, and we had a simply awful time trying to find something suitable for her. The only dresses left this late in the season are simply awful. Tacky, tacky dresses that I would not spend one penny on."

"Well, what do you suggest? I came to you for help. I thought you'd love this."

"Well, I suggest that next time you not wait until the last minute to get a date."

"I guess I'll just wear jeans." I knew that would get her panties in a bunch.

"Don't test me, Jessie," my mom said. "Let me think."

At this point I didn't even want to go shopping with my mom anymore, which was why the following suggestion didn't sound as ridiculous as it might seem.

"Have you looked in Bethany's closet?"

"Ugh," was all I could reply, remembering the suit I wore to the disastrous Boatwright tea.

"She's got at least a dozen formal dresses up there. Aren't the eighties back in style again?"

"Mom, that's a swell idea and all. Only you're forgetting that Bethany had boobs in high school and I do not."

"Come," she said. "Let's take a look-see."

So my mom and I scoured Bethany's prom archives. There were a lot of truly god-awful dresses up there. An iridescent purple *Gone with the Wind* ball gown. A white multilayered knee-length number that looked like a wedding cake. A skintight hot-pink minidress with ostrich feathers sprouting from the shoulders.

But then, in plastic, toward the back, was a red silk, one-shouldered dress with a swishy, asymmetrical bottom. It was so retro it was cool again.

"Ooooooh," my mom said. "I always loved this one. It's so fiery. So Carmen."

I held it up to me and was shocked that it looked like it could fit. I thought my sister was always way more bodacious than me, but my mom assured me that Bethany was as boobless as I was back in high school.

"She didn't fully develop until college," she confessed. "Neither did I."

"Really?"

"Really. We're a family of late bloomers here."

So there's hope that I'll be busting out of my A-cup bra yet.

I tried on the red dress, and would you believe it? With a slightly padded strapless bra, this sucker would actually fit me.

My mom burst out crying when she saw me in it.

"You're"—sniff!—"all"—sniff!—"grown"—sniff—"up!" She hugged me tightly and blubbered into the back of my head.

"Moooommmmm . . ."

"I guess"—sniff!—"you're old enough"—sniff!—"to decide what college is right for you"—sniff!—"even if"—sniff!—"your father and I disagree." Huge sniff!

"Thanks for finally realizing that, Mom." I was still stuck in her maternal headlock.

"It's just that"—sniff!—"we worry."

"Bad things happen everywhere, even close to home."

As soon as I said it, I felt horrible. Of course she knows this. My mom had every reason to be paranoid about my well-being.

Her only son died in his nursery while she slept less than twenty-five feet away.

I wish this was something we could talk about. Maybe one day she'll trust me enough to tell me how she feels about the loss. Maybe she never will. But it's not up to me to decide, now, is it? The only thing I can do is be the best daughter I can be to her. I'll fall short of her ideals, inevitably and often, but I'll just have to take Bethany's word about having kids: The blessings of being my mom's child outweigh the pains-in-the-ass.

"This was fun, Mom," I said, finally breaking free of her grip. "Thanks for your help."

"It was my pleasure," she said. "We should do things like this more often."

"We should," I said, so caught up in the moment that I actually meant it.

"I hear the shopping is outstanding in New York City."

"It is," I replied.

"Well, you'll have to show me around," she said, pushing a lock of hair behind my ear. "Big-city girl."

And this time we both sniffled through our tears.

the eighth

!!!

Here are some highlights from the Pineville High Senior Prom 2002:

So many girls were bent over at the waist, butt-clapping and body-slapping, that the administration couldn't even attempt to enforce the "no lewd dance moves" rule.

Sara and PJ were sent home before they even set foot through the hotel doors, as it was clear to the chaperones by the way they had taken turns vomiting in the parking lot that they had raided the D'Abruzzis' wet bar and gotten wasted before they arrived.

Manda was voted Prom Queen and Scotty was voted King. This caused more than a minor stir. The royal noncouple broke time-honored Pineville High tradition and danced with their dates (Len, of course, and some anonymous freshman Clubber Baby) instead of each other.

Bridget did not have an audition (another lie!) and went to the prom with Percy. They finally debuted as a couple, as she—as *they*—had planned all along, and Bridget was gracious enough to fill me in on all the major prom hoopla because . . .

I did not make it to the prom. It wasn't part of their master plan, but all involved parties were very happy, anyway.

Here, in dragged-out, dramatic detail, are several scenarios, all of which did indeed take place at the pre-prom party held at Sara's house, but only one of which is the real reason I did not make it to the prom.

SCENARIO #1: SKANK THANKS

"Can I talk to you?"

It was Manda, all heaving bosom, body glitter, and baby-blue chiffon.

"I never got a chance to apologize for what happened between you and Len," she said.

"Why now?"

"Because this is it, isn't it? It's never going to be like this again. We'll see each other from time to time, I'm sure, but it's never going to be like *this* again."

"Thank God."

"I just want you to know that Len and I are in love."

Quintuple ack.

"Manda, I understand that you want to apologize so you can go off to college with a clear conscience, but quite frankly, I don't really care about you and Len anymore."

"Then if you don't care, you can hear me out."

It was clear that she was hell-bent on unburdening her soul, so I gave her the go-ahead.

"Girls with low self-esteem have sex sooner, and more often, than girls with high self-esteem," she said.

"Oh, which must make me the queen of self-esteem." I snorted.

"Well, yes, actually . . ."

"Oh, Christ, Manda, I am not in the mood for any of your feminist bullshit."

"No, listen," she said. "But guys with low self-esteem postpone sex and have less of it than guys with high self-esteem."

I thought about this for a second. "Chicken or the egg."

"What?"

"Maybe the reason they have low self-esteem is because they're not getting laid. It's a chicken or the egg situation."

"Puh-leeze," she said, though I could tell I had stumped her. "That's not the point. The point is, I realized that Len and I were both suffering from low self-esteem, which seems to stem from our sexual histories."

"Or lack thereof."

"Right."

"Okay. That's fantastic. So are we done now?" I said, looking around for Percy.

"No. Listen," she said, grabbing my arm. "I realized we could help each other. And we have. I know you think that he's just another guy, but Len is the first one I've truly cared about."

I didn't say anything.

"I'm just sorry that it went down the way it did, and I want to thank you for being as cool as you've been about it."

This was as close to humane as Manda could ever get.

"Friends?" she asked as she extended her hand.

I know I was supposed to bypass her hand, bow down, and kiss her pedicured toes for her compassionate apology. Like hell I would.

Did I not make it to the prom because I bitch-slapped her across the face, thus starting the best girl-on-girl brawl since the infamous Bridget/Manda/Sara cheerleader cafeteria catfight of '00?

SCENARIO #2: JOCK SHOCK

"So you'd go to the prom with the Black Elvis, but you won't go with me."

Scottty was well on his way to a DUI.

"Yeah," I said.

"You look hot," he said, looking down the front of my dress. "You should dress like that more."

I must admit, I filled out the dress just fine, thank you very much. But it made me uncomfortable to know that Scotty had noticed too.

"That wouldn't be very practical," I said, crossing my arms over my chest.

"I mean, more like a girl. You wear jeans too much. You should show off your legs more often."

"Well, if you're done criticizing my appearance, I think I'll find my date."

"No," he said. "Wait. I didn't mean it. Fuck. Fuck. Fuck. I always say the most stupid fucking things in front of you."

"Yes, you do."

"I can't stop thinking about what you said to me when I asked you to the prom."

"What?" Whatever I had said had slipped my mind.

"You asked what happened to me."

"Oh, right."

"I know I've changed," he said. "And I know why."

"Okay. Why?"

"I was a pussy."

Oh, Christ. My eyes rolled around like triple cherries on a slot machine.

"No, seriously. Guys only care about two things—getting laid and getting respect from other guys. You only need to get one to get the other. Get laid, get respect. And being a pussy was not getting me laid."

"Here's a novel idea," I said. "How about getting respect from girls?"

Again, my retort had stumped its target.

"I liked the old you, the guy you call a pussy, but who I thought was a nice guy. I even respected that guy. That's where you lost out. You were dead wrong about nice guys not getting laid, because I just might have slept with that pussy, and I will never, ever in a bajillion years sleep with you."

Did I not make it to the prom because Scotty spent the rest of the night trying to reclaim his former pussiness in an attempt to get into my fancy prom panties?

SCENARIO #3: LIES SURPRISE

Chaos Called Creation hit the stage at 7:00 p.m. for a mini farewell concert. With Len off to Cornell in the fall, they've decided they just can't go on without him. I really wasn't all that eager to watch Len and Marcus revel in groupie glory for one last time. I told Percy that we should get going, since the prom was about to start and was about a twenty-minute drive from Sara's house.

"Everyone arrives fashionably late," he said with a curious edge to his voice. "What's the point in going there if everyone is here?"

It started to become clear why he wanted me to stay when

Marcus stepped up to the microphone. He had shaved off the rooster tufts, and the resulting buzz cut somehow made him seem more vulnerable and childlike. Or maybe it was the absence of his trademark smirk, which had been replaced with a beatific smile I had never seen before.

"Our first and last song for the evening is our only ballad," he said. "And it's the only song I'll ever sing. So I hope you're listening."

He looked straight at me, then stripped off the button-down he was wearing, under which, he was wearing a passion-red T-shirt that said: YOU. YES. YOU. Then he strummed the guitar and began singing his song for me. Yes. Me.

CROCODILE LIES

I confess, yes, our Fall was all my fault
If you kissed my eyes, your lips would taste salt
But you think my regret is a lie, and the tears I cry
Are the crocodile kind.
The sweat on your upper lip starts to boil
White-hot with anger, still convinced I'm your foil
You keep fighting me, though my eyes are free
From crocodile lies.
You, yes, you, linger inside my heart
The same you who stopped us before we could start
I didn't want to leave, but you began to believe
Your own crocodile lies.
The only person stopping you is yourself,

You won't accept that I want no one else,
So until you do, I'll let someone else have you
Every day, I live the lie
But not the crocodile kind.

How do you react to something like that? How? How do you react when you find out the exact opposite of what you've been telling yourself is true? Let's get more specific: How do *I* react when I find out that Marcus still wants me after all? Or maybe he doesn't and this is just another move in the Game? How do *I* react when *I* have no clue if Marcus is for real?

Dazed, I drifted in his direction.

"I wanted you to be happy," he said.

"Happy," I said.

"If you wouldn't be with me, I thought that you should be with the one guy I thought deserved you, my best friend," he said.

"Friend," I said.

"So that's why I had to help him out, and tell him the perfect presents to buy you and stuff," he said.

"Help," I said.

"Your unhappiness with him just proved that you and I should be together," he said.

"Together."

"But I was just as scared to be with you as you are to be with me."

Scared, I thought, but couldn't bring myself to say out loud.

"So what do you think?" he asked.

As if that was an easy question to answer. So I responded with an inquiry of my own.

"Why now?" I asked. "Why tell me all this now?"

"Because of Hope," he said.

Marcus went on to tell me that Hope had called him not too long after our last long phone conversation about all the reasons why Marcus was messing up my life. She called him to tell him she knew he couldn't have stopped her brother's death, and she was tired of hearing my unreasonable excuses for why I wouldn't let Marcus back into my life. She called him to tell him what I was too afraid to say out loud: that he was right, I was pushing him away because I was petrified of what would happen if he got too close. Hope called him to step in where she knew I wouldn't. The two of them—Marcus and Hope—got Percy and Bridget involved in this prom scheme too. But it was Hope's doing, mostly.

That's precisely why she is my best friend, and always will be no matter how much distance separates us.

I didn't realize that I had been standing there silent for a minute until he said, "Are you quiet because you're surprised or because you're repulsed?"

"Neither," I replied. "I'm quiet because we've done enough talking."

Did I not make it to the prom because I took his face in my hands and pressed my mouth to his, long and full and wet, right in front of the entire prom-going senior class? Did I not make it to the prom because we quickly hopped into the Caddie, never letting go of each other's hands, and drove back to his house? Did I not make it to the prom because we were all alone and unchaperoned because his parents were visiting his brother in Maine? Did I not make it to the prom because we, without speaking, and barely breathing, slowly and nervously and tenderly undressed each other, and even more slowly and nervously and tenderly made love in

*his bed, on black-and-white-striped sheets that smelled like smoky
cedar trees, exactly like I had imagined all this time . . . ?*

For the record, I was not under emotional duress.

While you know I can't write in detail about these things—
you know, *sex* things—especially when it's about me, I do feel
that after all this obsessive talk about dying a virgin and everyone
else in the world doing it but me, and wanting to wait for the perfect time and the perfect place and, most important, the perfect
person, I should at least say this to put your mind at ease:

It was well worth the wait.

Holy shit, was it worth it.

Right before I was about to fade into slumber, my eyes popped
open.

I suddenly remembered that I needed to ask him a question.

"Marcus?"

"Yes?"

"What's your middle name?"

"Armstrong."

Marcus Armstrong Flutie.

"Like Neil, the astronaut?" I asked.

"No," he replied.

"Like Louis, the jazz singer?"

"No," he replied.

"Then like who?"

"Like me."

"Thank you," I said, before drifting off into a long, uninter-
rupted, dreamless sleep.

the tenth

Is there anything more priceless than a yearbook picture of the Class Couple who are no longer a Class Couple? I nearly split my spleen when I saw that picture of Scotty and Manda making gooey eyes at each other. That alone was worth the seventy-five dollars.

But then there was the shock of seeing Sara in her Best Buddies and Class Motormouth photos, taken when she was still summertime skinny. Her weight gain was so gradual that it was impossible to pinpoint the day she was officially chunky again. It would have made an awesome subject for a time-lapse photography film.

Of course, the most excruciating photos were of Len and me, captured before there even was a Len and me. It was weird to see us in our Most Likely to Succeed and Class Brainiac pictures, the two of us not knowing what would happen between us this year. When the picture was taken, we weren't comfortable enough around each other to touch. In both pictures we're smiling and everything, feigning camaraderie, but keeping a safe distance. It's sort of how we act around each other now, as exes.

QUIZ! MATCH THE YEARBOOK QUOTE TO THE PERSON!

QUOTE	PERSON
1. "We've been through some tough times, sweetie. But I'm so psyched that we've put our differences aside. Who knew we'd both end up with rock stars???!!! Let's hang out this summer!!!"	A. Bridget
2. "I always knew there was something going on with the 'Brainiac' and 'Krispy'!!! But Manda says Len says that he's cool, so I guess he's cool with me too!!! Always remember me, your homeroom buddy!!! Let's hang out this summer!!!"	B. Len
3. "You are the smartest person I know. Congratulations on Columbia. I know you will succeed in whatever it is you do. I hope one day we can be friends again."	C. Manda
4. "I'm so happy that you and I got closer this year. I know things weren't easy for you after Hope left, but I hope (ha ha) I helped make things better for you. I know you definitely did for me."	D. Percy
5. "What am I going to do without you next year, my friend? *Mon dieu!* You're the only person who speaks the language."	E. Sara
6. "I hope I someday earn back your respect. And not just because I want to do you."	F. Scotty

Of course, looking at excruciating photos is only half the fun of yearbook-getting.

If there's anything I learned on prom night, it's that we seniors are compelled to kiss each other's asses before we graduate. Everyone's trying to mend fences and end feuds and basically get in everyone else's good graces, as if two weeks of nicey-niceties can erase nearly four years' dickheadedness. Ever notice how people wait until they're not going to see you anymore to say something nice to you? Nowhere is this more apparent than in how these people are signing my yearbook.

Notice how I'm playing games instead of writing about the most important thing in my life. It's because I haven't found a way to say it yet. Not right, anyway, which is why I'm glad Marcus did not buy a yearbook. He says he'll just look at mine whenever he's compelled to remember these people, which he does not anticipate happening very often. This spares me the humiliation of writing something sticky-sweet sentimental and trite.

This is what he wrote in mine:

Jessica:

There is nothing I can write in here that I won't be able to tell you in person.

Forever,
Marcus

the fourteenth

Tonight, when I came home from Marcus's house, I went upstairs to my bathroom. Showered. Dried off. Towel-squeegeed my hair. Put on boxers and the COMINGHOME T-shirt that still smells like him. Meticulously applied zit crap to my facial landmines.

All of this before sitting down and writing about an emotion I cannot express.

I cannot write about love. It's harder than writing about sex.

I found it even more impossible to talk about it with Hope on the phone, but I had to. I needed to know that she was okay with all this. I needed her to believe in Marcus and me as much as I do.

"If I didn't want you together," Hope said, "I wouldn't have gone through all that trouble."

That made perfect sense, of course.

"Are you okay with, you know, me not being a virgin any-more?" I asked.

Hope cackled into the receiver. "*You* were the one with the virgin complex, not me. I'll do it someday. But until then, I'll just have to live vicariously through you. You little vixen, you."

I'm so relieved that my relationship with Marcus won't come between me and Hope. Still, there are things that I will keep to myself. Like how I cut Senior Cut Day and spent it with Marcus instead. In his bed. Not the whole day, but the afternoon hours before his parents came home from work, which, quite frankly, was about as much as I could handle, as I am afraid of turning into a nymphomaniac.

As happy as I was to be alone with him, I couldn't stop myself from asking the question that needed to be asked.

"If I ask you to tell me the truth about something, will you?"

Marcus propped himself up on his elbow so we would be eye to eye. "I have never not told you the truth about anything," he said.

"That's subject to debate," I said.

"What subject *isn't* up for debate?" he countered.

"An honest answer to the question I'm about to ask you is *not* subject to debate," I replied.

"Okay. Ask me."

"What about the girls?" I asked.

"The girls . . ." he replied.

"How many girls before me?"

He buried his face in my neck and groaned. "Why do you need to ask me that?"

"Why do you need to keep the truth from me?"

His mouth was still on my neck. "Because I don't like to talk about it."

"Why? Because you feel guilty?"

"Not exactly."

"Then why?"

"I'm at peace with my moral failings."

"So you didn't think that anything you'd ever done was wrong?" I was about to gather my clothes and leave at this point.

"I just don't see the point in beating myself up. I think it's more productive to concentrate on being a better person right now than punishing myself for who I was in the past."

This was it. I'd been holding back for years about this. Hope may have forgiven him, but it was time for *me* to get it out of *my* system.

"How can you not feel any guilt when my best friend's brother—your best friend—died because of all the stupid things you did?"

"Heath is—" He caught himself. "Was not me. I was never into the heavy shit he was."

"You weren't?"

"No," he said. "I smoked up every day, did quite a bit of E, a little acid, some 'shrooms. Not that any of that stuff was healthy, but I never shot up. Ever. It just wasn't my thing."

I knew it was the truth.

"Why did you feel the urge to do anything?"

"To heighten my senses. Or to feel numb. Depending on the day, and the drug."

"Do you miss it?"

"Never," he said.

"Really? Not ever?"

"Never," he replied. "Life is actually more interesting without it."

"Why did you let people think you were hard core when you weren't?"

"Because I've learned that you can't control what other people are going to think about you. The best you can do in life is not piss yourself off."

That was a very profound observation, I thought. I would be much better off if I lived by it.

Then I started thinking. If the drug stuff wasn't true, maybe the stuff about the girls was all hype.

"So going back to my original question . . ."

"Jessica . . ." he said, biting into his pillow.

"How many girls? Or was that highly exaggerated too?"

He took my hand.

"Jessica, since the first time we really spoke, that time in the Cadillac outside your house, you are the only one who has ever mattered. I don't want to talk about the girls before you because none of those girls matter to me now, just like Len doesn't matter to you now. Fortunately for us all, love does not work on an exclusive first-come, first-served basis. Think of Gladdie and Moe, and everyone else out there who would've missed out if it did."

He wanted to say more, I could tell.

"What?"

I knew what he wanted to say. And I needed to hear him say it.

"So you aren't the first girl I've slept with. But it's the first time I felt like it was more than just fucking. It was making love, as cliché as it sounds."

It *was* totally cliché. But this time, I actually I wanted to hear it. I needed to hear him say it because I knew it was the truth. I finally believed it. I believed *him*.

"Knowing that you waited for so long, then picked me . . ." He stopped again. He pressed his face into the space above my navel, his hands grasping my hipbones, as it to brace himself for what he was about to say. "It means more than you will ever know that you picked me to be your first."

He moved up and up until our bodies fit together like a living, breathing ying yang symbol.

"I just wish I hadn't been so oblivious," I said.

"What do you mean?"

"We could've been together all year," I said. "Think of all the time we wasted."

"It's like I said before. There's no point in dwelling in the past," he said.

"But we could've spent so much more time together—"

"Jessica," he interrupted, pausing to lightly kiss the tip of my nose. "By going through what we have, we helped each other be the people we're supposed to be."

"But . . ."

"As complicated and confusing as our courtship was, it happened the way it had to."

"But . . ."

"Jessica, we were perfect in our imperfection."

"But . . ."

"We are the way we are supposed to be."

I placed my lips on top of his head, running them over his velvety crew cut. I breathed in his earthy and sweet scent and I needed to do more than kiss him. I needed to drink him. I needed to gobble him up. I needed—

"Jessica Darling."

"Marcus Flutie."

I want you to be the first and the second and the third and the last, I thought.

And then we looked at each other and started laughing. I loved that we were lying there naked and laughing for no reason other than the fact that we—and nobody else—were us.

Together.

The entire universe as an interconnected whole.

Samadhi.

the fifteenth

One last edition of *Pinevile Low*:

WHAT NOBODY FOOLED YOU ALL YEAR LONG?
TARYN BAKER, THAT'S WHO. SEE YOU NEXT YEAR IN THE
SEAGULL'S VOICE.

I called Taryn to congratulate her on her very brave confession.

"Remember, don't just slam people for the pure enjoyment of slamming them," I said. "It's fun for a while, but it gets old. And it isn't good for your karma."

"Right."

"Try to do some good. Try to make a difference in this crappy cesspool we call school."

"I'll try," she said. "Because someone has to be the next you."

The idea of anybody wanting to be the next me was, of course, laughable. Especially when I had tried so hard to be the *first* me all year.

I was ready to hang up when Taryn—apropros of nothing—said, "You and Marcus."

Me and Marcus. I still wasn't used to hearing others saying that out loud.

"You're together now."

"Yes," I said distractedly. I mouthed the words silently. *Me and Marcus. Marcus and me.*

"That was a long time coming."

"Yes," I replied, without really thinking about what I was saying. "Yes, it was."

There was a thoughtful pause before she said, "I don't know how I didn't see it until now."

As soon as those words came out of her mouth, I knew that she knew the truth. I knew she knew that I had peed in the cup to cover for Marcus. But I also knew, just as confidently, that our secret would never be revealed in *Pinevile Low, The Seagull's Voice*, or elsewhere—my reward for being the first person to listen to Taryn Baker, to treat her like a real person, to earn her trust.

"Thanks, Taryn," I said. "For everything."

"No, Jess," she replied with a tiny, tinny laugh, the first I'd ever heard escape her thin, repressed lips. "Thank *you*."

the twenty-first

It was strange, meeting Marcus's parents tonight. They weren't any weirder than your average parents, it was simply hard to believe that someone like Marcus even *had* parents. It seemed much more logical for Marcus to have been the result of a lab experiment, to see what *really* happens when you mix snips, snails, puppy dogs' tails, and Viagra.

I was nervous, of course, because I still haven't recovered from the knowledge that Mrs. Levy loooooooves Manda—a certified whore—yet would've had me drawn and quartered if the opportunity had presented itself. I was afraid Marcus's parents would automatically and inexplicably hate me too. Before my arrival, I tried to find out something, anything, about them that would aid in the conversation. All I knew was that his dad refurbished old cars and his mom worked in a day care center.

"My dad likes speed," Marcus said.

"Speed? Like meth?"

"No, like stock cars and motorcycles," he said. "It's impossible for him to sit still."

"Uh, okay."

"And my mom is into quilting and crafts and stuff like that."

It was interesting to think about how these traits manifested themselves in their son. The restless way he rattles coins in his pocket, or flicks open his lighter, or taps the table, etc. And how he personalized his T-shirts all year. I pointed this out to Marcus.

"I never really saw the connection before, but you're right," he said. "Now let me point out all the ways you are exactly like *your* parents."

"That's one analysis I really don't need to hear," I said before quickly hanging up the phone.

Mr. and Mrs. Flutie are indeed real people. They are also abnormally tall. Even Marcus's mom tops six feet, which kind of shocked me. I was expecting a delicate porcelain doll wielding a BeDazzler or something.

"Finally we get to meet the famous Jessica Darling!" she exclaimed, crushing me with a hug.

Mr. Flutie was zipping around the room, barbecue tongs in hand. "We kept waiting for you to shoot on over here," he said in a rapid-fire *rat-a-tat-tat* tone. "I kept on saying to Marcus, 'When's this new girlfriend of yours gonna shoot on over here?' Just the other day we shot past your house and I wanted to pop in for an introduction, but my son here said that wouldn't be cool, and the last thing I would ever want to do to my son is be uncool, so I said we'd just shoot on over there another time."

I learned very quickly that Mr. Flutie is always "shooting" to or from one place or another.

Marcus just stood there, massaging a wrinkled brow. I was seeing him in the midst of a brand-new emotion: total parental humiliation. It was very endearing to see that even the cool, calm, and collected Marcus Flutie could lose his shit in his parents' presence.

During dinner, I discovered where Marcus inherited his

haphazard conversational style. Over hot dogs, burgers, baked beans, and corn on the cob, Marcus, his parents, and I discussed, among other things, *Crossing Over*, pedophiliac priests, drilling in Alaska, Jews versus Palestinians, obese babies, and the New Jersey Nets.

The whole time, I was totally, completely myself. What's more, I didn't even have to concentrate on being myself. I just was. And you want to know the god-diggity-damndest thing? They loved me. Let me rephrase that: His parents LOOOOOOOOOOVED me. I know they loved me because, as I was getting ready to leave, Mrs. Flutie turned to her husband and said, "I just love this girl, don't you?"

"Marcus finally brought home someone who is smarter than he is."

"We love you, Jessica Darling!" enthused Mrs. Flutie as she bear-hugged me again.

Over her shoulder, I watched Marcus turn purple with embarrassment. Then he mouthed the words *I love you too*.

"And I love you," I replied, but I wasn't afraid to say it out loud.

the twenty-fourth

The only reason I am still in school is because extra days were tacked on to the school year to make up for the time wasted in September on account of the messed-up scheduling. I aced out of all my finals, so it has been a particularly useless week at Pineville High for me. Could there be a more fitting end to my academic experience, or lack thereof?

With the prom over, yearbooks signed, and finals a joke, seniors are compelled to be even more nauseatingly nostalgic than they would be.

"This is the last time I'll ever eat school pizza!"

"This is the last time I'll cut Spanish!"

"This is the last time I'll put out a cigarette on *this* toilet seat."

Manda and Sara have been particularly mopey, walking around with tears in their eyes all week. I think they know the truth: This *was* the best time of their lives, and it's almost over.

As much as I've bitched about not fitting in, and being an outsider among the insiders, I now realize that it was probably for the best. I mean, is there anything more pathetic than peaking at eighteen? Someone who counts down the decade until the next reunion? Someone whose mantra is "Remember when?"

I imagined Manda trying on her prom queen tiara when she's

thirty, Sara wanting to relive the days when her brainless scoop was a commodity, and Scotty, thick with frat fat, unable to run to the closest keg without getting winded, crying along with "Glory Days" on the radio because what Springsteen is singing is so true, *so true.*

If I ever, ever, ever miss Pineville High—with its dingy cinder block walls, moldy, asbestos-filled ceilings, and gray hot dog water cafeteria stench; with its clueless administration and counterintuitive zero-tolerance policies; with its hallways you can't walk down, bathrooms you can't use, and tables you can't sit at because of its oppressive social zoning laws that put Upper Crusters at the top of the high school hierarchy, followed by Jocks, Groupies, Clubbers, IQs, 404s, Dregs, Pineys, and Other Miscellaneous Bottom Dwellers Deemed Unworthy of Names; a place where any actual learning was purely by accident, and never took place inside the classroom—you have my permission to kill me.

Did I just write my graduation speech? Ha!

the twenty-eighth

I had already imagined how it would be next year.

I'd be at Columbia, and Marcus would move to Manhattan, or maybe one of the outer boroughs. I would study hard, and he would make money playing gigs at dingy bars. We'd spend countless hours going to clubs to see bands on the verge, touring obscure art exhibits, and sipping pot after pot of black coffee in hole-in-the-wall cafés. Many more hours would be spent lounging under the covers. We would never run out of witty and fascinating things to say to each other. Eventually, he'd apply to Columbia, and we'd be the type of well-educated, cosmopolitan couple that confuse the suburbumpkins who never leave Pineville.

I should have known not to get my heart set on anything.

"Jess, I've been meaning to tell you something."

While the rest of the senior class was celebrating their Pineville emancipation at yet another one of Sara's boot-and-rallies, Marcus had insisted on taking me to the Seaside Heights boardwalk.

"Come on, if it's good enough for MTV, it's good enough for us."

"I still can't believe that of all the resorts in the entire world,

MTV chose Seaside Heights, New Jersey, as its summer HQ," I said, shaking my head.

"It is the Home of Sunnin' and Funnin'," Marcus said, quoting the motto printed all over the boardwalk's brochures.

"Easy for you to say," I said. "You never had a toothless customer order a chocolate cone, then blow a burrito belch in your face."

"This is true," he replied.

"Millions of kids across the country are going to be sitting in front of their TV sets this summer thinking Seaside Heights is the coolest place on earth, wishing they could be here for all the sunnin' and funnin'—"

"When all you've ever wanted to do is get out of here," he said, completing my thought.

"Exactly."

"There's a lesson in there somewhere," Marcus said, sliding into a smile.

It turned out that MTV wasn't taping when we got there. If we had thought things through carefully, we would have figured this out before we got there. No way would Sara throw a party at her house when she could party in front of television cameras. She's promised to be such a fixture at the MTV house that her lust for nationwide attention might even threaten to cut into her tanning time. Anyway, the beach house was surprisingly dark and quiet, though that didn't stop dozens of TRL hopefuls from hanging around it anyway, hoping for a glimpse of a VJ.

"Oh, well," Marcus said. "I guess tonight's sunnin' and funnin' won't be televised after all."

Marcus beat me by 120 points in Skee-Ball, but I redeemed

myself by thwacking the bejeesus out of the little varmints in Whac-A-Mole. We both humiliated ourselves playing *Dance Dance Revolution* by not being able to keep up with the disco choreography that went with KC and the Sunshine Band's "That's the Way (I Like It)." We shared funnel cake and orange-ade. We giggled at countless fortysomething broads wearing age-inappropriate clothing in flammable fabrics, and the hirsute bennies who beer-goggle them. We even checked out how the Geek from Shoot the Geek was doing, though we refused to pay a dollar to launch paintball bazooka bombs at him, even if he was dressed like Osama Bin Laden. He was not as charismatic a geek as Percy was two summers ago, but he had mastered Percy's most impressive somersault escape maneuver.

With Marcus's help, I turned into what I thought I would never be when I slaved my sophomore summer away at Wally D's Sweet Treat Shoppe: someone who came to the boards to have *fun*. So yes, there was a lesson in all this. Who needed MTV? All I needed was Marcus.

It made me think about all the other possible places in the world that Marcus could help make fun for me. Little did I know that on the sky ride, a cable car suspended high in the air that afforded a gorgeous view of the ocean and an escape from the crowds and the chaos down below, the amusement would be short-lived.

"Jessica," he said, "I've been meaning to tell you something."

"What?"

"I'm going away."

"What?"

"I won't be around here next year. I'm going away to school."

I thought he was joking. He had to be joking. So I joked right back.

"Ringling Brothers reopened the clown college?"

"It's a new liberal arts school, Gakkai College."

"But you didn't even take your SATs."

"I know. That's the beauty of it. It's founded by a Buddhist sect and doesn't require SATs or any other admissions tests. All I had to do was write an essay about egalitarian ideals in the modern world. I guess they decided I was their spiritual brother because they offered me a scholarship."

"So where is this idyllic, intellectual haven?"

"Nuevo Viejo, California."

California. Of course it sounded a little *Let's put on our Nikes, drink cyanide-flavored Kool-Aid, and do the Helter Skelter* to me. California is the cult capital of the world.

Black waves crashed into the sand.

"Be happy for me, Jessica."

"That's . . ." I started.

Horrible. Tragic. Devastating.

"Awesome!" I managed to blurt out.

He didn't believe it for one second. Words that express excitement sound so weird coming out of my mouth. I am especially bad at expressing enthusiasm for others when I do not feel it myself.

"I'm not throwing my life away."

He was right. Shouldn't I want what's best for him?

BUT I THOUGHT WHAT'S BEST FOR HIM WAS BEING WITH ME!

Goddammit, I'm selfish.

"Awesome. Wow. Awesome."

"You are a terrible liar," he said.

"How do you expect me to react?" I said, looking down at the swarms of people below us, all of whom were still having fun,

fun, fun. "I thought we were going to have all this time together next year, and to find out that we aren't is just . . ."

I gurgled with tears.

"Jessica . . ."

"Why . . . didn't . . . you . . . tell me?"

He turned to face me directly, causing the car to quiver on the wire.

"Because I wasn't sure if I wanted to go. I knew that if I told you before I knew for sure, you would try to persuade me to go because it's 'the right thing.' And I didn't want my decision to be based on what you thought was the best thing for me, but what I thought was the best thing for me."

"How do you know that I wouldn't beg you to come to New York?"

"Because I know you."

He was right. I would never, ever beg. No matter how much I wanted to.

"So when do you leave?"

"Well, that's the thing." He paused. "I'm driving out next week."

"Next week? As in seven days from now."

"Six, actually."

"Six."

"Yes, Thursday."

I watched a frat boy try to urinate into a trash can.

"We won't even have the summer?"

"No." And then, very calmly: "But Jessica, we have all the time in the world."

Marcus truly believes this. He believes we have our whole lives together. Forever.

I was going to say how this is easy for him to believe because he is a romantic. I was going to point out how I am a realist. Actually, how I am a defensive pessimist. I always assume the worst, so if the reality is even a wee bit better than my disaster scenario, it's a cause for celebration.

I was going to say all of this, but then I thought, Marcus has never been wrong about anything so far. Couldn't he be right about us too?

I could fly out to see him next year when our family visits Bethany, G-Money, and the baby. Percy and I could take a cross-country drive together to see him and Bridget. Maybe this is all irrelevant, since we will be if we are meant to be, regardless of how often we see each other. If my experience with Hope has proven anything, it's that true friendship can survive, even thrive, despite the distance. Why can't it be the same for Marcus and me?

I shut up my mouth and my brain. I put my head on his shoulder and vowed to enjoy the rest of the ride with Marcus, no matter how long it lasted.

the thirtieth

Graduation Day: I am officially free. I finally feel it too.

As a reflection of just how much I don't care, I totally neglected to mention that Len beat me out for valedictorian by two-tenths of a point. Even with our history, this was absolutely fine by me because being at the tippy-top of the class meant way more to him than it did to me. When we lined up in our red and white graduation gowns, numbers one and two leading the rest of the Class of 2002, I very graciously congratulated him.

"You worked hard," I said. "You deserve it."

"Thanks, Jess."

"I mean, you really worked for it. You did hours of homework every night. I didn't bring a book home all year."

"Um."

Okay. So I wasn't thoroughly gracious. String me up.

Since I was number two, I got to give my speech first—you know, like the opening act to the headliner. As far as I was concerned, this was the advantageous spot. Despite my blasé acceptance of being second best, I wanted to blow Len's speech away.

I took my own advice about not slamming people for the sake of slamming people and opted against the tirade from a few pages back. Besides, that would've been too predictable. Instead, I surprised myself and the audience by saying something altogether unlike the Jessica they all thought they knew. I was inspired by Marcus's graduation gift, a custom-made T-shirt I wore under my gown that read: ME. YES. ME. I don't think anyone will even remember that Len got up there and stuttered his way through a very predictable quote from Thoreau followed by five minutes of canned "The future is ours" clichés.

The rest of the ceremony is a boring blur. As salutatorian, I got my diploma after Len, the second person out of 180. So I had a lot of time to sit and get hot under the blazing noonday sun. I might have fallen asleep if it weren't for the frequent head-bonkings from the beach balls that my fellow graduates had smuggled in under their gowns.

In accordance with alphabetical destiny, I watched Sara D'Abruzzi, Marcus Flutie, Scotty Glazer, Bridget Milhokovich, and Manda Powers walk up the stairs to the stage. I watched each one walk toward Principal Masters in their red and white gowns. I watched them reach for their diplomas and wave to their parents in the bleachers, despite how corny it was to do so. I watched them turn their tassels from one side to the other. I watched them walk down the stairs on the opposite side, grinning with freedom. I watched them and thought, *These are the people I went to high school with*. Some, like Manda, Sara, and Scotty, will never amount to more than that. There was no last-minute redemption for them, simply because it was a perfect opportunity for final forgiveness and understanding.

As for the others . . . well, I hope it goes without saying.

One hundred eighty caps flew into the air in celebration, and for a split second, the sky was red.

But not the same fiery orange-red I saw bounding toward me once the bleachers were cleared and the field was filled with camcorder-toting parents.

"Hey, *you!*" she yelled, from twenty yards away.

"*You!*" I screamed, sprinting toward her.

Hope. Hope was here.

"I wanted to surprise you!"

Roget could not come up with enough synonyms to adequately describe just how surprised I was to see Hope standing right in front of me.

"Omigod! Omigod! Omigod!" I shrieked as I bounced on my tippy-toes.

Hope's face fell. "Oh, I'm sorry, *Sara*," she said, gently mocking my Clueless Two-like enthusiasm. "I thought you were my old friend Jessica Darling. It's been a while since I've seen her, you know. I apologize for the error."

She turned and started to walk away, but I grabbed her before she made it two feet.

"I'm just so happy and totally shocked to see you here," I said. "I mean, this is even better than Jake Ryan—"

Hope knew exactly where I was going with this. "Surprising Samantha Baker after her sister's wedding—" she continued.

"At the end of *Sixteen Candles!*" We finished the thought simultaneously, before tackling each other into a hug.

As we held on to each other, I thought about how this is all I had ever wanted. My best friend. Right here with me.

When we finally separated, we just stood there, having far too much to say to actually start talking. Then I saw her eyes drift over my shoulder. And I knew why.

I knew Marcus and Hope had spoken on the phone—that,

in fact, she was responsible for the miracle of us getting together at all. I truly believed that she wanted us to be a couple. Yet I couldn't help but worry about what would happen when the three of us were together for the first time. Would they see each other as competition? As the enemy? Or worse?

But then all the fear and guilt and worry washed out with one simple gesture.

Hope held out her hand. "Hey, Marcus."

Marcus held out his hand. "Hey, Hope."

I stood there on the grass, watching the Darlings chatting happily with the Fluties, my two best friends pressed palm-to-palm, and a wave of calm washed over me. For the first time in my life, I wasn't thinking about what would happen in the seconds, minutes, hours, days, weeks, months, and years to come. I was right there in the moment, my world finally, albeit briefly, complete.

And I was happy. Deliriously, deliciously happy.

Jessica Darling's Graduation Address
Real-World Revelation:
A Malcontent Makes Peace with Pineville

I bet that a lot of you think I'm going to stand up here and go off on one of my anti–Pineville High diatribes, the likes of which I used to publish in the school paper, before I was unfairly silenced by the administration. I must admit that I've been looking forward to the opportunity to express my often-controversial opinions in front of a captive audience, since I was unable to do so all year long.

But I'm not going to do that today. I've vented enough about the shortcomings of this school. What I haven't done is consider what I gained from my experience here, and how going to Pineville High School has actually benefited me.

For the past four years, I've wanted nothing other than to escape this place. I couldn't wait to graduate, go to college, and get out into the real world that exists beyond Pineville. I longed for the place where I could finally be free of the social inequities and teen trivialities that dominate high school life.

But you want to hear something insane? I don't think I would change a thing about my high school experience. Not even the really bad stuff, like my best friend moving away, or my grandmother's death. If you're sitting next to two people having heart attacks right now, they are no doubt my parents, as this is probably particularly shocking news to them.

No doubt Pineville would have been a more pleasant place without all the backstabbing, social climbing, and cattiness. But the Jessica Darling standing in front of you today is the result of everything I've been through up to this point. Change one event, make a left instead of a right, and who knows where, or more specifically, *who* I might be at this moment. And here's the thing: I like who I am. I like the person I've turned out to be, and I know I'm not done evolving yet.

I believe that what we get out of life is what we've set ourselves up to get, so there's no such thing as an inconsequential decision. Our destinies are the culmination of all the choices we've made along the way, which is why it's imperative to listen hard to your inner voice when it speaks up. Don't let anyone else's noise drown it out.

Looking back on my four years here, I've realized that my lowest moments were the direct result of paying more attention to what other people were saying than listening to my gut.

That doesn't mean that you shouldn't ever take someone else's advice, or turn to others for guidance—just be sure they have your best interests at heart.

If there's one thing I've realized throughout my four years of Pineville High, it's that the real world, whether we like it or not, is right here, right now. All of this, every day, is important. Everybody matters. Everything we do has an effect on others, directly or indirectly, whether we realize it or not.

But even those who aren't looking out for you can end up helping you in the end. And as much as I don't like to admit it, I have to thank the Pineville High School Class of 2002 for the influence you've had on my life. For better or for worse, you have helped me become the person I was always meant to be: me. Yes. Me.

A Note from the Author

N ot many writers are rewarded with a reintroduction of their work to a whole new audience. Even fewer get the opportunity to address—and redress—their past mistakes.

It's fitting, actually. *Sloppy Firsts*—and the four books that follow—are all about making mistakes. As an author, it was vital to me for Jessica Darling to discover herself through trial and many, many errors. Countless readers have thanked me for creating an imperfect protagonist. Her numerous flaws, they tell me, are what make her recognizable and relatable. Fundamentally, Jessica Darling is good at heart. Yet that doesn't stop her from being snarky, self-absorbed, and—within the safe pages of her private journal—very, very judgmental.

Also very, very funny.

All five books were put out by an adult publisher, not young adult. In 2001, books for teens were still lumped together with children's titles. I knew that category was not appropriate for what I wanted to write, both in tone and content. This series was always intended for a crossover audience of older teens experiencing the daily indignities of adolescence and early adulthood, as well as nostalgic older readers who had graduated long ago. That choice provided freedom and flexibility to push boundaries in ways that would not have been possible at an imprint targeted to a younger audience.

Jessica's candid, caustic observations are written for laughs. And thankfully, her sarcastic takes on her classmates, crushes, and Y2K culture are as humorous now as they were back then. Except when they aren't. Imperfect people say and do imperfect things. And they hopefully learn from their blunders. I'm not referring to my fictional characters anymore. I'm talking about myself.

I wrote these books in real time. I was intentionally specific in the use of language and pop-cultural references (even the made-up ones) knowing they would date the series. Why? I hoped my work would ultimately serve as a sort of time capsule: *This* is what it was like for a young woman to come of age in the first decade of the new millennium. However, not all attitudes that were acceptable in 2001 should be tolerated today. And artifactual accuracy is no excuse for perpetuating potentially harmful stereotypes.

For that reason, I've worked with my team at Wednesday Books to make changes to the original text to reflect these more inclusive, diverse, and progressive times. This is a conscious decision to evolve in a manner that stays true to the spirit and integrity of the story. If we've done our jobs well, readers won't notice and certainly won't miss what we've removed.

So much has changed in the twenty years since *Sloppy Firsts* debuted. But the messiness of Jessica's journey into adulthood is timeless. She's both an outsider and an insider, wise beyond her years but exquisitely inexperienced in the ways of the world. I am so thrilled for this current generation of teens to see themselves—and others—in her story.

Acknowledgments

My agent, Heather Schroder, for always telling the truth and having better judgment than I do.

My editor, Sara Goodman, for believing Jessica's story is just as relevant now as it was 20 years ago. And the Wednesday Books team—including Jennie Conway, Meghan Harrington, Alexis Neuville, Melanie Sanders, Christa Désir, Michelle Li, Devan Norman, Gail Friedman, Olga Grlic, and Kerri Resnick—for putting your great and varied talents to work in bringing this series to a new generation.

Rebecca Serle, for writing an introduction that brought me to tears.

My readers, without whom this anniversary edition wouldn't exist.

CJM, for reminding me why high school is such a rich source of material.

And finally, Christopher, still my husband and best friend, for making me laugh more days than not.

About the Author

© Chiara Gold Photos

MEGAN McCAFFERTY writes fiction for tweens, teens, and teens-at-heart of all ages. The author of several novels, she's best known for *Sloppy Firsts* and several more books in the *New York Times* bestselling Jessica Darling series. Described in her first review as "Judy Blume meets Dorothy Parker" (*Wall Street Journal*), she's been trying to live up to that high standard ever since.